PALE GREY DOT

PALE GREY DOT

PALE GREY DOT

DON MIASEK

Raven Stone

Pale Grey Dot
© Don Miasek 2024

Published by Ravenstone, an imprint of Turnstone Press
Artspace Building, 206-100 Arthur Street
Winnipeg, MB. R3B 1H3 Canada
www.TurnstonePress.com

All rights reserved. No part of this book may be reproduced or transmitted
in any form or by any means—graphic, electronic or mechanical—without
the prior written permission of the publisher. Any request to photocopy any
part of this book shall be directed in writing to Access Copyright, Toronto.

Turnstone Press gratefully acknowledges the assistance of the Canada
Council for the Arts, the Manitoba Arts Council, the Government of Canada
through the Canada Book Fund, and the Province of Manitoba through the
Book Publishing Tax Credit and the Book Publisher Marketing Assistance
Program.

This novel is a work of fiction. Names, characters, places and incidents are
either the product of the author's imagination or are used fictitiously, and
any resemblance to actual persons living or dead, events or locales, is entirely
coincidental.

Printed and bound in Canada by Friesens.

Library and Archives Canada Cataloguing in Publication

Title: Pale grey dot / Don Miasek.
Names: Miasek, Don, author.
Identifiers: Canadiana (print) 20230586899 | Canadiana (ebook)
20230586902 | ISBN 9780888017772 (softcover) | ISBN 9780888017789
    (EPUB) | ISBN 9780888017796 (PDF)
Subjects: LCGFT: Novels.
Classification: LCC PS8626.I1454 P37 2024 | DDC C813/.6—dc23

*To my parents and siblings,
who gave me everything I needed to succeed.*

1

Jenna woke to the sound of arguing, audible even over the rain. Up above, water poured out of the gutters that ran down the sides of the housing complexes. Her internal chronometer showed 5:08 a.m., and the lights in the nearby buildings were still dimmed. Jenna's eyes settled on the man and woman.

They were now screaming at each other. She stole his ration chip, he said. He was a stain who couldn't tell a chip from his ass, she said. The man wore a tattered grey longcoat that blended in with the walls of the surrounding buildings. His breather was little more than scratched glass and cracked rubber. The woman had no breather at all, and her strained screeching was interrupted by a fit of hacking coughs. Her sagging skin and sunken eyes spoke of bad anti-ageing procedures long since abandoned. Her mouth had more gaps than teeth.

There were at least fifteen others huddled together in the laneway. Most were sprawled across the ground, sleeping under makeshift blankets, or propped up against one of the old shipping crates used for food distribution. Neither the screaming nor the rain woke them. Jenna had already marked and identified each one the night before. Even those with some fight in them knew better than to get in her way.

Jenna's joints ached as she climbed to her feet, turning away from the fight. Her fellow displaced were unstable after so many years of scavenging for survival, but at least they were predictable. Her drenched black hair obscured her vision as she stumbled out of the alley towards the street. Traffic was quiet, the curbs lined with auto-taxis waiting patiently for commuters.

The signs over each cab existed in the physical world as well as virtually for those with cybernetically enhanced eyes. *Thirteen minutes from downtown to the Bronx Port! Only twenty dollars!*

The sound of the argument faded as Jenna walked. *The homeless fight for petty reasons*, she thought. Every alley on the street was filled with this sort of nonsense. She took stock of her surroundings. Despite the hour and the downpour, a few brave, umbrella-wielding pedestrians strode past her. The rain had chased away most of the smog this morning, allowing citizens a chance to go without their breather masks. One man in a business suit and jacket took several steps to avoid being too close to her, wrinkling his nose in the process.

PALE GREY DOT

Time to see about stealing a fresh set of clothes, apparently. When the dredges started actively avoiding her, it meant they noticed her. Her stomach growled, but food was also something to worry about later—for now, she had to focus on her mission.

Up above, the glowing red light of a security checkpoint cut through the brown fog. The metal arch stretched from one side of the street, up and over to the other. It flashed its acknowledgement as each citizen passed underneath. Drones, no doubt managed by some cyborg in a darkened control room a continent away, watched her every move. A few hovered, fans beating against the rain, while others used their spidery legs to cling to the side of the arch. Old training helped Jenna keep her breathing and heart rate steady while her proxy identification program supplied a false name as she strode underneath. The arch flashed green, placated.

On the other side, Jenna backed into the nearest alley and rolled up her left sleeve, revealing ports and circuitry along a tarnished metal arm. She remembered how happy she'd been when she first received the cybernetic limb. *Such idiocy.* Digging into a soaked pocket, she drew out a small, gleaming data decrypter. Twisting it around, she braced herself before inserting it into one of her ports.

The instant she connected with SecLink, mixed in with the flood of information, came the Pull. For a moment, she wanted nothing more than to call the Earth Security Service and surrender. *You blame Her, but you know it was your fault. Make Her happy. Make yourself happy. ESS is your*

5

friend. They will help you. You know She only wants what's best for you.

"Piss off," she hissed out loud, though no one else heard her. Searing jolts of pain shot through her head the longer she resisted.

Fighting the desire to give up, she found what she was looking for. A map of Toronto filled her vision. A bright red mark appeared several streets over. Jenna pulled in every detail of the area. Every building, every car, every checkpoint, and every person was processed.

Disconnecting as fast as she could, Jenna breathed a sigh of relief. Any longer and her intrusion might have been detected. Worse, she might have fallen sway to the need to return to ESS's loving embrace. It'd taken years to design and build the decrypter. She almost thought it wasn't going to work. *Might never work again if they guess you have access.*

Shoving it back into her pocket, Jenna crossed the street, looking for her target. She hadn't been able to grab his full dossier, but what she had should be enough. Marcus Secor. ESS agent for one hundred and three years. Raised to operative status fifty-four years ago. Known to be stable and reliable. Expert in electronic interference, hijacking, and seduction. Combat training wasn't listed, but that always went without saying. Assigned to support the GreyCorp infiltration effort at the Jupiter locale. Though he'd become an operative during the end of the Athena Program years, Jenna didn't know him personally. As she passed by the slowly opening stores, she wondered if he would know anything

PALE GREY DOT

about the program. *Just what are they telling them about the Athena Six these days?*

The streets were slick, and the puddles cast reflections of the stratoscrapers above. None were taller than the Tower. The Earth Security Service's headquarters was as ugly as it was threatening. Asymmetrical and covered in black armoured plating, it was the centre of the web ESS cast across the entire solar system.

Though the sun wasn't strong enough to pierce the thick brown clouds, the city brightened as natural light usurped the artificial. More cars pulled away from the curb. There would be witnesses. Across the street, Jenna saw her target.

To anyone else, Marcus looked like a random pedestrian going about his business. He wore a black raincoat over a suit and carried a briefcase in his hand—real or a prop, Jenna couldn't tell. Even from here, she could make out his youthful features. She knew from his dossier that Marcus was well over a hundred, but he didn't look a day older than forty. *He isn't innocent,* Jenna reminded herself. *He's the enemy.*

Though Marcus looked as distracted as anyone else, Jenna knew better. Awareness training was the first thing every agent learned. Register every living being in sight, within earshot, and local electronic assets. Catalogue each for potential threats. Look for incongruences. Register any potential weapon, engineered or makeshift. Keep at least three escape routes available at all times. Assess the viability of any potential sources of cover.

Dressed in her ragged coat that was ill-equipped to deal

with the rain, Jenna played the part of a shuffling displaced woman while watching Marcus from the corner of her eye. She had no idea what his cybernetic enhancements consisted of, how diligent he was in his training, or where he was heading.

Jenna stopped at the corner opposite Marcus, pretending to wait for the light. She knew this would require perfect timing. Slowly putting her hands into her pockets, she gripped the signal disruptor tightly with one and her pistol with the other. Taking a deep breath, she squeezed the disruptor, and all hell broke loose.

Every wireless device was struck by static. Every eye ESS had in the area was blinded. Marcus and Jenna both reacted instantly. Pulling her energy projector pistol, she squeezed the trigger as Marcus hit the ground. Deep scorch marks spread across the corner of the building behind him.

There was chaos as pedestrians fled from the gunshots. Displaced, in the hidden safety of their alleys, huddled together in an attempt to go unnoticed. Transports, from the small auto-taxis to the larger commuter buses, slowed to a halt as their connection to the traffic controller was severed.

Jenna fired another shot as the enemy operative dove to the side. She cursed herself—had her internal cybernetics not degraded so much during the past fifty-odd years, this would have already been over. Her only hope was that Marcus was thrown off balance by the sudden disruption to SecLink.

He tossed his briefcase away as he rolled to a kneeling position. Jenna could see his face clearly now. He had the

PALE GREY DOT

stoic expression of a man who wasn't surprised at being ambushed. Raising his hand towards Jenna, his palm glowed as he charged an energy blast before her third shot struck him square in the torso. Falling backwards, Marcus hit the wet pavement, convulsing.

People were emerging from their vehicles. Someone in the crowd shouted at her, barely audible over the rain. Jenna raced across the street, kneeling before the downed operative. He was still alive. Good—his systems would start shutting down the instant he died.

Working fast, she pulled up Marcus's sleeve and began removing the data drives from his arm. Where her cybernetics had the roughness of tactical-grade equipment marred by decades of neglect, his were subtle, designed with a smooth sleekness to simulate civilian implants.

"… Jenna."

She froze.

Marcus twitched as he reached up with his free hand, feebly grasping at her shoulder. His eyes were unfocused, and his breathing had turned ragged. "You don't need to keep running. You can always go back."

Jenna removed the next drive and shoved it into her pocket. She met Marcus's eyes, cursing herself for lingering. Her disruptor wouldn't last much longer, and the instant ESS had access to their network of cameras and sensors again, she'd be lost.

"You know She will forgive you … She loves you …" Marcus murmured.

Don Miasek

"Shut up," she whispered. Jenna drew out a med-stim syringe and rested the tip against his chest. To save him, she knew she'd have to press down hard to break through the thin-weave armour beneath his suit. *No! Don't be stupid. If he lives, She will find you.*

Jenna swallowed hard. *You're wasting time,* she thought. *It's you or him.* "I'm doing you a favour," she muttered. Jenna withdrew the syringe and shoved it into her pocket, unused. Marcus's grip loosened and his breathing faded.

She wrenched out his last data drive. There would be witnesses. All the technological gadgetry in the solar system couldn't stand up against human eyes. Helicraft sirens sounded in the distance. A full lockdown of the sector would soon follow.

With no way to tell how long it would be before ESS's electronic eyes and ears returned, Jenna fled.

DC FORTRESS

WASHINGTON, EARTH

January 31, 2510

Re: Congratulations and concerns

Dear Premier Fairchild,

First, I would like to congratulate you on your re-election into high office. Earth and her territories, from Mercury to the extrasolar-system colonies, continue to prosper under your just leadership.

With your renewed mandate, I'd like to reiterate that we have the opportunity to eliminate a wasteful and dangerous section of our government. It is time that ESS is dismantled.

I won't mince words: ESS has a proven track record of failure. The Ganymede Blitz was a monumental disaster only rivalled by the bloodbath that was the Martian Insurrection fifty-one years ago. Allowing Her free rein has proven disastrous and may well jeopardize your administration's efforts to maintain unity and stability within the solar system.

With your approval, the United Fleet and the Ministry of Defence can be fully capable of handling all intelligence-related matters within three years. Let's use this opportunity to make Earth safe again.

Sincerely,

Sebastian Havoic, Minister of Defence

2

It was as if a switch went off in the back of his brain, and for the first time in fifty-one years, Cherny felt the Pull. He had a moment of near panic before his old training kicked in. Cherny gripped the refuelling hose tightly as he regained his bearings. Glancing over his shoulder, the bustling Hawaii Tsiolkovsky Spaceport filled his view. Jets fired under an orbital hopper, lifting the craft off the tarmac, while one of the big 4200 Series haulers, covered in maintenance personnel, rested behind it.

Cherny's gaze followed the hopper as it forced itself into the brown sky before vanishing into the darkened clouds. The Pull wasn't going away, he realized. This was it. This was finally it. A bewildered smile crept across his face behind his breather as the implications dawned on him. It took the shrill beeping of the refueller hose to snap him back to reality. Pulling the safety lock back onto the nozzle, Cherny

PALE GREY DOT

unhooked the connector from the engine and closed the hatch. As he dragged the hose away from the starliner, another man stood in his way.

"Christ! Thirty-six minutes for one goddamn MO-8 engine!" While he was only a little taller than Cherny, Minsk was a hell of a lot wider. He wore the same ugly safety-orange coverall and mask as everyone else. Only the blue card over his left breast pocket marked him as a supervisor. The man trudged up closer, and Cherny swore he could smell his boss's breath through the filtered air. "Alain had his done ten minutes ago! And his cybernetics are trash compared to yours."

After five decades of putting up with this lumbering sack of ego and abuse, Cherny's metallic hand twitched. It took everything Cherny had not to deck him. *The Pull doesn't mean you can unleash your frustration on this prick,* Cherny reminded himself. "I-I'm," he stammered, "I'm doing the best I can, Minsk." Cherny knew what a sad spectacle he must be right now. On any other day, this wouldn't have been an act. A few of his colleagues shot quick, nervous glances in their direction. He tried to ignore them as well.

"My great-grandma has a faster response time than you, and she's four hundred and fifty!" The supervisor grabbed Cherny's shoulder and turned him around to face the sprawling spaceport. The port was a small pond, but Minsk was the biggest fish in it. "Take a good, long look. There're plenty of people out there who would *love* your job." He drew out the word "love" mockingly. "One call is all it'd take. You'd be back on the street on your ass."

13

Don Miasek

Cherny shivered. Before the Pull, Minsk's threat would have genuinely terrified him. He had fallen so far over the past five decades. *Please let this be the last time I have to go through this,* he thought. "I'll do better," he promised.

Minsk grunted with obvious disbelief and looked out at the thriving port. It was his kingdom. "Or hell, maybe I'll get a drone to do your job. Cost me about ten bucks extra in taxes a day. What do ya think about that? Replace you with a goddamn calculator."

Cherny didn't say anything. It wouldn't take much for his sad excuse of a life to be destroyed.

"All right," Minsk finally said, letting go of Cherny's shoulder. "Get out of here. You're done for the day."

With a sigh of relief that was only partly acted, Cherny bolted, eager to get out of Minsk's sight. *That was the last time,* he repeated to himself. The doors to the terminal building slid open as Cherny approached, and as soon as he was through, he reached up and undid his breather's clasps. Even indoors, the air was putrid, but it was still good to be free of the mask.

The changing room was crowded with dock workers either preparing for a shift or just finishing. Cherny's coverall was filthy, stained with grease, dirt, and sweat. Undoing the zipper, he shed the garment and tossed it into the overflowing hamper before reaching for the towel in his locker. The circuitry and ports of his metallic left arm also covered half his chest, snaking about his flesh like veins.

"You're in a hurry, man."

14

PALE GREY DOT

Cherny looked up in surprise. A tall man with a wispy white beard was gearing up next to him. "I guess I am, José," Cherny replied with a chuckle. In the old days, he never would have been caught unawares. Being distracted by the long-lost Pull in his mind was no excuse, no matter how intoxicating it was.

"Got someplace to go?" José asked as he brought his tool belt up around his hips. The man was well over three hundred years old, and Cherny knew from his records that he had served at this post for nearly two hundred of them. If there was ever a poster boy of a dredge—stuck in the same job forever—José was it.

"Yeah, I might see about a trip to the mainland. I have a bit of cash saved up," Cherny lied.

"Mmm." José fumbled with his belt buckle for a few moments before the latch caught. "I've been thinking about that too. Me and Paul are going to see about getting our VR flick together. Paul's writing the script and I'm planning to direct and star. Just need an investor and we're ready to go. This is it. This is going to be my ticket out of here."

"Can't wait to see it." Cherny wrapped the towel around his waist. The Pull was growing stronger, going from a comforting sensation to one that made his head sore. Nevertheless, he stopped himself before stepping away. "Hey, you stay safe, José. You'll make it." *Lying is a skill you never quite forget,* Cherny mused.

"Thanks, man," José replied. Picking up his orange gloves, he headed for the exit.

15

Cherny watched him go. He wasn't proud of it, but it was comforting to see someone even more pathetic than he was. José was a cautionary tale, but now Cherny was on another path. A path back to greatness, luxury, and superiority over the dredges. A path back to Her. That last one terrified him, but it would be worth it. Setting the towel aside, Cherny stepped into the shower to get clean.

UFS *Starknight* shuddered as her boarding line contacted the broken primary hull of the freighter. Powerful shocks in the line compressed to distribute the impact evenly, but the vibrations were still felt up in the cruiser's command centre. Walls of monitors showed every inch of the captured transport. Someone had crudely painted *Sic Semper Tyrannis* across its hull. The demolished engine, sporting a gaping puncture wound, was surrounded by floating debris.

The command centre was cramped and sparse, like everything else on a military vessel, and supported only three crew members at a time. Wasting mass on creature comforts was unthinkable when that same space could be better utilized to improve ship performance. It could take months of living aboard a spaceship, surrounded by endless vacuum, to get used to it, and some never did. But Captain Ezza Jayens was born in space and spent the first six years of her life there. It was home.

Clipped into her zero-g harness at the command station,

PALE GREY DOT

she listened as her crew methodically and efficiently worked to take the freighter.

"All grapplers are green," Rachelle reported from the ops station. The woman carried a full suite of cybernetics. A dozen steel-grey cables ran from her station into ports along her body, granting her instant access to every scrap of data *Starknight* was receiving. When she turned to face Ezza, the hair-like wires running from the back of her head into the computer systems shimmered in the light.

"*Tyrannis* is stationary relative to our trajectory," Adams added, not looking up from his console. "All manoeuvring thrusters are disabled."

Ezza disapproved of the nickname the crew had given the other ship. The last thing she wanted was to make the Syndicate sound any tougher than they were. Compared to the true political powers in the solar system, Ezza considered them petty thugs with a sledgehammer, when a scalpel was needed to affect any kind of real change. Mentally flicking a switch, she accessed the ship's intercom and spoke in a commanding tone. "This is Captain Jayens to all hands. The Syndicate vessel has been disabled and grappling manoeuvres have been successful. Boarding operations will begin momentarily. Captain Jayens, out."

Severing the connection, Ezza looked in Adams's direction. "Tell Commander Gole his team can go in. Remember— no fatalities. Stunners and flashbangs only."

Heavily armed marines with power armour were overkill against whatever the Syndicate crew could scavenge

17

together. Ezza watched the progress from the command centre's holographic viewer. Twenty green dots denoting *Starknight* marines moved swiftly through the wireframe image of the freighter. Like any ship that wanted to simulate gravity when not accelerating, it was built with an even number of hulls rotating around a single fulcrum. It was big, bulky, and slow—a pack mule compared to *Starknight*'s cheetah.

"Is something wrong, Captain?" Rachelle asked. She was still plugged into *Starknight*, and Ezza knew from experience how distracting that could be.

"I'm trying to view this scenario from the perspective of the people on board that ship," she responded, tapping a gloved hand against the holographic display. "It doesn't add up."

"Oh?"

"The instant they spotted us, they tried to run. Fine. But then we locked on and managed to match their trajectory. From that point on, everyone knew how this was going to end. They couldn't outrun us, they couldn't outgun us, and they sure as hell can't outfight us." The way the green dots on the holographic freighter washed through the ship was proof of that. "Yet they made us chase them for two weeks. They didn't scuttle the ship, so it's clear they aren't suicidal. You'd think that surrender would have crossed their minds."

"Can't underestimate human stubbornness, Captain," Adams said. He still had a boyish smile at only fifty. "Maybe they were hoping we'd lose interest and leave 'em alone."

"Maybe," Ezza considered, unconvinced. Any other ship

PALE GREY DOT

suspected of carrying contraband would have either detonated their cargo or stashed their goods and prayed they'd survive the inspection. Illegal technology was always a possibility, though Ezza found it unlikely the Ministry of Science wouldn't have already detected and reported it.

Within twenty-five minutes, the fighting was over. *Starknight*'s marines had invaded with the efficiency and precision Gole had hammered into them drill after drill. Within two hours, Ezza's technicians had the freighter rigged up to operate under its own power again, and she made the trip over.

Ezza reached out, grabbing the handhold to pull herself through the freighter's wrecked halls. They brought back distant memories of her childhood on the Vesta Archipelago before she was transferred to a learning institute on Earth. The yellow lighting flickered, trash floated around her, and the distant sound of damaged machinery filled the halls. "Can't blame the battle for any of this," she muttered.

"Sorry, Captain?" Adams asked, too cautious to move quickly in zero-g. The man was still a few rungs behind her, face red from frustration.

"Never mind," Ezza said. "Don't worry about it, Lieutenant." She grabbed the nearest handhold and gently flipped around to face backwards, waiting for him to catch up.

Adams drifted to a halt, grateful for the break. "If you don't mind me saying, ma'am, you look pretty disappointed for someone who pulled off a terrific victory."

"Terrific victory, eh?"

Don Miasek

Adams wedged his leg behind one of the rungs to steady himself. "A full forty-five-degree telemetry shift at the velocity we were going, while simultaneously throwing up a mine cloud and deploying a full complement of missiles over the course of two days?" Adams illustrated the manoeuvres with his hands. "I'd have paid good money to have seen the look on the captain of this rust bucket's face when we pulled that off. Yes, ma'am, I'd call that a terrific victory."

"This was your first actual combat action, yes?"

"Yes, ma'am," Adams replied proudly. "Stunts like that are why I couldn't believe my luck when I got assigned to *Starknight*."

Was I ever that green? Ezza wondered. The Siege of Valles Marineris, the Lunar Blockade, and the Martian Insurrection seemed so long ago, but then, her participation in those assignments hadn't been while serving on a spaceship. "Overconfidence breeds complacency. This?" Ezza spread her arms and glanced around the dirty corridor. "This wasn't anything glorious. Just a broken-down freighter."

Adams shrugged but kept grinning. "Well, sure, but the Syndicate's got bigger ships out there. It's only a matter of time before we run into a real challenge."

Ezza smiled and shook her head at the young man's bravado. Before she could comment further, she was interrupted by the sound of muffled shouting.

"We've never carried anything illegal on this ship, technological or otherwise!"

The pair immediately pressed themselves against the wall

PALE GREY DOT

defensively. The shouts were joined by banging and crashing ahead of them. Ezza mentally pulled up the file on the freighter's layout. The grungy corridor led to the main common area, which then split off to the cargo hold, the command centre, and crew quarters.

"Our lawyers will have you crying like pigs when they're done with you!"

Soon a second voice joined the first. Though electronically modified by a marine's helmet and mask, it was still strong and commanding. "I need you to cooperate or I will take further action against you!"

From the hatch leading to the cargo hold, a marine shoved a struggling man into the corridor. The marine was decked out in grey power armour with the United Fleet insignia above her left breast. A helm and visor hid her features behind dark glass. The man wore beige civilian clothes, and despite having his hands bound behind his back, he was trying desperately to wrench them free from the marine's grasp.

"You bitch! There's nothing illegal about transporting hydroponics and cloning facilities!" the man yelled. He twisted around as far as he could and spat at the marine. Flecks of spittle landed harmlessly against her armour, while tiny globules drifted in the zero gravity.

"Do you have this under control, soldier?" Ezza asked as she sized the prisoner up.

Before the marine could reply, the man whirled around and glared at Ezza. Spotting the captain's bars on her shoulders, he hissed, "You! There won't be enough of you left to fill

Don Miasek

a piss pot by the time our lawyers are done with you!" With one final yank, the man broke free from the marine. Pushing off the wall with his legs, he charged headfirst at Ezza.

The captain pulled herself to the side with the help of a nearby railing and reached out to grab him with her other hand. Using his own momentum, she drove the man into the wall, hard.

He hit the metal bulkhead with a groan and turned awkwardly, but with his hands tied behind him, there was little he could do. Blood floated away from a gash on his forehead.

The marine had her stunner drawn, but before she could fire, Ezza held out a hand. "Wait!" Keeping a hold on the man's collar with a gloved hand, she forced him to look at her. "What's your name?"

"What?" He squinted at her, trying not to get any of the floating blood in his eyes.

"Your name."

"Bruce Arun."

"Well, Mr. Arun, let me explain something to you. Combining legal threats with an assault against a United Fleet captain doesn't tend to work. Next time, pick one and stick with it. Now, what do you mean by 'hydroponics and cloning facilities'?"

The marine answered for him. "The cargo holds in the secondary hull have been completely retrofitted. The entire place is jam-packed with farming and cloning tanks." After a beat, she hastily added, "Food-grade cloning.

PALE GREY DOT

Meat-processing facilities. Commander Gole said it was crammed so tight that his team could barely manoeuvre."

Adams glanced in the direction of the cargo hold. A look of confusion crossed his face. "Why so much food?"

"Neither are illegal! It's standard equipment!" Arun protested.

Ezza positioned the man so he'd have no choice but to look her in the eye. The realization dawned on her. "You were making a run, weren't you? All that food-production material was for the trip to Epsilon Eridani, wasn't it?"

Arun shook his head vigorously.

"Now why would a ship tagged to the Syndicate be trying to escape the solar system?"

Arun stayed silent, but Ezza pressed on. "Getting 'refugees' to Eridani is more along the Sympathizers' modus operandi. You're not secretly with them, are you?" At Arun's stony-faced glare, she added, "You can tell me now, or you can tell an interrogator later. I'd just as soon spare you the stress and myself the paperwork, but I suppose it's up to you." Ezza could see the resolve drain from Arun's face.

"We aren't delusional like them," he said. "The Syndicate isn't what it used to be. Alexander Reuben's control has slipped."

His mention of the disfigured leader of the Syndicate piqued Ezza's interest. "Really. What, did his people finally get sick of his anarchist rhetoric and decide to go back to being common criminals?"

Arun shook his head. "Don't laugh. Reuben kept everyone

23

under control. You'd miss him if he falls. I know I don't want to be here when it happens."

Ezza reached into the pocket of her uniform and drew out a white handkerchief. She dabbed at the cut on his forehead, wiping away the blood. "Thank you for your time, Mr. Arun."

The marine took hold of the man again, leading him back through the garbage-strewn corridor towards the airlock.

Adams watched them go as Ezza straightened her gloves.

"A Syndicate ship trying to escape the solar system," Adams whistled, amazed. "Damn, I never thought I'd see it. Think there's anything to this?"

"I don't know." Any trip out of the solar system, Ezza knew, was one-way. Epsilon Eridani didn't have the infrastructure to support repairing and refuelling a spaceship. Neither of the colonies did. "Come on, I'd like to see these food-production facilities. I'm curious whether they ever stood a chance of making it."

Before the pair could push off towards the cargo hold, Ezza felt a subtle vibration in her subdermal implants. Concentrating, she activated the incoming call and set it to full audio. "Captain Jayens here," she said aloud.

"Captain, this is Rachelle." There was an edge of worry in the cyborg's voice. Even Adams picked up on it, casting his gaze downwards.

"What's wrong, Rachelle?"

"One of the prisoners has asked to meet with you ASAP."

"So? Tell them no." Ezza prepared to push off in the direction of the cargo hold.

PALE GREY DOT

"He says he's an Earth Security Service operative."

Adams's face went pale, and he gripped the ladder as if he could fall off despite the zero-g.

Ezza took a deep breath. "I see. Credentials?"

"They all check out, Captain," Rachelle confirmed.

"Oh God," Adams said. His knuckles had turned white from holding onto the railing so tightly. "If we've stumbled onto some ESS operation ..."

Ezza waved at him to shut up. "Fine. I'll meet him in my office. What's his name?"

"Brylan Ncube."

Ezza didn't recognize it. Whether that was a good thing or not remained to be seen. "We're heading back to *Starknight* now."

"Captain, do you need me to be ...?" It wasn't like Rachelle to falter.

"No. I'll deal with this *alone*."

They made the trip back to *Starknight* in complete silence. Adams suddenly had nothing else to say, and Ezza was preoccupied with how to contain the situation. The last thing she needed was ESS's attention right now.

Her office was, like everything else on *Starknight*, small and functional. A metal desk pulled out from the wall, as did the visitor's chair just an arm's length away. With the ship still operating under zero-g conditions, harnesses hung from all surfaces to keep occupants from floating off. While other officers might have kept small mementoes or images of family vel-tacked to the walls for comfort, Ezza had nothing.

25

Don Miasek

She busied herself with reviewing Gole's combat report until there was a muffled knock from the corridor, and after a moment, the heavy door folded open. Brylan Ncube was tall, fit, and relatively young, with a full head of smooth black curls. In his dusty beige jumpsuit, Brylan would have fit right in with the Syndicate crew were it not for his swaggering movements that oozed confidence and power. Zero-g did not slow him in the least.

Without waiting to be asked, Brylan pulled the visitor's chair down from the wall and buckled in. "Ezza Jayens. My word. You, mademoiselle, are still a legend." His tone and grin matched his swagger.

Ezza set down her padd, fastening it to the magnets in the tabletop. "I'm afraid I've never heard of you, Mr. Ncube. Please close the door behind you." She rested her hands on the desk.

"Ah, yes, well, I joined after you left. And please, Brylan will do." He reached out with a foot and nudged the door. It clanged loudly as it folded shut.

"What can I do for you, Brylan?" Ezza asked, determined to keep this professional.

Ignoring the question, Brylan gestured around him with his hands. "Your ship is quite nice. Sometimes I wish ESS had some actual military assets. Your people were very effective in taking down the Syndicate crew. I was impressed." His tone suddenly turned dark. "It was inconvenient for ESS, though."

"If ESS had informed the United Fleet about your operation, then *maybe* I could have accommodated you."

PALE GREY DOT

Still grinning, Brylan pointed at her hands. "Your gloves. Are you cold, mademoiselle?"

Ezza said nothing.

His grin vanished. "Or is it to hide the cybernetics? I'm sure your crew already knows you have an advanced suite, but perhaps someone might notice just *how* advanced."

Ezza took a deep breath. "ESS never changes, does it? From the moment you floated in here, you were looking for weaknesses. You've sized up both me and my office. You're looking for any psychological defects I may have. No pictures of friends or family? Ah, I must be lonely and desperate." Ezza gave a thin smile. "My office door was closed when you arrived, therefore I'm cold and distant to my crew. I'm wearing gloves, thus I'm ashamed of my past. Allow me to give you some advice: Don't rely too much on character profiling. It is not as accurate as one might hope."

Brylan's smile was back, but this time it was sheepish. Ezza didn't buy it for a second. "I see you still remember your training," he said.

"Believe me," Ezza said, "you never forget it."

Giving an exaggerated sigh, Brylan shrugged. "Okay, I'll drop the act. It's so much more difficult when the subject doesn't instantly fear the Earth Security Service."

The act, Ezza knew, never drops either. "The fear is something you've cultivated well."

Brylan pointed at himself, and then at Ezza. "*We*," he corrected. "Something *we* have cultivated well, mademoiselle."

Ezza wished he would stop calling her that but knew better than to show weakness by asking him to stop.

"You know," Brylan continued, "I was serious when I said you are a legend. New recruits aspire to be as good as you. The United Fleet does not normally take kindly to people with nothing but state education and nearly a century and a half of classified nothingness on their record, yet here you are, a captain. I do not mind telling you that not everyone from the Athena Program has done so well."

"Really," Ezza replied, feigning disinterest. She would have loved to hear how the others were doing but refused to be baited into asking. "You still haven't gotten to the point, Brylan. What do you want?"

"You've seen the Syndicate ship."

"Yes."

"The focus on food production. I can tell you the engines and life-support systems are similarly prepped. You know what that means."

"Yes."

After a pause, he asked, "Well? Don't you want to know why a Syndicate ship would be making a run for Epsilon Eridani?"

"What makes you think I don't already know?" More than that, Ezza wanted to ask what Arun meant when he said Alexander Reuben's grip on the Syndicate was failing. ESS would surely know more than her about the organization's inner workings.

Brylan studied her face. "Nah," he said finally. "No,

mademoiselle, you don't know. Damn, though, you are good at the game. I can't tell you what a pleasure it is to go up against you."

"'Against'? Why Operative, I thought the United Fleet and ESS were on the same side."

Brylan waved his hand dismissively. "Don't insult either of our intellects."

"Then what, exactly, can I do to help you, Brylan Ncube? You will note this is the third time I've had to ask."

"I need a lift back to Jupiter Station."

"*Starknight* is needed elsewhere."

Brylan tsked. "You'll be getting orders from the Ministry of Defence in a few hours to head to Jupiter Station. You might as well prep to change course now. Save some time."

Ezza leaned back in her chair. She didn't doubt the truth of his words. "All right."

"After that, well, we'll see what you can do for ESS again."

"After that, Brylan, *Starknight* and I will be back on patrol. As you've enjoyed reminding me, I left the service." Ezza almost said "the service didn't need me anymore," but she caught herself in time.

"Oh, mademoiselle. You and I both know nobody ever really leaves ESS."

The door to Cherny's apartment banged shut. The automatic lights snapped on to reveal the overflowing trash can,

Don Miasek

crumpled clothes on the floor, and a stack of dishes on the counter. The Pull always started wonderfully, but the longer he delayed in his duty, the more it inched towards pain. Shoving aside last night's leftovers and empties from the comm unit— which he'd used as a placemat—he pressed his finger against its input pad and sat on the bed. Immediately, the unit lit up. Wiping the crumbs from the display, the call went out.

Transmission Open

Encrypting

Establishing Line to ESS—Earth Security Service HQ

Connecting

Connecting

Connecting

"Come on," Cherny urged. His leg shook and he tapped his finger against the comm unit, as if that would make it work faster. The display flashed its repeating message again, and for a second, Cherny feared the worst—that there had been some sort of mistake and his loyalty chip had been reactivated by accident. His fears were quickly allayed as the unit flashed again.

Connection Established

Line Open

Silence. After a brief hesitation, Cherny opened his mouth. "H-hello?"

PALE GREY DOT

"Operative," Her voice replied.

Cherny breathed a sigh of relief. It was rare for Her to speak aloud, but there was nothing more soothing. Or terrifying.

"I see you are still prospering," She continued.

Cherny glanced around his apartment with the bad lighting, the dirty clothes, the peeling wallpaper, and the broken electronics. If he stretched out, he could touch opposite walls at the same time. He wondered if She was being literal. It would have been trivial for Her to spy on him here.

"I took a moment to process your file since you left the service," She said, "though I have to admit, it did not take very long. Hired by the Hawaii Orbital Port Authority forty-nine years ago as a ship maintenance technician, and … well, that's about all there is, Cherny. Forty-nine years of nothing. Your social life is no better. I wonder if you still hold reservations about Sal."

Cherny rested his head against the wall of his apartment. *Please don't talk about her.* "I didn't leave. You threw me away. Me and everyone else in the Athena Program," he mumbled.

"An unfortunate situation," She replied, sounding indifferent to his plight. "But that's over now. You're reinstated to the rank of operative."

Cherny closed his eyes. It was like waking up from a nightmare. He tried to remember the mentality he used to have as an operative. The confidence, strength of will, and exactness would not come back easily to him. "Are you bringing the others back? Did you find Jenna?"

31

Don Miasek

"Do not worry about that yet, dear Cherny. We need to get you fixed up. Another operative is on her way for extraction. In one hour, there will be a car accident a few blocks north of your apartment complex. A glitch in the traffic controller will be responsible. The old you will be dead, and the new you will be on a flight to New York. The Tower awaits you. We will discuss matters during your trip."

"Does that mean …?" Cherny started to ask.

"Of course, Cherny. SecLink is ready when you are."

Cherny licked his lips and pulled a cord out from the comm unit. Rolling up his left sleeve, he inserted the tip into a port on his inner arm. Immediately, the whole world opened up to him. Cybernetics that hadn't seen use in the past five decades had new life breathed into them. He immediately felt stronger and faster, and he heard whispers from across the globe.

An operative was filing a report on ship taggings in the spaceport.

Bugs placed within the capital building in nearby Honolulu were recording a private conversation between a GreyCorp executive and the regional governor.

Agents in the Southern Manitoba Regional Governorship discussed the latest laws banning emigration to the two extrasolar-system colonies.

The movements of tens of thousands of Suspicious Persons were open to him.

All of Earth Security Service's information was at his fingertips.

PALE GREY DOT

//It feels good, doesn't it?// Her voice was now directly in his mind. It was Her preferred method of communication.

Cherny wondered if feeling was something She could do anymore. //Yes,// he admitted.

Cherny stood up from his bed. His dingy apartment now seemed smaller than before. It also now seemed utterly irrelevant. There were billions of crappy, run-down apartments across Earth, and Cherny would never have to live in one again. //Promise me You won't let me go again.//

//I promise I will always do what's best for you,// She sent. //You know you were always My favourite.//

33

WHAT WE AS A SOCIETY CAN LEARN FROM EPSILON ERIDANI
BY NIRALI KASHEM, IDEA

The latest transmission from Epsilon Eridani arrived yesterday, detailing all the challenges, dreams, and triumphs of our second extra-solar-system colony, and we wonder what we should be taking from this. For those who haven't had a chance to review the transmission, it is glowing—our colony is kicking ass!

Now, Governor Selezneva would have you believe that this is due to Earth's strong leadership, but longtime IDEA readers will know what silliness that is. The woman lives in the DC Fortress. She has about as much impact on Eridani as a butterfly flapping its wings.

No, Eridani is prospering for a very different reason: Earth *can't* control Eridani—the laws of physics are tougher than Earth's laws! It's a twenty-one-year round-trip delay before we hear the results of the Governor's proclamations. No wonder they aren't bothering to listen anymore!

That means they aren't bound by the same anti-technological bent of our illustrious government. Venus, Mars, Jupiter Station, Alpha Centauri, and Epsilon Eridani. We settled amazing places purely out of a sense of adventure and discovery. Now? Now we cower in fear of what technology can do to hurt us. Eridani won't be hampered by that.

Read on through this week's issue, true believers, and we'll explore how distance equates to unparalleled freedom, and how the Eridani Sympathizers may be doing more harm than good for our long-distance friends. Also, don't forget to donate for more articles like this!

3

It's amazing how quickly the old instincts come back,* Cherny thought. Three hours ago, he was working as a labourer, and now he was on a first-class flight to Toronto. Gone was his sweaty, stained jumpsuit and the dirt beneath his fingernails. Now he wore an elegant dark grey suit, and for the first time in ages, he felt truly clean. He eased back into the synth-leather chair, a glass of red wine in his hand, as a thousand data threads passed through his mind. There was so much to catch up on.

A woman slept in the seat next to him, oblivious to his SecLink connection. Two virtual reality cables—power and data—ran between her arm and the armrest of her chair. Socialite? Business exec? Some high-ranking government bureaucrat? It took Cherny a moment to remember that he no longer had to guess such things. He glanced at her face, and SecLink had the answers within moments. Her name was Kavitha Marcoccia, she lived in Toronto, and her schooling was online with GreyCorp, where she now worked. He knew with whom she last spoke, her favourite foods, her lovers, every VR experience she ever had, and more. He could know her entire life, if he desired it.

Cherny sipped his wine in satisfaction.

It felt good to be serving again. He wasn't sure if it was the loyalty chip or a natural reaction to missing his work. There was still something not quite right, though. He remembered SecLink perfectly. He often dreamt about it. But something was different. //Are You there?// he transmitted.

//Of course, Operative.// Her voice was in his head again. //I always have time for you.//

//You're keeping something from me. I can't find any of the others from the Athena Program. Where's Jenna? Ezza? Sienar? There's no information on them anywhere.//

//In due time, Cherny.//

Cherny frowned, setting down his glass. //I'm no good to You without all the information. Please don't keep me in the dark.//

She didn't reply. Silence was always a bad sign from Her, and Cherny worried he'd pushed Her too far. With one snap of Her fingers, he'd be back at Tsiolkovsky Spaceport, suffering whatever abuse Minsk saw fit to dole out.

//The Ganymede Blitz, Cherny. Tell me, did you hear of it?// She finally asked.

From anyone else, it would have been a simple question, but Cherny knew nothing was ever simple with Her. Woven

PALE GREY DOT

into the fabric of the question was a second one: did you manage to stay well informed throughout your exile, or were you helpless without Me? //No,// he reluctantly admitted. He didn't need another reminder of how much he'd always needed Her.

//Then allow me to educate you with the short version. It took nearly forty years of concentrated investigation for us to insert three of our operatives within the top ranks of the Syndicate. It took another four to carefully manoeuvre ships and personnel into the Ganymede region without arousing suspicion.//

//Sounds like You could have used us.// Cherny regretted sending it the second he did, but luckily She ignored the comment. Gazing out the window, Cherny could see the western coast of North America passing beneath them. To anyone else on the craft, Cherny appeared calm and serene, but he felt neither of those things.

//It was going to be magnificent. The culmination of the largest project in the past century. We lured all the top names. Ellaria and the Analyst. Members from the Comptroller's Guild. We even managed to draw Alexander Reuben himself out. Daniel, Sienar, and Ghanshyam had played their parts perfectly.//

Cherny couldn't help but feel disappointed by all the excitement he'd missed out on. Hearing these names brought back memories of the best times of his life.

//But when it came time to close the trap, it all went wrong. I will leave you to review the details at your leisure,

Don Miasek

but needless to say, every Syndicate leader assembled escaped unscathed, and Daniel and Ghanshyam are dead.//

Cherny jolted in his seat. The woman next to him snorted and glared at him through her VR haze. "Sorry," he muttered.

//It gets worse, Operative,// She continued. //Sienar has defected to the Syndicate.//

Impossible, he thought instantly.

Though it was so long ago, Cherny remembered when he'd first met Sienar. He remembered the long helicraft ride and being packed in with twenty-nine other kids ranging from four to seven. Cherny had pressed his nose up against the frosted window to catch a glimpse of the snowed-out landing pad. He had been excited and scared as the educators led them through the underground facility to their dormitories. But then they'd separated him from the others. His room wasn't with the others, they had said. Instead, they marched him to a special classroom. At first, Sienar was the only one there. He'd looked up from the toy plane he'd been playing with and handed Cherny the controller with a big smile. Sal had been added within the hour, and the three became instant friends. Over the following months and years, the remaining three had been added, and they were never separated again. Not until the Martian Insurrection, at least. There was no way that Sienar, of all people, would betray ESS. The man lived, breathed, and bled Earth Security Service.

Though She could not read his mind through SecLink, She must have sensed his doubt. //I am aware you and Sienar

PALE GREY DOT

were close. Closer than you were with Sal, perhaps.// The tone of Her transmission was cold and sterile, as if She only knew the concept of closeness in clinical terms.

//No. No, that's not a problem,// Cherny insisted. He knew what She was really asking. //My loyalty is to You, not them.//

//I never doubted you for an instant,// She replied.

Cherny let go of a breath he hadn't realized he'd been holding. //How do You know he turned?//

//The Syndicate was tipped off to our trap. Every solider and ESS agent sent in was slaughtered. All assets were accounted for ... except for Sienar.//

//But, I ... That's not ...// Cherny stopped to collect himself. //Maybe he was killed. If he went rogue, you'd have reactivated his loyalty chip. The Athena Protocols would—//

//Oh my dear, sweet Cherny,// She transmitted with a sigh, //you always did see only the best in people—especially those you care about—but you should know better than to think I could ever be wrong about something like this. Stand by, Operative.//

Cherny raised his glass and caught the attendant's eye.

"One in the air is two on the ground, sir," the attendant warned.

Cherny offered a weak smile. "I'll be fine."

The attendant nodded slowly and obligingly refilled his glass before moving onward, leaving Cherny alone with Her.

A file passed through his mind. //When Sienar went missing, we investigated. There were concerns of capture, of

39

course, which I could not allow. You know I would do anything for My agents.//

What She meant was that She did not easily give up what was Hers, Cherny knew.

//We scoured his history. We found uncertainty in his past behaviour. Conversations with fellow operatives—seemingly innocuous, but now we understand he was seeking friends he could trust. Had he found any, I am sure he would have coerced them into defection as well. Data forensics from the over-watches revealed secret transmissions to unknown locations, logs rewritten to cover his tracks. In the wake of the failed blitz, the Syndicate became emboldened. My agents began hearing rumours of new sources of information within their ranks.//

It pained Cherny to think that his friend could ever do something like this. //Why? I mean, there must be theories on why he'd do this.//

//Perhaps he felt disenchanted with our methods,// She replied. //As threats to the government's stability grow, our escalation must always be proportional. Or perhaps he was never the man we thought he was.//

Or maybe ESS wasn't the same without us, Cherny mused. The six of them had played, lived, and worked together since they were children. The Martian Insurrection had shattered those who'd survived. He hadn't spoken to them since. Cherny doubted it would have taken Sienar forty-nine years to defect if he'd simply missed them, though.

//There is more,// She continued. //Jenna has murdered one of my operatives.//

PALE GREY DOT

The name made Cherny shift uncomfortably in his seat. // This is why You brought me back,// he realized. Sal was long dead. Taylor too, though he at least deserved it. Sienar and Jenna had betrayed the agency. That left only him and Ezza.

//In part, Operative. The failure of the Athena Six during the Martian Insurrection was a disaster, but a disaster I could deal with. Now another one of you is responsible for the greatest catastrophe in the history of the Earth Security Service,// She replied. //Letting the rest of you go free was too merciful of Me. I am recalling you and Ezza back to service. One way or another, Cherny, we are going to wipe clean all the mistakes of the Athena Program.//

·

There was no greater symbol of projected power than Jupiter Station. Even the stations orbiting Earth paled in comparison in size and economic importance. Comprised of a dozen rings stacked around a central pylon, each housed a small city's worth of businesses, infrastructure, and people under gleaming domed windows. Jupiter Station's gentle rotation provided gravity to its berthed ships. It was the closest thing to a metropolis past Mars. "The last bastion of civilization," some called it. "The farthest reach of Earth," said others.

Ezza took a deep breath as she stepped out of the airlock. Compared to her *Starknight*, Terminal 3 on Ring 4 was a sprawling display of open spaces and comfort. There were thousands of people embarking or disembarking, and

41

thousands more waiting to greet or send off friends and family. Most wore the bright reds and blues that marked them as Jupiter Station locals, and Ezza spotted more than a few United Fleet uniforms, but ultimately, every corner of the solar system was represented somewhere on the station.

A restaurant with flashing neon lights beckoned anyone with a taste for the exotic inside. A man at a kiosk between the terminal's gates hocked souvenirs and jewellery "all the way from the asteroid belt." A man and woman were huddled over one of the display cases, deciding on engagement rings. Nearby, a woman led a small group through the throng. *Zeus Tours: The King of Tourism* was emblazoned on her jacket.

The wall beside the airlock lit up, displaying the face of an algorithm-approved woman. "Hello, Ezza Jayens," the avatar said in a singsong voice. "Would you be interested in hearing about Jupiter Station's delectable array of offerings? Hestia Way has the finest cuisine in the solar system. Martian? Venusian? Earthen? Hestia Way has it all! Craving action? You're a five-minute vacuum train ride away from Jupiter Station's zero-g central pylon! Interested in exotic getaways? See the volcanoes of Io up close with the Vulcanist Travel Bureau, gaze upon the sensational fish life deep within Europa, or relax on Ganymede, Jupiter's largest moon, at the system-famous Solatium Lodge."

Ezza stepped past the ad, focusing instead on taking in the sights. Looking up at the ceiling's bright domed windows, she could barely make out Ring 4's curvature. As much

PALE GREY DOT

contrast as there was between *Starknight* and the dock, she knew the real action would be on the station's Prime Hub— the most central ring in the station's structure. Members of her crew strode past her, eager to begin shore leave after the stress of battle. The station had all the comforts of Earth, but without the suffocating crowds or the noxious fumes.

"I love this place," Brylan said as he appeared next to her. Though only herself, Rachelle, and Adams knew of his status as an ESS operative, the man had kept to himself in the secondary hull throughout the trip. Nobody had wanted to field questions on why a Syndicate prisoner was now suddenly free to roam the ship. "So much loose information floating about, just waiting to be snatched," Brylan purred.

He wore a bright blue business suit with golden highlights. It was garish, yet it allowed him to blend in perfectly with the other Jupiter Station corporate employees. If she didn't know better, she would have sworn he was just another two-hundred-year-old veteran from the business sector.

"Well, Operative," she said, "you've arrived, safe and sound, as ordered." When Admiral Tolj gave the command for *Starknight* to set course for Jupiter Station, she hadn't been surprised to learn that Brylan had told the truth. "I assume you're off to tell Her all about your mission."

"Don't worry, mademoiselle. We've been in contact with one another the whole time." Brylan frowned slightly. "SecLink is always so awkward at long distances. Sometimes the speed of light isn't fast enough, you know?"

Ezza knew. "Personally, I always cherished the time lag.

43

Trust me when I say this: you don't want to be too close to Her at all times."

"Given your history, I'd have thought you'd have better insight when it comes to the importance of Her friendship." The operative glanced briefly at Ezza before sweeping a lock of his black curls aside. "See you soon, Captain. Thanks for the lift." Turning away, he joined the Jupiter Station masses, becoming just another man that had managed to escape Earth.

Good riddance.

Her thoughts were quickly echoed as Adams stepped up alongside her. "Thank God. If you don't mind me saying so, ma'am, I feel a lot safer without him on board."

"ESS is more bark than bite, Lieutenant," she replied. "The threat of pain has always been more effective than the pain itself."

"I've had personal experience that says otherwise, ma'am." Adams shook his head, staring in the direction that Brylan had headed.

Ezza looked back in surprise. "I didn't know you had a run-in with ESS."

They both scanned the teeming crowd of people in the terminal. The confused man looking for flight information on his padd could be an informant. The guide rattling off facts to her tour group about the significance of the station's construction could be a surveillance officer scanning new visitors. The trinkets being sold at the nearby kiosk could be fitted with bugs, scanners, or demolition charges. Jupiter

PALE GREY DOT

Station wasn't Earth; there was a modicum of freedom. But still ...

Ezza recalled that Adams was a Mars national. She wondered if he had been there during the strife of the Martian Insurrection—the brief alliance between the Martian city states against Earth. Ezza tried to put it out of her mind. *It wasn't your fault,* she reminded herself. *Or anyone else's.*

"Ah, Carmen's just sent the finished inventory list of what we'll need to resupply and rearm the ship," Adams said. "We should be able to start restocking within seventy-two hours."

Ezza appreciated the change of subject. Before she could answer, she felt a soft buzzing. Ezza switched the incoming call to full audio. Tapping a transmission was no harder for ESS than bugging the terminal. Still, Ezza and Adams took several steps back towards the airlock leading to *Starknight* for some semblance of privacy. "Captain Jayens here. What's the problem, Rachelle?" she asked.

"I've completed our link-up with the United Fleet office on Jupiter Station. There's some unusual movement of arms and personnel."

"What are you thinking, Rachelle?"

"There are all the hallmarks of assembling a new fleet. The *Athabaskan* and *Stalwart* are gearing up for flagship duty."

Any fleet centred around two battlecruisers would be bigger than anything seen in the past two decades, Ezza knew.

Adams furrowed his brow. "Something this significant would have been mentioned in our daily status briefs." He looked at his captain questioningly.

45

Don Miasek

"No," Ezza admitted, "I hadn't been informed of this." She had a growing suspicion as to why. "Adams, get back to the ship. Tell Carmen we're to arm for long-term fleet action. Rachelle, place a call to Admiral Tolj's office and tell them I'm on my way."

"What if he's unavailable?"

"He won't be," Ezza muttered. "He'll be expecting me."

She strode through the station terminal, ignoring the merchants and brushing past the tours. Given Jupiter Station's size and stacked layout, Ezza knew navigation was going to be a nightmare. Traffic to the Prime Hub, either by internal transport or star-car, could be an exercise in frustration.

Ezza climbed into the first cab she saw. Pressing her finger against the dashboard sensor, it registered her name and expense account. She transmitted her destination. Prime Hub. United Fleet Jupiter Headquarters. The computer beeped obligingly and merged into the heavy traffic. Ezza set the windows to one-way and gazed out.

The cab slowly kept pace with the cars in front of it. Its engine was nearly silent, leaving Ezza alone with her thoughts. She recalled *Starknight*'s capture of the Syndicate vessel a few days prior. She had initially dismissed Arun's threats and his idiotic plan to escape the solar system. But now, with a fleet being assembled, there was clearly more going on.

The cab passed underneath one of the expansive domed windows peering out into space. Silhouetted against the planet Jupiter was the *Athabaskan*. Its massive double-hull

PALE GREY DOT

structure was heavily armoured. From here, she could make out the missile ports and mine bays dotted alongside its hull.

No single ship could stand against a battlecruiser, and now the United Fleet was putting together a fleet containing two. Ezza tried to think of a target worthy of an armada like that. The Syndicate's piracy and other criminal enterprises always relied on speed and secrecy, not brute force. Chasing after anarchists wasn't a job for a single mass of ships.

The cab shifted onto another roadway, speeding up as it left the traffic behind. The great arched windows above the ring-connector corridors revealed more spaceships. A heavy-duty transport with slow but powerful engines was having its bays loaded with cargo containers on Ring 5. A starliner, bright hull reflecting the light of the station, was docked at one of Terminal 6's most upscale gates. A mining frigate pushed off from its mooring.

Ezza thought about all the people, from every corner of the solar system, going about their business. How many of them had she spied on for Her, she wondered. Whose pain and suffering were she and the others responsible for? Sal's and Taylor's, certainly, but also countless other faces and names she could barely remember.

She closed her eyes as she recalled Taylor, who was the second—and last—to pay the price for their failures. Ezza hoped the survivors had landed on their feet after the Athena Six broke apart, as she had. She wondered whether Sienar was still with ESS. He was the only good person there, as far as she could tell.

The next thing she knew, the cab's computer was beeping at her.

Ezza shifted in her seat, opening her eyes.

The cab beeped again, this time adding in a soft voice, "You have arrived at United Fleet Jupiter Headquarters. Thank you for your patronage with GreyCorp Cabs. GreyCorp Cabs aims to satisfy your driving needs."

Ezza rubbed her temples with gloved hands. *I must have been more tired than I thought.* The cab door slid up, and she stepped out into Jupiter Station's Prime Hub. If Ring 4 had been the tourism sector, then the Hub was the downtown core, entertainment district, and government affairs all rolled into one. Across the street was a park with real grass and trees. Ezza took a moment to watch the children playing. *They must actually have parents raising them*, she mused.

It was a sight far different from her own upbringing. As an unlicensed drop-off baby, she was enrolled in the state-run educational system on the Vesta Archipelago, an asteroid-based mining installation. It hadn't lasted long, though. Some calculation decided she had potential, and at eight years old, she'd been shipped off to Kazan on Earth. That was where she'd met the rest of her new family.

The Kazan Institute for Education had no grass or parks like Jupiter Station. Instead, it plugged students into VR terminals for hours, followed by physical training and lectures that taught the wonders of Earth's government and the dangers of revolution. Ezza hadn't minded it back then, and

PALE GREY DOT

a part of her still didn't. The control and discipline helped make her into the woman she was today.

Enjoy your years of freedom, kids, she thought. *After that, you get to join the workforce where you'll be stuck doing the same dredge job for half a millennium.* Common wisdom said that the farther away from Earth you were, the better your chances were of avoiding never-ending stagnation. She wondered if that held true for Alpha Centauri and Epsilon Eridani too. Ezza headed for the main gate.

The United Fleet's Jupiter headquarters was a flurry of activity. Ezza could sense the stress from the terse way the guard checked her credentials and waved her through. The soldiers walking the building perimeter eyed everyone with suspicion, and the number of scanner drones had doubled since Ezza was last here. The halls were filled with officers and enlisted personnel rushing to their destinations with a grim sense of urgency. ESS had deactivated many of her cybernetics' higher functions upon her exile, hampering her ability to eavesdrop, but the energy of the room spoke volumes.

Ezza stepped aside as a squad of marines jogged past her. Their faces were stoic, but Ezza recognized the demeanour of her colleagues preparing to march off to battle.

The United Fleet war room was the central hub of activity within the headquarters building. Circular and tall, half a dozen separate stations were manned by officers reviewing wireframe holographic ship schematics and maps charting local areas of space. A trio of full-convert cyborgs, plugged into huge data banks, methodically read out information for their colleagues.

In the middle of it all was a massive holographic display that dwarfed the others. Jupiter Station, coded in dark green, slowly revolved midair. White vacuum trains travelled through its terminals while short-range cargo ships ran between the station and its docked fleets, moving weapons, fuel, personnel, and more. The twenty-seven United Fleet ships were highlighted in bright red. Ezza's *Starknight*, in contrast to the others, was dull grey.

On a raised platform in the centre of the room stood Admiral Raymond Tolj, supervising it all. The admiral was well over four hundred years old, and the last century had taken its toll. Thin hair barely covered the liver spots on his forehead, and sagging skin lined his eyes and jaw. While most people his age opted to maintain a youthful appearance, Tolj instead cultivated an image of experience. Ezza once recalled him saying that it made people underestimate him, though how anyone could do that while he barked orders to three separate groups at once was beyond her.

Stepping aside to let an aide rush past her, Ezza remained content to watch the scene in silence. A major operation by her very own organization and she knew nothing about it. It never used to be like this. ESS spies often knew what the Admiralty was going to do before they even decided on it.

"And get a secondary line over to the *Raptor*, unless you want to personally oversee the paperwork that'll be generated when a missile destroyer can't keep up with the rest of

PALE GREY DOT

the fleet," Tolj warned an aide. His voice was a mixture of humour and authority. "So long as Captain Faulkes can—" The admiral suddenly glanced in Ezza's direction, and she instinctively stood up straighter. For the first time since her arrival, people seemed to notice her presence. "Gupta, take over."

Tolj slowly descended the steps from the supervisor's platform. As he approached, he broke into a wide smile. "Ezza, it's good to see you again." No one else could transition from your superior to your best friend like the admiral.

"It's good to see you too, sir," Ezza replied earnestly.

"Eight years is too long," Tolj said.

"I'd have to agree."

Tolj turned, looking out at the buzzing war room. "I know why you're here, Captain, and the answer is no." Ezza opened her mouth to retort, but the admiral simply raised a hand, cutting her off. "You'll be getting your written orders to return to normal patrol duties tomorrow. If you like, you can get a jump on that and start prepping for it now."

"Wait, sir, I can see what's going on here," Ezza said, putting together her thoughts even as they rushed out of her mouth. "We intercepted a Syndicate ship making a beeline out of the solar system with an ESS operative on board, and now you're assembling a fleet. You've stumbled across some sort of major threat—I don't know, maybe the Syndicate has gotten its hands on nukes—and are mobilizing to deal with it. What's more, *Tyrannis*'s captain claims Reuben's leadership is slipping. With the inevitable infighting, and

51

the United Fleet bearing down on the Syndicate, they probably decided to jump ship as deserters and leave the system before things get ugly."

Tolj stared at her in disbelief.

Ezza didn't slow down. "And you've excluded me from this mission despite my ship being one of the best tracker-fighters in the United Fleet. You've seen fit to include me in every major operation since I joined. Why not this time?" Ezza furrowed her brow, but then it came to her. "Ah, of course. Intel falls under the purview of ESS. That means whatever you're after probably came from them. Command still doesn't trust me," she said, indignant. "They think I'm still working for ESS, so they cut me out of the mission."

"That," he replied, "is an amazing bit of extrapolation based on zero evidence."

"Then I'm right?" Ezza's eyes brightened.

"No."

Ezza studied him, old habits kicking in. She heard his breathing, observed his eyes and the lines around his face, and measured any split second of hesitation. "But I'm right about ESS being involved, aren't I?"

"Watch it," Tolj snapped. Ezza suddenly became acutely aware of their height difference as he towered over her. The grandfather was gone. "We may be friends, Captain, but I'm still your commanding officer."

Ezza retreated, ashamed for arguing with the man who rescued her fifty-one years ago. "I'm sorry, sir. I was out of line."

PALE GREY DOT

"I'm not the only one in the Admiralty who made this decision, Captain," Tolj explained. "We have every reason to be cautious with ESS."

"If I may ask, sir, why was I allowed in the building if I was just going to be turned away?"

Tolj took a deep breath. A look of regret passed briefly over his face. "Because while I wasn't the only one to make the call, I *am* the only one who felt you deserved to be told face to face. Return to your ship, Ezza. You're not needed here."

To Cherny's cybernetically enhanced eyes, the quiet Toronto street corner was filled with violence. Pieced together from eyewitness footage and the finest forensic software in the solar system, the simulation of a fellow operative's last moments unfolded before Cherny. The shimmering image of Jenna knelt beside Marcus's fallen form, ready to plunge the med-stim into his chest. But then she muttered something—the witnesses hadn't been able to make it out—and returned the syringe to her pocket, unused.

They still had a few hours of darkness left, but the neon lights from the surrounding buildings were strong enough that Cherny could make out every detail as easy as day, even without cybernetic assistance.

"It must be hard to see an old colleague like this," said the woman with the tied-back blonde hair next to him. Clad in a black suit, Amanda watched the scene with apparent indifference. Like Cherny, she wore a sleek, high-end breather. Unlike his old industrial version, the filtered air from this device tasted clean and pure.

More than just a colleague, Cherny thought. He crouched, placing his hand where Jenna and Marcus had exchanged their last words. No sign of their lethal encounter remained. When he landed in Toronto, the news reported that a government-employed dredge had been attacked by a Syndicate terrorist, but that the culprit had been captured and would receive fair justice.

No, Cherny thought, *Jenna is still out there, and whatever she gets in the end, it isn't likely to be justice.* "The Athena Protocols affected us all differently," he explained to Amanda. "Taylor ..." Cherny searched for the words. He tapped his finger against the side of his forehead.

"Went mad?" Amanda suggested dryly. "Killed thousands during the Martian Insurrection?"

Cherny winced. It was hard to think of him as a murderer. Taylor had always been an asshole, even as a kid, but somewhere along the line, the Athena Protocols twisted him into something grotesque. And he dragged poor Sal down with him. "But the rest of us ..." he stressed, "I mean, the rest of us were fine. I thought Jenna had come through it okay."

"Mmm," Amanda said. "Perhaps the detrimental effects of the procedure were merely delayed with her. Or perhaps her early years in the Midwestern Wastes simply caught up with her. It is a testament to Her kindness that She ever let Jenna join our prestigious organization in the first place."

PALE GREY DOT

Jenna was better than you give her credit for, Cherny thought. "Yes, She was always good to us," Cherny quickly agreed. The last thing he wanted was to think about it. Cherny couldn't decide whether he loved the Pull or hated it, and its return had done nothing to make the answer clearer to him. For now, it was silent, and he knew it would continue to be silent as long as he did whatever She wanted him to do.

"Of course," Amanda replied, sounding unimpressed. Cherny knew that behind the breather, Amanda had sharp features, with high cheekbones and a narrow jaw. When they met at the airport, she had welcomed him with cold and unfriendly professionalism. Behind those dark eyes, however, Cherny thought he detected a hint of dislike for him. He had yet to see her smile.

Cherny motioned with his hand, and the virtual scene replayed. Jenna's form reappeared on the opposite side of the street. She looked so thin. He crossed the street, gesturing. "Look at this. Jenna is already heading towards Marcus. If you trace her path back, it's clear to me that she's been stalking him for the past, oh, ten minutes or so. She knew where he was and where he was heading."

Amanda slowly stepped across the deserted roadway, listening.

"Now, Marcus was planted within GreyCorp's head office. That's a class-five position and isn't available on the normal intranet, yet she found him anyway."

Amanda stopped in front of the frozen illusionary Jenna, staring at her. Cherny could almost feel her disgust for their

Don Miasek

wayward comrade radiating from the woman. Betraying the agency was abhorrent, and again he was reminded of Sienar.

Cherny motioned with his hand, returning Jenna to her crouched position next to the fallen agent. "She grabbed everything useful off his cybernetics suite without even having to check. So not only did she manage to track him down, but she knew his complete read-out of onboard systems."

Amanda stepped to the side, looking past Jenna towards Cherny. "You aren't suggesting what I think you are."

Cherny licked his lips behind his breather. "The fact that she managed to get into Toronto undetected by ESS makes it clear to me." He pointed to the twisted, black tower on the skyline. It was barely visible in the smog and darkness, only partially illuminated by the surrounding buildings. "Jenna had access to SecLink."

"I don't see how that's possible," Amanda replied. "She'd be noticed the instant she connected."

"Don't underestimate her skills. Never, ever underestimate her," Cherny warned.

Amanda crossed her arms. Even through the mask, Cherny could see her skepticism. "Jenna's loyalty chip was activated decades ago. Even if she somehow neutralized it, SecLink would feed her the Athena Protocols. If she reconnected to SecLink, she'd return to Her."

Cherny shook his head. "Jenna is the most resilient person I've ever known. If anyone is strong enough to resist, it's her." *Unlike me,* he thought. *Coward.* The virtual Jenna was now holding the syringe over Marcus's heart. He could

56

PALE GREY DOT

swear he saw her hand tremble before withdrawing it. Did a witness really capture that, or was he just hoping she at least hesitated before letting Marcus die?

Amanda looked down at the rogue operative. "I suppose it's possible. You certainly have a very high opinion of her."

"Ah, no," Cherny said, shaking his head vigorously. "I know where you're going with that, but my loyalty has always been to ESS, even over my fellow Athena Six members."

"Even Sal?"

Cherny did not hesitate. "Even Sal."

"I expected nothing less," Amanda replied coolly. "She has full confidence in both your abilities and your allegiance. Otherwise She would not have permitted your return."

"Right," Cherny said. "Good."

"I assume we're done here, then? Are you ready to visit the Tower?"

Cherny looked back at the skyline. Two of the six had now betrayed the agency, so he knew the hostility he would be facing. *No*, he thought. "Yes," he said.

57

4

Jenna sat on the bed, holding Marcus's memory drive between her thumb and forefinger. It was chrome, covered in circuitry, and no bigger than a grape. The actual data contained within was microscopic. The rest of the drive's size accommodated the transmitter and hardware-level encryption.

The motel room's lights flickered, but Jenna paid it no mind. The mould in the corners of the walls, the dirty sheets, and the dripping faucet in the closet-sized bathroom weren't important to her. She'd escaped Toronto and could rest while she planned her next move. Still, she knew it wasn't safe here. The man who rented the place to her had stared at her with shifty eyes. ESS could be tracking her right now.

She pushed her sweat-drenched hair out of her eyes, then rolled up her left sleeve, revealing the rough cybernetics of her arm. It used to be clean, shiny, and new, but decades

PALE GREY DOT

of self-surgery had left things a touch haphazard. For a moment, she hesitated. Developing the software to access an ESS memory drive had taken even longer than creating the data decrypter to access SecLink. After years of scrounging through GreyCorp trash bins for equipment, hacking EarthNet to co-opt whatever processing power was available, and ambushing low-ranked ESS agents, she'd finally found an operative's whereabouts. Marcus's vulnerability had been a stroke of luck, and successfully subduing him was an even bigger one.

This might not work. It might fry my brain. Then she remembered what happened to Taylor and Sal. *It's Her fault they're dead. This is the only way to avenge them, and the only way to get my surviving brothers and sister back. Do it for them.*

Jenna placed the data drive into one of her arm's slots. She heard the click and felt the connection take hold. "Let's see what you were thinking about before the end," she muttered.

Jenna's mind opened the instant her head hit the pillow.

The floor-to-ceiling faux windows overlooking the Toronto skyline through the smoke and smog were instantly familiar as Marcus sprinted through the Tower's halls. Real windows were a structural liability She never would have tolerated, so the "view" was merely a projected simulation. Agents and technicians ran to their posts, and Marcus ducked to the side to let a pair of security officers rush past in the other direction.

Jenna's subdermal implants were tingling—no, wait, they

Don Miasek

were Marcus's, not hers. The sensation of being connected to a greater whole came flooding back to her. Through her—no, his—implants, she realized the entire Tower was on lockdown. *When is this?* she wondered.

Barely breathing hard despite his breakneck speed, Marcus turned the corner and sped towards the heavy-duty door that led to one of the overwatch hideouts. The powerful mechanisms within the frame churned as the Tower's systems recognized him. The door unlocked with a deep, muffled clang.

Marcus slipped inside, letting the blast-proof door close behind him. The air in the cramped hideout was stuffy, but then, it was unlikely the two overwatches even noticed. Cables linked the man and woman to each other, and to the computer terminals bolted to the walls and hanging from the ceiling, which connected them to the Tower's central systems. Billions of ESS sources, spread across the solar system, flowed through their nervous systems.

"Well, well, how are my two favourite overwatches doing?" Marcus said, trying to lighten the mood.

Never turning from his dead stare straight ahead, the man raised his hand. The wires connected to it jingle-jangled against each other. "Hey, Marcus. Welcome to our abode," Adrian said grimly. Like the woman, his body was a tangled mess of wires woven around a thin metal frame. Calling him a full-convert cyborg would have been insufficient, for what little bodily flesh remained was covered by ports and circuitry. When he moved, the

PALE GREY DOT

cords attaching him to the surrounding computer banks twitched and jiggled.

Jenna had worked with plenty of overwatches during her time. As far as she was concerned, it wasn't devotion to the security of Earth that made them twist their bodies into these computerized monstrosities. It was the desire to live away from reality. A little voice in the back of her mind asked whether her motives for agreeing to the Athena Program were any different, but Jenna ignored it.

"If we weren't facing a disaster, I'd grab you guys a café. Or maybe something stronger," Marcus said. To Jenna's annoyance, his interest in his overwatches felt genuine. It would have been easier if he had been an asshole.

"The last thing Adrian needs is more drugs going through his system," replied the woman. Her voice was slow and distant.

"Jealous Esther," Adrian retorted. "You just wish"—the man halted mid-speech, but after a moment, he resumed as if nothing had happened—"you could hold your liquor like I can." His grin—one of the few natural parts of his body— was wide and toothy now.

"Focus," Marcus cut in. Overwatches were easily distracted, Jenna and Marcus thought. "Now, what have we got?"

Esther's pinky finger twitched, and the screen on one of the cramped walls lit up with a map of Olympus Mons—the Martian capital.

No. Please, no, Jenna thought. She knew what this was. It

61

was June 12, 2459. The day fifty-one years ago when everything went wrong. Back on the motel bed, she struggled to make her flesh-and-blood arm work, trying to get it over to rip the memory drive from its socket.

Olympus Mons was the first and largest above-ground city on terraformed Mars. Resting on the eastern cliffs circling the massive volcano that gave the city its name, it had once been a shining example of human ingenuity, spirit, and bravery. Within Marcus's memory, however, the city map was filled with markers indicating where fires had broken out.

It all looked so clinical from a planet away, but Marcus knew better. "Get me a news feed," he said curtly, keeping his voice steady.

Adrian's hand moved an imperceptible amount, and a pop-up of a stunned Martian newscaster appeared in the upper right corner. "The damage has spread across Liberty Way, bringing oxygen levels dangerously low. Authorities are pleading with all residents to stay indoors and gather emergency oxygen supplies."

Another twitch from the overwatch, and another pop-up appeared. Then another, and another. The voices rapidly overlapped.

"The Seneca Building's collapse has resulted in—"

"Possible terrorist activities—"

"Detonation has been detected at the Hippodrome—"

"Earth's involvement is believed—"

"No motive—"

Pale Grey Dot

"Reports are saying Demeter Sector has been engulfed in the flames—"

Marcus watched in horror, eyes wide and mouth agape. SecLink was barely comprehensible amid desperate cries for orders as information flew from one side of the solar system to the other. "I don't believe it," he breathed, raising his hand to steady himself against the wall. "How the hell did they screw this up?"

Jenna squirmed, closing her eyes in an attempt to block it out. As bad as it looked on the news, it had been so much worse in person. Jenna remembered parents holding their children and people fighting over breather masks. She remembered the losers gasping for air as the fires fed on the precious oxygen. Asphyxiation is a bad way to go. Jenna could feel Marcus's memories starting to fade. Thank God the data drive didn't have much more of this.

Out of the corner of Marcus's eye, another pop-up flared to life. *Mission Objectives*, it read. Jenna knew them by heart.

1. Defuse the Martian Insurrection via negotiation.

2. Failing that, defuse the Martian Insurrection via blackmail, extortion, disruption, or other non-lethal means.

3. Failing that, kill the Martian leadership with plausible deniability; frame a third party.

4. Failing that, kill the Martian leadership and accept Earthen involvement.

There were no parameters listed for destroying the entire city, and for once, the two overwatches were quiet.

63

Don Miasek

Marcus placed his hand on Adrian's mechanical shoulder. "Find me the Athena Six."

The overwatch nodded, and within moments, blue icons appeared on the map. Each was labelled, but Jenna didn't need to look. She remembered exactly where she'd been. Marcus and Jenna's vision began to fizzle, but the map and the fires were still vivid in her mind.

Marcus slowly shook his head. "That's only four of them. Where are the other two?"

Adrian's face darkened as he searched. "Operatives Taylor and Sal are no longer connected to SecLink. Last report has Sienar and Cherny searching their last known positions."

At that time of the year, there was a twenty-two-minute communication lag between Earth and Mars. Marcus had never felt so helpless. "That's it, then. The United Fleet wins." Marcus's voice faded into mental static. "It's over …"

The claustrophobic hideout slipped from Jenna's surroundings into nothingness. Now she and Marcus were elsewhere.

"Victoria, it has been too long." Marcus broke into a genuine smile.

Jenna quickly took stock of the new environment. The smell of roasting lamb and assorted vegetables made Jenna's mouth water in real life. This was a fine Toronto restaurant, though Jenna didn't recognize which. The warm notes of a violin, being played by a pretty woman in a gown, drifted through the air above the chatter of patrons.

While the overlapping conversations might be indistinct

PALE GREY DOT

to the normal observer, agents were trained to hear and process everything, and Marcus and Jenna were no exception. Within an instant, she recognized the ESS shop talk amongst the patrons. This was an ESS-secured lounge, she realized. Jenna refocused her attention on the two women sitting across from Marcus.

Not many women could captivate Marcus like Victoria could. Her lustrous black hair rolled over her shoulders, framing her heart-shaped face. While her lips betrayed no sign of emotion, her dark blue eyes shone mischievously, as if everything amused her. Marcus couldn't decide if the woman's black suit made her look more enticing, or dangerous.

Beside her was a taller woman whose blonde hair was tied straight back. Marcus recognized the hairstyle and her uniform as belonging to the Toronto Governorship Security detail. The blonde stared at him, as if studying him for weaknesses. All good agents were trained to do this to everyone they meet, Marcus mused, but it was bad form to be so obvious about it.

Jenna didn't recognize either of the women.

"Marcus, my dear," Victoria purred, "I only wish our reunion wasn't due to such dark circumstances."

Marcus shook his head at the shame of it all. "Where were you when you heard?"

"The DC Fortress. Minister Havoic was briefing the United Fleet Admiralty on the discovery of the Syndicate stronghold. 'An opportunity for the United Fleet to right

65

what ESS wronged,' I believe were his exact words. After the Ganymede Blitz, our sweet master ordered me home."

Marcus scoffed. "Just when you think you know a man, he goes and betrays everything he's ever stood for—everything we've ever fought for."

"I had the pleasure of working with Sienar," Victoria said. "Skilled. Professional. Loyal. Or so I thought."

Jenna had heard of the disaster at the Uruk Sulcus-132 outpost on Ganymede, and rumours across EarthNet spoke of some kind of ESS cover-up. But the idea that her brother had been involved in an attack there sent an electric jolt through her. "What did he do?" she whispered aloud.

But nobody in Marcus's fading memories heard her.

"I, for one, was unsurprised. Allowing Sienar to remain with ESS was too merciful of us," said the blonde, as if it were a forgone conclusion. She extended her hand, introducing herself. "Amanda. It is a pleasure, Marcus."

Marcus took her hand. "Likewise." Neither the woman's tone, nor the way she held the handshake, suggested she found much pleasure in anything.

All analytics and no tact, Jenna scoffed. Sal used to tease Jenna about having no tact back in the day. *No! Don't think about that. Remain focused,* she told herself. *Don't waste this opportunity. What happened to Sienar at Ganymede?*

Jenna then became aware of the awkward pause in the conversation, as if there was a topic they were deliberately trying to avoid. It was Marcus that finally broke it. He leaned in, lowering his voice. "I've been hearing that negotiations

PALE GREY DOT

amongst the ministries aren't going well. They're starting to openly talk about dismantling ESS."

"My contacts in DC have been telling me similar stories," Victoria replied. She held the stem of her glass tightly as she sipped.

Amanda steepled her hands. "It is unfortunate. However, I have been discussing matters with Her, and we feel we have it well in hand," she said.

Decades of training allowed Marcus to hide a wince at the mention of Her, but Jenna could feel it in his memories. *So*, she thought, *the current crop of agents is smart enough to fear Her like we did. Fear and love, always fighting.* Victoria looked away. For operatives constantly vying for superiority over one another, the ability to invoke Her name was a powerful one.

"Is that so?" Marcus asked, meeting Amanda's eyes. "Care to elaborate?" He didn't like being kept in the dark. It was a feeling Jenna knew all too well.

"I'm afraid not," Amanda replied. "However, She did ask me to convey to you the importance of your GreyCorp mission on Jupiter Station."

"I'll be happy to update Her over SecLink whenever She likes," Marcus replied evenly. "Jupiter Station's system network is an amalgamation of dozens of corporations—not just GreyCorp. With the time lag, manipulating it isn't easy."

Jupiter? Jenna scowled. *Who cares about a station halfway across the solar system? What does that have to do with Sienar?*

Victoria smiled that coy, confident smile of hers. "I'm certain Marcus will do a fabulous job, Amanda. You needn't worry."

The woman's voice was fading from Marcus's memory and Jenna's connection.

"I've worked with him for decades," Victoria explained, voice trailing off into static. "And he has never let me down."

Jenna struggled to force the data drive to show her what she wanted, but her hold on Marcus's memories kept slipping. Something had happened to Sienar during the Ganymede Blitz. Betrayal, Marcus had said. Jenna's cybernetic hand twitched. She could hear two men yelling at each other through the thin motel room walls. Outside, a car with squeaky brakes ground to a halt. Jenna ignored the distractions as best she could.

Victoria, Amanda, and the restaurant were now gone, replaced with a luxurious hotel room in Toronto. Marcus was alone. Through his eyes, Jenna saw him pull up personnel dossiers on a holo-projector. She recognized them instantly. There was Sal, the Silent One, with dark red lettering next to her name that read: *killed by Olympus Mons officers in Martian Insurrection.*

Jenna stared as the names and profiles scrolled by. *Why was Marcus following up on us? It's been fifty years since most of us were relevant.*

Jenna: AWOL. Surveillance unavailable.

Taylor: executed post-Martian Insurrection.

Jenna winced. Taylor didn't deserve his fate. He'd needed

PALE GREY DOT

help, not punishment. *I don't need another reminder of why She needs to die,* Jenna thought.

Jenna felt Marcus's emotions bleeding through—disgust for their failure, pity for their treatment, and jealousy for their legend. Marcus thought back to Her lavish pride for the Athena Six. They were meant to finally make the solar system safe. He looked away from the profiles, towards the hotel window overlooking the city, and Jenna was forced to look where he did.

No, you idiot! Get back to my friends. Get back to my family!

Marcus's gaze lingered on the smog-filled view for what felt like an eternity. Finally, he looked back, but Jenna could already feel the static. She was only getting bits and pieces now. Words describing the others drifted in and out of focus.

Cherny: potential recall to active service; full surveillance coverage.

Ezza: United Fleet. UFS Starknight. Jupiter locale. Surveillance unavailable; coercing to monitored location required.

Sienar: AWOL. Wanted for the murder of one hundred and thirteen ESS personnel at Uruk Sculus-132; surveillance unavailable. Marcus opened a secondary attachment on his dossier, and hundreds of documents and video footage alighted across the hotel room's walls simultaneously.

Sienar attacked ESS, she realized as the static overwhelmed her thoughts. *And Marcus was investigating him.*

The scene vanished, and images flashed before Jenna's

eyes. A corporate boardroom. A bloody fight in the back alleys of the Luna underground. Victoria's lips. The ranks and dossiers of key United Fleet personnel. Sweeping a Syndicate hideout with Sienar. The Tower briefing room and the holographic schematics of Jupiter Station. Planning an assignment with the overwatches. Upgrading his civilian cybernetics to operative grade. A desperate tryst in London.

The images came faster and faster. London. The Mare Serenitatis. A mining spaceship. Fighting. Loving.

Then the flashing stopped. Marcus and Jenna lay on the wet pavement in Toronto, staring up at the sky. His chest hurt. He fought for every breath. He was scared. Someone knelt beside them, pulling things from his arm.

"Jenna ..." he said, and he could barely see her looking down at him. He pitied her sad existence of living on the run and murdering Her people. Jenna and Marcus reached up with their flesh-and-blood hand to grab her arm. "You don't need to keep running. You can always go back."

Jenna met his eyes. To him, she didn't look any less scared than he felt. "You know She will forgive you ..." Marcus murmured. The last thing he saw was Jenna grabbing a med-stim, but he knew she wouldn't use it. His head fell to the side, and his vision faded into nothingness.

In the decrepit motel room, Jenna woke with tears and sweat streaking her face. Reaching over to her left arm, she tore the data drive from its socket and hurled it against the wall. Shivering as she covered her face, Jenna tried to keep a hold on her emotions. *You're not Marcus. You're*

PALE GREY DOT

you, she reminded herself. Slowly, she lowered her hands. Through the faded blinds, she could see that darkness had fallen. Hours had passed since she dove into Marcus's last memories.

Jenna nearly stumbled as she rolled over and stood up from the bed. The place stank, she realized. Her clothes stank, and she stank. Seeing how the old operatives lived was a stark reminder of how far she had fallen. Stepping over to the corner, Jenna picked up the memory drive and shoved it into her cloth backpack, burying it beneath everything else she owned.

As painful as it was reliving parts of Marcus's life, it gave her a new direction. She now knew Sienar had turned against the service and was on the run. And that the age-old rivalry between the Earth Security Service and the United Fleet was coming to a head, and She would be making the first move.

Jupiter Station, Jenna realized. *I have to get to Jupiter Station.*

From the back corner of the bar, Ezza ran her gloved thumb along the rim of her glass. The music was loud and awful at Nuke's Club, the dance floor crowded with drunken idiots in garish colours, and the air filled with aromatic smoke. While the other tables were packed with young partygoers, Ezza was the only one at hers. A surly glare warded off anyone who might have joined her. Not that she had many visitors;

71

Don Miasek

even in civvies, Ezza knew she still projected an authoritative air.

She'd never been one to patronize clubs by herself, but the beat beneath her feet and the smell of narcotics reminded her of the place they'd all snuck into back when she was thirteen. In some ways, it had been their first independent mission together. They'd successfully plotted the escape, snuck through the Kazan institute's vents, and trekked through waist-high snow, only to fail spectacularly at actually ordering a drink. It had been Taylor's idea, of course, and as usual, he'd managed to persuade the others. The educators were furious when they found out they'd left the facility without authorization and put them all on double workload for a month. It'd been worth it, though, and the nights out soon became a tradition for the six of them as they grew older, where they could laugh, drink, and be free without the spectre of work looming over them.

Ezza shook herself free from the memories, as pleasant as they were, and refocused on the here and now. The bartender was fidgety and he kept rubbing the back of his hand. He hadn't the cybernetics for Blue Scan; Naxx addict, perhaps? The pair one table over were having a hushed but heated conversation concerning freight schedules and local security; part of the Jupiter Station smuggling ring? One by one, she catalogued each of the forty-three individuals at the bar.

Ezza shook her head as she realized that her attempts at relaxation were doomed. She pushed her half-empty glass

PALE GREY DOT

away and stood. "Excuse me," she mumbled as she threaded through the crowd. Reaching the door, she sent a quick mental transaction to settle up. Turning, she nearly collided with a woman standing in her way.

She was barely five feet tall with brown, shoulder-length hair. Young, but Ezza didn't detect any signs of artificial de-aging. She looked up at Ezza and didn't move.

Ezza froze. Something was wrong. The woman's bright blue-and-white clothes were tailored but seemed out of place for a bar like this. She wasn't fit enough for the United Fleet, and her smile was far too warm and cheerful for a Jupiter Station bureaucrat. Ezza couldn't see any cybernetics beyond a standard civilian package. She could have been an operative were it not for the unsubtle way she was staring at Ezza.

"Pardon me," Ezza said evenly, stepping aside for her, but the woman didn't move.

Instead, she pressed her thumb and forefinger against her other hand's pinkie finger, and a soft blue light flickered on above her right eye, visible through the skin. "Captain Ezza Jayens?"

Ezza groaned. It was worse than she thought. "You're with the press." She glanced back, seeking escape.

The woman's smile widened but didn't lose its warmth. "Nirali Kashem, IDEA. It's a pleasure. I was wondering if I could ask you a few questions. Your *Starknight* docked just two days ago to join over a dozen other United Fleet ships."

"I have no comment, and I do not consent to being

recorded. You can contact the United Fleet Public Outreach Program via JupiterNet." Ezza rolled her eyes and pushed past the smaller woman.

"Is there anything you can say about the mass resupply effort here at Jupiter Station?" Nirali asked. She had to jog to keep up with Ezza's long strides.

Ezza stepped out into the Prime Hub. Several ships were visible through the windows overhead, resting at their docking stations. The streetlights were dimmed, as the sector was under simulated night, though the neon sign for Nuke's Club bathed the street in crimson. The blaring music and pounding beat could still be felt through the deck, but at least now it was muffled. "No comment," Ezza repeated, eyes scanning for a cab.

"Every United Fleet ship docked at Jupiter Station has been receiving dozens of shipments per day except for yours," Nirali went on.

A cab slid up to the curb in front of Ezza, and she tapped its side with her finger, prompting the gull-like door to slide upwards.

"Captain, does your sudden arrival at the station have anything to do with Brylan Ncube and ESS's operations here?"

Ezza paused. After taking a moment to steady herself, she sent the cab away with a wave of her hand and turned back. "Let's talk, Ms. Kashem."

Nirali beamed triumphantly and followed Ezza as she led them around the side of the bar.

PALE GREY DOT

Ezza pointed at the glowing blue light above Nirali's eye. "First, turn that thing off."

Nirali hesitated before tapping her pinkie finger, stopping the recording.

"Thank you. Now, what did you say about Brylan and ESS?" Ezza asked, keeping her voice low.

Taking the cue, Nirali spoke in a hushed tone. "My agency has been following up on ESS activities," she said. "Cases of abuse of power, unlawful searches and seizures, violent interrogation techniques."

Ezza burst out laughing. Taking a step back, she looked at the reporter with a mix of disappointment and amusement as she fought to regain her composure. "Are you being serious? 'Abuse of power'? Exactly how long have you been investigating ESS?" Ezza wiped a tear from her eye. "Heh, you actually had me thinking that you were onto something there. You aren't the first one to think you're invincible because of some press pass. It doesn't work that way. If you're investigating them, then they've already investigated you. The fact that you're still here is proof that you might as well be shouting into the void."

Nirali frowned, straightening her jacket. "But—"

The deck heaved beneath their feet. The sound of tearing metal screeched as Ezza was thrown off balance. Just before the back of her head struck the deck, Ezza caught a brief glimpse of one of the spaceships beyond the upper windows tilting before being violently wrenched free of its mooring.

A split second later, Nirali crashed on top of Ezza,

Don Miasek

knocking the wind out of her. Ezza wheezed, pushing the reporter off her. The music in the club went out, replaced with panicked screams.

"What's happening?" Nirali shouted. She started to reach for the wall for support, but a second rumble in the deck sent her stumbling to the side.

I don't know, Ezza thought, unable to reply as she gasped for air. She forced herself to her feet, keeping her centre of gravity low to maintain her balance. Her head hammered with waves of pain. The cab she had nearly entered had been knocked onto the curb, and people were flooding into the streets.

A moment later, the lights flickered, and everything went dark. The shouting intensified, and Ezza could hear heavy footsteps as people ran. A long five seconds passed before the station's emergency lighting activated, and an automated voice rang through every speaker and cybernetic device capable of audio.

"MAY I HAVE YOUR ATTENTION, PLEASE. THIS IS A PRIORITY ONE MESSAGE FROM STATION ADMINISTRA-TION. THERE IS AN EMERGENCY IN PROGRESS THAT WILL BE HANDLED BY STATION AUTHORITIES. PLEASE REMAIN CALM AND HEAD TO YOUR ASSIGNED SHELTER. THANK YOU FOR YOUR COOPERATION. THE ADMINIS-TRATION APOLOGIZES FOR THIS INCONVENIENCE."

Though loud, the voice was far too calm and reasonable, and its polite request went unheeded in the rampaging hysteria.

Finally able to draw in a lungful of air, Ezza quickly ran

PALE GREY DOT

through her options. Something was happening to the station—an attack or malfunction, she didn't know—but safety was her first priority. Glancing up, she could no longer see the spaceship that had broken free of its dock. Ezza could have sworn it was a military ship. Tapping her forefinger and thumb together, she tried to raise *Starknight*—nothing. Rachelle would have the watch, and Ezza hoped she'd be able to deal with the crisis. A call to the United Fleet HQ went similarly unanswered.

"What's happening?" Nirali repeated. The poor woman was frozen with fear.

Ezza grabbed the journalist's arm. "Come on. My ship is docked at Ring 4, Terminal 3. It's our best bet." Leaving her behind in the midst of a disaster didn't feel right. A man in bright red shoved Ezza in his panicked attempt to reach somewhere safe, and she had to jump to the side to avoid being trampled by another. The station rumbled again.

As the automated announcement from station administration repeated, Ezza and Nirali reached an intact cab. Pressing a hand against the door only elicited a loud buzzing noise.

"Dammit," Ezza said. "Transit's down."

"MAY I HAVE YOUR ATTENTION, PLEASE. PRIORITY ONE EMERGENCY PROCEDURES ARE IN EFFECT FOR PRIME HUB SECTORS 1, 2, 3, AND 4. ACCESS TO TERMINALS 1, 4, 6, 7, 8, 9, 11, AND 12 ARE RESTRICTED. PLEASE REMAIN CALM AND HEAD TO YOUR ASSIGNED SHELTER. THANK YOU FOR YOUR COOPERATION. THE ADMINISTRATION APOLOGIZES FOR THIS INCONVENIENCE."

Don Miasek

"I don't understand. Who would attack us?" Nirali breathed.

Ezza glanced back at her and saw that her hands were shaking.

"I've lived on Jupiter Station my whole life. I've run reports on the safety procedures," Nirali explained. "This isn't an accident!"

Sparing only a moment to run down the list of suspects, Ezza finally shook her head. "I don't know, but we can worry about that later." Smoke poured from Nuke's Club. There was a loud crack above them as a support strut sagged before collapsing entirely. The beam's impact exploded against the deck, shattering a pair of cabs beneath it.

Both women hit the ground, and Ezza felt a switch go off in her head.

Nirali climbed to her feet. "Here." Se reached down to help her up, but Ezza waved her away.

"No, no, no ..." Ezza wheezed. "Not now ... Not now ..." The sensation that she hadn't felt in over half a century had returned. The Pull—the need to do whatever it took to fulfill the desires of the Earth Security Service—was back.

Nirali stared at her fallen protector in horror and confusion.

Slowly, Ezza reached out with a shaking hand towards Nirali, gingerly accepting her help. "We need to get to a comm station."

"What? Two seconds ago, you wanted to go to your ship!"

Ezza ignored the comment. *What would ESS want me to*

PALE GREY DOT

do? Find out who's attacking? It'd been so long, Ezza wasn't sure if she could even reach SecLink to report any discovered information. *No! Don't cave so easily! Think of Taylor! Think of the suffering he went through at Her hands! ESS doesn't deserve your loyalty!*

Nirali pulled Ezza close, eyes wide with panic. "What's wrong with you?"

Ezza gave her a blank look. It was so hard to concentrate all of a sudden. The sound of a shattering support beam rattled her brain again, and both women stumbled. "Where's the nearest transmitter facility?" she demanded, ignoring the reporter's question.

"Three blocks over." Nirali pointed down the street. Ezza launched into a sprint through the crowd with Nirali close on her heels. People fled in every direction around them. Most sought anything that looked like safety, but more than a few had smashed through storefronts to grab what they could. The women dodged around panicked bodies and scattered goods before skidding to a halt before the transmitter facility's entrance.

Though the building looked like countless others within the Prime Hub, Ezza knew access to the transmitter would be tightly controlled and given only to the station's technical staff or security force. All data transfers extending beyond the station needed to be routed through here. A reinforced door barred their way.

Ezza pressed her hand against the metal. It was warm to the touch. She crouched down next to the access terminal.

79

Don Miasek

"What are you doing?" Nirali asked.

Again, Ezza didn't bother answering. The terminal needed station authorization that her United Fleet credentials wouldn't cover. Gently popping open the hatch beneath the panel, Ezza looked at the mess of wires and circuits. Sal had taught her so much about lock picking. Slowly, Ezza reached over and slid off her left glove, revealing the metal cybernetics of her hand and arm.

Nirali stared, though Ezza couldn't tell whether she understood their significance.

Ezza smiled as she ran her finger along the metal limb, feeling every groove and port along its surface. She hadn't used them since she left the service. But now? Now doing so felt right. Now it felt like what She would want her to do. Why had they ever fought?

"MAY I HAVE YOUR ATTENTION, PLEASE. PRIORITY ONE EVACUATION LIFEBOATS ARE AVAILABLE IN TERMINALS 1, 4, 6, 7, 8, 9, 11, AND 12. EVACUATION LIFEBOATS ARE AVAILABLE IN PRIME HUB SECTORS 1, 2, 3, AND 4. THOSE IN THE AFFECTED SECTORS MAY PROCEED TO THEIR NEAREST LIFEBOAT. THANK YOU FOR YOUR COOPERATION. THE ADMINISTRATION APOLOGIZES FOR THIS INCONVENIENCE."

"Please hurry, Captain," Nirali pressed, looking out at the fleeing civilians.

Ezza pulled one of the plugs from her wrist, drawing out a cable behind it. Squinting into the dark maintenance hatch, she inserted the plug into an empty socket.

PALE GREY DOT

"It's really been too long," she murmured. "She's going to be so proud."

"'She'? Who …?"

Ezza smiled in return. Rumbling loudly, the door jolted inwards and slid to the side.

The transmitter station's interior was illuminated by a single yellow emergency light, but it was more than enough for Ezza to see where she was going. Built for maintenance personnel, the room was a tangle of wires and access hatches. A series of holographic monitors rested on one wall beneath a terminal. Ezza didn't bother using them, instead sliding off the terminal cover and plugging in directly.

"MAY I HAVE YOUR ATTE—" the automated voice squawked before dissolving into static. A moment later, and it was gone.

"Ahhh," Ezza sighed, closing her eyes.

Nirali crouched down low behind the sole desk in the station, peering out through the smoke-filled doorway. The shouting pedestrians were growing louder.

"Emergency power still functions. I have access to the station's network and to JupiterNet," Ezza announced. "Let me see if I can find out what …" she trailed off. The realization of what had happened shocked her out of her stupor. Using her free hand, Ezza held onto the terminal to avoid falling over. The station rumbled again, but this time she knew the cause. "The fleet … They're all gone."

"*Gone?*"

"*Dominus*'s primary and secondary hulls have collapsed.

81

Raptor is being abandoned. *Korolev* has collided with Terminal 8. *Astrum Viator*, *Warsaw*, *Orion* ..." Ezza twitched her fingers, searching for the fate of the two battlecruisers the fleet was built around. "*Stalwart* has broken apart. *Athabaskan* is fighting an overload in its nuclear pulse engines. Their entire secondary hull has been evacuated."

Nirali took a deep breath as the consequences dawned on her. "What about the station itself?"

"Fourteen sectors have been exposed to open space." The preliminary estimates of the dead passed through Ezza's mind, but she refrained from reading them out. They reminded her too much of the disaster on Mars fifty-one years ago. "I can't get any information on United Fleet headquarters, but I'm getting a line to *Starknight*." It felt selfish to be relieved that her ship was intact and her people were alive when so many others had been obliterated.

"Raise your hands and disconnect any and all cybernetic links immediately!" a voice roared.

An armoured man stood in the open door, aiming a rifle at them. A breather obscured his face and modulated his voice, amplifying it over the crackling fire that had broken out in the concourse. Ezza eyed the emblem on his uniform—a bright red circle on a dark blue field—that marked him as a member of Jupiter Station Security. She marked the rifle as a standard-issue heavy stunner. Beside her, Nirali's hands were already in the air.

"Officer, p-please," Nirali stammered, "this is Captain Ezza Jayens with the United Fleet. We're—"

PALE GREY DOT

"You on the left—hands in the air! Disconnect immediately and power down any and all cybernetic implants or I will shoot!" The man trained the gun on Ezza.

Ezza glanced at him for only a moment before looking over his left shoulder. Her hands remained right where they were.

The guard started to squeeze the trigger an instant before his right shoulder and torso burst into bright white light. Nirali screamed, but the man didn't make a sound as he collapsed. The end of his arm, along with the stunner, landed away from the body.

Through the smoke emerged a tall man in a dark blue suit, with a backpack slung over his shoulder. He returned a dull, silver energy projector to its inner-jacket holster. The breather he wore didn't hide his curly black hair, and Ezza recognized him immediately.

"Hello again, Brylan."

The operative stepped over the corpse. "Hello, mademoiselle. I trust you've already had a full analysis of the situation?"

Nirali stepped towards the security guard but shied away upon seeing the pooling blood. She looked back at Ezza and Brylan, horror in her eyes.

"The station has been attacked and is no longer structurally sound. Nearly every ship in the fleet is damaged or destroyed," Ezza said.

"How are you okay with this?" Nirali demanded. Her hand trembled as she pointed at the guard.

83

Don Miasek

Ezza paused to consider the question. Brylan shot the guard in the back. Murdered him. *Why am I not outraged?* Panic seized Ezza as she realized what was happening. The Pull—born from the Athena Program's loyalty chips—was already altering her outlook. She knew that She would be fine with the guard's fate, and somehow that was all Ezza needed.

The operative looked over at the reporter as if noticing her for the first time. "Who is this?"

"My name is Nirali. I'm with IDEA," she answered. She stepped towards him, a mix of fear and anger in her eyes. "Are you ... Brylan Ncube?"

"IDEA?" Brylan furrowed his brow, ignoring her question. "The conspiracy site?"

Ezza reached into the terminal's access hatch and disconnected herself from the station's network. "She's right, Brylan. That wasn't necessary." Even to her own ears, Ezza realized how apathetic she sounded.

The operative shrugged. "We don't have time to waste. I've reached the same conclusion as you. The station isn't going to last, and your ship is the best way out of here." Reaching into his backpack, he drew out a second breather and tossed it to Ezza. "Leave her and let's go," he said, gesturing at the shorter woman.

"What?!" Nirali yelped.

Ezza caught the breather and slipped it on in one fluid motion. She looked over at Nirali. There was no logical reason to bring her along. There was no doubt that She would agree with Brylan. Still, Nirali knew Brylan Ncube's name.

PALE GREY DOT

Part of Ezza argued that She would want to know why, and so they should keep her around. The other half argued that if Ezza was going to fight against Her influence, she'd need to know what Nirali knew.

Ezza laughed out loud at the absurdity of opposing parts of her mind arguing for the same course of action for different reasons.

Brylan looked at her, apparently confused by the sudden outburst. "She isn't going to survive anyway. The smoke is going to kill her, along with everyone else."

Ezza crouched beside the fallen security guard, gently removing the breather from his face. Stepping up to Nirali, she slipped it over the reporter's head and pulled the straps as tight as they would go. It was huge on her, but the seals appeared intact. "She's with me, Brylan." Ezza placed a hand on the smaller woman's shoulder. "Don't worry, Nirali. I promise you we'll get through this."

Still shaking, Nirali nodded.

Brylan watched the exchange carefully. "There is something different about you, mademoiselle."

For the first time since the Pull returned, Ezza found herself questioning what caused it. The timing was too perfect to be coincidental. "You can't be that surprised that I'm disagreeing with you, Brylan," Ezza replied, desperately trying to reclaim her calm, unflappable persona. The Pull did not make it easy.

Striding out of the transmitter station into the smoke-filled concourse, Ezza tapped the side of her mask. Her vision immediately cleared.

85

Don Miasek

"Nirali, are you familiar with the service tunnels?" Ezza asked.

"I used to play in them when I was a kid," Nirali replied, voice modulated by the breather.

"*Starknight* is berthed at Gate 15. I'd like to avoid any violence."

Nirali guided them to a closed hatchway, which led into the service tunnels that ran throughout Jupiter Station. They were large enough for a child to stand comfortably, but an adult would have to stoop.

As Brylan crouched to remove the cover, he noticed the reporter staring at him. "Yes?"

"You *are* Brylan Ncube ... aren't you?"

With a loud clang, the cover disengaged from the wall, and Brylan set it aside. "Yeeesss?" he repeated. The operative was doing nothing to hide his disapproval of bringing a living ball and chain along with them.

"You're with the Earth Security Service. You're an operative." It was somewhere between a question and a statement.

"You, my dear, are a paragon of inductive reasoning and investigative skill," Brylan said with a snide smile. "No wonder IDEA is as respected and relevant as it is."

Nirali went quiet, and Ezza knew exactly what was going through her mind: the countless rumours of politicians falling under ESS's sway, of never being sure if a private conversation was just that, or of friends and family members speaking out against Earth's government, only to soon vanish.

PALE GREY DOT

Brylan stood up again and stepped to the side, gesturing to the open hatch. "Oh, don't give me that look. If it makes you feel any better, your saviour over there is an operative too."

"That's not—" Ezza cut herself off and cursed under her breath as Nirali whipped around to look at her. *Don't let him get to you,* she reminded herself, but the grin behind Brylan's breather didn't make it easy. "Go ahead, Nirali. Gate 15."

The service tunnels were cramped and designed with twists and forks that branched off into seemingly random directions. While she and Brylan struggled in the low corridors, Nirali barely had to crouch. The hard metal grates were rough on Ezza's hands and knees, and the claustrophobic environment reminded her of *Starknight*. There was something comforting about being cocooned by layers of nearly impenetrable metal. The emergency lighting in the tunnels was woefully inadequate, but the night-vision optics in Ezza's breather showed the way.

Were the station's network still functional, Ezza could have pulled up a map of the service tunnels. It served as a good excuse to keep Nirali along. The reporter's memory of the maze-like passageways was as good as Ezza could have hoped.

"If you two are ESS operatives," Nirali called back to them, "then I have a hard time believing you don't know who's attacking and why."

"Oh, we will find out," Brylan replied sternly, grabbing the handrail to pull himself along. The heat in the tunnels was intense, and the man's face was covered in sweat.

87

Don Miasek

Ezza was glad the reporter was asking the questions she couldn't. *Just don't push him too far*, she silently urged.

"I thought the justification for ESS's reign of terror was to protect us from things like this," Nirali retorted.

Brylan grunted as he crawled around a sharp corner after her. "Spare me the middle school sociology argument. You have no idea how many organized threats the solar system faces. Without unwavering surveillance, you'd have much more to fear than us. If we did not have total control, we'd have total anarchy."

Ezza had witnessed this firsthand. She remembered when she and Sienar tracked down the Blue Scan operation on Luna. She remembered when she, Sal, and Taylor destroyed the Syndicate human smuggling ring in Sydney. Human beings could cause so much pain, and she remembered all the times the Earth Security Service's resources prevented that. Then she remembered the Martian Insurrection and steeled herself.

There was the sound of an access hatch sliding open in front of them, and Ezza leaned to the side to see past Brylan. Nirali climbed out of the service tunnel and into the terminal.

Brylan followed, stretching to his full height once he was out. "I'm pleased to see you didn't get us lost," he told the reporter, taking the time to straighten his suit. "And we're in luck. A clear run to *Starknight*."

Ezza gripped the side of the hatch and pulled herself out. To her relief, Terminal 3 was in better shape than the Prime Hub. There was no smoke, no looting, and no dead

PALE GREY DOT

in the streets. Yellow lights still whirled, and emergency sirens wailed to guide any lingering citizens to the nearest lifeboats, but there was no one left besides them. From the automated damage reports, it seemed incredible that Terminal 3 was untouched. In a flash, Ezza realized why, and looked up.

Brylan stepped next to her, following her gaze. "Yes, I see it too."

"See what?" Nirali asked, squinting. She had to raise her voice to be heard over the klaxons.

Smiling as he undid the straps of his breather, Brylan pointed through the sprawling windows, into the blackness of space above them. "Think, Ms. Kashem. The evidence is all around you," he said like a schoolteacher trying to educate a particularly slow pupil. "Right there would be Terminal 4. That tiny point of light? That would be the *Cerberus* burning in space. And that there? *Stalwart*'s shattered secondary hull. On the other side? Terminal 5 and *Venture*—a Martian mining scraper. Not a mark on her. That's only what we can see, but if you have been listening to the evacuation orders, we know exactly which rings and terminals were hit, and therefore every ship affected."

Nirali looked over at the operative. "The station's wireless is down. Did you memorize where every ship was berthed or something?"

"You didn't?" Brylan asked, feigning incredulity. "And you call yourself an investigator. Always know your surroundings, Ms. Kashem. It is clear to me that the United Fleet was

89

the target. From the list of damaged terminals, every ship in the fleet was hit simultaneously. And yet ..."

"And yet?"

"And yet mademoiselle's ship is unscathed," he prompted. "Come along, Ms. Keshem."

Nirali had to jog to keep up with his stride. She frowned, working it through. "It's the only ship that wasn't receiving supplies to join the fleet they were assembling."

"And so now we have a theory for how they staged this attack. Ah, but there is more. We can begin reviewing what position and level of security one would need to supplement military shipments with explosive devices and consider how many would be required to destroy each ship. Then we start reviewing the files on every member of the United Fleet stationed here. Look for potential weaknesses. Either sympathetic tendencies with hostile elements, potential blackmail or extortion material that a third party could exploit, or even recent changes in their behaviour which could suggest they are compromised.

"With all due respect to our dear captain"—Brylan waved a dismissive hand towards Ezza—"the United Fleet is not known for their counterintelligence."

Nirali opened her mouth as if to say something, but then stopped. Despite her efforts to hide it, it was clear she was impressed.

Ezza picked up the pace towards *Starknight*. Once aboard, she'd be able to get in contact with Her and see how she could help. No, she could remind Her of their deal and demand

PALE GREY DOT

that She deactivate her programming. Or at least hear Her out. Given the circumstances, She may have vital information about this disaster, which had harmed so many of her friends and colleagues.

A wave of relief washed over Ezza as her subdermal implants buzzed. "Captain Jayens here," she said out loud. "It's good to hear from you, Adams. What's your status?"

Nirali and Brylan stopped.

Adams's voice was barely audible over the emergency klaxons. His flat tone was that of a man still in shock. "We, uh, lost contact with Jupiter Station's headquarters immediately after the bombs went off. Eighteen ships have been lost, and another fourteen are in various states of emergency."

A pang of worry shot through Ezza. She had hoped Admiral Tolj and the others at HQ weren't hit. "What about civilian casualties?" Ezza snapped her fingers at Nirali and Brylan, motioning for them to keep moving.

"Half the station's rings have been evacuated, and with the structural damage that's been done, The commander thinks it's only a matter of time before the rest follow suit. She's been trying to coordinate a rescue effort for the civilians, but most spaceworthy ships have already fled. I … Captain, we've gotten so many calls for help …"

Ezza could imagine the frustration of watching a disaster unfolding while being powerless to do anything. "Adams," she said in a softer tone, "just focus on what we can do for now. Don't worry about what we can't. Have we heard from any flag officers?"

"Uh, none in local space. Admiral Cheng-Visitor is enroute, but she's seven days away and the time delay …"

Ezza tried not to think about Admiral Tolj. Up ahead, she could see the airlock leading to *Starknight*. A pair of heavily armed marines, clad in dark grey armour, stood watch. "Tell Rachelle to grant two additional requests to the access manifest. Nirali Kashem and Brylan Ncube."

Brylan marched up to the marines, giving each a stern nod. Nirali slowed, staying behind Ezza.

Adams's reply was not instantaneous. "Yes, ma'am."

"Start preparing the ship to undock. Jayens, out." Ezza closed the connection and stepped through the airlock doors. As they closed, separating her, Brylan, Nirali, and the marines from the desolate station, the gentle tug in her brain reminded her that ESS was the best chance she had to find out who was responsible.

All I need to do now is call Her, Ezza decided.

5

Jenna watched the shuttle hoppers land and take off for hours. She was one of hundreds waiting behind the chain-link fence separating them from the tarmac. It was a bad one today, and the smoky, polluted clouds were thick enough that her old, creaking breather did little to get the stale, metallic taste out of her mouth. Only by their dark silhouettes was she able to discern the make and model of each hopper.

The dredges around her were no better dressed. Their tattered longcoats stuck to their bodies in the heat. A woman next to her coughed and wheezed, nearly doubling over.

Jenna saw that she had goggles on but no breather. *She's going to die*, Jenna thought. She wondered if it would be days or weeks. *That will be sad*, Jenna decided after a moment's consideration.

Every few minutes, a figure would emerge from the

smoke on the tarmac and approach the fence. The dredges would shout out their credentials, describing how they once served on an asteroid scraper just like that one, how their cybernetic suite allowed them to run an entire spaceship with one data port, that their amazing resume was available to view online, and my, wasn't that a fine-looking vessel they had there. Anything to earn a berth on a ship heading off-world.

Each time, the spaceship's captain or staffing officer eyed them all with contempt, asked a few questions of the likely candidates, and gave some lucky bastard a job that spelled their escape from Earth.

Each time, Jenna remained silent, letting the other dredges clamour for the jobs. The ore hauler wouldn't be heading where she wanted to go. The bulk freighter would need another week of maintenance before leaving. The captain of the fueller had the look of a deviant about her.

Finally, Jenna saw what she'd been waiting for. Grabbing onto the chain-link fence, she climbed up and over, landing on the other side in one smooth motion. Jenna heard a voice behind her call out.

"Hey! The hell are you doing? You can't just—"

But Jenna ignored it, striding purposefully across the grimy tarmac, past the repair carts, the thick, rubbery fuelling hoses, the labourers in safety-orange coveralls, and crew members readying their ships for departure.

With a mental flick, Jenna saw not just the hoppers themselves, but also the overlaid image of their counterpart

PALE GREY DOT

spaceships high in orbit. It was these ships she needed to see, the ones that never delved into Earth's disgusting atmosphere.

Jenna walked past the small ships for Earth-only transport, and barely gave a second glance to the building-sized behemoths that couldn't even pull 0.05g. Instead, she headed to the large, angular shape by the main refuelling tanks.

The virtual image of the starliner looked as out of place as Jenna did, but for entirely different reasons. Where Jenna wore rags, the starliner's twin hulls wore gleaming white armoured panels from bow to stern. Real transparent windows ran along its dozen decks. The liner was sharp in the front, curving out in the middle before tapering off at the end, and its thermal radiators were stylized in the shape of wings. It was a sleek and aerodynamic frame for a ship that needed to be neither. Style over function.

Jenna, though, could see the creaks and cracks beneath the paint, the subtle stress fractures along the docking collars, and the faint scratches on the hull plating. A mediocre ship looking to rise above its station, she decided. She wondered how many wealthy passengers were taken in by the ageing ship's slick disguise. Jenna strode underneath the image's wings to the hopper, where she found a big man reading from a tablet.

"I don't need any dredges today," the man said in a mildly annoyed tone. He did not so much as glance up from his reading.

Though the man wore a rough longcoat and a heavy

Don Miasek

breather, Jenna could see fine clothes peeking out beneath his collar. But with a thick red beard and sagging eyelids, he looked too rough for someone ferrying the rich around. Jenna examined the white underpanels. "Going to Jupiter, aren't you?"

The man just grunted, still not looking up.

"I can tell. You're scheduled to leave in thirty-four hours. Considering the land-to-orbit time for an Aquarius-class shuttle hopper, with the modifications you've made, of course"—Jenna gestured towards the ship's rear—"Earth's rotation will put you in perfect position to meet up with Gagarin Station. Assuming a not-unreasonable day's layover, and you'd have a good trajectory on your way to Jupiter."

Now the man looked up.

Jenna tried to read his expression. She used to be so good at that, but since fleeing the service, she found it more and more difficult. *Smile*, she reminded herself. *Normal people smile.* "And I think you do need dredges. Way more cost effective to keep your hopper in orbit. Avoid wasting all that fuel getting this bucket off the ground. No, you want to hire your dredges down here on Earth, away from the prying eyes of the richies."

The man's beady eyes narrowed. "Exactly what do you want, dredge?"

"Why wait until tomorrow to hire? I'm available now. Interfaced with everything from a United Fleet battlecruiser to a lifeboat." This was one of the few things Jenna did not need to lie about.

PALE GREY DOT

"Is that so," the man said. His coat made a rustling noise as he approached her. He was tall and wide enough that even Taylor would have been intimidated. Looking her up and down, he gestured into the smog towards the fence keeping the rest of the dredges away. "How about you come back tomorrow and I'll see."

"Really rather get a secure job now," Jenna replied. Her smile fell away. Carefully, she rolled her left sleeve up as far as it would go, exposing the machinery beneath. "These go all the way up. You're not going to find anything better in that lot," she nodded towards the fence.

The man took one look. "Looks like they're in crap condition."

Jenna said nothing.

The man took a deep breath, his mask wheezing against the thick air. Jenna could tell he was weighing his options between not wanting to set a precedent for other dredges to hop the fence and skip the line, or simply hiring Jenna now to save himself the trouble of finding someone in the throng tomorrow. "You have accreditation with the Ship Overseers' Guild?"

Jenna nodded, though she hoped he wouldn't test her forgery.

"Any gear or belongings you need to get?"

Jenna shook her head. Her backpack held everything she owned.

After a moment's thought, the man jerked his thumb towards the hopper's boarding ramp. "All right, get your ass

97

on board. You bunk in the secondary hull with the rest of the workers. Check in with Jo-Ann and tell her Hecktor said you're training for third watch."

Jenna turned towards the boarding ramp. "Thank you. You made the right choice."

Hecktor grunted in reply and went back to his tablet.

◆

Cherny sank into the padded chair, wearier now than after a dozen consecutive shifts at the Tsiolkovsky Spaceport fueller lines. Disaster had struck Jupiter Station, all but destroying it and the United Fleet armada mobilizing there. The past twenty-four hours had been a nonstop attempt to contain the information. It would inevitably get out, though, and they would have to be ready.

The Tower lounge had a view that only the two-hundred-and-fifth floor could provide. Even with the simulated windows filtering out the sky's swirling grey clouds, it was still hard to see much of anything on the ground.

Though his eyes were blurred from exhaustion and his limbs were heavy, Cherny had never felt more alive. Leaning his head back against the chair, he opened his mind and connected to SecLink.

An operative was serving as advisor to the Minister of Defence. "Don't worry," he said, "ESS can conduct a thorough investigation of the United Fleet to root out any potential collaborators."

PALE GREY DOT

Sixteen overwatches were working in tandem, monitoring all transmissions from the Jupiter site, filtering out all those deemed damaging to Earth's regime.

Quietly, emergency containment units and police forces across Earth, Mars, Venus, and other key holdings were activated. Riots would be inevitable, and civil disobedience was not something Premier Fairchild would tolerate for long.

Assets implanted across the financial sector prepared for the inevitable economic fallout that would result from the homeworld's now weakened reach beyond the asteroid belt.

An informant sent a report about a small racer-craft in the vicinity of the attack that was on its way to the 704 Interamnia asteroid with firsthand knowledge of the incident. The ship would be impounded, communications silenced, and crew detained upon arrival.

One of the several compromised crew members aboard Admiral Cheng-Visitor's battlecruiser gave full readiness reports on the admiral's ability to help the survivors.

Cherny was proud to be part of this amazing coordination effort. Dozens of operatives, a hundred overwatches, and billions of assets—human and machine—all worked to protect Earth and its interests when the news broke.

Though it hadn't taken him long to slip back into the role of a loyal ESS operative, Cherny had spent the first three hours after his arrival at the Tower reviewing his half-century-old files stuck in ESS storage. Paperwork, most of it, but it still brought back memories of the days when he and the others were together. Just reading the reports and communiques almost made him feel like he'd never left. One file, however, was a mere image. The date and time stamp read October 15, 2455. The location was marked as an ESS safe house in the British Regional Governorship. It was of him and Sal, dressed in civilian beiges. Her long brunette hair rested over one shoulder, and there was a bright smile on her face. It was a few years before they had all gone to Mars for their first mission with their freshly installed Athena Protocols. Cherny had closed the image and moved on.

He was not alone in the Tower lounge. Assets drifted in and out. Each of them, though, gave Cherny a wide berth. Even the odd overwatch would occasionally emerge from their lairs with their wires dragging behind them, but none approached him. Whether it was out of reverence for his work with the Athena Six or contempt for his downfall, Cherny couldn't tell. They'd come around, he decided.

As he admired the work of his colleagues, Cherny narrowed his focus in SecLink. //Are you there?// he asked.

//Of course, Cherny. I am always here.// If the stress of the impending crisis was affecting Her, She didn't show it.

//I wanted to thank you again. For the opportunity.//

//My dear Cherny, you know you belong here.//

Cherny smiled, breathing deep. //Yes. Yes, I do. It's just amazing being able to do some good again. To be part of a team again.//

//Have you rested since the attack?// It wasn't like Her to show compassion for Her operatives' well-being. No, that wasn't what She was really asking.

//No, I'm fine. I feel like I can keep this up forever.//

//You know what could happen if you get overstressed.//

Cherny shook his head vigorously. //I'm good. Really. It won't be like before. You know I'm one of the stable ones.// *Taylor was the one that went mad. Not me.*

She did not reply immediately. Was She mulling over what to do with him, or just enjoying tormenting him? //All right, Operative. I trust you.//

Cherny gave an audible sigh of relief.

//Now then, the premier is expected to break the news in two days' time. You and Amanda need to have a lead on Jenna and Sienar before then. My resources will be committed to containing the news until then.//

Cherny pushed himself up from the chair, determined to prove his boast. //I'll go see Amanda right now.//

//I would wish you luck, Operative, but I expect that you do not need it.//

Cherny strode out of the lounge, ignoring the wary glances of those he passed. Many levels down, Cherny pressed his finger against the side of the blastproof door leading to an overwatch lair. The metal groaned as the door accepted his credentials and swung open.

If the hideout was cramped enough for two, it was extraordinarily uncomfortable for four. Only Cherny seemed to mind, though, as he pressed himself against one of the monitor-filled walls. Amanda appeared unfazed, and the overwatches rarely cared for creature comforts.

Adrian and Esther were the ones assigned to Marcus, Cherny knew. *Poor bastard.* "What have I missed?"

The overwatches did not reply with anything more than a servo twitch. Cherny wasn't sure whether they noticed his arrival.

"Adrian has an estimate on what Jenna may have been able to pull from SecLink during the timeframe of her attack," Amanda said. "You truly believe she found a way to connect?"

Cherny folded his arms, leaning back against the monitor in an attempt to make more room for himself. "Never underestimate her." When he had first made the suggestion, nobody thought it remotely possible. Still, the overwatches had applied a dozen patches to SecLink to shore up any potential weaknesses, no matter how unlikely.

Amanda looked at him with cold disbelief, but Cherny stood firm. Finally, she shook her head. "Very well. Pull up the file."

The mess of wires that was Esther's left hand twitched as the command was processed. "Here you go."

The monitors on the opposite wall lit up. Text and images scrolled past, both physically and in the operatives' minds. Cherny stumbled forward, reaching out and grabbing Adrian's shoulder for support. The metal plating was cold to the touch.

"Mars ..." Cherny whispered.

PALE GREY DOT

Adrian shifted in his seat, but with the dozens of cables between him and the computer, he couldn't move far.

"Are you all right?" Amanda asked, though she made no motion to help.

Cherny waved his hand dismissively, pushing himself back up. "Yes. Yes, I'm fine." He watched Amanda's reaction, knowing full well that she had no faith in him or his abilities. *She thinks I'm going to fall apart when the trouble starts. She'll learn,* he decided.

Apparently uninterested in pursuing the matter, Amanda looked at the scrolling text. "In addition to his duties monitoring Jupiter Station, Marcus was involved in the search for Sienar. This included reviewing the events around the Martian Insurrection. If Jenna successfully accessed his full dossier, then she likely knows this. Perhaps that is why she selected him—he was investigating your wayward colleague."

"*Our* wayward colleague," Cherny corrected. "Sienar was a member of ESS and the finest operative we've ever had."

"The finest operative does not turn against us. Do you know how many of our people died in the Ganymede Blitz?"

"That's not … That's not what I'm talking about," Cherny argued. Out of the corner of his eye, he saw Esther and Adrian exchange quick glances. Operatives did not bicker with each other in public. "Look, let's just focus on the mission."

"Agreed."

"So Jenna knows that Sienar went against the service," Cherny said, thinking out loud. "Maybe she has all the

103

Don Miasek

details and maybe she doesn't. In my mind, it's clear she'll be searching for him. He was a brother to her." *We were all family to her, once.* "And she'll see finding him as the best way to hurt the service."

"You may be right."

"It only matters what Jenna thinks, and Jenna knows that Marcus was also interested in the Jupiter locale. And if she's aware that Sienar's defection"—Cherny hated saying the word out loud—"took place on one of Jupiter's moons, then that will be another reason for her to head there. I don't know if she's bypassed the information blackout on Jupiter and found out about the attack, but either way, it wouldn't dissuade her."

Amanda nodded slowly. "In fact, it may give her further incentive to set out for Jupiter's locale."

"What do you mean?"

"Surely you've made the connection." Amanda glanced towards Esther. "Bring up the timeline overlay on the Syndicate's assets."

"Sure thing," the overwatch replied. Her wires rattled against each other. A holographic display of the solar system appeared before the two overwatches. Red icons listed known Syndicate assets. Earth was virtually clear.

Amanda spread her hands towards the map. "At their core, the Syndicate is a bunch of anarchists acting out against perceived slights by the government. They've always been an annoyance, but large-scale operations have been rare. Now Sienar defects"—the map shifted, and the Syndicate icons

PALE GREY DOT

doubled in number—"and suddenly their fortunes begin to grow. His experience and knowledge in ESS's methods have aided them greatly. The destruction of Jupiter Station is going to cause chaos, both here on Earth and throughout the solar system. We can thank your friend for that."

"Oh, come on!" Cherny blurted. "You can't know that Sienar is responsible for—"

"No, you're right. I don't," Amanda interrupted. "But your other friend, Jenna, may think it likely. Another reason for her to head to Jupiter."

Cherny scowled, fuming silently.

"Should I go ahead and arrange passage?" Esther asked, sounding unsure about interrupting the conversation.

Amanda raised a hand, signalling Esther to wait a moment, and then went silent. After ten seconds, she finally replied. "No. As luck would have it, She already has two operatives near Jupiter. Likely three, soon enough."

Cherny glanced at the overwatches, but if they had any reservations about Amanda's connection with Her, they didn't show it. "Who?" he asked.

"The first is Brylan Ncube."

"Is he any good?"

Amanda's reply was not instantaneous. "He's acceptable. Trained in infiltration and combat assignments. The second is Bev Stroud. New to operative status, but I have high expectations should we need to pull her in. The potential third you already know: Ezza Jayens."

Cherny drew in a sharp breath, momentarily stunned by

the news. "You've reactivated Ezza." Of the Athena Six, she had always been the most level-headed. Cherny hadn't been surprised to find out that she was the only one to land on her feet after being expelled from the service. A captain in the United Fleet. Cherny couldn't help but be proud of her success. *No fifty-year career pumping fuel for her.*

"Reactivated, yes," Amanda replied, "though she hasn't connected to SecLink yet. She's with Brylan, so we know she's still alive and well. I am curious—do you think she would try to remove the Athena Protocols, as Jenna must have?"

Cherny shook his head. "I doubt it. Ezza doesn't have the technical skill that Jenna does. More to the point, Ezza isn't crazy like her." *So why hasn't Ezza phoned in?* Cherny wondered. He absentmindedly scratched his cybernetic arm as he thought about trying to resist the Pull. "The damage to Jupiter Station's comm network must be preventing her from making contact," he said.

"Perhaps," Amanda replied. Cherny couldn't tell if she was being dismissive or genuinely agreeing with him. "In any event, Brylan can carry the investigation in the Jupiter locale."

Cherny struggled to hide his discomfort. This all used to be so easy. Letting someone else deal with Jenna didn't sit well with him. This Brylan might be inclined to shoot first and ask questions later. He hoped Ezza would take care of her. "All right," he reluctantly agreed. "We can focus on Sienar."

PALE GREY DOT

"You were the data analyst of your group, and you knew the man perhaps better than anyone else alive. Where would Sienar go?" Amanda challenged.

"There are twenty billion people in the solar system, Amanda," Cherny complained. "I don't think it's reasonable—"

"Cherny," Amanda interrupted. The woman stepped past the silent overwatches. She was tall—taller than Cherny by at least a head—and looked down at him. Her voice maintained that cold, firm tone. "You know that She brought you back because She had faith in your abilities. She believed you were the best person for this job. Was She wrong?"

Cherny's eyes widened, but never broke contact with Amanda's gaze. He fought back a flash of anger. *Think, Cherny!* he urged himself. *This is your chance to prove yourself. You were the best the Earth Security Service had, and you can be that again!* In an instant, it came to him. Cherny smiled. "I … No, She's never wrong. But you're going about this the wrong way."

Amanda sighed impatiently but waited for him to continue.

"We don't need to find Sienar. He was the most loyal person I've ever known." Cherny cut Amanda off before she could object. "Loyal to us, Amanda. The Athena Six. To the people he cared about." He turned towards the overwatches. "Esther, please focus on Mars."

Within an instant, the red planet loomed before them. The time lapse showed a once modest Syndicate presence rapidly expand into holdings covering the entire planet. Known cells, Suspicious Persons, potential informants, and latest movements all scrolled through the hologram. Olympus Mons, the Martian capital, was depicted as ruins.

"The investigation suggested Sienar was trying to find out who he could trust. He was looking for friends to join him, and he sure as hell didn't find any here."

Amanda watched the slowly rotating planet with an unreadable expression.

Careful now, Cherny thought. *Make this convincing.* "We don't have to know where he'd go. We just have to know where I'd go if I wanted him to find me."

Amanda was silent. *Is she talking with Her again?* Cherny wondered. *Does that woman do nothing without consulting Her?* Finally, she nodded. "It is a good plan." The hostility was gone. "Prepare for our immediate departure to Mars."

Cherny hid a smile as he stepped aside to let Amanda exit the room. He knew once he found Sienar, his brother could explain why he defected. Or Cherny could decide whether to help the man in earnest. His head throbbed. *No, helping Sienar is out of the question. Bringing him in safely is the way to go.*

As he planned, he found his gaze lingering on Olympus Mons. The enemy really had grown stronger since the Martian Insurrection. *It's not your fault, though,* he told himself. *It was Taylor's. The whole idiotic plan was his idea to begin with. He coerced Sal to help him.* Cherny rubbed his forehead in frustration.

PALE GREY DOT

"Cherny?"

"Yes, Adrian?"

Both overwatches had awkwardly turned in their linkup seats to face him. "Do you mind if I ask a question?"

"I think you just did." It was such a lame joke, but the overwatch smiled anyway. Some operatives preferred to keep their support personnel at arm's length, treating them as cogs in the network, but Cherny never felt that was an effective approach. The human connection was as important as the mechanical.

"Why did Jenna kill Marcus?"

"I'm ... sorry?"

"Why did Jenna kill Marcus?" Adrian asked again. "Everyone is always talking about how she operates, what her capabilities are, and where she might go now, but nobody is talking about why she's doing this."

Cherny studied Adrian's face. The overwatch was staring, not quite at him, but through him, as if he couldn't quite make out Cherny's form. Only his connection with vast computer network running through the Tower—and thus, the planet—mattered. For Cherny, it was distracting enough to browse SecLink while maintaining some awareness of the real world. For overwatches, it must be damn near impossible.

"It's complicated." *No, it isn't.*

The overwatches just looked through him.

"The, ah, it's the Athena Protocols. The loyalty ..." Cherny searched for the right word. "Programming" was the term

109

most people used, but he never felt it was apt. "Conditioning" wasn't right either. How to describe the wonderful sensation that came from being able to serve ESS? He tried again. "The loyalty that comes with it ... Not everyone in our group was able to"—*adapt? Cope? Stay sane?*—"handle the stress."

Cherny remembered how Sienar once put it. It was shortly after the surgery. "Your every desire is to do what's best for ESS," he had said. "What's 'best' isn't so easy though, is it?" Sienar had smiled and shaken his head in his deep, contemplative way. "You can try to convince yourself that what you want to do is best for ESS. Maybe you'll succeed, and maybe you won't. But you can't cheat, can you? If you know in your heart what She would want you to do, then that's that."

Cherny leaned against the nearest wall monitor. "Look, it goes back to Mars. The six of us were sent to put an end to Governor Griffenham's insurrection. It should have been straightforward. Find dirt on Griffenham and blackmail him, disrupt his organization from within, infiltrate and alienate its members ... Lots of ways to go about it. But then Taylor got some stupid ideas in his head, and it turned into a bloodbath."

I should have told them to mind their own business, Cherny thought bitterly, but he was too far into the story to stop now. "After we got back, we found out Taylor was to be executed. Jenna bolted. I know Marcus was your friend, but it isn't her fault. Jenna and Sal are just casualties."

"So the protocols made her crazy, like they did with Taylor."

PALE GREY DOT

"No, no. Look, she blames ESS for what the Athena Protocols did to us. Wrongly, of course," Cherny quickly added.

Adrian frowned. "But Jenna created the Athena Protocols."

She did. Cherny wondered if she blamed herself for what happened. *She shouldn't. Taylor was the one who wasn't strong enough. The rest of us were fine.* "That wasn't her fault," Cherny said.

Adrian nodded. "We understand."

Do you? Cherny wondered. Grateful for the chance to escape, he grabbed the door latch. But then a thought came to him. Looking back at the pair of overwatches, he asked, "What's the local opinion on my old team? How … What do people think of …?"

The servos at the edge of Esther's mouth tugged downwards, and Cherny noted her discomfort.

"It's all right," he said. "I'm used to hearing bad news."

"Taylor and Sal rebelled against Her," Adrian said in a quiet voice, as if not quite trusting Cherny's reassurance.

"Betrayers," Esther said.

Sal wasn't, Cherny thought. *Sal was innocent.* There was no one warmer or more thoughtful than her. If Cherny hadn't been there to see it with his own eyes, he'd have never believed she was capable of it. *It was Taylor that led her astray.*

Adrian shifted uncomfortably, and the wires draped over the back of his chair slid from side to side. "Thought the Athena Six survivors got off easy. But you are nicer than I would have figured, Cherny."

111

Don Miasek

"There may be hope for you and Ezza yet," Esther mused. "We'd like it if you both could come back. Heal old wounds."

"Right. Me too," Cherny replied, though he didn't feel reassured. "Could I ask you two for a favour?"

"You can ask," Esther replied. The pair had settled back into their seats, now looking forward towards nothingness.

"Pull up all the files you have on Amanda," Cherny said. "I want to know everything there is to know about my new partner."

Ezza didn't realize how tightly she was holding the little orange bottle until she saw her knuckles had turned white. *Cerebrol Acetaminophen,* the label read in clinical black letters. Through the shaded plastic, two dozen little white pills rested in a chaotic jumble. *It might help against the Pull.*

With her cybernetic hand, Ezza pinched the bridge of her nose. Her head was pounding. Half of her wanted sleep. Half of her wanted to order Rachelle to charge up the transmitter for a direct connection to the Tower on Earth. For the past twenty hours, neither side got what it wanted. She told herself that the rescue operations required her full attention. A flotilla of arriving civilian and governmental ships needed coordinating, and it would be days before a flag officer could arrive to take over.

Ezza turned her head slightly, now gazing at a second bottle resting on her desk. The stimulant was effective at keeping

PALE GREY DOT

her active and awake. She knew the moment she slept would be the moment she'd surrender to the Pull, though for the life of her, she struggled to remember why she shouldn't do just that.

Ezza set the bottle down. She tapped the screen of her padd, and a list of reports from her department heads scrolled past her eyes.

Debris from *Stalwart*, one of the two battlecruisers in the fleet, had slammed into Ring 2. Adams and Gole had led a team to find any survivors.

Chief Engineer Carmen reported that the main nuclear pulse engines on *Starknight's* secondary hull were fully repaired after their emergency departure from the station.

Another search team confirmed there was no sign of Admiral Tolj. MIA, the official profile said, but the reigning belief was that he and everyone else in the regional headquarters had perished.

News of the attack had broken across the solar system a few hours ago. Shortly after, two separate declarations came across the Net from the Syndicate. The first claimed responsibility for the attack. The other claimed innocence. *Just what is going on over there?* Ezza wondered. Intelligence, she reminded herself, was under the purview of the Earth Security Service. *It would be irresponsible not to fill them in. Perhaps even put* Starknight *at Brylan's disposal for the investigation. Surely that would make sense. Surely it's what She would want.*

The longer she fought against the Pull, the worse her head felt. Transmitter or pills. Slowly, she reached forward.

113

Don Miasek

A sudden knock snapped her out of her daze. Unlike those from her crew or Brylan, this knock was soft and timid. Ezza hastily cleared the bottles from her desk and slipped her gloves on. With a mental flick, the door to her office opened. "What can I do for you, Nirali?" She could hear the raggedness in her own voice.

The journalist glanced over her shoulder before entering. Without a change of clothes of her own, someone had loaned her an orange technician's jumpsuit that was a few sizes too large. "Hello again, Captain," she said quietly.

Reaching across her desk, Ezza undid the latch to the visitor's chair and swung it down from the wall. It was nothing more than a cold metal bench, but Nirali gratefully sat down, slipping a cloth backpack from her shoulders and setting it on the desk. Then, after a moment's thought, she leaned over and closed the door leading out into the hallway.

Like Ezza, Nirali looked exhausted. "I, um, wanted to thank you."

Ezza raised an eyebrow. She kept her hands clasped together and tried to keep her breathing from sounding haggard. Maintaining the indomitable image of confidence that leadership required was getting harder with each passing hour.

"For rescuing me from Jupiter Station, I mean." Nirali placed her hand on Ezza's desk.

"You are very welcome, Nirali."

"My family also got to safety thanks to a United Fleet rescue team."

PALE GREY DOT

"Helping others is part of the job." It felt like someone was repeatedly hitting her skull with a hammer. *Wham, wham, wham.*

Nirali smiled weakly. "Brylan Ncube certainly didn't seem to think so."

"He had his reasons," Ezza quickly replied. "ESS operatives are trained to be pragmatic during emergencies. I'm sure he was only thinking of the best way to save as many people as he could."

The journalist peered at Ezza. "You really respect him, huh?"

"I ... what?" Ezza sputtered. Her cool demeanour cracked. The pounding in her skull didn't hold back.

Nirali gave her a confused look. "Sure. You brought him on board, you've agreed with just about everything he's said. He's been bossing your people around. He's had full access to your communication and scanning stations. And according to your chief engineer, he hasn't shared anything he's found with the rest of the crew."

Ezza shook her head, but that proved to be a mistake, so she waved her hand instead. "This is a crisis, Nirali. Cooperation. We need to have cooperation. The United Fleet and ESS have been at each other's throats for too long." *Wham, wham, wham.*

Nirali leaned forward slightly. "Is it true what he said? That you're an operative?"

Ezza broke into a halting laugh. "Hah, no, that isn't right. It isn't, Nirali."

115

Don Miasek

"You used to be, then?"

How is this woman pushing me around? Ezza thought through the haze in her mind. "Listen, I brought you on board, but there are conditions for you to stay here," Ezza retorted.

"What's wrong?" the reporter asked, feigning innocence. "I thought you were fine with being on his side. United Fleet and ESS"—Nirali held up her hand, crossing her fingers—"nice and close with one another."

Ezza closed her eyes, trying to clear her head, but the Pull was agony. She thought back to when she and Cherny had been exiled. All of her contacts had abandoned her. Only Tolj had come forward and given her a shot in the rival United Fleet. He had taken such a risk, Ezza knew, and he wouldn't want this. And yet, giving ESS their full support felt logical, good, and right. *Wham, wham, wham.* "I know you mean well, Nirali, but you're way out of your depth. The United Fleet has been crippled—possibly irreparably so. We aren't going to be able to keep the peace in the solar system for long. We need the Earth Security Service's help to find out who's responsible."

Nirali snorted. "I figure ESS was behind it."

Ezza's eyes widened. "That will be all, Nirali. You're dismissed," she said firmly.

Nirali started to protest, but quickly changed her mind. The reporter stood, grabbing her backpack as she did. Undoing the strings that kept it closed, she reached in and drew out something large and black. Nirali set it down on the desk with an audible thud.

PALE GREY DOT

The empty eyes of the breather mask that once belonged to a Jupiter Station guardsman looked up at Ezza. She met its stare, spotting flecks of dried blood still on the straps from when Brylan casually murdered its owner.

It took her a minute to realize Nirali was gone, and that she was alone again. Her hand shook as she slid open the wall compartment and took out the bottle of Cerebrol. It took a couple tries to unscrew the lid.

Ezza opened her eyes twenty minutes later. The pill had muted the banging in her head. She still felt tired and sore, but the fog in her mind had started to lift. Ezza folded up the chairs and desk, slipping the bottle into her uniform pocket before stepping out into the hallway.

A passing crew member in a stained refueller's suit moved aside, saluting.

Ezza stepped past her, returning the gesture as if on auto-pilot. *They're just as tired as you are*, Ezza thought. She wasn't sure if it was the fatigue, the Pull, or the brief respite on the wide-open Jupiter Station that made the corridors of her cruiser seem like they were closing in on her. Ezza pressed her hand against the wall, stopping for support.

A tingle ran through her implants. The call was from Brylan. With some satisfaction, Ezza ignored it and pressed on. *Remember the mask*, she told herself.

Starknight's war room doubled as a recreation facility and meeting room for the ship's officers. Since the attack, it was a full-time nerve centre for the rescue and relief oper-ations. Centred around a fold-out table with a holographic projector, Rachelle and Chief Engineer Carmen immediately stopped chatting and stood straight.

"Commanders," Ezza said, keeping her voice firm despite the clouds in her mind.

"Captain," Rachelle replied, nodding her head. She looked as exhausted as Ezza felt. The silver machinery adorning the cyborg couldn't hide the dark rings around her eyes. Her lips were dry and cracked, and she soon returned to hunching over the holo-projector. The cables running from her frame into the ship's computer sagged under their own weight.

Even Carmen couldn't hide her fatigue. Though her grey uniform was pressed and fitted as perfectly as ever, her eyes had lost some of the bright sharpness she was known for. With one hand, she pushed her long brown hair behind her ear. With her other, she cradled a steel mug of café as if her sanity depended on it.

"Let's get right to it," Ezza said. She hoped they couldn't see her own weariness. "What's our status?"

Rachelle's fingers twitched. Ezza knew that every scrap of data *Starknight* received, from its internal systems to any transmissions it picked up, ran through those wires and into the cyborg's mind. "We have an updated survivor count: twenty-two thousand, seven hundred and twenty-seven civilians, and two hundred and sixty-four United Fleet personnel—not including our own. Terminal 2 has been secured as a refugee centre."

"We're up since the last round of searches," Carmen muttered sarcastically. "Yay."

PALE GREY DOT

Ezza ignored her, focusing on her second-in-command. "And the fleet?"

"Recovering the *Integrity* has been unsuccessful. The ship is technically still berthed at Terminal 4, Ring 4, but the salvage teams have decided it is a total loss."

And so Starknight *is the only United Fleet ship still intact until reinforcements arrive,* Ezza thought grimly. "Have the teams on Rings 4 and 6 completed their searches?"

Rachelle shook her head. "The re-mapping is done, but it's revealed more internal breaches than we expected. The search teams are going to have to EVA over ninety percent of the interior, and we don't have the equipment."

Ezza considered this for a moment. It felt good to have a problem she could focus on. "Is the *Venture* still in local space?" The mining scraper was one of the few ships lucky enough to survive the attack unscathed.

"For now, but Captain Volpe's already sent in an official request to be allowed to depart."

"Make the captain an offer," Ezza replied. "She loans us two dozen interior-grade EVA suits and I'll make a call to speed up her application." Hopefully Volpe wouldn't want a face-to-face discussion about it.

Rachelle nodded, silently composing the letter.

Ezza turned towards her engineer, who immediately spoke up.

"I already know what you're going to ask, Captain. It's still going to be three days minimum before we're ready for long-distance flight." The woman failed to keep the

119

annoyance out of her voice. "Everything was shut down when we docked for refuelling."

Deciding not to endure yet another speech from Carmen about the complexities of safely starting a nuclear pulse engine, Ezza nodded. "Let me know if I can help in any way."

"Will do. Thanks, ma'am," Carmen replied. She raised her mug and drained the contents.

Ezza moved on. "Have the searchers had any luck finding the perpetrators?"

"Not yet," Rachelle said. "The Ministry of Public Safety has announced that ESS will be leading the investigation."

Nirali's words echoed through Ezza's mind. *"I figure ESS was behind it."*

Impossible. What would they gain by crippling the United Fleet? No mere inter-governmental rivalry would account for this. Even through the Cerebrol, Ezza's headache started to throb. *Wham, wham, wham.* She decided not to think about it.

Ezza suddenly realized that Carmen and Rachelle were looking at her, waiting. "I'd like to have our searches of the rings completed before more ESS assets arrive," she said, maintaining an even tone.

"God," Carmen muttered, "this is going to be such crap. Hell, the United Fleet probably won't be able to maintain our patrols anymore."

Rachelle turned to the engineer. "I have been thoroughly monitoring fleet communications. Nearly every reserve member and functional ship is being activated."

PALE GREY DOT

"Won't be enough," Carmen retorted, folding her arms.

"Speaking of communications"—Rachelle now fixed her glassy eyes upon Ezza—"we did pick up a transmission an hour ago. It was encrypted, but my United Fleet codes are invalid."

Carmen raised her hand. "Hold on, Commander. I know where you're going with this."

"We have to ask," Rachelle replied. "You said it yourself—the United Fleet may no longer be capable of providing adequate security for the system. We may need to rely on the Earth Security Service."

Ezza used her hands to support herself as she leaned against the holo-projector. "Bring it up, Commander. I'd like to see it."

The projector hummed. Encoded text scrolled past Ezza's widening eyes. "It's an ESS code."

"There, you see, Carmen? Let me open a line to Brylan Ncube."

"No." Ezza's eyes were glued to the projection. "That won't be necessary." She looked at her left hand. The synth-leather glove was creased and cracked after years of use. It almost felt as much a part of her as her own skin did. *Didn't take long to start relying on these again, did it?*

Gently, Ezza tugged at the fingers, slipping the glove off. Rachelle and Carmen watched. Her cybernetic suite was no secret to her crew, but she was never sure if they knew just how advanced they were. Rachelle, she suspected, would have recognized them as far beyond standard military grade.

121

Don Miasek

For now, the cyborg was silent as Ezza took a cord from the projector and slid the connector into her arm. Codes and electronic warfare were never her specialty, but Ezza couldn't help but feel nostalgic when she used her ESS-given gifts. Even her headache seemed to subside just a little bit.

"Ma'am," Carmen started slowly, "how did you recognize that these were ESS codes by sight alone?" There was suspicion and fear in her voice.

Though neither Rachelle nor Ezza responded out loud, the obvious answer was there.

"Decryption complete," Ezza finally said. "This code is decades old. I don't know why anyone would be sending ... Ah." The answer came to her in a flash as the scrolling text shifted and became legible. "Jenna," she breathed.

```
*** Ezza. We haven't seen eye to eye on everything,
but now there're bigger problems than you being a
colossal bitch. We have a chance to hurt ESS real
bad, and we need your help. Sienar is missing. He
went AWOL and killed a lot of ESS people at Ganymede.
Uruk Sulcus-132. I knew he was still on our side. ***

*** They're looking for him. It's like Her personal
crusade now. Moreover, they have some kind of plan
for Jupiter Station. Don't know what yet. I'm on my
way to Ganymede now. Sienar might be hiding there.
Get your ship and help. ***

*** Will see if I can grab Cherny. It'll be just like
old times. We're going to be a family again. ***
```

122

Pale Grey Dot

Ezza felt the stares from her chief engineer and second-in-command. Her arm tingled as she calmly drew the connector out and pulled the glove back over her hand. "I think," she said slowly, "that I owe you an explanation."

DISPATCH FROM THE PREMIER OF EARTH

*** HIGH PRIORITY ***

All residents within the solar system need to be aware that an attack has occurred at Jupiter Station targeting twenty-seven United Fleet spaceships. Though the damage to the ships and the station is extensive, disaster management is underway to limit the death toll. This is a joint venture between the Ministry of Defence and the Ministry of Transportation and will include new travel restrictions to the Jupiter locale.

I have instructed Minister Richter of Public Safety to dispatch the Earth Security Service to confirm the Syndicate's involvement and bring them to justice. Full cooperation is expected from all citizens involved in their investigation.

Time and time again, our grand government has been challenged by those seeking to replace it with anarchy for their own benefit, and time and time again, Earth has withstood them. This shall be no different.

When we stand together, we are unbeatable.

Mary Fairchild, Premier of Earth

"Jenna! Jenna, you stupid girl, wake up!"

Jenna's eyes snapped open. The sheets of her bunk were hot and twisted around her body. *Have you forgotten how to sleep in a bed?* The workers' quarters on *Étoile* were cramped, the air was musty, and the lights were too bright. Jo-Ann's nasally screeches did little to add to the room's comfort.

Sitting up and dangling her legs over the edge, Jenna had to hold her hand up to avoid hitting her head on the bunk above her. In truth, the bed wasn't hers—not really. She had to hot bunk with Larry, one of the cooks, and Betty, one of the engine room twerps. When they worked, she slept, and when she worked, one of them slept. It had only been three days since they departed Gagarin Station over Earth, but the mattress and bed bag were already beginning to smell.

Jenna carefully pushed herself to her feet—*Étoile* was still

Don Miasek

under only 0.15g of thrust. As she did so, she became aware of the buzzing from her cybernetics. One of her internal alarms was going off. "What's happened?" she asked Jo-Ann in a hoarse whisper as she connected to the network.

Jo-Ann's dark hair was scraggly and unkempt, though she was able to tie it back in a semi-elegant fashion when she had to mingle with the passengers. Her skin was splotchy, and she had a puggish nose. When she stood up straight, wore a clean, white uniform, and set a prim and proper expression on her face, she could almost look regal. But when stuck in the secondary hull with the dredges, she looked like one of them.

What she couldn't hide, though, were the badly installed and poorly maintained cybernetics circling her left eye and ear and running down her arm. *That's what you get for shopping around for the lowest price,* Jenna had thought when she first laid eyes on her.

"Get moving. There's news from Earth!" Jo-Ann exclaimed.

Jenna quickly slipped on her official *Étoile* uniform. In reality, they were given two: one they had to keep clean for when they ventured to the primary hull, and one they could damn well do whatever they wanted with. The clean one included a paper hat with *Étoile, Explore in Style!* written across the front in navy blue.

They arrived to find that the workers' lounge was already full. Jenna didn't like crowds—not of the civilized variety, at least. She'd have preferred to review the transmissions alone,

Pale Grey Dot

but knew it wasn't socially acceptable. None of the crew already present were at the kitchen or the couches or the RecSystem. Instead, they huddled around the image above the projector. Jenna's heart skipped a beat when she realized it was the broken and battered ruins of Jupiter Station. Several of its rings were torn and shredded, and the wreckage of spaceships littered local space.

"Sources within the Syndicate have claimed responsibility for the attack, along with conflicting statements denying responsibility." In the corner of the projection, a mustachioed reporter spoke in a focus-group-approved voice. "Initial accusations of Eridani Sympathizer involvement have pro—hold on." The man paused. "The premier's dispatch has just been posted."

Jenna received the file and quickly scanned it. Typical political rhetoric. *Fear not, citizens—the great and wonderful government, with its armies and intelligence agencies, has you covered. What nonsense.* There were other dispatches as well. There were initial travel advisories from the Ministry of Transportation, and the Ministry of Extrasolar-System Affairs was drafting a notification to the colonies at Alpha Centauri and Epsilon Eridani.

Ralph took a step over to her and smiled nervously. Even in the secondary hull, he still wore that stupid white paper hat with the *Étoile* slogan. Underneath it, curly red hair framed a freckled face. "Don't worry, it'll be okay," he said, as if he had any clue whether that was true.

"All right," Jenna replied dryly. She only needed part of her

127

Don Miasek

focus to placate him—the rest of her attention was directed at absorbing data through the ship's network, downloading every scrap of information sent by the news.

"Oh my God ..." someone whispered in the crowd, covering their mouth with their hand. A clattering of voices rippled through the crowd and immediately drowned out the projection. It was a mix of subdued panic, horror, and anxiety.

"Without the fleet, who's going to protect us?"

"Are we still going to Jupiter?"

"I sure wouldn't want to be listed as a Suspicious Person right now ..."

Ralph looked up at the ceiling in thought. "I think I might have a cousin on Jupiter Station." He looked at Jenna. "What about you? Any family near Jupiter?"

Jenna shook her head. "No," she lied. In truth, she didn't really remember anyone biologically related to her. But they weren't her family anyway. She met her real family at the learning institute in Kazan when she was ten, and now they were either killed or scattered to the four corners of the solar system. She did know Ezza was near Jupiter with a warship, though. She hoped her sister got her message.

As a half-dozen separate conversations broke out, Jenna tried to think about what to do. Though she'd been out of the game for over half a century, Jenna didn't believe the Syndicate theory. *I need more information.*

You could try to reconnect to SecLink, she thought. Jenna instantly shivered at the idea. She had barely resisted it in

PALE GREY DOT

Toronto. The idea of succumbing to that tormenting Pull and returning on her hands and knees to beg Her to be let back into the fold was abhorrent. *"Help me, help me! I never should have doubted you!"* Jenna imagined herself pleading. Just the thought of being near Her almost made Jenna sick to her stomach.

"Huh!" came a deep voice from the lounge's entrance, and with that, the chatter instantly ceased. Hecktor Ramirez stepped in. If *Étoile*'s captain looked big out on the spaceport tarmac in his longcoat and breather, he was gigantic in the smaller confines of the ship's secondary hull. Without the breather, the man cut an impressive figure. His mean, beady eyes constantly squinted at whatever he looked at, and his red beard was thick and wiry. Hecktor was smiling, though it did nothing to make him appear less imposing. Instead, it was the thin smile of a vicious man.

Hecktor stepped forward towards the projector, and the workers moved aside to let him through. As the captain, he always had to wear the clean, white cruise liner uniform, though Jenna noted that his stupid hat was much fancier than everyone else's.

A news analyst was pointing out the damage on a wireframe model of Jupiter Station when Hecktor stopped. "Huh," he repeated. "So they finally did it."

Someone in the back raised a hand. "Hecktor, are we still going to Jupiter? I mean, with the attack and all?"

Jenna froze. This could annihilate her chances of getting to Ganymede. But to her relief, Hecktor laughed.

Don Miasek

"Lad, we don't have the fuel for another round of accelerating and decelerating. Not if we want to dock sometime this year. Besides, I want to see this for myself." Hecktor stroked his beard in thought. "The news'll be breaking in the primary hull. I'm going to head over there to reassure everyone. Pretty sure I can convince them that it's perfectly safe. Heh!"

Murmuring rippled through the gathered workers.

"Come on, Hecktor. You aren't saying this is a good thing," Jo-Ann said, rolling her eyes.

Hecktor waved his hand, but his smile didn't fade. "Nah … nah. Tragic, really. All those poor bastards on the station. Lemme ask you all something, though. Anyone here really have a problem with Earth's control getting dealt a bloody nose?"

Numerous shaking heads and chuckles answered his question. With that, the tension was broken. A little less governmental oversight had its appeal.

"Didn't think so. I'm heading back up. Jenna!" He whirled towards her. "The guest in Suite 7G says her terminals have gone out again. Looks to be a problem at the source. Grab a clean uniform and let's go."

"Okay," Jenna said.

"And as for the rest of you," Hecktor continued, "we've got a day and a half before we cut our thrust and start up rotational gravity. Start prepping to cool the engines and tie everything back down to the outer walls." The big man gave one last glare to his crew before turning away.

Jenna started after him.

PALE GREY DOT

"Jenna, wait!" Ralph called out, reaching into a lounge cupboard. "Don't forget this." He unfolded the white paper hat and placed it on her head. "There!" he said proudly.

"Thanks," Jenna deadpanned.

Like most ships designed for long-distance travel, *Étoile* was built around a double hull configuration, though Jenna had rarely seen a ship with such contrast between them.

The connection shaft, like the workers' quarters in the secondary hull behind her, was made of dark grey metal. Warning lights flickered, casting shadows off the corridor's plating. Crawling was easy at 0.15g, but Hecktor still struggled in the tight confines of the shaft. He grunted and sweated as he pulled himself along two handholds at a time, compensating for his great bulk with his strength.

Pausing, perhaps to catch his breath, Hecktor glanced behind him. "Jo-Ann tells me you're being mouthy about our network setup," he said.

"Jo-Ann isn't very smart," Jenna replied matter-of-factly from several rungs back. Unlike the captain, her scrawny figure gave her plenty of room to move.

Hecktor's huge hands gripped the handholds so tightly that his knuckles turned white. "Listen, dredge, don't start thinking you're home free just because we're off Earth. You were brought along to do a job and that's it. If I don't like what I'm seeing, you'll be gettin' off this ship a lot sooner than Jupiter, if you catch my drift."

Jenna bit her tongue. Sal would have told her to keep her chin up and to appreciate that she now had three square meals a day and a roof over her head. Taylor would have flashed that grin of his and joked about throwing Hecktor out the airlock.

Having to deal with people again was proving harder than she remembered. Part of her missed the alleys, Netcafes, VR sims, and wastelands on Earth. There, she didn't have to rely on anyone but herself, she didn't have to put up with nagging shrews, and she definitely didn't have to wear stupid paper hats.

"Well?" Hecktor asked. "We going to have a problem or not?"

"No," Jenna replied. "We won't have a problem."

Hecktor grunted his acknowledgement and got moving again.

As they made their way to the primary hull, Jenna silently hooked back into the ship's network. A part of her was delighted to watch everything She and the others had worked for crashing down around them. Their grand society was showing its cracks. *Ezza better be all right,* Jenna thought. Hopefully she and Cherny had gotten her messages. Making use of *Étoile*'s transmitter without the other ship overseers knowing about it was child's play, though she had needed to keep the notes short.

Getting to Ezza was no problem. Slipping a message in

PALE GREY DOT

with all the civilian and governmental transmissions a typical United Fleet ship received was something Jenna could do in her sleep.

Cherny, however, was a different matter. She knew from Marcus's memories that he was with ESS, but Jenna knew it wasn't so simple. Cherny would never betray his family. No, this was another one of his cunning plots to gain intel on the enemy. If there was one thing that that man knew, it was loyalty. Getting a covert message to him involved weaving through thousands of intermediaries, all of which needed to be reliable and secure. He should get it, but it could take a while.

Jenna's feet hit the deck shortly after Hecktor's.

"All right," Hecktor said. His entire demeanour changed as he softened his usual grimace and relaxed his shoulders. "Smile." Jenna couldn't tell if he was talking to her or himself. The man pushed open the door and the pair stepped out into the passenger hull.

The ship's cafeteria—the advertisements called it a "restaurant"—was packed, as usual, with passengers at nearly every seat around the long, thin tables that filled it. Harried servers struggled to attend to the demands of the guests. Where *Étoile*'s secondary hull had been cramped, musty, and dirty, the primary was brighter and bordered on clean. It fell short of being truly luxurious, however, because of the veneer of fakeness. The furniture looked like wood, but still had that plastic sheen to it.

Jenna was unsurprised that the heated conversations

around the cafeteria were of Jupiter Station. She could hear passengers arguing about what this meant for them, their friends, and the solar system as a whole. A crowd at the forwardmost table was getting rowdy as a thin man in a blue suit stood up and shouted at a woman across the table.

"Captain Ramirez, did you hear?" came a feminine voice. The woman was either around forty or had some very effective anti-ageing techniques. Jenna couldn't spot any of the subtle lines, faded wrinkles, or tightness around the eyes that gave it away. She wore a smart grey suit with azure highlights running down the lapels. Silvery cybernetics crisscrossed between an ocular enhancement above her left eye and the tips of her fingers. It was artistry mixed with functionality. Her blonde hair cascaded down her back, with a few locks resting on her shoulders.

Hecktor, standing tall, prim, and proper, as a good cruise line captain should, nodded solemnly. "I did, Ms. Noble. Grave news indeed."

Jenna watched with amazement. Hecktor was a completely different man. Though still powerful and imposing-looking, refined elegance had replaced his brutish tendencies.

"The crew is working to bring all transmitters online for those who wish to contact home," Hecktor continued.

"Is there any danger?" Noble asked, leaning in as if she needed to whisper the possibility of a threat. "I've been in contact with the board and they're asking that all non-essential travel be halted. Are we thinking about turning back?"

Hecktor gave her a warm, reassuring smile. "The Ministry

PALE GREY DOT

of Transportation has assured us that the route to Jupiter is still heavily patrolled by the United Fleet. The travel advisory has not extended into our path. If I may be so bold, Ms. Noble, this ship has the finest crew in the solar system, and we work every day to make it the safest it can be."

Jenna thought of Ralph the idiot, Jo-Ann the nagging witch, the gaggle of twerps in the engine room, the VR addicts running the custodial service, Ben from the kitchen who kept wiping his hands on everything, and Kathy, the ship overseer on the shift before her, who couldn't code her way out of a wet paper bag.

Noble, however, looked placated. "Thank you, Captain. Please let me know if there's any way I can help."

Jenna couldn't imagine what possible value the woman could contribute if a Syndicate ship decided to fire a few long-ranged missiles their way. She'd already reviewed *Étoile*'s defensive systems and found them wanting. Jenna wondered why Hecktor didn't seem more concerned.

"I will, Ms. Noble," Hecktor confirmed. "Now, if you'll excuse me, I do have to prepare an announcement for our remaining guests." Gesturing towards Jenna, he added, "Ensign Jenna will be happy to help you with your suite's terminal."

"Ensign"? Jenna thought.

Hecktor gave Jenna a final wary look before stepping towards the arguing passengers.

Jenna wondered how he'd deal with them. When she had first come on board, Jo-Ann had drilled her on the expected behaviour of every crew member when interacting with guests. Uniforms must be immaculate at all times. Guests always have right of way. Speak only when spoken to. Offer no opinions. Yes, ma'am. No, sir. If it pleases you, ma'am. We're here to serve, sir.

Jenna ignored all that and sized the other woman up. "Suite 7G, right?" Noble had every marking of a moderately high-ranking executive. She looked powerful and relatively well off, but with a hint of impatience. The cybernetics were a high-end CrossNet enterprise package. GreyCorp, perhaps? Geodynamic Industries? There were countless reasons a business exec might get sent out to Jupiter Station.

Noble nodded pleasantly enough, but Jenna could detect the condescension behind the smile. "The network access terminal just stopped responding to my commands. Here, I'll take you there."

Jenna was half tempted to let Noble know that she wouldn't steal anything from the suite but restrained herself. *Focus on the mission,* she thought.

As she followed Noble across the cafeteria, Jenna found herself comparing the clean, fake surroundings to her time in the service. They had all the best things back then. The Tower itself had luxury that would put *Étoile* to shame.

Jenna also had to resist the urge to roll her eyes at the chatter filling the room.

"I have faith that Fairchild will see us through ..."

"Those poor, brave soldiers of the United Fleet ..."

PALE GREY DOT

"... Fairchild will need to pull all funding from Jupiter's moons and local asteroids, of course ..."

Jenna ducked to the side to let a server with a plate of "certified authentic meat" past. The fine print of the vessel's Travel Disclosure Agreement admitted it came from the cloning tanks back on the secondary hull.

"I honestly don't understand why the Syndicate would want to harm so many innocent people," Noble said.

"Dunno," Jenna replied. *To gain some semblance of freedom.*

If she had any problem with Jenna's casual tone, Noble didn't show it. She spoke as if she was used to lecturing others. "It really is a problem with the solar system, isn't it? We spread out so much and lost our ability to relate to one another. Our culture is diverging, Ensign."

"Uh-huh." Jenna eyed a trio of execs poring over a holographic analysis of the Jupiter Station damage. Jenna fought the instinctual urge to run and hide.

"How is a man from some asteroid supposed to understand a woman from Paris? Or a man from Mars and a woman from Venus?" Noble smiled at her own cleverness. "And the colonies! The decade of comm lag makes it impossible. The cultural differences are going to be extreme in the not-too-distant future. Mark my words.

"Oh, and I don't just mean physical distance either, Ensign. Have you ever gotten a good look at a full-convert cyborg? I don't see how someone who experiences taste, touch, and smell is going to relate to someone who knows

137

Don Miasek

only of electricity, magnetic senses, and wireless interfacing. It's getting to the point where the news is so bad, it's all I can do to ignore it. It's not like we can do anything about it anyway." She led Jenna around the corner into the habitation halls.

Jenna ran through her old awareness training. Mark every individual. Catalogue threats. Plan escape routes. Look for incongruences. Identify potential weapons. The fat man there looked slow and awkward in this gravity. He could be used as a hostage, but he also looked like the panicky type. The old woman chatting with him had shifty, suspicious eyes. The airlock-grade door to the side led to a maintenance area and could be locked from behind.

"Well, Ensign? What do you think?" Noble asked as the pair turned off towards the first-class guest quarters.

It took Jenna a moment to think back on what the exec had been talking about. *"Offer no opinions,"* Jo-Ann's nasally voice echoed in her mind. "Humans don't need many differences to start murdering each other. Cybernetics and distance are just others in a long line of excuses."

Noble sighed, "I suppose you may be right. Terrifying as they are, it's a good thing we have the Earth Security Service to protect us."

Jenna gritted her teeth.

The woman stopped in front of the double doors leading to her suite. Pressing her finger against the display screen, the doors emitted a melodic chime and slid open, revealing a stunning suite.

PALE GREY DOT

One of the walls of Noble's living room was a floor-to-ceiling window looking out into space, while the other walls cycled through decorative planetary landscapes, from Mars to Neptune. The deck covering was a mix of blues woven with greens into an intricate design. Soft music played as they entered.

Spying the broken terminal resting on the carved desk near the window, Jenna trudged over. Pulling a cable from it, she jammed it into a socket in her arm. It took a few tries to get the plug to fit right in the bent and rusted port. "Yeah, the router isn't able to connect to the network. Let me reset this thing. And ... done."

Noble gave her a blank look. "So all you did was turn it off and on again?"

"Pretty much."

Noble shook her head. "And I thought my job was bad."

Yes, it must be awful to be so helpless when faced with the simplest of problems. No wonder the richies are such big fans of ESS; it means they don't have to do anything about their own safety. Jenna marvelled at the contrast between her past and now. She used to topple corporations and help chart the course of the solar system. Now she was making house calls to fix people's Net connections.

Noble thanked her profusely and complimented her nice uniform and hat, and Jenna returned to her duties.

139

Don Miasek

Her days on *Étoile* were filled with petty technical problems and avoiding her crewmates. The nights were spent in the too-warm bunk. Her shifts in the secondary hull's control room were her only respite from the morons running the ship. The eight hours of peace and quiet gave Jenna time to reflect, plan, and sink her claws into *Étoile*'s systems.

The control room wasn't much bigger than an outhouse, with only enough room for a ship overseer to connect directly to the ship's computer, and for any other crew member who didn't mind getting cozy. The only chair was carefully moulded to allow the user to recline and relax as they carefully watched over the ship. Though its upholstery was ripped in several spots, Jenna still found it far more comfortable than her squalid living conditions on Earth.

A projector displayed screens for Jenna, but she preferred the direct connection. A dozen wires ran from the bent and twisted ports of her left arm to those on the control room wall. Jenna liked to keep the room dark, though there were enough blinking red and blue lights along the access panels that she could still see.

Checking the comm logs, she found no answer yet from Ezza or Cherny. *Soon*, she figured, as she worked to build access points and scripts into the ship's key functions. Nuclear pulse engines, manoeuvring thrusters, network, defences … The list of things she might need was a long one.

The one good thing about the ship was that the incompetence of *Étoile*'s network staff meant she had free reign over the ship's systems. She had to keep the messages short, but

PALE GREY DOT

that was fine. With Hecktor fearlessly willing to finish the trek to Jupiter, she decided that picking this ship had been a stroke of luck.

Jenna watched the alerts as they scrolled through her mind. A message, purportedly from Alexander Reuben of the Syndicate, had claimed no responsibility for the attack at Jupiter Station, contradicting those from other Syndicate leaders earlier. *Hah. Nice try.*

Syndicate piracy reports had increased, neatly coinciding with the attack on Jupiter Station. Raids had taken down a dozen United Fleet and militia targets throughout the system. A bomber blew up a luxury liner, taking one hundred and thirty souls with her. *Certainly adds credence to the claims of responsibility,* Jenna decided. She idly wondered how she'd destroy an entire fleet if she had to. Something to plan for, she supposed.

Back in her day, the Syndicate never would have been organized enough to pull this off before being shut down. She knew that ESS had taken a hit after the Martian Insurrection, but they must have really fallen far. *Good*, Jenna thought with smug satisfaction.

Jenna smiled at what She must be going through. *Not so great at keeping the system secure now, are You?* She thought back to Marcus's words. *"That's it, then. The United Fleet wins."* Jenna wondered what She was feeling right now—if She even *could* feel anymore.

Fear. She hoped it was fear. That was an emotion Jenna wanted Her to become intimately familiar with.

141

*** **FLEET-WIDE TRANSMISSION** ***

*** **SOURCE: UFS *PRAVEDNI*** ***

*** **RESTRICTED TO CAPTAIN (RANK O-6) AND ABOVE** ***

Ladies and gentlemen, official orders will be coming through shortly, but I wanted to give everyone a report. The fleet at Jupiter Station is, from a hardware perspective, a total loss. This represents a quarter of the active fleet. Personnel are still being recovered, but casualties are high.

Now, there's going to be a lot of talk coming from the media about security across the solar system. We all know that maintaining control is going to be difficult, and we've already seen a rise in illegal activities. Consequently, all spaceworthy vessels and reserve forces will be reactivated. Furthermore, Defence Minister Havoic is planning to grant expanded powers to the local planetary militias to cover any territory we lose. Expect extensive reassignments.

While ESS will investigate, I think we're all confident of the Syndicate's responsibility. Reports suggest the explosives were hidden amongst the cargo loaded onto the resupplying ships. I want every precaution taken when dealing with external partners. Don't let anything on board without your or your crew's visual inspection.

Stay strong and stay alert. We'll get through this.

Admiral Gabrielle Cheng-Visitor

7

Mars was worse than he remembered.

Cherny leaned on the balcony railing of his fif-teenth-storey hotel room, looking out over the darkened city. The air smelled foul, the low gravity made his steps awkward, and the sky was too dim. Cherny remembered what Sienar once told him: "It took our greatest minds to bring Mars up to Earth's level—and the same minds to bring Earth down to Mars's."

Cherny rested his wine glass on the railing. He watched the sparkling purple hue of its contents glinting in the low, early-morning light. *Suddenly a non-renewable resource,* Cherny mused. He doubted there was another decent bottle anywhere in the city.

Olympus Mons was nothing compared to any Earthen metropolis. On Earth, cities had no choice but to grow up into the sky. On Mars, going underground had been the

143

best chance to survive the planet's high levels of radiation, but once the terraforming efforts kicked in, the virgin lands had made the sprawl inevitable. The rounded building tops rarely exceeded ten storeys.

From his vantage point, Cherny could see all the way to the Altis Legislature, despite the hazy atmosphere. They had fixed it up well. Cherny remembered back when the polished metal roofs were brilliantly decorated with every hue of the rainbow. Nowadays, the paint was faded, scoured by dust and wind to reveal the dull brown beneath that matched the planet's soil.

He could even make out the ramshackle encampments and shelters cobbled together in Olympus Mons's back streets. With enhanced vision, he spotted more than a few displaced mulling about. Fighting. Scavenging. Scurrying to and from the underground passages. *Doing whatever it is they do between ration drops. Another tribute to your idiocy, Taylor.*

Leaning over the railing and craning his neck, Cherny could make out the steady surge of auto-trains flowing from the Nix Olympica cliffside mines to the Propylaea space elevator. From there, Cherny knew, it would be a one-way trip to feed Earth. In the other direction, just before the boundaries of the city's radiation shielding, were the great wind farms. An army of tall, monolithic structures stood, slowly turning in their endless mission to power the city.

Taking a deep breath, Cherny looked up. The most beautiful light in the heavens this morning was the pale grey

PALE GREY DOT

dot—Earth, the biggest stage in the vast cosmic arena—alongside its lunar companion. *The aggregate of all joy and suffering,* Cherny thought as he stepped back inside, making sure to grab his glass on the way.

The Excalibur Hotel was one of the better ones in the city, though that no longer meant what it once did. Sitting on the worn couch, Cherny sorted through the alerts passing through his mind via SecLink. Since the premier revealed the news two days ago, it was like decades of pent-up aggression had finally boiled over. Cherny read reports of riots on the planets and attacks by the Syndicate in space. Olympus Mons, at least, was relatively quiet.

Cherny drained his glass and reached for the bottle. His job wasn't the containment effort. His job was to track down Sienar. *Track him down and join him.* Cherny rubbed his forehead. He could feel his eyes watering from the Martian air. *Track him down and bring him in,* Cherny decided.

An alert pinged and Cherny sat up straighter. It had all the hallmarks of a notification from ESS, but there was something about the encryption that made him wary. Cherny furrowed his brow, but a knock on his door snapped him out of his trance.

Mentally setting the file aside, Cherny strode to the door and peered through the security camera. Sighing, he opened the door. "Welcome to my humble abode, Amanda," he said, gesturing to the suite.

Amanda stepped in, sparing a second glance at the bottle on the coffee table. Like Cherny, she had dressed as the locals did. The long, brown coat from shoulder to boots kept the dust and chill away. Her hair was still tied back perfectly, without a blonde strand out of place. She gently pulled off her gloves, folded them, and placed them in her coat pocket. "I trust you're ready."

Cherny noted that she shared Her habit of asking questions that sounded an awful lot like statements. "Yeah." He led her back to the couch. He sat. She stood. "I've mapped out every potential contact for Syndicate recruitment and started making noise on MarsNet to complain about Earth. Thirsty?" He held up the bottle.

"No."

Cherny shrugged, filling his own glass. "I've been working remotely with Adrian and Esther to finalize my new past. Anyone who wants to do some digging on this potential recruit will find all the signs of a disgruntled dredge who's finally ready to take a stand after a few hundred years."

"Yes, I reviewed your mock-up. Martian expatriate who's spent the past fifty-one years on the refuelling lines in Hawaii after the insurrection." Amanda raised an eyebrow. "A bit close to home, no?"

"The best lies, Amanda, are close to the truth." It'd be an easy part to play. "But forget about me. How are you holding up?"

Amanda frowned. "Pardon?"

Careful, Cherny warned himself. "We're at a twenty-four-minute round-trip delay from Her." He feigned hesitation. "I'm sorry, it's just I know how disconcerting that

PALE GREY DOT

can be when you're used to being able to reach out to Her whenever you need to."

Amanda stared. Apparently detecting no malicious intent, she shook her head. "You do not need to concern yourself. I am fine." Then, after a moment's thought, she added, "Thank you, though." The words sounded foreign coming from her lips.

"Operatives look out for one another," Cherny reassured her, draining the contents of his glass. There was no point in letting it go to waste, he reasoned. He stood up. "Well, wish me luck. Time I met some of my new friends face to face."

At ground level, Olympus Mons reminded Cherny of old-fashioned towns he'd seen in period pieces. The buildings, ranging from shops to housing units, topped out at five storeys. Every few minutes, an auto-taxi rumbled down the pockmarked streets. Deep cracks ran through the sidewalks, reminding him of abstract jigsaw puzzles.

"Gimme a dollar."

Cherny barely turned his head. The man had his hand out. His fingers were smudged with brown dirt, and he had scrapes running up his arm. He wore no breather—instead, the skin around his throat was missing, revealing cloudy tubes and small pistons that contracted whenever he moved his head. From the wheezing sound they emitted with each breath, Cherny didn't think the cybernetics were enough to handle the atmosphere. "I said gimme a dollar," the man repeated in a louder voice when Cherny failed to immediately respond.

147

Don Miasek

"Sorry man, I don't have anything," Cherny muttered without slowing. Fake Cherny had no patience for the displaced.

"Hey, screw you! I was in the mines before they replaced me with a goddamn machine!" the man shouted. From the lack of audible footsteps, Cherny could tell he wasn't following him. "All I need is a dollar, man! You think my payment transfer isn't secure? The transfer's secure! It's j—" His voice broke as the pistons in his throat jammed. The man coughed and shook his head. With a stutter, the pistons began moving again. "—ust a dollar!"

Cherny kept moving, leaving the man behind. To his right were the inhabited alleys. To his left were the streets. The sun crested over the edge of the horizon, bathing the city and the volcano that dwarfed it in light. Taxis were now on the roads, passing him by.

Turning a corner, Cherny spotted his destination. There was no physical sign, only a virtual one visible to those with cybernetically augmented eyes and a connection to MarsNet. Those without such enhancements weren't likely to patronize this place. *The Virtual Retreat,* the sign read. Convincing the Syndicate he was simply another dredge meant living the life, just in case he was being watched.

These places are disgusting, Cherny thought as he pushed the door open. His systems automatically connected to the shop's network as it transmitted a soft ping to announce his arrival. In reality, the single room was as dark as it was quiet, but the network fed him all the light and sound he

PALE GREY DOT

needed. Three rows, alcoves on both sides, ran from the front to the back of the store. In each alcove was a series of network access ports. Thick cords, designed for maximum data transfer, ran from the ports into the mechanical flesh of each alcove's inhabitant. A virtual icon showed that two out of thirty-six VR alcoves were free.

As Cherny slowly walked down the central row, he watched the individuals plugged into their ports. Though there were seats, some had just curled up against the wall, hands wrapped around their legs and chins resting on their knees. None of them moved—they could have passed for dead.

Back in Hawaii, there were three VR shops within walking distance of his old apartment, each much larger than this. Plenty of his coworkers spent their lives there. Work. VR. Work. VR. Cherny had been perturbed to learn how many had arisen in Olympus Mons in the past few decades. As he passed each inhabitant, Cherny wondered what they were experiencing. Was that woman a famous musician? Was that man an action hero? How did they design their better lives?

At the back of the store, a ragged woman behind a counter unplugged herself from her network with an unsteady hand. Her grey hair was long and stringy. Her skin was pale, and her T-shirt was ripped in several places. Even with Martian gravity, she needed to use her hands to push herself to her feet. She was skin, bones, and metal. *Much like how Jenna had looked.* "Hey," she said as Cherny approached. "Ten dollars

149

Don Miasek

an hour. One-twenty for fifteen." Her voice was barely over a whisper. "We got an EZ Dispensary in the backroom. No food in the main room unless it's intravenously."

"I, uh, don't actually have a job yet," Cherny said. He kept his voice low. His cover identity wasn't proud of being here.

The woman's eyes didn't quite focus on Cherny. "We also have variable rates. You know, if your eventual job schedule is erratic."

"How much for something long-term?"

"Months?" she asked. "Years?"

Cherny remembered having conversations like this back on Earth. It was only a desperate hope that his exile from ESS would come to an end that kept him from signing up. "Five years, probably," he mumbled. It was far too easy to slip back into the mindset of a pathetic shell of a man.

"'Kay," the woman replied. She glanced back at her station behind the counter longingly. "Well, the rates get more complex the longer you go, and whether you're okay with wireless when all the alcoves are full."

"No, no. I … Definitely wired," Cherny let a hint of pleading into his voice.

She shrugged. "All right, but priority access is way more expensive."

"I'll pay for it," Cherny insisted.

"Oh," the woman said, looking back at Cherny. "Sweet rig you got there. They don't make them like that anymore." She pointed at Cherny's metal left arm. "Earthen?" From the way

PALE GREY DOT

her eyes didn't follow her bony finger, Cherny suspected she was looking up his specs through the network connection.

Cherny held his arm out and flexed his hand. "Yeah, got them a long time ago. Been in Hawaii for the past fifty years. Born here, though," he hastily added.

"Huh." Even a VR addict shared the same dislike of Earth as the normal Martian residents. Apparently, his answer piqued her interest enough to continue a real conversation. "How're you adapting to home?" Though her eyes remained unfocused, Cherny knew she'd be looking him up on MarsNet.

Without missing a beat, Cherny mentally pulled up the file on the woman and reviewed it. Zhou Lawson. Fifty years ago, she was a different woman. Back then, she had all the telltale indicators of a true Martian loyalist. She'd been here during the stand against Earth and the bloodbath of the insurrection. No criminal record, though, even through the worst of the riots. Soon after, she was hired at The Virtual Retreat, and that was all there was. Forty-nine years of nothing followed. Her dossier showed her portrait over the decades, degrading from a vibrant, smiling woman into a thin wretch with no expression at all.

Cherny wondered if the heart of a revolutionist still beat beneath her machinery. *Would she so much as glance up if Mars had another shot at autonomy?* "Honestly?" *Hah.* "The gravity is taking a bit to get used to again, but I can't tell you how great it is to be home. You can't breathe on Earth, you know?"

The corners of Zhou's mouth twitched upwards a tick.

Don Miasek

"Yeah." Now her eyes were on him. "Following the news? In the real world, I mean? Bad, huh?"

Cherny studied her face, but VR addicts were always so unreadable. "Personally, I think those poor bastards on Jupiter Station paid for Earth's sins. This is just the first sign that their precious control is starting to slip away from them."

"Yes. Should be Earth facing the fire. Not people past the asteroid belt."

"It's what always happens," Cherny said grimly. "They tighten their grip, we resist, and we're the ones who suffer."

Zhou went silent for several long, awkward seconds, until she finally spoke. "If you want a long-term VR pack, you can negotiate the price online."

"Right, thanks. I've got jobs lining up, so I'll be back," Cherny said with a sigh. "So, uh, thanks for helping me."

"Welcome home," Zhou said. The woman dragged herself back around the counter, sagging into her seat. She reconnected the cables to her arm with practised ease.

Cherny tightened his jacket straps as he walked back through the rows of the almost dead and out into the sunlight. His internal cybernetics whirled as he breathed in. Hell, maybe the air really was better here than on Earth.

Opening a line to SecLink, Cherny began composing a brief report. On Mars, the link felt different. The twelve-and-a-half-minute delay between here and the homeworld meant he was always trying to play catch-up with information. //Amanda,// he wrote, //I'm heading to meet my contacts

PALE GREY DOT

now. Expecting a mute field shortly, so may be on radio silence. Let Her know.//

The centre of Martian high class and culture had been reduced to a slum over the past half-century. The once vibrant and clean streets were now cluttered with trash and debris. A displaced, leaning against the side of a building, stuck out her hand as Cherny passed by. Her long, tangled hair, ragged coat, and dark, bloodshot eyes cut a sorry figure. Cherny didn't slow down.

Up ahead, in the shadow of one of the huge tubes that contained an auto-train line, stood a man and woman.

The man was short and squat, and either his coat was padded, or he was. His boots were stained with Martian dirt. His large chin and puffy cheeks made him look out of shape, and he moved awkwardly when he stepped over to speak to passing pedestrians.

"We're here to mark the fifty-first anniversary of the Martian Insurrection! The grand unification of the city states! You, sir, take a pamphlet. Virtual or physical. No? Ma'am, are you interested in a pamphlet that will tell you of a political freedom that we co—okay, ma'am, thank you anyway. Sir, learn about the amazing history of the Martian gov—yeah, all right, sir. Ma'am, are you—Christ, easy on the swearing, lady. We're all on the same side here."

The woman beside him sat on an old plastic crate, legs dangling as she watched her partner fail to hand out pamphlets for download. Her head and features were hidden

153

behind a cap and goggles, but her thin chin and tight suit suggested she was a looker.

This would be the first time he'd meet his contacts face to face. He stopped in front of them, and the man instantly approached. "You, sir. Care for a pamphlet? It's a small download that will change your life. It was on this very spot that Governor Griffenham stunned the solar system and gave his 'Stand Up and Say No' speech. He and so many others gave their lives for that all important 'no.'"

Cherny smiled confidently. "I know all about the insurrection already."

The man nodded his understanding. "Everyone who lived in Olympus Mons during those trying times will understand the struggle better than anyone else in the solar system."

"Hey," the woman broke in. Her voice was heavily modulated, and Cherny could pick up the energy signatures of heavy-duty cybernetics within her. "You looking for a good time?" She flicked her hand outwards, and holographic images of her product shone brightly in front of Cherny, clad only in their imaginations. "Women? Men? Both?"

Cherny gave it a quick glance. They came in all shapes and sizes, from tall and thin to thick and curved. "I appreciate the thought, Lori, but no thanks."

Both immediately went quiet. The woman's eyes narrowed behind her goggles, but before she could reply, the man stepped in between them. "You have us at a disadvantage, sir."

"Name's Cherny. Pleasure to meet you finally, Ben." Cherny extended his hand.

PALE GREY DOT

Obvious relief washed over the man's face as he clasped the hand with both of his. "Christ, Cherny! You had me scared for a moment. Damn, it's fantastic to meet you face to face. The Net forums are way too impersonal."

Lori eyed Cherny for another second before flicking her wrist, shutting off the projector. To anyone else, it would be imperceptible, but Cherny felt the mute field activate, severing any wireless communication.

Grinning, Cherny joined Ben in leaning against the train tube, looking out at the passing crowds. "You having any luck with them?"

Ben scoffed and shook his head. "The fire is there. You know, in their hearts. But there isn't the impetus to risk another bloodbath. Can't say I blame anyone."

Cherny nodded and gestured with his hand. "You know, you weren't wrong about the Griffenham speech. I was here when he gave it. See there? The barricades had been set up at the corners, blocking off the Altis Legislature. Griffenham was up there, on the stage, flanked by militia."

Ben's gaze followed Cherny. "We all thought they were invincible. That even Earth would think twice about challenging us. Never thought Earth's response would be so brutal. I actually believed Fairchild when she said they were open to talking." He closed his eyes as if imagining that fateful day.

"Remember the crowds?" Cherny asked. "From here all the way to the Echo Stoa."

Ben looked away, shaking his head. "Yeah," he replied. His voice cracked.

Don Miasek

"I thought you worked in Ascraeus Mons back then, Cherny," Lori said.

Cherny wondered if she was challenging his backstory. "I did, but I knew the real action was in Olympus Mons. Wanted to be here when history was made."

"Not the history you expected, huh?" She idly kicked the blue plastic crate she sat on with the backs of her heels.

"'Fraid not." Cherny let his smile fade. The best lie was close to the truth.

"Let's, uh, let's get out of the open, eh?" Ben suggested. Lori hopped off her crate.

Cherny pretended to look around, just in case someone was watching them. He knew it wouldn't matter, though. ESS's reach, even on Mars, was considerable. Though SecLink had marked every hidden camera, compromised network, and human asset in the region, he'd have to go without updates while the mute field was active.

Ben spoke in a hushed tone as he led them through the streets. He talked about the supposed surge in support since the Jupiter Station attack. Nobody really wanted to see those past the belt suffer, Ben insisted, but to them, this felt like the first domino that could bring Earth to its knees. There was excitement in his voice that he tried to suppress.

Cherny nodded, chuckled, and agreed at all the right times as he followed the pair. He silently reviewed what he knew about his contacts. Ben was born a Nix Olympus miner and would probably die a Nix Olympus miner. He was one of the lucky ones, skilled enough to manage the

PALE GREY DOT

drones that now ran the mines, and yet he still fought for further Martian employment. ESS confirmed he fled to the Tharsis province shortly after the riots began.

Lori, on the other hand, was hardcore Syndicate through and through. ESS had her marked as a Suspicious Person for the past six decades, but the decision was made to track rather than eliminate. Following a known Syndicate member to monitor the group's progress had proven a hundred times more valuable than simply removing someone who could easily be replaced. It was Lori, Cherny knew, that he'd have to impress.

"You remember what Hippodrome Plaza was like?" Ben was asking.

"Sure do," Cherny replied. The trio turned onto the street that housed the great stadium. "Mars has always had the best sports in the solar system. Weak enough gravity for stunts without any of that floaty Luna crap."

"This was the height of Martian culture," Ben said. "The shops, the bars, the nightclubs, the museums. The bright and cheerful alternative to the homeworld."

"And then the detonations began," Cherny said. "The number of people ..." He didn't have to act to make his voice quiver.

Looking up, the great Martian Hippodrome stadium loomed before them. An eighty-thousand-seat structure modelled after the old Roman Colosseum, its windows with rounded tops fit in well with the rest of Mars's architecture. It'd been a long time since it drew that many people, though. Cherny took several steps to the side, nearly onto the roadway. Taxicabs slowed down as a precaution. "I was right here," he recalled. "I didn't see the first explosion, but I felt it. The ground shook, we fell, and I ..." Cherny shook his head.

"Easy," Ben said as he reached over and put his arm around Cherny's shoulders.

Even Lori's eyes softened. "If you two are done crying about the past, let's meet the others."

They led Cherny into one of the few taverns not boarded up, though the inside was no livelier than the outside. The sign—both physical and virtual—marked it as Dionysus's Lament. Only a few patrons had turned out. Not a lot of demand for pub food this early, Cherny supposed.

A tired bartender gave the three a knowing nod, studying Cherny just a little longer than the others. Cherny followed the pair to the backroom, where two women and a man played a game of Scraps. He mused that the weak gravity must make it harder.

Cherny soon found that the gathering was more of a support group than any sort of organized resistance. After warmly greeting Cherny, they reminisced about the Mars of old and whispered in excited tones about winds of change now that the Syndicate had dealt a crippling blow to the United Fleet.

Ben and Lori's friends asked Cherny how life was Earth-side, and he found the words describing the dull, unending misery tumbling from his mouth. Mars was becoming the new Earth, they felt, with its job scarcity, roving bands of displaced, and slum sectors of entire cities.

They blamed it on Fairchild's automation laws. Mars had

PALE GREY DOT

prospered up until she decided to relax the regulations on drone-to-cyborg ratios and allow advanced robotics into the mines. Millions would be out of work, they had argued. Then the Martian Insurrection turned into a massacre, and Fairchild got her way after all.

Cherny knew the root cause wasn't that simple, though—Earth desperately needed Mars's resources to function. Millions out of work, or billions starving. But he nodded anyway when they said that the premier cared only for her precious homeworld.

"We may not be Earth," Ben muttered, "but thanks to them, we're on the same path, heading the same direction."

The group, Cherny had long ago decided, was mostly harmless. If he were on any other assignment, he'd have marked them for ESS to monitor but not take further action against.

Here, though, he kept his eye on Lori. She was the link from innocent venting to action. When Cherny described his old job fuelling spaceships at the Tsiolkovsky Spaceport, her eyes darted his way. When he mentioned that he knew the man in charge of outgoing customs inspections, she nodded. As he expressed his sympathy for Alexander Reuben, the disfigured leader of the Syndicate, he saw the cracks of a smile. He hit all the right notes of a potential recruit—competence, pent-up frustration, and the impotent urge to take action.

Before long, Cherny realized four hours of swapping stories had passed. Ben ended the meeting with a toast: "To the memory of Governor Griffenham, and to the prosperity of Mars."

Cherny left the bar feeling good. The bait had been left

Don Miasek

dangling in front of the recruiter, and he knew all he had to do now was wait. If she pulled him in, then surely Sienar would find out about it. The streets of Olympus Mons were brighter now that the sun was shining overhead. Those with jobs were going about their daily lives. The auto-train tunnels hummed, bringing workers to the mines, and hauling ores from them. *There's a light at the end of the tunnel,* Cherny told himself.

As he walked back towards the hotel, he reconnected to SecLink. The day's standard dossiers and updates filled his cybernetics. A report from Operative Brylan Ncube revealed that Ezza still hadn't reconnected. Her ship, *Starknight,* remained parked at Jupiter Station, assisting with the relief effort. Brylan was requesting additional assets to help.

What are you doing, Ezza? Cherny thought. She must have a good reason, though he couldn't imagine what it could be. Nevertheless, resisting the Pull for much longer should be impossible.

Threading his way through the lunchtime crowds, Cherny brought the mystery file from this morning to the forefront of his mind. Its encryption methods were old but familiar. With a thought, the file unravelled into coherence.

Cherny stumbled, nearly colliding with a man in a grey coat and breather.

"Watch it, dickhead," the man muttered, backing away.

Cherny pushed himself up against the side of a building. The bricks were cold to the touch. Text scrolled past his vision. "No …" he whispered. "No, Jenna." His breathing turned ragged.

PALE GREY DOT

*** Cherny. Sienar has gone AWOL from ESS. Heard you might be getting back in with ESS. Clever idea, to infiltrate. I've got a ship called *Étoile* and am heading to Ganymede to find him. Ezza is already there. Can't miss this chance to hurt Her. ***

*** Stay with ESS. Keep spying on them. Say all the right things that made Her proud of us. Don't let Her find out. ***

*** I miss you all. We're going to be a family again. ***

"You stupid ... stupid!" Cherny hissed. People were now avoiding walking past him. "Idiot! Why the hell did you think you could trust me?" *More time. I thought I'd have more time!* There was no avoiding it now. Cherny tried to think of a reason that She would want him to keep Jenna's message a secret. *Maybe Amanda can't be trusted. Maybe Jenna would catch wind of his betrayal if he reported in. Maybe ...* Cherny rubbed the tears from his eyes, knowing it was in vain. The Pull was already turning into agonizing pain the longer he delayed.

Sienar's words echoed in his mind. *"You can try to convince yourself that what you want to do is best for ESS. Maybe you'll succeed, and maybe you won't. But you can't cheat, can you?"*

As he opened a line in SecLink, the pain began to subside. //Amanda,// he transmitted. //I know where Jenna is.//

Cherny looked up at the sky as he leaned against the brick wall. He could breathe again. *I'm sorry, Jenna.*

"You have been very busy, mademoiselle."

Ezza stopped. Brylan blocked her way. *Starknight*'s corridor was not quite wide enough for two people to pass without somebody pressing themselves against the bulkhead, and neither she nor Brylan was interested in backing down. She'd managed to avoid this confrontation for the past week by concentrating on the relief effort but had known her luck wouldn't last forever.

The man had ditched his Jupiter blues in favour of beige off-duty wear, presumably borrowed from one of the crew. He was smiling, but Ezza could guess what he wanted.

"Brylan," Ezza replied. Ten minutes ago, her insides had felt like they were crawling. Another Cerebrol put an end to that. *Remember the mask.* "I haven't seen you in the primary hull since we boarded. Carmen tells me you've been spending most of your time in the transmitter room."

PALE GREY DOT

"Yes, I have been coordinating with my colleagues. Speaking of which ..." Brylan trailed off, as if to prompt a reply from Ezza.

"Yes?" Ezza feigned confusion.

Brylan hesitated, if only slightly. "I think you'll agree that ESS and the United Fleet are in this together ... no?"

You poor, dumb bastard, Ezza thought with satisfaction. *You want to ask me why I haven't reconnected to SecLink. It must be driving you crazy. Hell, it must be driving Her crazy.*

"Of course, Brylan. Is that all you came to ask me?"

Brylan stared at her, and for a moment, Ezza thought she saw a hint of recognition pass across his face. Brylan opened his mouth to speak, but Ezza cut him off.

"Speaking of which, Admiral Cheng-Visitor's battlecruiser has begun deceleration operations. I've spoken with her, and she's agreed to take you on board."

Brylan slowly closed his mouth. Any pretence of civility vanished. "Let's talk in private."

"Of course, Brylan." Ezza was grateful he suggested it. With four dozen crew members crammed into *Starknight's* twin hulls, it was only a matter of time before the pissing contest became public. Admiral Tolj once told her that nothing flies faster than a rumour through a ship.

Ezza transmitted her credentials to a nearby door. The sound of moving metal echoed through the hull as the hatch unlocked.

The pair stepped into *Starknight's* vacant medical station. The bay was centred around four metal beds with plastic padding, with a hatch leading to the surgical room. Rows of white, plastic supply cabinets lined the walls, each meticulously labelled both physically and virtually for cybernetically enhanced eyes. Ezza knew exactly where the remaining bottles of Cerebrol were stored.

Brylan closed the door. "I think it would be better if I stay with *Starknight* for the time being."

"Why? Any coordination work you're doing would be better served on Admiral Cheng-Visitor's flagship."

"I think staying here is what She would want." Brylan paused long enough to gauge Ezza's reaction.

Ezza knew the words all too well. *He's been briefed on the Athena Protocols,* she realized. *Remember the mask.* "If She wishes you reassigned, then She can petition the Ministry of Defence and let the Admiralty decide."

Brylan continued to stare at her.

There's no way he doesn't know. He can probably read it on my face.

"If we must go through the formal process, then of course we will, mademoiselle, but I would have thought that a special request from Her would be sufficient. Given your shared past, that is." The man's face was stone. Any hint of the charm he displayed when he first came on board *Starknight* was gone.

"When I left the service"—*when I was fired*—"She and I agreed that it would be permanent. There would be no further obligation to ESS. Are you calling Her a liar?" Ezza kept her voice even.

PALE GREY DOT

Brylan's mouth twitched. "Of course not."

Aha, Ezza thought. *So the newer operatives are just as terrified of Her as we were.* "My association with ESS ended half a century ago, Brylan. It's over."

"Your overwatch seems to have a different opinion," Brylan replied.

Now you're getting desperate. Ezza could feel the tide turning her way, cutting through the fog in her mind. "Commander Rachelle Eday is not an overwatch."

"I'm sorry?"

"She's the executive officer on this ship."

"She's a full-convert cyborg. There's not much of a difference."

"Warmth, human compassion, and the social skills to deal with others," Ezza replied. "Those would be the main differences."

Brylan shook his head. "Well, whatever you call her, your executive officer sees the logic behind ESS and United Fleet cooperation. The more data we share, the smarter we both become. To be honest, I do not understand why you're unwilling to work with us."

"There's simply a process to follow. Contact the Admiralty and have them approve it."

"Do you know what I think?" Brylan took a step towards her, lowering his voice to just above a whisper. "I think you're simply bitter. You and your Athena compatriots were raised to be Her favourites. The shining example of everything an operative could be: smart, capable, and above all, loyal. She

165

loved you. You fought for Her, risked your life for Her, and agreed to have your brain tinkered with for Her. But then your crew screwed up, and so She tossed you aside and replaced you in an instant. You haven't gotten past that."

Replaced us? Ezza had to force a smile through that thought. "I've warned you about character profiling before."

Brylan tsked. "Tell you what. Since trust requires one of us to make the first move, I will volunteer. ESS has reason to believe that the perpetrators of the attack against Jupiter Station can be found on Ganymede."

"Why?" Ezza asked a little too quickly.

Brylan smiled at her eagerness. "Ah, so now you're interested in what ESS can do for you. Let me stay on board. Prep the ship for the journey to Ganymede and we can pool our resources."

Ezza was silent for a few moments. The idea that Brylan would want to go to Ganymede stunned her. There was no doubt in her mind that he knew more than she did. Finally, Ezza spoke in a low, even tone. "Six hours before Cheng-Visitor arrives. Then you're off this ship."

•

Ezza stumbled and leaned against the lavatory cubicle's sink, wheezing as she desperately tried to suck in air. With fumbling hands, she reached into her uniform pocket and drew out the small orange bottle. *Two ought to do it*, she decided.

PALE GREY DOT

Ezza popped the pills into her mouth and swallowed with a handful of water.

She slid the door open, already feeling better, and dabbed the sweat from her forehead with the sleeve of her uniform. At the sound of footsteps, she straightened up and palmed the bottle. Lieutenant Lassiter, Adams's second, passed her on the way to the officers' quarters, saluting as he went. Ezza could only hope that her mask was effective.

She started towards the primary hull's command centre. The exchange with Brylan had left her feeling dirty, and her uniform clung to her flesh. He said he wanted them to go to Ganymede. *Jenna thought Sienar was there. Brylan might think the same.* A nervous thought crossed her mind—either Brylan intercepted Jenna's message or ESS had independently concluded that Jupiter's largest moon held Sienar's hideout. Jenna had said their old leader had gone AWOL and killed members of the service, but she had been awfully light on details.

She and Jenna had fought more times than Ezza remembered, but they were basically sisters. *Sisters fight. It's normal.* Ezza never found out what happened to her after the surviving members of the Athena Six returned to Earth. Jenna had slipped out of the Tower and vanished. Somehow, though, she had resisted the Pull. *Did she go the drug route?* Ezza wondered. Without the Cerebrol, she knew defying it would have been impossible. Even with them, surviving for decades didn't seem likely. It was Jenna's technical brilliance that generated the loyalty programming to begin with, and Ezza knew better than to underestimate her.

167

Navigating *Starknight*'s tight corridors as though she was sleepwalking, Ezza thought of the other two survivors. She hadn't heard from either of them since the fallout. *Did they reactivate Cherny?* As for Sienar, if Jenna's message was anything to go by, he had stayed with ESS until recently.

Pausing long enough to steel herself, Ezza unlocked the command centre hatch and pushed it open. Rachelle and Adams were at their posts. Rachelle's eyes were glazed over as she sent data through the dozens of wires connecting her to *Starknight*.

Adams looked over from his console with weary eyes.

"Lieutenant," Ezza began, "welcome back. Jupiter Station Security wanted me to pass along their appreciation for your work with the search teams."

Adams nodded. "Thank you."

Ezza stepped into the command station, leaning over towards him. "How was it?" she asked, dropping the formal tone.

Adams shook his head. "It's really bad. Most of the rings are filled with debris. They've set up safety shelters throughout the station, but they're temporary at best. A lot of people lost their homes and families."

Ezza had seen the shelters, teeming with survivors, on the internal United Fleet feeds. She knew what conditions the man had been working in. "And the Prime Hub?" she asked.

"We had to use drones just to get through the wreckage, but then ..." Adams took a deep breath. "I know the official report hasn't come out yet, but I can't imagine how anyone

PALE GREY DOT

could have survived. No movement, no cybernetic transmissions, no heat signatures … There's nobody left."

Poor Tolj. She'd known his chances of surviving were slim to nil, but hearing Adams's assessment gave her a feeling of finality. She reached out and put her hand on his shoulder. "You did a good job over there. A lot of people are still breathing thanks to you and the search teams. From here on out, it's all about moving forward to prevent this from happening again."

"Yeah," Adams said after a moment's thought. "Thanks."

Ezza nodded. She wondered who she was channelling there—Sienar or Admiral Tolj. Ezza hoped she projected even a fraction of the warmth and leadership that they had. Then she remembered what Jenna had said. That Sienar had gone AWOL and killed a lot of Earth Security Service people. The thought made her shudder.

"After all that death and destruction on Jupiter Station, I'm starting to see why people put up with ESS," Adams muttered. "Doesn't make them right, but I'm starting to understand it."

Though Ezza didn't take her gaze off him, she heard the rattling of cables as Rachelle shifted at her station, listening in. Ezza recalled her recommendation to bring Brylan into the fold. She briefly wondered if he could be getting his intel from her, but immediately dismissed the idea. "No, it definitely doesn't," Ezza agreed.

With a gloved hand, Ezza pressed her finger against the console, connecting to the ship's intercom. "This is the

Don Miasek

captain to all hands. With the Jupiter Station disaster under control, we'll be preparing to depart local space for a short-range trip. Acceleration protocols will be going into effect thirty hours from now. We'll be 0.3g for four hours and fifty-six minutes, after which we'll begin our deceleration. No rotational manoeuvres throughout. Our destination is Ganymede Orbital Station over the Nexus. Captain Jayens, out."

Ezza mentally let go of the connection. "Rachelle, I want you to get a team together and sweep the ship for bugs. I'll send the details of what to look for. Operative Ncube will be leaving once Cheng-Visitor arrives."

Rachelle nodded, swaying at her station. "Yes, ma'am." When Ezza had told her and Carmen about her work with the Earth Security Service and the Athena Program, the cyborg had merely listened quietly, staring straight ahead while the chief engineer peppered the captain with questions.

Ezza had been selective about what she revealed. An ex-operative is one thing, but involvement in the disastrous Martian Insurrection was something else entirely. Carmen had been wary at first, but Ezza was confident that her engineer still trusted her. Rachelle was much harder to read.

Revealing secrets and going against the Pull in such a fundamental way made it hard to concentrate. *Do what She would want you to do.* This was definitely not it.

"What about the reporter?" Rachelle asked.

"I've made my decision on Ms. Kashem. Have her meet me in my office."

PALE GREY DOT

As she made her way through the cold metal halls of *Starknight*, Ezza reviewed Nirali's dossier again. The woman was born on Jupiter Station and never strayed past its moons in any of her thirty-seven years. After skimming a few of Nirali's articles, Ezza had decided she was a standard Net hack—long on preaching the gospel, short on action. For someone who never actually visited Earth to see it in person, she had an awful lot to say about its conditions. That ESS had never moved against her or IDEA was proof enough of their ineffectiveness. There was value in permitting small pockets of dissent to show your tolerance—but only so long as it was impotent.

Ezza had just gotten settled behind her desk when the door to her office folded open, revealing a nervous Nirali. The shorter woman stepped through the threshold into the room. She had managed to scrounge up a set of civvies that more or less fit.

"You kept it?" Nirali asked with wide eyes.

Ezza followed her gaze to the cramped office wall and the breather mask of the Jupiter Station guard. A strip of vel-tack affixed the mask's straps to the wall. Its empty eye sockets and blunt breather apparatus stared back at Ezza. *It is,* Ezza realized, *my first personal keepsake.* "Ah, yes," she said slowly. "I've found it useful."

Nirali gingerly reached over and lowered the fold-out visitor's chair from the wall before taking a seat. "I heard your announcement," Nirali ventured. "Why Ganymede, of all places?"

171

Don Miasek

"Nirali," Ezza began slowly, not answering the question just yet. She leaned forward, resting her elbows on the fold-out desk. "I want you to stay on *Starknight*. At least for the time being."

The reporter blinked in obvious surprise. "Why?"

Ezza glanced at the breather mask. "You remind me of what's important. What do you say? Come with us to Ganymede. You'll get to see us in action as we find out who's responsible for the attack on Jupiter Station."

Nirali hesitated, so Ezza offered, "Yes, ESS. It seems possible to me as well." The throbbing in her head had returned. *Wham, wham, wham.* Ezza wished she had paced her pills better before having this meeting.

Nirali peered at her, as if to gauge her reaction to her next words. "You were an operative, weren't you?" she asked. To Ezza's surprise, her tone was sympathetic rather than accusatory.

"That's right," Ezza replied. "It was a long time ago, but it didn't work out. The United Fleet has been a much better fit." *Don't push me on this, Nirali.*

The reporter took the hint and nodded. "But again, why Ganymede? The place isn't exactly easy to get around."

"You remember Uruk Sulcus-132?"

"Yeah," Nirali nodded. "I know IDEA wanted to run a piece on it, but our team couldn't even get close."

"Yes, I'm sure the investigation was marked as classified."

"No," Nirali replied, placing her hands on the metal desk. "When I say we couldn't get close, I don't just mean we

PALE GREY DOT

weren't allowed. Literally, we couldn't get close. Ganymede is a hellhole—nothing but cracked ice, subhundred-degree temperatures, and impact craters. Taking the space elevator to the Ganymede Nexus is one thing, but getting out to the base? The trains will get you part way, but the tunnels were nothing but wreckage over fifty kilometres out. The team had to turn back."

Ezza couldn't help but be amused by the thought of a bunch of witless IDEA members trying to dig into the destruction of Uruk Sulcus-132. ESS would have been tracking their every movement. Ezza wondered what She would have done had IDEA's reporters gotten close. "Well, an old colleague of mine has suggested we pay it a visit."

"An old colleague," Nirali repeated. "So an operative."

Ezza was silent for a moment as she considered how much she should reveal. Telling an outsider anything felt like anathema to her old training. "Ex-operative, like me. Jenna and I ..." *How to describe it?* "We didn't see eye to eye on everything, but I do trust her. She's the last person in the system who would ever be loyal to ESS." *Assuming she didn't finally succumb to the Pull.* "If she says we need to go to Uruk Sulcus-132, then that's where we're going."

Nirali looked doubtful. "If we can make it."

"Well, we aim to make it the full distance, and I'd like you to come with us."

Nirali looked at her with obvious disbelief. "I ... Sure, but I can't help but ask again—*why?*"

173

Don Miasek

Because you help me remember the mask. "I like your outsider's perspective."

Ezza didn't know if Nirali believed her, but the journalist smiled nonetheless. "Yeah. Okay, I'll go with you."

"Thank you, Nirali," Ezza said. Her voice was just above a whisper. Ezza held out her hand.

Nirali took it. "Well heck, thank you for saving my life back on the station."

Don't thank me yet, Ezza thought as she shook Nirali's hand. *If there's any hint of what truly happened on Ganymede remaining at Uruk Sulcus-132, then there's no way She would have left it unprotected.*

●

And so, Cherny told her.

Sitting on the run-down couch in his Excalibur Hotel suite, he told Amanda about the message Jenna sent him. Ganymede. She thought Sienar was there. She was in contact with Ezza. As the words poured out, his head cleared, his muscles relaxed, his cybernetics purred, and his nerves settled. The refilled glass of wine in his hand didn't hurt either.

Amanda sat on the couch's matching footrest, though the upholstery had been patched with pieces from some other fabric. She stared straight at him throughout the explanation, registering no emotion. Her hands were clasped together as she rested her elbows on her knees.

PALE GREY DOT

The edges of the woman's longcoat were covered in Martian dust. Cherny knew she would not have been idle while he was working.

When he finished, Amanda finally unclasped her hands and shifted in her seat. "Jenna trusts you despite knowing you're working with us. Remarkable." She sounded surprised at the notion.

Cherny scowled, knowing there was an accusation in her words. "Misplaced trust," he muttered, fighting to keep the shame off his face. *You've failed Jenna like you failed Sal.*

"Mmm," Amanda replied in a noncommittal tone. Standing up, Cherny felt her connect to SecLink and send a transmission. //Priority 1. Suspicious Person: ex-operative Jenna Doe. Spaceship: *Étoile*. Aquarius-class liner. Make: Langston. Model: 2458.//

Cherny glanced at the ship's preliminary history. SecLink would need over twenty minutes for the full report to arrive from Earth, but *Étoile* looked like any other moderately expensive cruise liner. Cherny had to fight the instinct to shake his head as he saw the ship's latest flight plan, inventory, crew and passenger rosters, and cargo manifest. It was everything they'd need for an easy takedown.

I have to warn her. As soon as he thought it, Cherny regretted it. He grunted and leaned forward, raising his hand to his head as the Pull racked his mind.

Amanda eyed him with a cold, suspicious look.

"This Martian air is headache-inducing," Cherny explained. It wasn't really a lie.

Amanda closed her connection to SecLink. "You've done well, Cherny."

"And here I thought I was being so clever, setting myself up as bait for Sienar—turns out I'm bait for Jenna as well."

"We all do what we must for the safety and security of the solar system. It is not always glamorous work, hmm?"

Cherny looked around the hotel room. Sure, the drapes were faded, and the couch was patchwork, but compared to the stench of failure that permeated his old closet apartment in Hawaii, this was paradise. "I'm still wondering about Ezza," he said, sidestepping the question. "Jenna seems to think she'd be on her side, but then ... she thought the same of me."

"An interesting question for Brylan Ncube to deal with," Amanda replied.

"Yeah, I did a background check on Ncube and, frankly, I wasn't impressed," Cherny said. "You really think he's up to the task of helping Ezza?" *Helping.* Even as he said it, the word didn't feel right.

"I've already discussed these concerns with Her, and we are activating Bev Stroud to assist," Amanda said. "In the meantime, we have our own mission. How did your meet go?"

Cherny was grateful for the change in subject. *Keep talking about Ezza and you're liable to betray her next*, he thought. The Pull's reward couldn't fill the pit he felt in his stomach. Cherny resealed the bottle of wine. Suddenly, he didn't feel like drinking anymore. "Went well. Lori's definitely interested. Give it half a week for them to run a background

PALE GREY DOT

check and I'll be in." *If Sienar is paying attention, he'll know I'm on Mars.*

"What's the status of this cell?"

"Oh, it's way too pitiful to call it that. It's just a bunch of old protesters remembering the glory days. Lori's the only one who's actually with the Syndicate." Cherny remembered reading a report released by the Ministry of Public Safety that showcased what a tiny, insignificant fraction of the population actually had ties with the Syndicate. Near as Cherny could tell, the figures had been truthful. The ministry never released any figures on the poor dredges like Ben and Zhou who were just waiting for that spark to ignite them into action, though.

"Very well," Amanda replied. "I will recommend to Her that Ms. Lori Wallace remain free for surveillance."

"I wonder how She's handling all this," Cherny said. He tried to make it sound like idle musing.

Amanda raised an eyebrow. "What do you mean?"

"Well, She's suddenly got a solar system of chaos to deal with. The last time this sort of thing happened"—Cherny gestured around them—"was right here, in this city, fifty-one years ago."

"She is more than capable of dealing with stress," Amanda assured him.

"Oh, I know. Trust me, I know. But when a crisis happens, sweeping changes tend to follow. Martian Insurrection—throw the Athena Six members out. Ganymede Blitz—bring 'em back."

177

The edges of Amanda's mouth tugged downwards. "You don't really think She simply threw you out. Taylor's actions killed over a thousand innocent people. Of course there would be ramifications. That he was merely executed is a tribute to Her mercy." Cherny could swear her features softened, even if it was just by a micron.

"Right, but he was the only crazy one," Cherny retorted. "The rest of us—"

"Sal went with him," Amanda interrupted. "And Sienar and Ezza were in command, yet they failed to see his instability. And Jenna designed the Athena Protocols in the first place. If you are looking to place blame, look to those other than Her. She risked Fairchild's wrath by standing by you. She loves all Her operatives." Amanda mouthed the word like she didn't know what it meant.

Cherny silently fumed. He couldn't help but feel it was true—She did love them, in Her own way—though whether that was from the Pull or his own natural instincts, he couldn't tell. "I know," he said quietly. Cherny glanced up at her. *Time to take a risk,* he decided. "How long has it been since She took direct control?"

Amanda raised her chin. She hesitated—if only for a moment—before replying. "How long have you known?"

"I've suspected it since before we left the Tower. I went over your history. Your dossier showed a young, vibrant woman who was popular with her friends and colleagues. Then you changed. No offence, but 'vibrant' and 'popular' doesn't exactly describe what I've seen. I took a look at the

PALE GREY DOT

SecLink logs, and you reach out to Her a hell of a lot more than anyone else. We both know She isn't one to just give up when something goes wrong. The loyalty chips didn't work out as planned with the Athena Six, and so the next step would be to exert influence over someone with a straight connection."

"I see," Amanda replied. Her voice had softened.

"Plus, you have the classic background of Her favourites."

Amanda frowned. "What do you mean?"

"Well, I was born on a rig during the Arctic oil rush and left behind when the bust swept through. I never knew my parents, so I got sent to the state-run learning institute in Kazan. Jenna was born into the gangs of the Midwestern Wastes and arrived around the same time. Sal's parents dropped her off the first chance they got. Want me to list us all? Her favourite operatives have no family."

"She has always had an eye for talent," Amanda replied. "Monitoring the school system is only logical."

"Did you know your parents?" Cherny pressed.

"Many in this day and age don't," Amanda said.

"It could be a coincidence," he admitted. When Amanda didn't immediately reply, he leaned forward on the couch. He knew he shouldn't ask but found he couldn't resist. "What's it like?"

"It's ..." For the first time since Cherny had met her, she seemed at a loss for words. "It's wonderful. I had the procedure that linked us done three years ago, and since then, it's like being a brand new person. When I'm on Earth, our

179

thoughts are one. I've never been so in tune with another as I am now with Her." She smiled.

"But here on Mars?" Cherny prompted.

Amanda shook her head. "The time lag ruins the connection. Instead of merging our thoughts and feelings, it's more like receiving a letter with advice. It isn't the same."

Cherny nodded. A part of him couldn't help but be jealous of the bond she shared with Her. *You're looking at your replacement model,* he realized. *But a model with clear limitations.*

Amanda straightened again, regaining her composure. Cherny wondered if she regretted her comments. Her face had returned to its normal, unreadable expression. "Good luck on your assignment, Cherny. I'll be in touch." She let herself out.

Cherny leased an apartment that day. It was dirty, the landlord kept coughing while she showed him around, a girl sold Naxx in the back alley by the electrical transformer station, and at least four neighbours were obvious VR addicts. The lighting was too dim for his liking, forcing Cherny to lean on his cybernetic vision for comfort. It was the perfect residence for an old Martian national returning home to start over.

The Martian diurnal cycle was close enough to Earth's that Cherny didn't need much time to adjust, and soon he fell into a routine. Wake up. Visit The Virtual Retreat to ingratiate himself with the community. Fire off a dozen résumés looking for cybernetics work in the Nix Olympica mines. Drink with Ben, Lori, and the others at Dionysus's Lament.

PALE GREY DOT

Every night, Cherny found the pale grey dot in the sky and wondered how Jenna, Ezza, and Sienar were doing. Amanda kept him updated as best she could. Brylan had "failed to convince"—that was the phrasing he used—Ezza to reconnect, but Jenna's ship was due to arrive at Jupiter in mere days. He prayed Brylan would have better luck with her.

Then Cherny would fall asleep on a lumpy mattress, listening to the low buzzing of the electrical station next door.

Four days later, as he peeled the wrapper off a boiling cup of insta-pork, Cherny glanced at the day's incoming messages. *Ah. There you are.*

```
*** Mr. Cherny Fender ***

*** It has come to our attention that you are
interested in making our solar system a place worth
living in again. We believe you could have an
important part to play. ***

*** 36188 Caledonia at 2438 hours. It is the start of
a new solar system. ***
```

Cherny grinned at his success as he slurped a forkful of noodles. //Amanda,// he sent, //looks like they're going for the bait. We should have viable results soon.//

Well, Cherny thought as he looked over the disgusting apartment. *Four days isn't so bad. Better than the fifty years I had to endure.*

Caledonia was on the other side of the city, near the great field of wind turbines. Though largely unscathed by

181

the fallout of the Martian Insurrection, the economic reality of Olympus Mons had hit it hard. The factories and shipping warehouses that once powered Martian society were now derelict shelters for the lost, abandoned by their corporations.

As he downloaded the latest neighbourhood schematics to his cybernetics, Cherny checked the charge on his energy projector and holstered it, ensuring the weight was properly balanced to avoid visual detection. He took one last look at the apartment and headed out into the night.

The streets in Caledonia were bare. The string of overhead lights failed to illuminate the alleys, and though he could see movement with his cybernetic vision, no one stepped out to confront him.

He shivered and pulled his coat tighter as he made his way towards the meet. His cybernetics churned, slowly increasing his body temperature and regulating the impact of Mars's radiation levels. The constant hum of hundreds of wind turbines melted into background noise.

36188 Caledonia was an old distribution centre once used to store raw materials drawn from the Nix Olympica mines and sold by Geodynamic Industries. There was nothing in its history that suggested Syndicate ownership. No, this was just one of a hundred empty buildings in Olympus Mons where witnesses weren't likely.

//Amanda,// he transmitted as he rounded the corner. //I'm nearing the meet-up site. Expect a mute field shortly.//

//I am tracking you,// she replied. She and Cherny had

PALE GREY DOT

picked out a sniper position for her eight hundred metres away. Neither were thrilled by the field of view, but Caledonia didn't offer much in the way of high vantage points.

As he stepped up to the old Geodynamic Industries front doors, Cherny felt his connection to SecLink turn to static. He stared at the faded sign with faked confusion before reaching out and rapping his knuckles against the door. To his surprise, he didn't see any signs of squatters. "H … hello?" he called out. The door rattled. He craned his neck upwards, as if trying to see if there were any lights on.

Click.

Cherny didn't immediately react to the distant noise behind him. Concentrating, he heard the footsteps of four individuals, picking them out from the background hum of the power generators.

Finding the door to the warehouse locked, Cherny turned and spied the four figures across the road. His optics whirled, revealing a wealth of data. The heat signatures on all four glowed an eerie, bright red against the darkness of their surroundings.

Their presumptive leader wore a large pistol—an energy projector, from the looks of it—on his belt. The second had a long ponytail resting over her shoulder and a satchel that registered explosives warnings. The third had a snub-nosed ballistics rifle. The last, though, worried Cherny the most. A full-con cyborg, who was clearly the source of the mute field.

Outwardly, Cherny waved towards the advancing figures.

Don Miasek

"H-hi?" he called out. "Are you …?" he trailed off. A potential recruit shouldn't be too confident.

Inwardly, Cherny focused on the full-convert. Military-grade armouring, sensors, and hidden weaponry. Though she wore a coat similar to those of her comrades, the bulges and creases told of the metal limbs and chest within. Silver optics peered out from behind a metal mask that looked like it was bolted on. Some full-cons were built to serve as a computer interface. Some to recover from debilitating injuries. Not this one, though—Silver Eyes was built to fight.

This is a remarkable amount of expensive hardware for a simple recruitment meet, Cherny mused.

He took one step towards them, ensuring to stay within line of sight of Amanda's distant perch. Now that they were closer, Cherny was able to get a better look. Clean dusters. Not a smudge on them. He and Amanda had made sure their clothes had that lived-in feel to pose as locals, but these four hadn't been so careful. They wore breathers that hid their faces. *Off-worlders, then?*

"Are you Cherny?" The apparent leader stepped forward.

The ponytailed woman with the satchel shifted her weight from one foot to another. She sized Cherny up and down with unreadable eyes.

Despite the breather distorting the voice, the leader's accent was pure Martian. Pavonis Mons, if Cherny wasn't mistaken. *Locals receiving funds and equipment from off-world, then.* "Yeah? I, uh, I'm here to meet someone. Are you from—"

"Sorry about this," the leader interrupted.

Pale Grey Dot

The heat signature on the energy projectors and cyber-netics spiked. Time seemed to slow as half a dozen events happened in quick succession.

The leader reached for the pistol on his hip. Silver Eyes lunged towards Cherny, arms outstretched. He could see now that her hands had been replaced with powerful steel claws.

Knowing exactly what his distant partner would do, Cherny leapt backwards, raising his cybernetic left hand as power flowed into it from his other systems. Two great flashes lit up the night sky. The first was the leader's upper torso disintegrating, causing melted goo to splash into the dirt. The second emanated from Cherny's hand, the electro-magnetic pulse enveloping all five of them in white light.

The cyborg seized up, but her momentum kept her tilting forward until she crashed into the ground. "Dammit!" she hissed. Her voice was heavily modulated. Craning her neck, she glared at Cherny impotently.

Turning, he sprinted back towards the warehouse. The EMP would only keep them off balance for a moment. His own systems weren't immune to the effects, and Cherny grunted with the effort of carrying so much dead metal within him. Fifty years ago, when he was in shape, this wouldn't have been such a problem, but now Cherny was gasping for breath. Lowering his shoulder, he smashed through the doors.

Behind him, Cherny heard the sound of weapons charging but failing to fire. Heavy servos began to whirl as Silver Eyes

Don Miasek

started to recover. The ballistics, however, worked just fine. A spray of bullets ricocheted off the doorframe behind him.

Without the usual cybernetic assistance, Cherny's eyes took a moment to adjust to the lobby's darkness. A lone receptionist's desk sat facing the door, covered in dust. The wallpaper was peeling, revealing bare concrete and metal beams beneath. Cherny dragged himself past it and into the corridors beyond.

Stupid! Cherny thought. *They'll follow you in here, where Amanda won't have line of sight.* Still, staying out in the open didn't seem to be an option.

"ATTENTION."

The voice over the intercom made Cherny jump. Lights flickered on behind him in the lobby, rapidly expanding through the corridor and into the rest of the building. Cherny squinted in the bright glare.

"THIS GEODYNAMIC INDUSTRIES DISTRIBUTION CEN-TRE IS CURRENTLY CLOSED TO THE PUBLIC. IN ACCOR-DANCE WITH THE OLYMPUS MONS CRIMINAL CODE SECTION 177, WE WOULD REQUEST THAT YOU PLEASE VACATE THE PREMISES."

Cherny wheezed. Power slowly started to flow through his circuits again. //Amanda,// he sent.

Nothing.

Cursing, Cherny sprinted onto the main warehouse floor. Empty shipping crates taller than three men and wider than a tank stood stacked on one another, creating a veritable maze. Either his onboard transmitter wasn't stable enough

PALE GREY DOT

yet to reach Amanda or that mute-emitting cyborg recovered a hell of a lot faster than he had hoped.

"THIS GEODYNAMIC INDUSTRIES FACILITY MAY CONTAIN MATERIALS DEEMED HAZARDOUS BY LOCAL AUTHORITIES. SECURITY MONITORING STATIONS HAVE BEEN ACTIVATED AND THE POLICE HAVE BEEN NOTIFIED. WE APPRECIATE YOUR COOPERATION."

That damn automated voice had better actually be connected to MarsNet. He stood up straighter as he felt his remaining systems starting to reboot. Propping himself up against the corrugations in the nearest shipping crate's side, Cherny reached into his inner coat pocket and drew out his pistol. He held his breath, listening intently.

Heavy footsteps—metal striking metal—were audible even through the thick walls. Silver Eyes was outside. Trying to circle around quietly and doing a bad job of it. Cherny wondered where the other two were.

Crunch, crunch.

There! At least one of them. Cherny crouched low behind a massive, automated drill bit that was once used to bore into the Olympus Mons volcano, but now was rusting out the rest of its existence, forgotten.

The footsteps stopped, but Cherny saw the flickering of shadows through the maze. He tried to remember his own path and calculate where the attacker would be. Ponytail or Rifle Man? Gripping his pistol with both hands, Cherny slowly began to retrace his steps, careful to avoid casting shadows ahead of him.

187

Don Miasek

A loud crack and a flash of heat ripped through the warehouse floor, knocking Cherny off his feet and into the side of a crate. In an instant, Cherny realized what had happened. A demolition charge. Ponytail's satchel.

Lying on his back, Cherny saw the three-storey stack of cargo containers tilting towards him. He forced himself to his feet and sprinted.

The sound of the collapsing metal rivalled that of the demo charge. Shrapnel flew in all directions, and Cherny fell to his knees, grabbing his right side as searing pain tore through it. When he withdrew his mechanical hand, it was slick with blood.

Decades' worth of dust floated in the air, and Cherny hacked and coughed. His enhanced vision showed brief bursts of static. With his free hand, Cherny fumbled for his gun amidst the shattered metal. Finally feeling its grip, he struggled to his feet.

Through the hazy static, Cherny spied movement. Reacting in an instant, he twisted and squeezed the trigger. The energy projector flashed. There was a crash and a loud thump as something hit the floor.

Cherny gritted his teeth and held his side again. Hobbling forward, he stepped through the wreckage in the direction of his downed target. His coat was in tatters and each breath produced a spasm of agony.

What the hell provoked this? He scoured his mind, but the pain kept breaking his concentration. *Did the Syndicate figure me out?* Alexander Reuben was crafty, so it didn't seem

PALE GREY DOT

out of the question. Still, surely ignoring his infiltration attempt would have been a whole lot cheaper.

Cherny grunted as his foot hit something soft and wet. Kneeling, he set his pistol on the ground long enough to feel the long locks of the woman he shot. Ponytail. Dead.

Grabbing his gun, Cherny stood back up again on wobbly legs. *Amanda,* he thought, *you had better be hauling your sorry ass over here.*

//Cherny.//

It wasn't Amanda. It was a text-only message, routed through the building's security systems. Cherny staggered towards what he hoped was cover. He didn't need his onboard life-support monitor to tell him how bad it was.

//Cherny,// the message repeated. //I can help you. The detonation breached one of the outer walls. The cyborg is moving there now. You have approximately ninety seconds before she reaches you.//

//Who are you?// Cherny felt a twitch in his chest as his internal transmitter struggled to send the message.

The reply ignored the question. //Your other assailant is moving back to the front door. He's the immediate threat. He is armed with a Shadow Arms E-78 rifle. His cybernetics suite is a custom variation on an older CrossNet design, but it looks like your EMP knocked it out. His visual, reflex, and audial acuity will be human norm.//

Grunting with each step, Cherny lurched back towards the lobby, grateful that the static in his vision had cleared somewhat. Stopping at the receptionist's station, he fumbled

189

with his flesh hand, pulling out a small device from his metal arm and affixing it to the underside of the desk. Cherny could already hear Rifle Man sprinting outside, mixed in with distant sirens and the stomping of Silver Eyes.

//Don't go back the way you came. Take a left at the washrooms. The cyborg will be blocking the other route soon.// The text scrolled past his eyes as fast as Cherny could read it.

He limped out of the lobby and to the right, fighting lightheadedness. The air in the hall was at least clean.

Rifle Man stormed into the lobby.

Listening to the footsteps, Cherny remotely activated the charge, engulfing the front waiting room in fire. Even from here, he could feel the heat. It made his side scream in anguish.

//Good work, Cherny,// said the message. //Now, the cyborg is another matter. You don't have anything capable of stopping it.//

//Amanda—tell her where I am,// Cherny sent desperately. //She can fight it.//

//Your partner will be on the premises shortly; however, it's best she does not get involved. Keep following this hall. There's a loading dock at the end of it, just beyond the offices.//

"OPERATIVE!" bellowed a heavily modulated voice that must have been heard across all of Caledonia. "You can't run forever!" Cherny heard metal hit concrete as Silver Eyes smashed her way into the warehouse. His benefactor had steered him in the right direction, as she sounded distant.

PALE GREY DOT

The distribution centre's loading dock consisted of a single hydraulic lift and a massive garage door covering the far wall. Cherny wondered if he could get the rusted mechanism to open. The sirens grew louder, and Amanda would be on her way. With her help, they'd have a chance.

//The door on the east side leads to the underground auto-train tunnels, and straight into Nix Olympica.//

Cherny hesitated. Stumbling into the centre of the bay, he rested against the broken-down chassis of an old fueller truck. In a daze, he peered up at the ceiling, noticing the micro-lens watching his every move. *That's how the messenger is working,* he realized. *They'd need a hard-line network to bypass the mute field.* Cherny's gaze fell, and he could see the thin trail of blood left in his wake.

//Cherny, you don't have time to waste. You have to get out of there.//

Despite the protests of his wound, Cherny hobbled towards the door leading to the underground tunnels. The lock had long since rusted away, and Cherny was able to force it open with a smash of his metal hand. There, as promised, was a grated staircase leading down.

Cherny kept his hand on the concrete walls as the light behind him faded. Guided by touch and half-broken eyes, he reached the bottom. It was cold down here, and Cherny shivered uncontrollably while keeping pressure on his bloodied side. The auto-train tunnel, two storeys high and just as wide, seemed to go on forever. From the broken tracks and crumbling ceiling, it was clear this line was long abandoned.

Don Miasek

//Are you still there?// he transmitted.

There was no response.

//Amanda? Anyone …?// Cherny fell to his hands and knees as both flesh and machine grew weak. He reached forward, clawing at the ground in an attempt to drag himself farther. His vision failed him, and everything went dark.

Cherny opened his eyes. Mouth agape, he desperately sucked in as much air as he could. His side was numb. He was on a medical slab, and he lifted his left arm and found it unrestrained. The metal armouring covering the cybernetics had been removed, revealing the new, clean components of a recent repair job. Reaching over, he felt bandages covering his wound.

The room was the same shade of brown as the train tunnels, but here, the walls were covered in screens and terminals, and the room was lit by overhead floodlights. New cables and computers had been installed next to the decrepit pipes and grates. Three other cots with white sheets had been pushed to one wall next to a small, humming power generator. Dripping water could be heard in the distance.

A man in a tan vest turned from the main terminal and stepped towards him with a comforting smile on his lean face. "Welcome to the Resistance, Cherny," Sienar said.

The walls of the Ganymede Nexus groaned but held against the slowly shifting glacial ice. Each time the frigid outside world convulsed, the floor trembled. Though Ezza had been told the exterior walls of the hub were a metre thick, it still felt like the next rumble would be the one to tear the place apart.

"Feeling all right?" asked the man across the table from her and Nirali. He had the slimy smile and thin, frail look of someone who had resigned himself to never experiencing normal gravity again.

"Just fine, thank you," Ezza replied. Even here, in the insulated travel bureau, her thick civvy jacket wasn't enough to keep the chill away.

"Mmm. Now then, let's take a look at your application, shall we?" said the man. He waved his hand over his desk, conjuring up the travel request. His eyes followed the scrolling text.

Don Miasek

Ezza glanced over at Nirali. The journalist looked every-where but at the man. The holographic sign hovering over his desk read *Dilton Rowe, Primary Adjunct to the Director of the Ganymede Travel Bureau* in steel-blue letters. Each of the bureau's alcoves had an assistant with the same blue-and-sil-ver suit and tie, a metal desk, and exactly one personal item. Rowe's was a small holographic stand projecting a frumpy but happy-looking woman attached magnetically to the desk.

This place could use some colour, Ezza thought. *I'd go back to Earth if I wanted nothing but variations of grey. Some plastic plants, maybe.* Ezza had surreptitiously downed three Cerebrol after the space elevator touched down, and she had to concentrate to stay focused.

For her part, Nirali looked lost. She shifted uncomfort-ably each time the floor shuddered. Tiny windows in the walls, up where they met the ceiling, gave a glimpse of the outside world. Apparently, they were there to reduce feelings of claustrophobia, but the constant sight of endless waste-land wasn't exactly comforting. According to the station's introductory guide, the windows had to be placed up high to avoid ice building up over them.

Rowe hummed as the application's map flashed open, dis-playing a highlighted route. A dark red X appeared over the destination. "Ah, yes, I see why they asked you to speak with me," he said. He traced his finger along the holographic map. "You've requested clearance to the Uruk Sulcus sector, but as you can see, that entire section of track was shut down two years ago. After the accident."

Pale Grey Dot

Waving his hand over his desk, the map vanished, replaced with images of smiling people in colourful sweaters relaxing fireside, gazing in wonder through frosty windows at the rugged Ganymede terrain while Jupiter shone over-head. It looked a hell of a lot nicer than this dismal place.

"If it's a romantic getaway you're after, I could make several better suggestions," Rowe said. "From Pacem to Solatium, our lodges have all been rated A and above by the Virtual Tourist. You'll find that Ganymede gravity is perfectly tuned for extreme hikes or cozy relaxation."

The station emitted another moan as the ice ground against it. Nirali jolted upright in her seat, prompting another amused smile from the travel advisor.

Watching the newbies squirm must be what passes for entertainment on this rock, Ezza thought. *That and escaping to Naxx and virtual reality every night. Being a dredge isn't confined to Earth anymore.*

"Uh, this trip isn't for pleasure. We're here on business," Nirali said. She glanced over at Ezza nervously, who just nodded back in support.

"And exactly what business could you have in Uruk Sulcus?" Rowe asked, settling his hands on the desk in front of him.

"It's United Fleet business," Ezza said. Her voice sounded raspy. Last night, she needed another two pills just to get to sleep.

Rowe's eyes lit up. "Ah! You must be with the warship that docked at the elevator orbit-side."

195

Don Miasek

"Captain Ezza Jayens, yes," Ezza confirmed. She ignored Nirali's surprised look. Hiding her identity wasn't going to be possible here. "Now, my team and I need to get to Uruk Sulcus-132. Four people, us included."

"Well, I'm sorry, but it simply isn't possible," Rowe said, shrugging his shoulders in mock helplessness. His smile, however, spoke of his glee at being able to shoot down a United Fleet officer. "The Regional Ganymede Board of Transportation declared those train lines off-limits to everyone. Even if I granted your request—and believe me, I am not—the lines out that way are in complete disrepair from the accident. Not to mention, transferring a train from another line would entail a service disruption we simply can't afford. This isn't Earth, Captain. In some places, these tunnels bore through ice half a kilometre beneath the surface. You don't just"—Rowe swept his hand dismissively—"swap trains willy-nilly."

Ezza's glare could have melted half that ice, but Rowe was on a roll.

"Now, if the Ministry of Defence wishes to make an official request to the Ganymede Transport Commission, then by all means. But until then, the Ministry of Transportation is not at the beck and call of the military, Captain."

Ezza took a deep breath to keep herself from strangling the man. All the Cerebrol in the solar system couldn't save her from her growing headache. Her voice was barely above a hiss. "In case you haven't noticed, Mr. Rowe, our fleet has come under attack. I would think that at a time like this—"

PALE GREY DOT

"You'd be better off patrolling the space lanes?" Rowe interrupted. "I'm sorry, Captain, but I cannot help you. Please have your superiors contact my superiors and go through the proper process. Now, unless there was anything else?"

Nirali glanced at Ezza expectantly. When she didn't answer, the reporter leaned forward, placing a hand on the man's desk. "Mr. Rowe, please, can't we work something out? We both know there are special accommodations that can be granted under extenuating circumstances. I have contacts in the Jupiter Station government who would be happy to put in a good word to your supervisors."

Ezza wondered how long it would take to go through the proper channels. Days. Weeks. Admiral Cheng-Visitor hadn't been thrilled by her request to go to Ganymede and was even less impressed when she heard Ezza's suspicions of what she'd find there. Her parting words had been concise: "Seven days, Jayens. That's all I'm giving you. Tolj is no longer around to put up with your crap."

As Nirali and Rowe haggled, their words were drowned out by the pain in her head. *Wham, wham, wham.*

The Pull is getting worse, Ezza realized. *The Cerebrol isn't working like it once did.* Ezza wished she knew the technical specifics of the Athena Program's mental conditioning as well as Jenna had, but the cybernetic sciences were never her forte.

Ezza knew what She would say, were she connected to SecLink. *"Science may not be your forte,"* She'd say, *"but*

197

taking command of a situation is. Use the gifts I have given you. You aren't a United Fleet captain. You're an operative. Seize control."

Ezza reached forward slowly and plucked the holographic projection stand off Rowe's desk, holding it up to her eyes to get a better look at the woman.

"It's a tempting offer, Ms. Kashem. I'll forward it to my superiors, but I highly suspect your application will still be denied." Rowe said. He frowned at Ezza. "Excuse me, Captain, but if you could just put that—"

"If Nirali's offer isn't sufficient, then we'll go the formal request route," Ezza interrupted wearily. "Proper channels and everything, Mr. Rowe. But it won't be a request from the Ministry of Defence. No, it will come in the form of an Earth Security Service investigation into this entire pathetic excuse of an outpost. Do you know what happens to someone labelled a Suspicious Person, Mr. Rowe?"

"I-I..." Rowe stammered, confused. "But you're—"

"Your life is scoured. Every place you've visited, every cab you've taken, everything you've purchased, everything you've sold, and every person you know goes under the microscope." Ezza placed the holographic woman back on the magnetic holder with a loud thud. "And that's just the beginning. Your cybernetics package. A SineWave 85X, if I'm not mistaken. Every visual and audial scrap of information it's ever held is sitting on an ESS server right now. How hard do you think it would be for me to pull that up? What do you think I'd find?"

PALE GREY DOT

Rowe went pale.

Nirali stared at her, but Ezza kept her focus on Rowe. "Now then. Have another look at our application. Talk it over with your superiors. I'm going to arrange for the formal request that you've asked for. Should a train to Uruk Sulcus somehow become available by the time my team is ready to depart, then clearly, my petition won't be necessary."

Ezza stood. "Thank you for your time, Mr. Rowe." Storming out of the travel bureau wasn't an option with Ganymede's gravity, so a half-skipping gait had to suffice.

Nirali followed, struggling to keep up with the taller woman.

The Commons was at the heart of the Ganymede Nexus. The outpost ran ten storeys deep into the ice, with different sectors splitting off into their own wards. The deck was a sleek silver, reflecting the overhead lights to create an ambient blue glow. Leaning on a railing overlooking the atrium, Ezza watched as pedestrians on the lower levels headed to Bulwark Arms, GreyCorp Distribution, the Governmental Affairs offices, and beyond. She saw tourists heading to the train lines on the lowest levels. *Bet they're glad they picked Ganymede and not Jupiter Station.*

"Nirali, you make an excellent good cop," Ezza commented as the journalist joined her at the railing. She unzipped her jacket. It didn't feel so cold in here anymore.

"I think I could have talked him into helping us without the threats," the reporter replied. "What was that back there? It was like you were in a trance."

199

Don Miasek

Ezza smiled. "Just a bluff. Nothing more."

"Yeah? I'm not so sure. You looked like you enjoyed that a little too much."

I did enjoy it, Ezza realized. A life in the United Fleet was one of red tape and protocol, but an operative could do whatever was needed. It might just have been the Pull rewarding her for using her talents, Ezza mused, but it still felt so damn good. "Let's see how Adams and Gole are making out."

There was a soft hum as they waited for the elevator to arrive. The locals were used to simply hopping from the upper levels to ones below in the weak gravity, but Nirali hadn't felt up to the challenge yet. The outpost rumbled again.

"I don't think I'm ever going to get used to that," Nirali murmured as the glass doors slid open to accept them.

"It must be overwhelming, this being your first time off Jupiter Station," Ezza said.

"I went on assignment to Io once. Hated every minute of it." Even though the elevator accelerated slowly to account for the gravity, Nirali instinctively grabbed onto the railing as if her life depended on it.

"I would have thought you'd be experienced with this. Jupiter Station's zero-g central pylon is one of its main attractions."

Nirali crinkled her nose. "Nah, I was never really into sports." Her knuckles were turning white.

Ezza chuckled. "Well, this won't be like Io."

"I guess not." Nirali looked upwards.

PALE GREY DOT

Both the elevator and the roof of the atrium had skylights, allowing the two women to peer straight into the heavens. Though she couldn't quite spy the gas giant, Ezza could make out the elevator cable stretching up and out of view.

"What do you think we'll find at Uruk Sulcus?" Nirali asked.

Ezza thought for a moment before replying. "Jenna seemed to think another old colleague of ours, Sienar, fled the service during the 'accident' two years ago."

"So that's three ex-operatives I've learned about in the span of a few days. You know, from the outside looking in, ESS is a terrifying, faceless, and impenetrable organization that can do no wrong, comprised of superbeings who swoop in, enforce the will of the government, and vanish back into the ether."

"Everyone's human, Nirali. Even those in ESS. With flaws, pettiness, and fears. Even ..." *Even Her.* Ezza bit her tongue. "Even their most capable operatives."

The elevator doors slid open to reveal a mid-level floor. Ezza wondered if the Nexus was always this crowded. A pair of soon-to-be hikers, wearing safety suits and helmets, pushed past a couple trying to make sense of the holographic maps emitting from their arms. The queue for the Java Café Dispensary curled around the corner. Ezza overheard a trio complaining about the ghastly state of the "so-called luxury liner" industry these days. A man in the Java line was arguing with someone over JupiterNet about the delays to refuel his freighter.

201

"I still have a zillion questions about this," Nirali said, raising her voice to be heard over the chatter as the pair navigated through the horde.

"We'll have twenty hours on the train. I'm sure there'll be time," Ezza replied.

Up ahead, the bright azure *Arctic First Supplies* sign floated above the storefront. A holographic man and woman smiled perpetually while the clothing around them fizzled, shifting from custom bright blue clothing to heavy-duty orange surface suits. As the women approached, the holograms blinked out of existence and were replaced with their images. Fake Ezza proudly displayed hiking spikes on her gloves and feet. She looked ready to tackle anything Ganymede could throw at her. Fake Nirali wore one of the colourful sweaters they saw back at the travel bureau, looking relaxed and at peace. Ezza could swear the reporter was two inches taller and had more defined musculature in the projected form.

Hiding really is impossible in this solar system, Ezza fumed. There was no doubt in her mind that She was already aware of their presence. The security camera hidden in the holographic camera. The bored-looking woman overseeing the store. The automatic credit-checker system. Any of them could be Her assets.

For a brief moment, Ezza considered reconnecting to SecLink. Just long enough to catch a glimpse of what She and ESS were thinking. *I'd know what to expect at Uruk Sulcus,* Ezza thought. There was a Heliopause Telecom station one level down. Ten minutes, at most. Or less if she went

PALE GREY DOT

through the Ganymede Nexus wireless. Thirty seconds, Ezza calculated. That's all it would take to be back.

"Ezza? Are you all right?" Deep concern marred Nirali's features.

It took Ezza a moment to focus on her. "What?" They were in the store now, but she didn't remember stepping past the threshold.

"You look terrible." Nirali reached out and held her arm.

Ezza realized she was sweating. Raising her gloved hand, she wiped her forehead with the sleeve of her jacket. "I'm fine," she whispered.

Nirali gave her an appraising stare but was interrupted before she could respond.

"Captain, over here," Adams called out from one of the rows of vacuum-hiking equipment.

Ezza held her hand against Nirali's before taking it off her arm. "I'm fine," she repeated as they approached the men. *Remember the mask.* "It's 'Ezza' while we're grounded, Adams," she said in a firm tone. "Just four more tourists."

"Right. Sorry, ma'am. Ezza." Adams said. The name sounded foreign coming from him. He and Gole were inspecting the pressure suits needed for survival beyond the Nexus. The heavy suits were a mix of silver and white material, with coloured armbands for easy identification. The outfits were padded, both for external protection and to cushion the wearer. The helmet faces consisted of blank, curved, two-way faceguards from chin to hairline.

"The store has our specifications and measurements

on file," Gole said. "Four suits, by tomorrow. Adams and I bought enough rations to last two weeks, along with camping supplies. But if what we've been hearing about the train lines to Uruk Sulcus is true, we'll be hoofing it for at least the last fifty kilometres. The lines are supposedly in bad shape."

Ajay Gole was a towering man, with a dark beard and darker eyes. The commander of *Starknight's* marines was a veteran of the Lunar Blockade, and he looked the part. While others sought to remove any scars, he wore his like badges of honour. Ezza always wondered if he was slumming it on *Starknight*. Heading up boarding operations to capture ships like the *Tyrannis* seemed beneath his station.

"We heard the same," Ezza replied.

"The accident," Rowe had called it, but Jenna said Sienar killed a lot of ESS personnel there.

"Ezza managed to convince the transport authority to get us a train," Nirali piped up. "But a fifty-kilometre hike …"

"Don't worry, Ms. Kashem," Gole replied. "It's just one foot in front of the other. It'll be over before you know it."

Gole seemed cautious around Nirali, and Ezza didn't blame him. A civilian suddenly taken on board and brought everywhere the captain goes was more than enough to raise a few eyebrows. *I need her here, though,* Ezza thought. She had told neither Adams nor Gole of her past affiliation with ESS. While both men were too professional to ask why they were travelling to an old monitoring station destroyed in an accident two years ago, it clearly weighed on their minds.

PALE GREY DOT

"Ezza?" Adams was asking. After a moment, he added in a quieter voice, "Captain?"

Ezza blinked. "I'm sorry?"

"*Starknight* has sent us the travel bureau's latest expected weather forecasts. Apparently, the Governmental Affairs office doesn't distribute condition reports for Uruk Sulcus."

"Yes. Right," Ezza replied.

Adams and Gole exchanged glances.

Ezza had been thinking about the telecom station one level down. It was just a few mental clicks away. It'd be so easy. "Let's head back to the Habitats and get some sleep," she said, changing the subject. "Adams, keep an eye on the train lines. Make sure it looks like they're prepping one for us. Gole, you're going to have to stop by here tomorrow to check if our gear is in order. If we'll be hiking part of the way to Uruk Sulcus, then we'll need to travel light. I want to be ready to board at oh-six-hundred hours, *Starknight* time."

The two men nodded their assent before setting off.

"Nirali, a moment," Ezza said.

The reporter hung back with her. A remote shopper drone hovered by the holographic mannequins, now displaying the latest visitors to the shop.

Ezza pulled off her left glove, holding it between her arm and side as she rolled up her sleeve. Her cybernetics made an audible click as she removed a one-inch device from the underside of her arm. Quickly, she handed it to Nirali.

The reporter held it up to her eye, confused. "Your transmitter? I don't understand."

Don Miasek

"Just keep it for now," Ezza replied in a hoarse voice. "I'll get it back from you tomorrow."

"Why don't you want—"

"Just keep it. I'll explain later," Ezza lied.

Nirali shook her head but tucked the transmitter into her pocket as she followed Ezza towards the elevator. "You're the weirdest United Fleet captain I've ever met."

The Habitat rooms were the cheapest on the Nexus and no bigger than the quarters on *Starknight*. Two by two metres, there was only room for a bed bag, a ChargeAll unit, and a GreyCorp locker. The communal bathroom was down the hall. The rooms were cheap in both senses of the word.

The moment the door slid closed behind her, Ezza knelt before the locker chest. Without her transmitter, she had to manually input her credentials, but the inconvenience was worth it to keep from connecting to the telecom centre down below. Lifting the lid, she reached in and pulled out a United Fleet duffle bag. With shaking hands, she found the pouch with the four bottles of Cerebrol.

Staring at the two little white capsules in her palm, Ezza hoped it would be enough. It should be, she reasoned, unless the Pull got worse. Ezza added a third and fourth pill to the mix, tilted her head back, and swallowed.

Stripping down, Ezza climbed into the bed bag and zipped up the sides. The lights flickered off, leaving her in complete darkness with her thoughts. As exhausted as she was, her mind raced. Jenna said she was on her way.

PALE GREY DOT

Ezza's sister had been the last to join them at the Kazan Institute for Education. They hadn't known it then, but the six of them had already been selected as potential recruits for the Earth Security Service. Jenna was intense and withdrawn in the beginning—a reflection of her upbringing in the Midwestern Wastes, no doubt. But soon enough, she'd come out of her shell. Ezza remembered racing with Jenna in the tunnels beneath the school and squabbling over toys. More than a few of their snowball fights had turned vicious. Their competitive spirits didn't change much as they grew up and found themselves drafted as agents. But ultimately, Ezza trusted Jenna. There was no question in Ezza's mind that Jenna loved all of them, and if she said to go to Uruk Sulcus, then that was all the reason she needed.

Ezza wondered if Jenna felt any guilt over working to develop the Athena Protocols in the first place. Ezza hoped she didn't—it wasn't her fault how everything turned out.

As she lay on the mattress, looking up at the ceiling of her Habitat room, she wondered why Taylor and Sal had suffered from the Athena Protocols more than the others. *Luck,* Ezza finally decided. *It was just luck that you didn't go mad right along with them. You're no stronger than Taylor or more reliable than Sal, yet they succumbed. There's no good reason you stayed sane. Here's another chance to fail.*

After an hour of anxious tossing and turning, she fell into a restless sleep and dreamt.

Don Miasek

●

Étoile's massive nuclear pulse engines steadily fired as they worked to slow the craft. Even from the control room, deep within the primary hull, Jenna could feel each detonation. After sixteen days on the ship, she had finally gotten used to the comforts of the control chair. Its foam padding was thick enough that she could really sink into it, and the chair swivelled in a pleasing fashion to face whichever screen she wanted—not that Jenna needed them. With a tangle of cables running between her arm and the computer, it felt like the ship was an extension of her own body. From its primary hull to its secondary, Jenna saw everything that happened inside and out. Using one of *Étoile*'s external cameras, she could gaze into the blackness of space. The control room's walls were no more than two metres apart, but all the machinery made it feel smaller. She kept the overhead lights off, and so it felt like it was just her, the glow of the computer screens, and the stars. It was peaceful.

As far as dredge work goes, Jenna mused, *it could be a whole lot worse.* She even found she was starting to get used to the civilized people on board, with their petty grievances and annoying tendencies. The ship's inefficiencies were another matter. Shifting from acceleration gravity to rotational and back again was a pain. The crew had to move everything

PALE GREY DOT

from the floors to the walls during the brief period of zero-g. They could have avoided it by accelerating to the midway point and then decelerating, but Hecktor was too damn cheap with the fuel. Why the ship had so much furniture not bolted in place was beyond Jenna. Luxury breeds weakness, she decided. Nevertheless, it had been easy work.

Despite how the ship's comforts were growing on her, Jenna knew this wasn't the life for her. *Not while She still drew breath.* Last night, Jenna dreamt of storming the Tower with a rifle, kicking down the door, and blasting every agent and operative she saw. Her gun never ran out of energy, and no matter how much they shot back at her, they could never find their mark. Old rivals and hated enemies fell with each squeeze of the trigger. She'd had the supreme confidence of a dreamer that nothing could stop her as she carved her way down to the building's sub-levels to face Her.

Then Larry the idiot cook had shaken her awake, yelling that it was his turn to sleep.

Still, the dream had Jenna in good spirits. It was just a matter of turning all that into reality. Step one was to make it to Jupiter's locale and meet up with Ezza. Together, she knew, they'd be able to reform the remaining Athena Six survivors and take the fight to ESS. It wouldn't be long now. Another four hours of 0.15g deceleration and they'd be in Europa's orbit. *Étoile*'s scanners were already picking up the fleet at Jupiter Station. The news feeds reported crews of civilian and rescue crafts working tirelessly to provide relief

Don Miasek

at the station, all led by a United Fleet battlecruiser. But neither the news nor *Étoile's* scanners showed any sign of Ezza's *Starknight.*

Ezza got her message—of that, Jenna was certain—but did she listen and go to Ganymede? Ezza could be as stubborn as a mule sometimes. Maybe calling her a colossal bitch hadn't been such a good idea after all.

The rest of the news didn't concern Jenna. Defence Minister Havoic had made a few vows about tracking down those responsible and rebuilding the fleet, while the Minister of Public Safety, Richter, had pledged the full cooperation of ESS forces in achieving both ends. *Typical political drivel.*

Jenna wondered how the hell the relationship between Richter and Her worked. In theory, ESS fell under government jurisdiction like any other department, and so She would report to him. Somehow Jenna couldn't imagine Her having an actual boss, though. Just what do a politician and an abomination of technology talk about? *"How's the weather? Catch the calvball game last night? Corrupt any orphans lately?"*

Jenna snapped out of her newsgazing as an alert rang in her ears. Incoming transmission. High priority. Governmental origin. Jenna's blood turned cold. Clenching her metal hand into a fist, she brought the alert up before her. Her eyes darted back and forth as she processed it.

*** TRAJECTORY ADJUSTMENT REQUIREMENT ***

*** SPACESHIP *ÉTOILE*, A NEW FLIGHT PLAN HAS BEEN

PALE GREY DOT

ORDERED BY THE MINISTRY OF TRANSPORTATION. YOUR APPROACH TO EUROPAN ELEVATOR ONE IS DECLINED. UPON DECELERATION TO MANOEUVRING SPEED, YOU ARE TO DIVERT COURSE AWAY FROM THE STATION TO RENDEZVOUS WITH UFS *PRAVEDNI*. COORDINATIONS AND TRAJECTORY CALCULATIONS ENCLOSED. ***

*** SEND IMMEDIATE ACKNOWLEDGEMENT OF MESSAGE RECEIPT. ***

The electronic signature at the end of the transmission was signed by Admiral Gabrielle Cheng-Visitor. Jenna gaped at the monitor as if she could change the message by sheer willpower alone. *They found me out. They must have.* Jenna tried to think of how this could have happened. She had been so careful on Earth, and her forged ID had passed inspection at customs. Surely if the authorities had always known she was on board, they would have stopped *Étoile* at Gagarin Station. There were other ships at Jupiter Station, but Jenna could see none of them had been given course adjustments.

No, she decided. *It's me they're after.* Jenna's mind reached out to every corner of the ship—nuclear pulse engines, oxygen regenerators, rotational engines, the electrical grid, and security locks were all at her fingertips.

Unclenching her hand on the worn armrest, Jenna switched into action mode. Throughout *Étoile*, network access ports shut down. Watching through the internal cameras, Jenna could see the workers down in the engine

Don Miasek

room react with immediate confusion. She saw one man— Jon, if Jenna recalled correctly—step away from his console towards his supervisor. The woman next to him rolled her eyes, stepped forward, and pressed her hand against it. But when her access failed, her brow furrowed. "The hell?" she muttered.

A shudder ran through *Étoile* a second later as the nuclear pulse engines shifted into standby. Powerful thrusters along the ship's secondary hull fired, beginning a slow one-hundred-and-eighty-degree turn. Decelerating was now the last thing Jenna wanted *Étoile* to do. Jenna watched the cameras as passengers and crew stumbled in shock, thrown off balance by the shifting g-forces.

"Jenna!" Hecktor's voice came through the intercom. "What's going on? Why are we changing course?" His voice was already full of suspicion.

Jenna peered at the man through the cameras. He was in the crew mess hall, where his dinner of vita-noodles had apparently been interrupted. She briefly considered ignoring him, but then decided to buy herself another thirty seconds. "Looking into it now," she lied, switching off the intercom. It was only after she spoke that she remembered she should have feigned a confused and concerned tone. With a flick of her wrist, the control room's interior doors snapped shut, magnetic locks engaging.

Checking the scanners, Jenna saw a warship at Jupiter Station already beginning to move. That would be UFS *Pravedni*. The transmission said Cheng-Visitor was in

PALE GREY DOT

command. As she locked out the controls across the ship, Jenna crafted a quick response.

*** THIS IS HECKTOR RAMIREZ OF THE SYNDICATE VESSEL *ÉTOILE*. THERE ARE TWO HUNDRED SOULS ON BOARD THIS SHIP. I'LL DROP THEM OFF SOMEPLACE SAFE IF YOU HALT ALL PURSUIT. IF NOT, THEY DIE. ***

There was no question in Jenna's mind that She would happily let them all burn if it meant getting what She wanted, but maybe Admiral Cheng-Visitor wouldn't. Jenna recalled the admiral's broad shoulders, shortly cropped silver hair, and fierce eyes that gave the impression of a woman uninterested in compromise. Her careful planning and blunt attitude had been legendary in Jenna's day, and she doubted that had changed in the past few decades. Then again, Cheng-Visitor might not have any say in what was going on. If she'd been told to detain *Étoile*, then it'd be on ESS's request.

"JENNA!" Hecktor's voice roared through the intercom. "What do you think you're doing?"

Jenna frowned. Pulling up the mess hall camera, Jenna saw his face, red with fury. Behind him, over his left shoulder, her fellow ship overseer knelt in front of the RecSystem access port. Kathy had managed to tap into the ship's transmitter and reactivate the intercom.

Not so incompetent after all.

"I have zero affiliation with those pirates!" Hecktor hissed. His beard shook with every word he spat at her. There were other *Étoile* crew members Jenna recognized behind him, all standing around uselessly, unsure of what to do.

"It doesn't matter," Jenna replied, dropping any pretence of innocence. "Your anti-Earth sentiments. I'm sure you've spoken them before in civilized space. I'm certain ESS already had you tagged long before I came along."

The big man looked ready to reach through the camera and strangle her.

Jenna returned her focus to tightening her grip on *Étoile*'s systems. There was a rumble as the nuclear pulse engines started once more. The course was an obvious one—slingshot around Jupiter to build up enough speed that an extended pursuit wouldn't be worth it. A battlecruiser like *Pravedni* was unmatched in a straight-up fight, but with the entire solar system in chaos, Jenna prayed she was a small enough fish to not bother chasing for long.

Hecktor turned away from the camera. "Jo-Ann, get a team over there with torches," he snapped. "Kathy, find out how the hell she's doing this." The woman looked away from the access point long enough to nod nervously. Hecktor gave the camera one last glance with fire in his eyes as he growled in a low voice, "First, I'm going to cut you out of that control room." It was almost a whisper. "Then I'm going to cut out your miserable heart. I should have let you rot on Earth, you little bitch."

Jenna ignored him and took a deep breath to calm herself. *Étoile* was designed with a full crew in mind, and micromanaging every system was exhausting. The two twerps in the

PALE GREY DOT

secondary hull's engine room were now trying to unscrew the hatches that led to the power cables feeding the engines while their chief watched.

Jenna activated the room's speakers. "Clever. Dangerous. But I wouldn't do that if I were you."

The lead engineer looked up at the camera in horror. Her frizzy red hair was tied back in a ponytail, and she had freckles on her cheek. "Why are you doing this?" There was a growing panic in her voice.

Jenna didn't answer the question. "If you cut into the power cables, I'll blow the heat shielding around the radiators. You'll burn."

The engineer turned white. "Why are you doing this?" she pleaded again. "There are hundreds of people on board!"

"Then you'd best not touch the power cables. Cooking is a terrible way to die," Jenna hissed, terminating the audio. Other cameras showed Jo-Ann and two other crew members trying to cut through the locked bulkhead doors. The control room was well secluded from the populated areas of the ship—Jenna calculated six bulkheads they'd have to carve through. They'd get through eventually, but by then, it had better not matter. An alert pinged in Jenna's mind. *Pravedni*'s latest transmission was straight from Cheng-Visitor herself. Included was a request for video communication, but Jenna ignored it in favour of the text. *Please,* she thought. *Please believe the bluff.*

*** HECKTOR RAMIREZ. TELEMETRY HAS OUR MISSILES

REACHING YOU WITHIN THIRTEEN MINUTES. YOU HAVE UNTIL THEN TO BEGIN DECELERATING AGAIN. ***

*** YOU AND I BOTH KNOW THERE'S ZERO CHANCE OF YOU ESCAPING *PRAVEDNI*. THE LOGICAL CHOICE—YOUR ONLY CHOICE, FRANKLY—IS SURRENDER. ***

*** ACCEPT MY VIDEO REQUEST AND WE CAN DISCUSS THIS. ***

So it didn't work. Jenna knew everything the admiral had sent was true. A single volley of thirty missiles were already en route. Six and a half minutes for them to accelerate, and six and a half to decelerate if they were to avoid obliterating the ship. *Étoile* had no mine clouds, no point defence lasers, no speed, no jamming equipment, and no hope. All Jenna had were empty threats.

Running the ship by herself was proving to be damn near impossible, but with a fraction of her mind, Jenna glanced at the cameras. Jo-Ann and her helpers were almost half-way through the first bulkhead. At the rate they were going, Jenna had less than forty minutes before they reached the control room. The engine room trio were staying put, successfully cowed by her threat.

Jenna shifted uncomfortably in the control chair. Its upholstery had grown slick with sweat from her back. Diverting power from other systems, Jenna ignited the engines. The rumble of distant nuclear explosions impacting against the shock-absorbing plate at the ship's aft could be felt throughout both hulls. *Étoile* surged in its new direction as Jenna pushed the engines, accelerating to 0.5g. She

PALE GREY DOT

felt herself being pressed deeper into the chair's padding. A dozen red system warnings flashed in Jenna's mind, and she struggled to deal with each simultaneously.

Another alert pinged, and Jenna could barely spare the split second to activate Cheng-Visitor's latest transmission.

*** CAPTAIN RAMIREZ—ASSUMING THAT'S WHO IS REALLY RECEIVING THESE MESSAGES—I HAVE NOT RECEIVED ANY REPLY TO MY DEMANDS. ***

*** MY MISSILES ARE NOW NINE MINUTES AWAY. WE'VE TRACKED YOUR COURSE AND KNOW YOUR PLANS TO SLINGSHOT AROUND JUPITER, BUT IT ISN'T GOING TO WORK OUT FOR YOU. ***

Jenna rubbed her forehead with her flesh hand.

*** MY ORDERS ARE TO DETAIN ONLY ONE MEMBER OF YOUR CREW. I HAVE NO INTEREST IN YOUR SHIP OR THE REST OF YOUR CREW. LET'S DISCUSS THIS FACE TO FACE. ***

Again, Cheng-Visitor attached the video request, but again, Jenna ignored it. The last thing she needed was the distraction of bantering with the admiral. Any hope Jenna had that Cheng-Visitor wasn't after her specifically had been shattered. *She wants me alive. It will never come to that.* Her struggles were sporadically interrupted by pings as Kathy broke through and regained control of a minor system—the secondary hull ventilation systems, the ship-wide comm system, the rotational systems—or Jo-Ann's team hacked their way through another bulkhead. Jenna was careful to

217

Don Miasek

intervene whenever they had a chance to reach something important.

Six minutes before *Pravedni*'s missiles would hit; thirty before Jo-Ann sliced into her cocoon; forty before Kathy re-engaged the network's security, taking away her control over *Étoile*. It would be over four hours before Jenna could even start to benefit from Jupiter's orbit. She fought to suppress her panic. There were threats all around her and she couldn't think of a way past any of them.

*** WE BOTH KNOW THIS ISN'T HECKTOR RAMIREZ RECEIVING MY TRANSMISSIONS. IF YOU'RE AS SMART AS THEY SAY YOU ARE, YOU'VE CALCULATED WHAT MY TECHNICIANS HAVE—YOU CANNOT OUTRUN OUR MISSILES. I HAVE THIRTY IN THE AIR BUT COULD ADD ANOTHER HUNDRED AT A MOMENT'S NOTICE. THERE'S NO REASON TO PUT OTHERS IN HARM'S WAY. LET'S DISCUSS SURRENDER FACE TO FACE. ***

Jenna set her jaw. There was a solution, she decided. There must be. Maybe there was some way she could fake a critical situation elsewhere for Cheng-Visitor to deal with. Maybe she could trick her into thinking she wasn't on board. Jenna glanced at her left arm. Among its many tools was a low-level energy projector. Maybe she could ditch the control room, fight her way to the ship's lifeboats, and escape. Maybe she could push the engines harder. Maybe ... Jenna knew none of her options stood a chance.

Through her connection to *Étoile*'s network, she suddenly

PALE GREY DOT

realized that the ship's transmitter had been activated by a different user ID. "No!" she shouted, angrily smashing her fist against the controls.

*** *ÉTOILE* TO *PRAVEDNI*. THIS IS THE REAL HECKTOR RAMIREZ. OUR SHIP HAS BEEN HIJACKED BY A DREDGE NAMED JENNA. WE WILL CO— ***

Jenna severed the transmission, but she already knew it was too late. "No, no, no," she whispered. Her earlier empty threats passed through her mind again. They weren't going to be enough against Cheng-Visitor.

Hecktor's face filled the mess hall camera frame as he stared daggers into it. "That got your attention, eh?" he snarled. "I'm betting Cheng-Visitor won't care what shape you're in by the time she gets here."

Jenna didn't answer. Her attention was focused on the ship's generators. The three engineers nervously monitored the ship's systems, but they still hadn't taken action following Jenna's threats to blow the heat shielding. She could drop the shields all the way from the generators to the struts that connected the primary hull to the central pylon. The damage to the primary hull would be catastrophic—the passengers wouldn't stand a chance. Her words to the chief engineer came back to her. *"Cooking is a bad way to die."* Cheng-Visitor's *Pravedni* would definitely pick up the heat flare on their scanners. *Kill half the hostages; threaten with the remaining half.*

Jenna's arm twitched as she brought up the mental

Don Miasek

commands for the heat shielding. A red emergency light flashed in the engine room as her access to the system was detected. The virtual button, labelled *Activate* in crimson, hovered above the switch. Jenna reached out towards it ... and thought of Noble, Ralph, and the other idiots she knew on board. *No!* Jenna thought. *Don't let compassion make you weak again! You almost made that mistake with Marcus!*

The reminder of the operative brought Jenna back to his memories. Back to when he and his overwatches had seen the horrors on Mars. It had been genuine fear and concern that the man felt over the deaths of so many. Deaths Jenna and her team were responsible for.

Jenna cursed herself and closed the heat shielding controls.

She couldn't outrun *Pravedni*. She couldn't keep control of the ship away from Kathy and Hecktor. She couldn't stop Jo-Ann's torch-wielding team. They were all hopeless causes. It was only a question of which one got to her first.

A sudden warning jolted Jenna out of her thoughts. "No, no, no," she whispered. In her distraction, her lock on the ship's manoeuvring thrusters had been taken away. In the mess hall, Hecktor looked over Kathy's shoulder with grim satisfaction. System after system slipped from Jenna's grasp—the ship's network, the power relays, the external transmitter ...

Jenna could only watch helplessly as Cheng-Visitor's thirty missiles, backed by some of the most impressive AI ever devised, split off from one another, slowing down so

PALE GREY DOT

they were just above *Étoile*'s velocity to avoid obliterating the liner with sheer kinetic energy. They worked in concert with one another, with four targeting a specific spot on *Étoile*'s nuclear pulse assembly, while the remaining twenty-six hung back in reserve. Jenna reached out and gripped the control room's safety bar as tightly as she could. The ship shuddered as the warheads collided with *Étoile*'s rear. The plating along the central pylon that connected the primary and secondary hulls tore apart. A fireball ignited before quickly burning off into nothingness.

Jenna's connection to the ship's systems flickered in and out of existence. Through the static, a stream of damage reports flowed past her vision, colour-coded to indicate severity. The nuclear pulse engines were no longer firing, and a desperate mental calculation told her that they hadn't built up nearly enough speed to escape Cheng-Visitor's *Pravedni*. Instead of the deep rumble of explosions, there was only the impotent sound of clicking.

"Hear that?" Hecktor said as he gripped a handhold tightly. With the engines cut, the ship's gravity had failed. "That's the clock ticking down how much time you have left."

Jenna's breathing turned ragged. She felt like an animal snared in a trap. On her monitors, she watched as *Pravedni* methodically matched the velocity, angle, and rotation of *Étoile*. The battlecruiser, with its bulky, grey armour plating, dwarfed the sleek, white liner. Through her stuttering connection to the ship, she felt every grappler that launched from *Pravedni* and burrowed itself into *Étoile*'s primary

221

Don Miasek

hull, slowly but roughly bringing the two ships together. The United Fleet's crew went by the book, and within ten minutes, three dozen marines were slicing through the hull. Each soldier wore power armour with a full breather helmet and were armed as if they were going into war.

Jenna frantically struggled to figure out where it all went wrong. Her upper lip curled at the thought of how She had bested her, and Jenna slammed her fist against the control panel in frustration.

The armoured soldiers rapidly and efficiently took the ship, guns drawn as they swept through, ordering the passengers and crew to clip to the walls and floors to be searched. As they swarmed the mess hall, Hecktor gave one last victorious smile in the camera's direction before turning away. A marine ran a scanner over his body for weapons, and the captain did not resist.

Three minutes, maybe, before they reach the control room and burn their way through to me. How many power-armoured soldiers could I kill? she wondered. *Two? Three? Five or six with some luck.* Then she'd be sent back to Earth, where She would violate her mind, twisting her into a happy, loyal minion. There'd be nothing left of the real her anymore. *It will never come to that.*

Jenna tasted bile in her mouth as, one by one, she yanked out her connections with *Étoile*'s network. Her body was numb as she raised her metal arm, diverting all the power her cybernetics had into her energy projector.

The marines had now reached Jo-Ann and her team.

PALE GREY DOT

The woman was almost gleeful as she pointed towards the control room. They rapidly moved into position around the heavy door that led to Jenna's cocoon.

A light flashed on *Étoile*'s controls as, once again, Admiral Cheng-Visitor requested face-to-face communication. *What the hell,* Jenna thought. *One last chance to spit in the eye of authority before the end.* She accepted the request.

She could hear them now—not just through the ship's sensors, but with her own ears. The sizzle of a torch filled the tiny control room. Jenna pushed herself from the chair and pressed herself against the wall behind it. She had only moments left. Her cybernetics signalled the full charge of her energy projector. Jenna lifted her hand towards her own neck.

The screen flickered to life, but instead of Admiral Cheng-Visitor, it was a pre-recording of a familiar man with thin, greying hair. It was not addressed to Jenna, but to the admiral herself. "Gabrielle," Sienar began. "I need your help to save one of my friends ..."

Jenna gasped as the marines broke through.

223

10

"We have tissue nanites knitting you back up, but the materials to print off more are in short supply. We don't have Jenna's magical touch, so you need to take it easy." Sienar looked, to Cherny, much like he had when he'd last seen him, after the Martian Insurrection. There was a little less brown and a little more grey throughout his hair, but his eyes were as sharp as ever. He was dressed in a tan synth-leather vest over a white short-sleeved shirt that revealed his telltale metal left arm. "It was touch-and-go in the tunnels. I worried you weren't going to make it."

Cherny looked up at the overhead lights. Exposed wiring ran from the fixtures along the ceiling to the wall. "What …" His mouth was dry. "What happened?" Cherny found himself gasping for air with each word. *Jenna. Sienar had mentioned Jenna.* Cherny struggled to hide the guilt on his face.

PALE GREY DOT

"Hah, now that is a question with a lot of different answers," Sienar replied with a grin. "Do you mean what happened after you passed out? What happened to the venerable ESS during your exile? What happened during the Ganymede Blitz?" Sienar sat down on a wheeled stool and pushed himself over to the medical bed. Leaning forward, he added in a softer voice, "I assume you were told about the blitz? Or at least, one account of it?"

Cherny didn't answer. A second man stood at the far wall console, tall and thin with dark, cropped hair and a stubbled chin. Both his legs were thick metal starting just above the knee, and when he turned towards them, Cherny could hear the soft sound of machinery grinding against itself. The man gave him a look of fear loaded with suspicion.

Cherny focused his attention back on Sienar. He wanted to give him a hug. After being separated for so long, it was almost like being home again. A flood of memories—old missions, celebrations, victories, and even defeats—came rushing back to him. Together, Cherny knew there was nothing they couldn't do.

A sudden surge of pain in his head caused Cherny to raise his flesh hand to his forehead. "The Pull," Cherny whispered. "It'll make me betray you." He gritted his teeth from the pain. "Like I ..."

Sienar met Cherny's eyes. His confident smile had been replaced with a look of deep concern. His voice became firm, as if he were giving out orders. "Cherny. Listen to me very carefully. I know you think you need to bring me in, arrest me, kill me, or whatever She told you to do, but you're in no condition to do it right now. You nearly died. Tell me, what would She want you to do in this situation?"

Feeling his face turning red from exertion, Cherny tried to focus. "Gather intel. Keep you talking. Find out information to use against you later."

"Convenient," Sienar replied, "because I'm in the mood for talking. We'll chat now and you can betray me later."

The man with the cybernetic legs winced.

Cherny almost laughed despite the pain. "You're the one who told me it's impossible to cheat the Pull."

"No," Sienar said slowly, "I said that *you* couldn't cheat the Pull. *I* can do whatever I want." He flashed that smile of his.

"They tried to reactivate your loyalty chip."

"Mmm, I bet they did." Sienar spread his arms, gesturing to his ramshackle base of operations. "These tunnels are deep enough that no external signal can reach me here. Since the Ganymede Blitz, I've travelled in lined containers with heavy scramblers. She can flick the switch as much as She likes—I won't be able to hear it. Hell, I haven't been outside in two years."

Cherny shook his head in amazement. An attempt to connect to SecLink resulted in only dead air.

The man with the robotic legs stepped towards them. His right knee joint caught for just a moment with each step he took, making him limp. "Sienar, it isn't a good idea, telling him all this," he said softly. "He's too dangerous."

Sienar turned grim. "I'm aware, but if we can help him,

PALE GREY DOT

we should. I owe him that much." His voice was stern as he looked back to Cherny. "You need to stop thinking of the Pull and the Earth Security Service as being omnipotent, because they aren't. It's technology. Technology and people. Both of those things are and always will be fallible."

"I don't think it's quite that simple," Cherny said.

Sienar sighed. "It really is, but I don't know how to convince you." He glanced over at the medical scanner hovering over Cherny, checking on the progress of the nanites.

Cherny nodded towards the unknown man. "Who's your friend?"

He answered for himself. "My name is Kyle. I'm Sienar's husband."

Cherny's mouth fell open. "You're married?"

Sienar took Kyle's hand in his and smiled up at him before returning his attention to Cherny. "I'm curious, what do you think of Her, given all that's happened in the past half-century?"

Cherny was silent for a moment as he collected his thoughts. "I owe Her everything. We all do. We'd have grown up like anyone else and been assigned some crap governmental jobs if it weren't for Her. When I found out that the six of us were being moulded to join ESS, it was the proudest day of my life. She raised us from the state system and made us who we are. There is no higher calling than the service." *And no other way to escape a life of dull desperation.*

"That doesn't answer my question. You were our prime analyst. What do you think of Her?"

227

Don Miasek

Thinking about it made Cherny's head hurt. Questioning Her didn't feel right. "She's, uh, smart. Brilliant, really. How She manages the billions of technological and personnel assets under Her is something I'll never know. She genuinely cares about us. About Her people. Loves us."

Kyle shook his head in disappointment. "It's like you said, Sienar. He's brainwashed. Reuben isn't going to go for this." He sounded ready to give up and released Sienar's hand.

"I was promised a chance to get through to him, and I aim to make the most of it." Sienar's expression remained neutral as he kept his focus on Cherny. "And Her motivations? What does She want?"

Cherny felt sweat beading on his forehead at the mention of Alexander Reuben, the leader of the Syndicate. *So Sienar truly did defect.* "I'm not a—" he coughed, which sent stabbing pain through his ribs. "I'm not going to help you fight Her."

"Fair enough. Let me answer for you, then," Sienar said, leaning back on his stool.

She wants to be loved, Cherny thought.

"She wants to be feared," Sienar said. "And yet She is a terrified woman." At Cherny's expression, Sienar raised an eyebrow. "Oh, you don't believe me? Everything She does is for control and Her own safety."

"Says the man who betrayed us to Alexander Reuben and his fanatics," Cherny muttered. He strained, trying to push himself up off the cot.

Sienar ignored the accusation, helping his old friend to

PALE GREY DOT

his feet. "Careful. One foot at a time." Sienar slowly let go, smiling as Cherny kept his balance. "There you go."

"How many of our people did you kill in the Ganymede Blitz, Sienar?" Cherny couldn't hide the accusatory tone.

"One hundred and thirteen," he answered instantly. "Far less, I assure you, than would have died had I not taken action. Come on, I'd like to introduce you to someone, and you need some exercise. Let's kill two birds."

Kyle frowned and took an awkward step backwards. "You aren't going alone with him, are you?"

"I'll be fine, dear," Sienar assured him. At Kyle's doubtful look, he smiled. "Trust me."

You should listen to him, Cherny thought. *If I see an opening, I'll have no choice but to take it.* Cherny gingerly stepped after Sienar as he gathered a silvery satchel and slung it over his shoulder. Though there were a few more wrinkles on his face, Sienar's eyes still blazed with the passion of a man supremely confident in his own righteousness. Kneeling in front of a metal chest bolted to the floor, Sienar pulled out a thick, brown, synth-leather jacket and tossed it Cherny's way. "You'll need one of these. I didn't have a chance to get the bloodstains out of your old one."

Catching the jacket, Cherny winced as he manoeuvred each arm through the sleeves. It was only his flesh that ached, though. His cybernetics were repaired, though he noted his combat systems were still disabled. Sienar was right—he wouldn't stand a chance against him. That made the choice to talk rather than fight that much easier. As he

Don Miasek

forced the jacket over his shoulders, Cherny saw Kyle staring nervously at him. He wanted to tell him that it would be all right—that he would never hurt the first and best friend he'd ever had—but found he couldn't bring himself to lie.

As they set out, Cherny noted that the base had been built within an old vacuum train substation. There were plenty of abandoned vacuum train lines crisscrossing the planet, relics from Earth's initial colonization efforts on Mars. Cherny wondered if they were still in Olympus Mons.

There were others here too. They wore Martian garb, as tattered and worn as those he and Amanda had used to fit in with the locals. Cherny followed Sienar through the station's cafeteria, where a small crowd was finishing the lunch shift. The metal tables looked like they were original to the derelict train station. His attackers in Caledonia had top-of-the-line equipment, but these people were barely surviving. Cherny caught the glances cast their way and recognized the unmistakable respect directed at the man he was following. Cherny knew the feeling—it was hard not to be taken in by Sienar's brand of kind leadership.

When they looked at Cherny, though, their eyes burned with hatred. *They know who I am. They look at me and see every ESS operative who's ever fought against them and their loved ones.* Cherny had no doubt that they would kill him in an instant if they got the chance. *Sienar's protection is the only thing keeping me alive.*

As they walked, Sienar spoke in a calm, conversational tone. "You'll be interested to know that your new partner

PALE GREY DOT

took down that cyborg. There's a terrific broadcast on the Net showing bits and pieces of it. Far as I can tell, the video hasn't been doctored, though they really did a number twisting the story around to make it seem like it was a valiant ESS operative stopping a Syndicate attack."

"Amanda's Her new favourite," Cherny said. He found himself breathing heavily, hobbling as he tried to keep up. Sienar didn't slow, though. It was his way of encouraging him to try harder, no doubt.

"Yes, I noticed," Sienar said.

"You know what that means," Cherny pressed.

"The next iteration of loyalty programming. More than just a chip urging us to further Her goals. A direct connection between Amanda and Her. Believe me when I say you're better off not being Her focus. Amanda used to be normal. Or as normal as any of us ever got."

Cherny doubted if Sienar felt the same bitterness over those past five decades as he did. Sienar hadn't been exiled like he and the others had been.

The station's old reception area had been reconfigured into a comm centre. Each computer and access point was a different model from its neighbour, as if each had been scrounged from different sources. Opposite many of the terminals sat people of varying cybernetic conversion. Up above, bundles of cables were stapled to the ceiling. The station's inhabitants could only communicate with the outside world via their own wired network, Cherny remembered. To his left, a formidable glass window dominated the length

Don Miasek

of the wall, overlooking the train platform and tunnel. A small barricade had been set up with bored guards and bolted-down drones serving as sentinels. The tunnel's curved walls stretched into the darkness in both directions. Cherny wondered if the line ran directly to where he'd fallen.

Sienar pushed open a door leading to a grated stairwell that ran deeper into the station. A single shimmering light provided illumination, and their shadows danced with each step they took. "Do you have any idea how much that cyborg cost?"

"Three million. Maybe four," Cherny guessed. "And yes, I've ... uh ... noticed the disconnect between her and the sad state of affairs here." He groaned with every step. *How big is this place?* If he had access to SecLink, he might have been able to match the layout with a location, but his local files were insufficient.

"Good. Maybe that'll make it easier for you to accept the truth," Sienar replied casually as he pulled the door open on the next level. The rooms in this hall were laid out like barracks, and some had signs of recent excavation and expansion. "You haven't asked me who I wanted you to meet yet," Sienar noted.

"I assumed it was another husband."

"Hah!" Sienar laughed. He stopped in front of a steel door with an electronic lock and looked back at him. "That's the Cherny I remember from the old days." He grinned. "Yeah, I never considered myself the marrying type either, but we met shortly after the blitz. Kyle was a physician with the Core

PALE GREY DOT

Miners Group before a collapse took his legs. He couldn't afford decent cybernetics, and so that was it for his job. Before Earth jacked up the automation ratios, he might have been able to keep working, but now? He bounced around awhile before winding up with the Syndicate. You can thank him for patching you up, by the way."

Sienar reached out towards the lock with his metal hand, but then stopped himself. "You know, one of my biggest regrets of being an operative is how much time I wasted trying to be an emotionless robot. We were always so focused on the mission. We never took enough time for simple human warmth." He nodded in Cherny's direction. "It's something you should consider."

"Uh-huh," Cherny replied. "So who is it, then?"

"Alexander Reuben."

Cherny coughed. He pressed a hand against his wound, but as far as he could tell, the tissue reconstruction was holding just fine. "Reuben is *here*?"

Sienar answered by tapping the door. The lock flashed green before the door swung open. "After you."

The first thing Cherny noticed as he passed the threshold into the room was the chill. He instantly realized why Sienar had given him the jacket. Though the lights were kept low—rumour had it that Reuben's remaining eye was sensitive to light—Cherny was able to see his breath each time he exhaled. Only a single dull red bulb shone down on them from above. Cherny had to rely on his cybernetic vision to see clearly.

Don Miasek

The room itself was sparsely furnished. Reuben had no need for decorations; a smattering of consoles lined the walls, and a lone computerized desk containing his life-support system was bolted to the centre of the floor. Sitting behind it, the face of the Syndicate cut a grotesque image. Clear tubes, cycling red and black fluids between the desk and his body, swayed each time the man moved. ESS records marked him at six foot six, and his physical afflictions hadn't made him any less imposing. When he rose to his feet in a halting manner, he towered over both men. Reuben studied them with his organic left eye and robotic right, his bald head gleaming under the red light. He had no jaw—not anymore. Instead, a metal guard with thin slots serving as vents connected his face to his neck. Cherny was reminded of a knight's helm. Reuben's skin was pale, as if the blood had been drained from his body. His clothing was strategically cut along the upper half of his torso to expose the metal beneath.

"Cherny Fender," the man intoned, looking down at him. "One of the six that Sienar speaks so highly of." Whether by design or necessity, his booming voice failed to rise or fall in pitch as he spoke. There were no pauses for Reuben to draw breath, for he no longer needed to.

Cherny looked over his shoulder at Sienar, who was closing the door. *How much did you tell him?* he wondered. Looking back at the cyborg, he tried to keep his mind focused. There were many conflicting stories on how the man received his injuries, but the one thing they all agreed on was it had been

234

PALE GREY DOT

violent, painful, and only served to drive Reuben's anarchist passions further. *Show no fear,* he told himself. Standing this close to Reuben, he could feel the intense heat emanating from the machinery. That was likely why the room needed to be kept so cold.

Sienar stepped next to Cherny.

Reuben's optic telescoped as he focused on them. "You should thank your friend. He is responsible for your continued existence."

"Thank him?" Cherny said. "For what? Killing over a hundred loyal agents at Ganymede?"

"Your friend believes he can convince you to join us," Reuben continued, as if Cherny hadn't said anything. "But I believe you would sooner kill him."

Cherny wondered which of them would eventually win that wager. "Sienar betrayed everything he stood for to join your band of murderers and thieves."

Sienar's smile flickered.

"Murderers. Thieves." Reuben was perfectly still, as if the act of sitting back down would be as difficult as it was for him to stand. "Surely you are not so delusional to believe that is all the Syndicate stands for."

Sienar put his hand on Cherny's shoulder. "You know me better than that. I wouldn't have turned against Her unless I had a damn good reason."

"Ah. Yes. Her," Reuben said. "It is a cruel and vicious woman who enjoys pulling the strings of Her puppets, only to throw them away when they malfunction. You lay blame

Don Miasek

and assume the worst of a friend whose judgement you know to be sound based on flawed information. It is unjust of you. Tell me, Operative, what you were led to believe about the blitz."

Cherny recalled what She had told him. "It was the result of a major infiltration effort by the Earth Security Service. It aimed to gather all the Syndicate leaders and eliminate them in one fell swoop. But then Sienar turned on them and got everyone involved killed, letting the Syndicate leaders—including you—escape."

Sienar shifted his weight from one foot to the other and took his hand off Cherny's shoulder, saying nothing.

"Half truths. Half lies," Reuben declared. "It misses the crux of the equation. The Ganymede Blitz did not target all the Syndicate leaders. It targeted *half* the Syndicate leaders."

"So?" With his eyes adjusting to the darkness, Cherny could better make out more of Reuben's form. He was built like a tank, with rivets and hydraulic cylinders running along the outside of his mechanical limbs. Cherny wondered how easy it would be for the man to crush him with his bare metal hands.

Reuben didn't answer. Instead, Sienar stepped between them. Cherny felt him reach out wirelessly to him. "Read."

It was a file. A large one. Cherny took it and uncompressed its contents. There were videos, documents, cybernetic sensor data, news reports, and ESS intelligence reports on Syndicate activities over the past half-century. He skimmed their contents.

PALE GREY DOT

"You see it?" Sienar asked.

"Yeah, I see it," Cherny replied, closing the files. "Looks like Alexander Reuben's hold on the Syndicate is finally slipping. Now some new hotshots are coming along and proving more capable than him."

"Dammit, Cherny," Sienar hissed. "It took me ages to gather all this data. Really look at it! ESS has been allowing the rise of cell leaders that they believe they can influence. Permit the leak of a vulnerable ship here, allow a few tech shops to operate without interference there, maybe let slip details of the shipping lines of a United Fleet armada at Jupiter Station ..."

"Or maybe Reuben's rivals are smarter than him," Cherny shot back. "I know I wouldn't settle for living in a hovel like this place if there was a better option out there. Hell, maybe you should see if some of these guys are hiring."

Cherny couldn't remember the last time he'd seen Sienar look so disappointed, but he forced himself to hold firm.

"It is the Athena Protocols," Reuben declared. "They are preventing him from even considering that She would aid the enemy. My 'murderers and thieves,' as you so ineloquently stated, have been fractured, and all the shattered pieces are waging civil war."

"Looks to me like you aren't winning."

"No," Reuben conceded.

"This train station is all you have left, isn't it?" Cherny asked.

Reuben took an angry, lumbering step out from behind

his desk, wires dangling between him and his life support. His body made a horrible ratcheting sound as the gears strained against his bulk, but Sienar motioned for him to stop.

Cherny thought of the confusion following the Jupiter Station attack. "The Syndicate breaking apart? Fine, that I believe. But She'd never risk something like this."

"Desperate times result in desperate actions," Sienar replied. "ESS isn't as secure as it once was. It's like I said. She'll do anything to protect Herself."

"Do you know," Reuben said, "the line I had to walk to cater to the Syndicate's conflicting desires? Anarchists. Revolutionists. Murderers and thieves, as you say. I have been a member of the Syndicate for one hundred and ninety-seven years. Since humanity's spread across the solar system outstripped any government's ability to exert authority over it. 'Murderers and thieves.' An accurate statement, back then. Intergang warfare and violence soon followed. Such pettiness left me as you see me now. But the authorities did not lag for long. Survival requires evolution, and when I came to lead the Syndicate, I forged us into a force for change. The change was slow. The change was painful. So many conflicting ideas. So many conflicting goals. Easy prey for your master.

"I have earned my subjects' loyalty. You, on the other hand, were nurtured to produce compliance from childhood. But even that is not enough for Her. She seeks control over Her subjects through technology, conditioning,

PALE GREY DOT

and fear. Your Athena Protocols are an abomination to humankind."

"Do you have a way to stop it?" Cherny asked a little too quickly.

"I wonder," Reuben mused, "whether your question is motivated by eagerness to be free or fear of losing Her. No, little operative. I cannot undo Her programming. Another avenue She has bested me at. Three survivors of your original six, however, have succeeded where you have not."

Cherny looked at his brother. "What does he mean?"

Sienar took a step towards him. "My contacts have told me that Ezza still hasn't reconnected to SecLink. In fact, she expelled the operative who was attached to her and is already on Ganymede. She's heading for Uruk Sulcus-132."

"She's investigating the blitz? What's she going to find?"

"The truth, I hope," Sienar replied. "The base wasn't exactly in good condition when I left it. I did leave Ezza a message, though. I hope she gets it."

"Captain Ezza Jayens's resistance is commendable, but unsustainable," Reuben proclaimed. "She will fail. The wicked side effects of your master's loyalty programming. Sienar told us how your affiliates were driven mad. How your actions led to the Martian Insurrection bloodbath."

How Taylor went mad. Only him. "We weren't forced into the Athena Program. We volunteered," he protested.

"That," intoned Reuben, "fails to make it right."

Sienar glanced first at Reuben, and then at Cherny. "Gentlemen, if we could focus. Cherny, I lost track of Jenna after the insurrection's fallout. Her loyalty chip was reactivated shortly thereafter, but she didn't return. I have no idea how she's avoided the Pull, but somehow she has."

Cherny opened his mouth, but no words came out. *I know where she is. She's on a spaceship. Heading to Ganymede. She's looking for you. ESS knows.* As much as he wanted to, he couldn't speak the words.

"What is it?" Sienar was now giving him a critical eye.

Cherny closed his mouth.

"You alluded to another betrayal earlier." Sienar's expression was deadly serious. "It's been two years since the Ganymede Blitz, but you've only been reactivated recently. Something else has happened."

Cherny tried to keep a neutral face. Staring forward, he met Reuben's mismatched eyes. The cyborg did not respond.

"Jenna has killed again, hasn't she?" Sienar raised a hand to his forehead, closing his eyes. "Oh, I'm such an idiot. I've never been able to guess what She would do after the blitz, but now it's so obvious. Reactivate the others. Use them as bait against me and Jenna." He turned towards Reuben. "And it would have worked perfectly on Jenna as well."

Reuben said nothing but watched intently.

Sienar grasped Cherny by the shoulders and forced him to make eye contact. "I need you to concentrate."

"He does not have the strength of will to resist Her," Reuben stated.

"Alex, please," Sienar said sternly.

PALE GREY DOT

Reuben went silent.

"Where is Jenna?" Sienar asked softly, keeping a firm grip on his brother.

Cherny stared into his eyes. "I don't know what you're talking about." He had no idea if his lie sounded convincing—or if he even wanted it to. Cherny felt an ache in the back of his mind.

"Jenna, who was the last to join us in Kazan. She was so shy at first. Remember when she and Sal vanished for eight hours, and we all had to go searching? We found them hiding in the subbasement, giggling and trading dolls. Jenna, who was with us during those long, cold nights during the Siege of Valles Marineris." Sienar's voice rose. "Jenna, who suffered the most for our benefit on 94 Aurora. Jenna, who would do anything—anything, Cherny!—to protect her family. To protect us!"

Cherny gritted his teeth. He tried to wrench himself free from Sienar's grasp, but he didn't have the strength. "She needs to be recaptured, for her own good," he breathed. "ESS will take care of her."

"You know damn well that is a lie!" Sienar snapped. His fingers were beginning to hurt Cherny's shoulders. "As soon as She has Jenna back in Her hands, she'll be broken down and rebuilt into a puppet again. You know Jenna would rather die than let that happen."

"I …" Cherny felt like his head was going to split open from the pain.

"She's somewhere out there, Cherny." Sienar lowered his

voice to a whisper, pulling Cherny in close. "She's probably alone. She's probably scared. Help her."

Cherny forced the words out as fast as he could. "*Étoile. Ganymede.*" *Again!* His mind raced. *Again, you've betrayed. First Jenna and now Her.* He frantically wondered if this was what Taylor went through during the insurrection.

Sienar's eyes softened, and he brought Cherny into an embrace. "Thank you. I know that wasn't easy." Letting go, he turned towards Reuben. "Cross-reference *Étoile* and anything in the Jupiter locale. Sounds like a ship to me.

"Processing," Reuben intoned. It didn't take him long. "Acquired. Spaceship *Étoile*. Flight plan was confirmed with the Ministry of Transportation twenty days ago. Destination: Jupiter Station. Two course alterations logged since the Jupiter attack: the first to Europan Elevator One, and the second to rendezvous with UFS *Pravedni*. Military action against spaceship *Étoile* is scheduled upon deceleration."

Sienar rushed towards the console on Reuben's desk, connecting his metal left hand to its data port. "Alex, power up the base's transmitter and get Kyle in here to help Cherny. I need to get a message to Gabrielle."

"Ill-advised. The danger of interception and—"

"Please," Sienar insisted. "We need Jenna on our side. Message begins: Gabrielle, I need your help to save one of my friends ..."

Cherny's shoulders slumped as the Pull punished him for his disloyalty. He raised his hands to his head, trying to force the pain from his mind. Despite the agony, he tried to decide

PALE GREY DOT

if Cheng-Visitor stood a chance of getting Jenna to stand down. *Maybe Cheng-Visitor will turn her over to ESS anyway. Maybe Jenna will escape.* Cherny couldn't decide which he hoped for. He just knew this wouldn't be the last time he'd betray whichever side he chose.

Ezza dreamt of fifty-one years ago.

The grand unification between the Martian city states had come to a violent end. Governor Griffenham was dead, as were over a thousand others. The Tower had suddenly felt like a foreign place to her. At least here, down in the lower levels of the cellblock, she did not have to suffer the accusing eyes of former friends and colleagues. *They all know it's our fault,* Ezza had thought.

His cell was at the end of the row, separated from the others. Ezza stopped in front and looked in through the bars. The man was seated on the metal slab, on the far side. His head had been in his hands, but he looked up upon hearing her footsteps. His eyes were red. "Ezza," he breathed. He looked broken.

"Taylor," she had replied. Ezza could still remember their conversation word for word.

Taylor stood, but the cell didn't give him much room to pace. He had been a big man, but now looked thinner and frailer despite it only being a week. They had dressed in him in the threadbare, short-sleeved beige shirt that marked him

243

as a prisoner. They both knew they were not truly alone here. There could be no doubt that She would be listening in. It was Taylor who found the words to break the silence that had fallen over them. "How are you doing, little sister?"

Ezza gave a sad smile. Even now he was trying to cheer her up. "I've seen better days, big brother."

Taylor stepped up to the bars, squeezing his fingers through to clasp hers. "Jenna?"

Ezza shook her head. "She's gone. Skipped out last night."

"And Cherny?"

This was harder to answer. "I … He …"

"He didn't want to come," Taylor finished the words for her.

"Taylor …"

"It could be my last goddamn day in this system, and he wouldn't see me."

"Taylor."

Taylor pulled his hand back and clenched it into a fist. His face darkened into a scowl.

"Don't be mad at Cherny. This isn't easy for him," Ezza pleaded. "He's being exiled because of this."

"Oh, exile. That's rough," Taylor snarled. "He's not in here, is he? He's not here, waiting until they drag him out and stick a needle in his arm, is he? Exile!"

Cherny didn't start the infighting, Ezza had thought. Cherny also hadn't been the one to convince Sal that stopping the Martian Insurrection had to be done by any means necessary, regardless of how many perished. Cherny hadn't

PALE GREY DOT

been the one to decide that the last fail-safe of their mission parameters—killing the Martian leadership—permitted wiping out a city. Cherny hadn't been the one to turn against the rest of them. Ezza couldn't say any of that, though, so she said nothing.

Taylor finally stopped fuming. He scratched his cheek nervously. Two days' worth of stubble had grown in, though Ezza didn't know if they'd refused to give him a razor or if he simply hadn't seen the point of shaving anymore. The man took deep breaths, calming himself, as he looked back to Ezza. "What, ah, what's going to happen to you?"

"Same as Cherny—tossed out. I don't know what he'll do, but I'm going to talk with Admiral Tolj. See if he doesn't have something for me."

For the first time in a long while, Taylor gave an inkling of a genuine smile. "Then the family will live on."

"Sienar is staying, though. I think She still sees value in him. Wants to keep him around."

"At least Sienar had the decency to visit. Can't believe She isn't kicking him out too, though." Taylor shook his head. "But this isn't his fault."

Is it yours? Ezza had wondered. She'd always suspected Jenna hadn't known as much about her creation as she'd claimed. "They've turned off our Athena Protocols, and She's promised not to reactivate them so long as we stay out of ESS's business."

Taylor grunted. Neither thought the promise meant much. Silence again filled the cellblock. Again, it was Taylor

245

Don Miasek

who finally broke it. "Listen ... Ezza ... I want you to know I didn't mean for any of this to happen. It just ..." He rubbed the side of his head. "This Pull ... it should be simple. Do what She would want you to do. But what She wants isn't always easy to know. Sometimes what She wants and what I want is the same. Sometimes you can ..." Taylor looked pained just speaking of it. "Sometimes you don't know what She'd want. So you resist. You fight it. Then the pain begins. It gets hard to think straight. So you go back to doing what She wants. What you think She wants."

Ezza doubted even She wanted so many innocents dead on Mars.

"'Do what She wants.'" Taylor slumped down onto the metal slab once more. "What vague nonsense that is. How the hell do you live your life with goddamn rules overriding your every thought? One mistake and a thousand people are gone."

I had the same protocols installed, Ezza had thought, *but never felt any madness.* So long as she had focused on the mission, she had been fine.

"They're going to kill me," Taylor sighed.

Ezza nodded. There were tears on her cheeks.

"But the rest of you will live on," he repeated.

Ezza said nothing.

Taylor looked back up at her. "If you ever see Cherny or Jenna again, tell them I'm sorry." There was no more anger left in him.

"I will," she promised. She could hear her voice cracking.

PALE GREY DOT

"Thank you, little sister. I wish I could've apologized to Sal too."

Ezza's implants buzzed. It was time to go. "Goodbye, Taylor." The last memory she had of her brother was the image of a terrified man sitting against the wall of an otherwise empty cell.

The buzzing intensified, but it wasn't her signal to leave the cellblock. It was her internal chronometer, waking her from her dreams. She remembered where she really was—the cold and distant Ganymede Nexus with a twenty-hour journey ahead of her. It was time to go to Uruk Sulcus-132.

247

//SECLINK DIRECT CONNECTION TRANSMISSION #ZMFTAWX5//
//DATETIME STAMP: 2510-02-23 14:53:10//
//OPERATIVE AMANDA TO HEAD OF EARTH SECURITY SERVICE//

//I'm sorry … Cherny is gone.//

//I tried my best to keep him safe, but the ambushers forced him into a nearby warehouse. Although all attackers were dealt with, I couldn't find him. A thorough investigation of the warehouse revealed a blood trail—Cherny's—leading to the train tunnels beneath Olympus Mons.//

//The forensics team believes that Cherny collapsed before being carried. There was no evidence indicating the direction he travelled, and his beacon must have been disabled. I've dispatched drones throughout the tunnels but there are enough dead zones that tracking his current location might be impossible.//

//The combat cyborg has been identified as Dova Cyprus. My interrogation has revealed she's one of those who fled the Syndicate during their fracture. It appears she's affiliated with Cherny's contact, Lori Wallace, who has shifted allegiance to Ellaria's splinter group, and Ellaria apparently did not take kindly to Cherny's infiltration attempt. Note this means that Reuben's power base continues to erode.//

//On a more personal note, I'm finding the time lag between us disconcerting. Interplanetary SecLink transmissions aren't the same as having Your mind added to mine. Once I finish here, I want to return to You on Earth as soon as possible.//

//Please, let me know.//

//Amanda//

11

Ezza retched, leaning on the metal sink for support as she emptied her stomach into it. The bathroom stall was no bigger than those on *Starknight*, refusing to even give her enough room to take a step back. The rumble of the train's engine caused the water to splash as she ran it. Looking up at the mirror, she saw the colour had drained from her face, and beads of sweat dotted her forehead. Her hair was matted and clung to her skull. *Wham, wham, wham.*

They know something's wrong, Ezza decided. She looked over her shoulder at the door. The hall beyond it led to the train's front cabin where Gole, Adams, and Nirali would be. *They have to know by now. They're probably talking about me.* Digging her hand into the pocket of her pressure suit, Ezza drew out the bottle of Cerebrol. She fumbled with the lid before shoving four pills into her mouth.

Come on, she urged. *Do something!* Her cybernetics had

been warning her of a racing heart rate ever since she woke up, and she knew the drugs weren't helping like they once did.

Ezza reached for the old towel hanging on the rack and wiped the sweat from her face, trying to make herself presentable. *It won't be long now.*

She undid the latch and pushed the door open.

"And I say it's a hunk of junk," Nirali was saying as Ezza entered the front cabin. She had taken the assistant engineer's seat to the right of Adams, though the train essentially ran itself.

Adams grinned at the woman. "Actually, she's in a lot better shape than I thought she'd be."

"You must be joking," Nirali replied, aghast. "The hull looks like it was stripped."

Ezza recalled when they had first laid eyes on the train. The Ministry of Transportation had only seen fit to include the boxy locomotive section without any of the cars. The outer plating was missing in a half-dozen spots, and the exposed engine looked corroded around the edges.

"Commander Eday and I went over the transportation infrastructure last night after you and I talked," Adams told the reporter. "Fairchild's cut funding three times in the past decade to divert cash back to Earth. Tourism isn't enough to keep this place self-sufficient, Ms. Kashem."

Ezza's eyes shifted between them. *Adams and Nirali met last night. Then he spoke with Rachelle. All behind my back.*

"I already told you," Nirali replied with a smile, "call me Nirali."

PALE GREY DOT

"You got it, Ms. Kashem," Adams said. "This poor girl is probably pretty typical among her sisters. Not enough love and care put into her maintenance these days." He patted the console like it was a lost pet.

Ezza took a seat in the back row opposite Gole and looked through the front window. "It doesn't have to be pretty," she said. "It just has to get us there."

Gole nodded in agreement. "No points for style."

"We don't get points for suffocating to death when an air-lock seal fails either," Nirali said.

Gole snorted. "That's why I told you to always keep your helmet in arm's reach, Ms. Kashem. Ganymede is an inhospitable wasteland that no sane person would ever want to visit. Yet here we are. That suit and helmet are the only things you can rely on to keep you alive."

Nirali pulled the sleek white helmet off the dash and placed it on her lap as she looked through the window. The train was building up speed now. An endless wave of structural support posts, each poorly illuminated by the train's external lights, flew past them. "It's so grey ..." she said.

"What did you expect?" Ezza muttered, though it came out louder than she'd intended.

The reporter hesitated. "I'm not sure, to be honest."

"That view is all we get for a good long while," Gole said. His eyes then fell upon Ezza. "Captain, I'd like to check our equipment before we reach Uruk Sulcus-132."

Ezza caught the look and nodded. "I'll join you. Adams,

251

you and Nirali take the first watch." The support posts were a blur now.

At the other end of the hall was a backroom that served as a joint living space and cargo bay. Two alcoves, each with a bed bag, were set against the far wall. A small, busted RecSystem rested next to the computer terminal that would have normally shown the status of any attached cars. Unlike the cab, there were no windows.

"Captain, if you don't mind me asking, are you feeling all right?" Gole asked as he began sorting through the weapons brought over from *Starknight*.

"I feel fine," Ezza said, forcing a smile.

Gole glanced up from the crate to study her. "You don't look fine."

"I feel fine," she repeated.

"Is there a reason we brought Ms. Kashem along? Surely a few more marines would have been better suited to picking through the ruins of some remote outpost than a reporter who's barely stepped outside her home station." Gole shook his head. "Not to mention the security risk …"

"You're going to have to trust me on this one."

After a pause, Gole nodded. "Of course, ma'am. Is she with the United Fleet Outreach Program, then?"

Ezza had considered trying to make Nirali's presence official but decided it would have raised more questions than it'd be worth. "No," she admitted. "Why? What are you getting at?"

"I … Nothing, ma'am," Gole said, taken aback.

PALE GREY DOT

"Commander Eday told me she came on board along with Brylan Ncube during the Jupiter Station disaster."

I knew it! Ezza thought. *They've been conspiring. My mission is to get to Uruk Sulcus. No one can get in my way.* She took a step towards him. "What else has Rachelle been saying?"

The marine drew up to his full height. "To be perfectly honest, Captain, I'm concerned, and I'm not the only one."

"Listen, Ajay, Brylan Ncube is a dangerous man, and I threw him off my ship the first chance I got. As for you and Rachelle, just focus on the mission." *Wham, wham, wham.*

"And what *is* our mission?" He lowered his voice. "You still haven't told us what we're trying to accomplish here. I understand special ops. I've done the whole 'need to know' thing more times than I can count, but none of this feels right."

Ezza could feel her face becoming warm. *Remember the mask,* she reminded herself. "Very well. We're here because ESS may have played a role in the accident two years ago at Uruk Sulcus-132. If so, we're to find evidence of it."

Gole drew in a sharp breath at the mention of ESS. "I understand, ma'am. I'm sorry to have doubted you." Ezza wasn't sure if he looked convinced, but he asked no further questions.

The hours on board the train were dull. When on watch with Nirali, Ezza kept her eyes closed, as the continuous blur of support struts against the grey walls did nothing to help her relax. She checked her internal chronometer. Eight

253

hours since they set out. It would be another twelve at least until the tunnels became too ruined to continue. A part of her almost hoped they wouldn't make it. Either Sienar was a defector or Jenna was wrong and sent her here on a fruitless chase. Ezza wasn't sure which would be worse. That Brylan Ncube seemed aware Sienar may be here didn't help.

"Well, that's it," Nirali said. "We are officially out of range."

Ezza opened her eyes and found the reporter looking at her from the assistant engineer's chair. "Excuse me?"

"From connecting to the Ganymede branch of JupiterNet. We passed its outer limits thirty seconds ago." Nirali dug a hand into the pocket of her pressure suit and pulled out a small device. "I imagine you'll be wanting this back."

Ezza took her transmitter from Nirali's outstretched hand. Snapping open her suit's left arm seal, she slipped the device back into place.

"You know, my brother was addicted."

"I didn't know you had a brother." *Or I must have forgotten*, Ezza thought. It didn't seem important when she ran Nirali's background check.

"You never asked."

"And addicted—what? What are you going on about, Nirali?" Ezza sat up straight.

"Eighteen years ago, Lohit was on a serious VR trip. Twenty hours a day at minimum. Sometimes days at a time. Just …"—Nirali gestured with her hands as she wrestled with the words—"stuck. The station had plenty of VR cafés. JupiterNet is small and not so great for VR, I'm told, but

PALE GREY DOT

he was in deep. I was just a kid then, but I'd have to track him down whenever he went missing, and I'd inevitably find him in some dark corner, curled up with a hardline between him and the system. Each time he was a little thinner, a little frailer than before.

"I did everything I could to keep him out, but he'd always slip back in. If he couldn't get a hardline, he'd go in via the wireless. One time, I convinced him to give me his transmitter. You know, to stop the easy temptation, but it didn't last."

"I'm sorry to hear that," Ezza replied softly. "What happened to him?"

"One day, he boarded a spaceship heading to Earth, and I never saw him again," Nirali said. "Better infrastructure there, I guess. Billions instead of thousands of people to connect with. I've tried making queries to find his location but never had any leads. I wouldn't know where to start looking."

Ezza didn't reply. Instead, she looked out at the grey tunnels before them.

"Do you have any family?" Nirali asked.

Ezza nodded. "Of course. My crew. My old team."

"I meant growing up," Nirali said.

"Like I said, my old team," Ezza replied. Her voice was growing raspy again. "I was an unlicensed asteroid drop-off baby. Met the others when I transferred to Earth at eight." Ezza hoped Jenna, Cherny, and Sienar were all right. She wondered if they were as lost and scared as she was feeling right now.

The pair sat in silence, hearing only the soft rumble of the train's engine before Nirali spoke again.

255

Don Miasek

"Did they do something to you? ESS, I mean."

Ezza stared back at her.

"You seemed so in charge on Jupiter Station, until suddenly ..." Nirali snapped her fingers. "And then that jerk Brylan showed up."

Ezza considered saying nothing but eventually spoke. "We volunteered. The Earth Security Service isn't just a job. It's a way of life. When you're tasked with protecting an entire solar system, it's understood that sacrifices have to be made, and that your own personal liberty might be one of them." Her head had started to hurt again, but she resisted the urge to slip into the bathroom for a few more Cerebrol.

"I think I'd go crazy if I were forced to think a certain way," Nirali said.

Ezza had no answer for that.

"If you don't mind me asking, what's it like?"

Ezza felt a jolt of pain in her head. The ache ran down her neck and into her arms. *Remember the mask. Don't succumb like Taylor and Sal.* "It's not ... It isn't like a direct ..." Ezza shook her head. "Sometimes I think that I could fix it. Maybe I could influence ESS back into shape or ... I already have ideas, Nirali. It's so clear in my mind. Plans on how to restructure, initiatives to weed out anyone in it for their own personal gain, ways to actually work with the United Fleet instead of against it. Then the idea of going back suddenly doesn't seem so bad. I mean, She can be reasoned with, and we were always Her favourites."

PALE GREY DOT

Nirali frowned in confusion. "'She'?"

"But I can't tell if that's me doing the thinking or this … Pull," Ezza continued. "I think I just have to keep reminding myself of all the horrible things ESS has done."

"Ahhh," Nirali nodded as if a great revelation had dawned on her. "Albert Chan-Reynolds."

"Who?" It was irritating, the way Nirali could push her around sometimes.

"I did some research, and that's the name of the man Brylan Ncube shot on Jupiter Station."

Ezza noted the hyphenated name. "He was married?"

"For ten years—a pretty darn good run. Even had a kid. Wife and daughter managed to get off the station, at least."

Ezza stared back out into the Ganymede tunnels. Killing in the line of duty was one thing, but Chan-Reynolds had just been an innocent guard doing his job. "Thank you," she said.

"What about you, Captain? Any marriages in your past?"

"Has this suddenly become an interview, Nirali?" Ezza asked wearily.

Nirali laughed. "No, I promised I wouldn't record you, and I'm standing by that. Just idle curiosity." She glanced towards the door to the backroom where Gole and Adams would just be waking up before leaning in close to whisper, "But there's an awful lot of people that walk around the barracks in their skivvies. Think of the shenanigans you could get up to …"

Ezza couldn't help but smile. "Against many United Fleet

257

Don Miasek

regulations, and I assure you, *Starknight* is about as unsexy an atmosphere as it gets."

Nirali tsked in disbelief. "If you say so."

"To answer your question, no. No marriages, no partners, no serious relationships."

Nirali scrunched up her face. "You say that like it's normal."

"It's like you said. I'm the weirdest United Fleet captain you've ever met." Besides, love for anyone that wasn't Her was frowned upon.

Before Nirali could fire back, the cab's back door swung open. "Reporting in for the next watch," Gole said, helmet tucked under his arm. Adams was right behind him.

Nirali grinned at the pair. "You're just in time. We were gossiping and swapping our worst ESS stories. The captain here didn't have anything interesting, but I told her about the time one of my IDEA colleagues got shoved into lock-up for two years. We used to have staff meetings to review which politicians we could criticize and which we couldn't, and on which subjects."

"Don't even joke about that," Gole said, sitting at the engineer's station. "That sort of talk is a good way to suddenly vanish."

"We're about as far into the middle of nowhere as we could possibly be," Nirali pointed out. "It doesn't get any safer than this."

"It's a bad habit to get into," Gole replied.

"What about you, Lieutenant? You mentioned some

PALE GREY DOT

troubles in the past," Nirali said, twisting in her seat towards Adams.

"Ah, no. Nothing to add," he said nervously. "Sorry."

"Gole is right," Ezza said. "It's not a good idea to get used to mocking ESS." Out of the corner of her eye, she saw Gole and Adams shooting each other a look.

The next four hours were spent preparing to infiltrate the outpost. Gole made Nirali seal, unseal, and run through the basic functions of her suit a dozen times until he was satisfied that she got it. After a brief discussion, they gave her a stunner pistol instead of a real firearm. Nirali looked relieved. Adams reviewed the known layout of the base with the team, and Ezza explained the various security features they'd likely encounter. No one asked how she knew.

Finally, the locomotive creaked and groaned to a halt as the tunnels became too rough to continue. In the backroom, they performed final checks of their suits in grim silence. Ezza slipped her helmet over her head and felt it seal at the neck. The train's airlock cycled, and she took her turn stepping through. Everything went quiet except for the hum of her pressure suit and the sound of her own breathing.

As Adams activated the comm system, Ezza set a watch protocol to monitor their transmissions. She wanted to know if they were talking amongst themselves.

After helping Nirali down from the train's steps, Ezza walked over to where the tunnel's ceiling had collapsed. Jagged blocks of ice and rock barred the way.

Once they squeezed through the cracks in the icy

Don Miasek

barricade, they settled in for the ten-hour hike. Gole took point while Adams kept watch with his pressure suit's scanners. Nirali, for her part, contributed by talking nonstop.

"So you never got around to telling me about how you joined the United Fleet, Lieutenant," she said over the comms. Her footsteps became less cautious as her confidence manoeuvring in the low gravity grew.

"There's really not a lot to tell, Ms. Kashem," Adams replied. "Military service was my best chance to get off Mars. Exploring the solar system versus living in a hole."

"So has it been everything you thought it would be?"

Through the two-way faceguard on his helmet, Adams grinned. "Well, my commanding officer is about three metres away from me, so I'm going to say yes—working for the United Fleet is the greatest job in the history of humankind, and you should immediately head to your nearest recruiting station to see if you qualify."

Everyone laughed except for Ezza. Her mind kept returning to the chaos plaguing the solar system, the war between the United Fleet and the Syndicate, the threats facing her old team, and the constant nagging in her brain. Her head pounded while Nirali chatted about her life on Jupiter Station, about the latest premier elections, about her theories on secret multi-planetary corporation ownership, and about seemingly anything else that crossed her mind. She didn't bring up the topic of ESS again.

Two hours in, the group emerged into a clearing where the tunnel's ceiling had collapsed entirely, leaving

PALE GREY DOT

nothing between them and a view of the heavens above. Nirali stopped, and the others followed suit. The infinite points of starlight reminded Ezza that they were just four specks of chemicals on a ball of ice, hurtling around a ball of gas, hurtling around an even larger ball of gas. Just one out of a hundred billion spheres rolling through the cosmos. It all suddenly seemed so petty.

"Do you think ..." Adams said as he took it all in. "Do you think they're doing all right out there? Alpha Centauri and Epsilon Eridani?"

"Sure," Nirali replied. "Their latest transmissions say they are."

"I bet it's different on the colonies," Adams said with a sigh. "I bet they don't have someone looking over their shoulder, watching every move they make."

Maybe, Ezza thought, *but it's just as likely that as soon as the infrastructure made it possible, someone would set up their own version of ESS.* Again, Ezza wondered if anyone was watching them right now. She couldn't shake the idea that the only way they'd have gotten so close to Uruk Sulcus-132 was if ESS had let them. "I think," Ezza replied, changing the subject, "that we should keep moving. Another hour and we're there."

Where are they? Ezza silently asked as they trudged back into the dark tunnels. There was no way that her warship docked at the Nexus would go unnoticed. Ezza thought of Rachelle, back on *Starknight*. If she had been the source of Brylan's information, then ESS would have already known

261

Don Miasek ·

her plans to reach Uruk Sulcus long before they arrived. If not Rachelle, then Ezza could think of a dozen other ways—technological or human—that She could have found out.

Ezza wondered whether there was anything left at Uruk Sulcus-132. Maybe that's why ESS had done nothing to stop them so far. Jenna was clever but not infallible. She could be wrong. *Jenna wants me here to investigate,* she thought. *No, surely ESS would want me to ensure there was nothing here that could implicate them.* Ezza focused on the latter idea. The more she rationalized their presence as fulfilling Her wishes, the more the Pull faded into a dull ache in the back of her head.

"One hundred metres."

Gole's sudden interruption nearly made Ezza trip, but she recovered at the last second. Her suit beeped, warning her again of an increased heart rate, but she ignored it. Her helmet's HUD showed pockets of heat up ahead where the tunnel expanded into a full train station. Even from here, she could see the gaping hole in the outer airlock doors.

As they made their approach, Gole took point again. "This doesn't mesh. The accident was a breach on the upper level, but this door looks like it's been blown outward. Decompression happened as a result of this breach, not before it."

Adams stepped up to the entrance, pressing his gloved finger against the blackened seals. "Evaporator torch, if I had to guess."

The inner airlock was in no better condition, leaving

the corridors exposed to the vacuum. With each step, Ezza could feel small shards of debris crunching beneath her feet. She activated the night-vision HUD overlay as she stepped over the threshold. Turning back to her comrades, she saw Adams helping Nirali up through the doorway.

"The accident's follow-up should have included returning airtight stability to the base," Adams said. "But it doesn't look like that—or frankly anything—was done."

Ezza's hopes fell. *Jenna must have been wrong—there's no way Sienar is here.* "Let's head to the comm centre. Maybe there's something left in the network."

Though the halls were dark, their suits' HUDs made everything clear. There were burn marks and shattered walls. Several doors had been broken through, and more than a few network terminals had been destroyed.

Despite the destruction, Ezza saw that the base was remarkably uncluttered. The monitoring station had supposedly been home to a hundred people. There should have been personal effects, pictures, creature comforts, or other signs that people once lived here. Maybe it was stripped clean by the accident investigators—or maybe that had never been the purpose of Uruk Sulcus-132. *There has to be something here,* she thought. *Evidence of where Sienar is or what he's doing. Dammit, Jenna. This had better not have been for nothing.*

They passed by the station quarters, past the recreation rooms, past the scanner suites, and past the observatory. All showed signs of violence.

Don Miasek

As they descended the stairs leading into the heart of the station, Ezza stumbled.

"Captain, are you all right?" Gole reached out and held her shoulder, helping her regain her balance.

"I'm fine," she mumbled. She hoped the others couldn't see the sweat pouring down her face through her faceguard. Being here felt like a betrayal. *Why would you seek to hurt someone who's done so much for you? Doesn't She deserve better?* "It's just … I'm fine. Keep moving, Gole."

They soon reached the comm centre. The door had long since been blown open. The room held a dozen holographic monitors and data ports filling the far wall, interrupted only by a supply closet to the side. It was a cramped space for four people wearing pressure suits. Of all the rooms they'd explored, this was the first to have no signs of disruption.

Adams knelt in front of one of the wired stations, pulling out a cord and plugging it into one of the ports on his suit's arm. After a moment of silence, he shook his head. "I'm not getting anywhere. I can't get past the login module. United Fleet credentials should be sufficient, but …" Even through the two-way faceguard, Ezza could see the frustration on his face.

"Adams," she said, "stand aside." Reaching out with her cybernetics, Ezza accessed the login protocols. Three user IDs flared up in her mind: *Cherny Fender, Jenna Doe, Ezza Jayens.* The first, she saw, had already been accessed.

ESS must have Cherny's credentials. Does that mean he succumbed to the Pull? Ezza prayed some other explanation hid within the computer banks as she selected her own name.

PALE GREY DOT

An image of a man shimmered into existence before them. All four instinctively took a step back. Gole gripped his gun tighter, ready to react at a moment's notice. The hologram was rough, as if hastily recorded on substandard equipment.

"Ezza," Sienar began. "I don't know when you've activated this, but know that I'll be happy you're on ESS's trail. Assuming I'm still alive, that is." Sienar wore a mismatched set of combat armour, and Ezza could barely make out the sound of gunfire deep in the background of the recording.

"Who ...?" Nirali started, but Ezza waved at her to shut up.

"In two minutes, I'm going to go against a hundred and fifty years of ESS training and stop their attack on the Syndicate leadership," Sienar continued. "A lot of good people are going to die as a result of this, and it's important you understand why. In recent years, I've come to suspect that She's been working to influence the Syndicate and overthrow Alexander Reuben. Not to destroy it, but to keep it controllable. From there, She can ensure ESS's—and more importantly, *Her*—indefinite survival. I've included the files on what I've found so far. It's circumstantial, I'll admit, but I'm working on finding out more."

Sienar clasped his hands behind his back, staring straight ahead as he spoke. "I used to think we were the good guys, even if our methods were occasionally heavy-handed. Hell, even She might have once been motivated by benevolence, though somehow, I doubt that. But this ... this vindictive, self-serving plan is unacceptable." Sienar waved his hand.

265

"Forgive the rambling—my plan to stop this takeover of the Syndicate has been rather rushed."

A rumbling sound came across, and Sienar paused long enough to attend to one of the monitors before addressing the camera again. "Once the ESS attack has been stopped, I'm going to see about departing with Alexander Reuben."

Through the comms, Ezza heard Gole draw in a sharp breath.

"I honestly don't know where I'll be by the time you get this, but once I find out you're back in the game, you can bet I'll be on the lookout for you. Below, you'll find a list of Syndicate-secure codes on the Net that I'll monitor in case you need to reach me." Sienar smiled, but Ezza thought she could see uncertainty in his eyes. "I'd rather not say farewell, so ... see you soon." Sienar gave one final nod before vanishing, casting the room into darkness once more.

Adams was the first to break the silence that followed. "Then it's true. Nirali was right—you're ESS," he said. To Ezza, it sounded like an accusation.

Ezza whirled around, glaring at the reporter. The pain in her head had returned with a vengeance. *Turn this data over to ESS!* her thoughts screamed. "You told them! What else have you been saying?" She took a step towards Nirali. Instinctively, she diverted power towards her cybernetic arm.

The reporter backed up, bumping against one of walls. She raised her hands defensively. Even through the helmet's faceguard, Ezza saw Nirali's eyes go wide. "What? I ..." She looked past her towards the others.

PALE GREY DOT

"Captain!"

Ezza felt a hand on her shoulder. "Back off, Gole. This is between me and Nirali."

Instead, the commander pulled her around, and Ezza found herself face to face with the man.

"You have to stop this," Gole said. Though his tone was soft, his grip was tight. "Let's head back to the Nexus. We can download the server contents and analyze them on *Starknight.*"

Ezza took deep breaths, sucking in as much air as she could. *Remember the mask. Focus on the mission.* She tried to convince herself that Nirali had only been doing what she thought was best, but her treachery seemed unforgivable. *It's your fault,* she thought, *for trusting her in the first place.*

"We can get you help," Gole continued.

Ezza tried to pull away, but he held on. Suddenly, her subdermal implants buzzed with an incoming alert. "I just felt something." She reached over her shoulder for the rifle pinned to the backside of her suit. "A signal, not far from here."

"Captain ..." Gole said.

"Wait, Commander. I detect it too," Adams said. He was at Nirali's side, supporting the frightened journalist.

Ezza's helmet buzzed as a transmission filled her ears.

"Captain Jayens," the voice said. "This is Operative Bev Stroud. You don't know me, but I need you to know that She would like you to stand down."

Ezza yanked herself free, but she doubled over before she

267

could reach the doorway as a wave of nausea hit her. She fell to her knees, dry-heaving into her helmet. Her rifle hit the deck beside her. She heard Gole and Adams shouting, but they sounded distant, and she couldn't make out their words. On her HUD, she saw their rifles unlock. *Focus on the mission,* she urged herself.

Operative. Bev said she was an operative. She'd want you to help your fellow operative. Ezza shook her head. *Against! Fight against your fellow—no!—against the enemy! She's your enemy!*

WHAM, WHAM, WHAM!

Ezza felt herself starting to hyperventilate. Even if she could reach her pills, she had no way to take them with her helmet on.

The sound of gunfire, simulated by her helmet, rang through her ears, but Ezza found she couldn't stand.

"Drone!" Gole shouted. Ezza caught a flash of his shadow before his icon flickered bright red on her HUD. Adams's swiftly met the same fate. Through the dizziness, Ezza struggled to reach for her fallen rifle.

Just as her fingers brushed against it, a silver boot entered her view, casually kicking the weapon aside. Ezza looked up at a figure clad in combat armour, wielding a small pistol. Her HUD's thermal imager showed that the weapon had been recently fired. The suit was pristine, designed for long-term exposure. Behind her, crawling along the wall, were two pairs of combat drones. Their silver legs telescoped in and out as they skittered down to the floor, stopping just

PALE GREY DOT

behind the woman. Their movements were graceful, carefully calculated to maximize efficiency. Each drone had a small energy projector at its tip which darted back and forth, looking for any signs of movement.

The figure stared down at Ezza, though the blank faceguard hid what lay behind.

"Ezza Jayens," Bev said. "Thank you for decrypting another one of Sienar's messages for us. It was more useful than I thought it'd be." She aimed the pistol downwards towards Ezza's face. Her drones followed suit with their energy projectors. "Now then, I need you to ask yourself something: what would She want you to do in this position, hmm?"

Ezza stared up at the barrel. *Lie!* she told herself. *Surrender now and fight later!* Ezza found herself shivering uncontrollably as she lowered her head. *WHAM, WHAM, WHAM!*

"I surrender," she whispered into the comms. As soon as she said it, Ezza realized she meant it. A calm warmth passed through her body, and the pain in her head vanished. She could think clearly again.

"Good," Bev said, though she didn't lower the pistol. "If you could gather your last associate for me?"

Ezza pressed her hands against the floor, pushing herself back to her feet. She hadn't felt this steady in weeks. She saw the fallen forms of Adams and Gole. *Avenge them later. Or don't.* It didn't seem important anymore—Bev had done what was best for ESS, after all. "Nirali," Ezza called. Her tracker showed that the woman was barricaded in the

269

comm centre's supply room. Ezza stepped up to the door that separated them, leaving her rifle where it lay. "It's over, Nirali. Come on out."

Nirali didn't reply.

"A door isn't going to stop me. Save us both the trouble."

"Captain ... Ezza." Even over the comms, she sounded scared out of her mind.

Come on, Ezza silently urged. She found she no longer had a grudge against the reporter. The solar system felt right again. She was back with ESS. Back where she belonged. "I'm giving you five seconds. I promise we won't hurt you."

"Ezza, you don't want to do this," she pleaded. "Please, we can still help Adams and Gole. We can work together to—"

Ezza sighed and mentally accessed the centre's locking mechanism. The door opened, revealing Nirali crouched in the corner beside a rack of tools, stunner pistol out.

"I'm warning you. I'll shoot!" Nirali backed as far against the wall as she could.

"Oh, Nirali," Ezza said with a smile. "It's almost sweet of you that you'd try to save me." She nodded towards the pistol. "But I remotely deactivated that thing thirty-five seconds ago." Ezza brought her cybernetic arm around and backhanded Nirali into unconsciousness.

//SECLINK TRANSMISSION//
//SOURCE: Overwatch Control//
//FROM: Overwatch Douglas//
//DESTINATION: SecLink High Priority Bulletin//
//TO: All//

Hi all,

Below are the steps for tonight's SecLink implementation, as covered by Activity Record AR81243532987399348. All times are locally adjusted.

Step 1 || Emergency Outage Broadcast || Overwatch Control || 7:30 p.m. to 8:00 p.m.

Step 2 || Shut Down SecLink || Overwatch Control || 8:00 p.m. to 8:05 p.m.

Step 3 || Apply Patch || Overwatch Control || 8:05 p.m. to 8:10 p.m.

Step 4 || Bring Up SecLink || Overwatch Control || 8:10 p.m. to 8:15 p.m.

Step 5 || Request and Verify All Individual Access Credentials || Overwatch Control and All Operatives || 8:15 p.m. to 8:30 p.m.

Step 6 || Post-Implementation Verification || All Operatives || 8:30 p.m. to 9:00 p.m.

Any operatives outside of communication range will be contacted individually to confirm their credentials. We know everyone is super busy lately, what with society collapsing, so thanks for bearing with us through all these security patches. While I think we all agree that SecLink is impregnable, it's better to be safe than sorry.

Overwatch Douglas

12

Jenna stared at the cell door, unblinking.

Though her cybernetics had been disabled, she knew it had been six hours and twelve minutes since Cheng-Visitor's marines tore her from her control room, smashed her against the cold, hard floor, shackled her arms and legs, and shoved her through *Étoile*'s halls to where the boarding collar had sliced through the primary hull. From there, it was a long trek through *Pravedni* to the cellblock, where they forced her into a chair and left her alone. The marines had been rough, but she didn't blame them. She'd have done the same.

Another minute passed. Six hours, thirteen minutes since she received the transmission that stopped her from mentally pulling the trigger. Jenna knew because she had counted each second.

It was cold in the cell. Cold and dark—only a thin sliver

PALE GREY DOT

of light shone through the gap between the door and floor. Jenna knew from experience that it was intentional. When the marines ripped off her control suit, they had only given her a pair of faded cloth pants and a short-sleeved shirt to wear, which provided no warmth. Nor had they given her anything to eat or drink. That, Jenna knew, was also intentional. Demean the subject. Make them uncomfortable. Let them linger in one place, all alone, with nothing but their thoughts and fears to erode their will. Jenna had no doubt they were watching for signs of weakness.

But she wouldn't let them have the satisfaction. She'd suffered worse with the gangs in the Midwestern Wastes. And during her time in ESS. And living as a fugitive for the past half-century. Compared to that, this was child's play.

Six hours, fourteen minutes now since she took the risk of being taken alive. The sight of Sienar had given her a glimmer of hope that she might escape this without being returned to mindless servitude. No wonder Cheng-Visitor had been so insistent that she accept the video request. A ripple of fear ran down her spine as she, not for the first time, considered whether it had been an elaborate trick.

Jenna heard footsteps. Within moments, the cell door swung open, and three individuals entered.

The first was Admiral Gabrielle Cheng-Visitor—Jenna recognized her immediately. She had a wide, powerful build, and the look she gave Jenna was impenetrable. If there was any hint of an ulterior motive stemming from

Don Miasek

her last-minute transmission during the takedown, it didn't show in her dark brown eyes.

The second person wore power armour and had light hair and a square jaw. Marine jock, Jenna decided. She had met plenty in her time. The soldiers who took her from *Étoile* wore helmets, so she couldn't tell if he was one of them. *That's a lot of firepower for a prisoner interrogation,* she thought. *Are they worried I'll break my chains and strangle each of them to death?*

The last had curly black hair and, unlike the others, did not wear United Fleet garb. Instead, he wore a fine grey suit. Jenna did not recognize him, but from the way he walked and the way he smiled, he looked confident and in control.

Cheng-Visitor stepped aside, letting him take the lead. A United Fleet flag officer deferring to a man in civilian clothes. That meant …

"Hello," the man said with a smile that did not look as warm as he probably thought it did. "I am Operative Brylan Ncube."

Operative. The word nearly made her shiver. He was one of Hers.

When she did not reply, he crouched down to get at eye level. "And you are the famous Jenna Doe. You, my dear, are still a legend. Your techniques are taught to new recruits." Brylan took a deep breath. "'Pragmatic ruthlessness.' That is what She calls it."

Jenna resisted the urge to shift in her chair. She was so close to being returned.

PALE GREY DOT

"You know, there are entire classes back home on what went wrong with you. One theory says that there was still too much of the old Midwestern Raiders left in you. A little bit of wilderness that didn't quite get beaten out by the educators. If She has any faults, it's that She's too kind. Perhaps Her love blinded Her to your instabilities.

"But personally, I like the simpler theory—that your protocols led you astray. Whatever madness overtook your colleagues Sal and Taylor wormed its way into your mind. But don't worry—it's fixable. Here is what is going to happen: in a few hours, we will board another ship heading back to Earth—to the Tower. You have malfunctioned, but we will help you."

Jenna thought back to when the Athena Protocols were first installed. She knew every detail of the procedure. The wires implanted in one's head, the biochemical modifications to one's brain, and the chip that kept everything humming along smoothly. She had designed it, after all.

"But before we leave, there are a few matters to discuss," Brylan continued. "First, Marcus Secor. The operative you ambushed and killed."

I want to kill you too—you seem like the asshole Marcus wasn't, Jenna decided. She met Brylan's eyes, trying to ward him off with willpower alone.

Instead, Brylan moved closer until his face was inches away from Jenna's. "Why assassinate poor Marcus, hmm?" he whispered. "I get that you're bitter about being tossed from ESS. Hell, who wouldn't be? But you got what you

275

Don Miasek

wanted. Fifty years ago, after you and your colleagues turned what should have been a quiet and bloodless operation into a massacre, you simply fled. You proved you could escape us indefinitely. So, Jenna, why come back? Why suddenly come out of hiding?"

Jenna glared at him. She could smell his breath when he spoke.

"Oh, come on now," Brylan exclaimed, standing back up. "You aren't just going to give me the silent treatment, are you? Your friend Cherny was a lot more receptive to the idea of returning to the fold. It certainly didn't take him long to turn you in."

Jenna's eyes widened, and Brylan caught it immediately.

"Seriously?" Brylan arched an eyebrow. "You can't be surprised. He was working some dead-end job pumping fuel. Of course he'd jump at the chance to be amongst the elite again."

He's lying, Jenna knew. *Cherny is family. This operative has simply fallen for Cherny's tricks.*

Cheng-Visitor gave a grunt. "Brylan, this dick-measuring contest isn't accomplishing anything. You'll have all the time in the world to interrogate the prisoner on your way back to Earth. You can do"—the admiral waved her hand—"whatever it is that ESS does with their runaways." She looked vaguely disgusted.

Jenna looked up at her, but again found no solace. She was her only hope.

Brylan turned to Cheng-Visitor, speaking to her as if

276

PALE GREY DOT

she were a child. "Admiral, this woman murdered an Earth Security Service operative right under the nose of the Tower just four weeks ago. She has been on the run for a very, very long time. The information she has on Syndicate activities may save lives. Your fleet is crumbling as it is."

"I am well aware of our tactical situation, thank you," Cheng-Visitor replied.

"You should be happy we even let you take part in this interrogation." His smile remained glued to his face. "Do we need to contact the Minister of Defence again and have him sort this out?"

"No ..." Cheng-Visitor said, backing down. She and the marine briefly glanced at one another.

Jenna wondered if she could have ever gotten away with talking to an admiral like that back in the old days. She knew from Marcus's memories that the balance of power between ESS and the United Fleet had shifted towards the latter, but this suggested something else entirely. Jenna thought back to what Noble had said to her on *Étoile*. *"It's a good thing we have the Earth Security Service to protect us."*

"Let me ask you something," Brylan said. The man's cheerful demeanour remained unfazed as he turned his attention back to Jenna. "How do you think we caught you? You had successfully evaded us for fifty impressive years. Then you contact your dear friend Cherny, and pop!" Brylan spread his arms. "Suddenly, you're in a cell with me."

A trickle of doubt entered Jenna's mind. Her cheap cloth outfit and the walls of the cell were starting to feel like they

Don Miasek

were closing in on her. She tried to move her arms, but the chains held tight. *Cherny would never break ... It's impossible.*

"So, I've gone ahead and given you some useful information, and I think it'd only be fair if you returned the favour," Brylan said. He reached over and tapped Jenna on the forehead with his knuckle; somehow, she managed not to recoil. "How have you evaded your Athena Protocols, hmm?"

Jenna would have spit in his face had her mouth not been so dry.

Brylan reached behind her, unlocking her left arm from the chair. With his cybernetically enhanced strength, he forced the arm up in front of her, inspecting the dirty ports and twisted circuitry that ran along it. The marines had removed every chip and peripheral she had. "This is in terrible shape," Brylan said. "It was a gift from Her and look how you've treated it." He let go of the arm as if he were discarding a broken toy.

Jenna wanted to hit him, but she knew it was a trap. Without functioning cybernetics, he'd overpower her in seconds.

"Is that it?" Brylan asked. "You hacked your implants until the loyalty chip couldn't affect you? Or did you slice it out entirely?" He ran his hand through her greasy black hair, feeling for any scars.

Jenna shuddered at his touch. Out of the corner of her eye, she could see Cheng-Visitor looking away.

"Why would you do such a thing? For someone who hates the Athena Protocols so much, why would you have

PALE GREY DOT

even designed them in the first place? They're a testament to your genius. To your dedication to ESS." Brylan drew his hand back, apparently not finding what he was looking for. "A cranial scan should show us what's going on in there," he muttered. He stood straight again and glanced briefly at Cheng-Visitor with a renewed smile. "I'm going to grab a few instruments from the med bay, Admiral. Please let me know if our wayward operative decides to break her silence."

Cheng-Visitor nodded grimly. The armoured marine stepped aside to let Brylan through.

Jenna listened until his footsteps faded into the hum of the ship's systems before letting go of a breath she hadn't realized she had been holding. After five seconds of silence had passed, she finally looked up at Cheng-Visitor and spoke for the first time since being shoved into the cell. "Ezza hasn't succumbed." Her voice sounded weary, even to her own ears. "If she had, he wouldn't need to know how I beat the protocols."

The admiral cleared her throat. "She's been out of communication range for three days now. I don't know if she has or hasn't. All this 'Athena' nonsense is new to me."

Jenna struggled to say the next words, and they came out as a whisper. "Did Cherny betray me?"

Cheng-Visitor shook her head. "Sienar mentioned working with someone by that name."

A wave of relief washed over Jenna. Cheng-Visitor had no reason to lie now. The transmission—the one that stopped her from ending it all in the *Étoile* control room—was real.

279

Don Miasek

"Sienar always told me it was important to have friends in high places." Jenna shook her head. "Wish I'd listened."

Cheng-Visitor looked to the marine. "O'Brien."

The man quickly stepped behind Jenna. "Hold still, please," he said. Within a moment, Jenna felt her shackles release.

Now standing, Jenna looked at the admiral. "Get me out of here," she pleaded. "Before he comes back."

Cheng-Visitor dug a hand into her uniform's pocket and drew out a small data jack that reminded Jenna of the memory drive she stole from Marcus just a few weeks ago. "Review this on the way."

Jenna took it in her hand and turned it over. It looked like a standard United Fleet drive. After a moment's hesitation, she gingerly inserted it into a slot in her arm and followed after Cheng-Visitor and O'Brien.

The instant the connection was made, an image appeared, visible only to her. The lean, tall form was instantly recognizable. *You're still alive,* Jenna thought with a wild grin.

"Gabrielle," the image of Sienar said. "I need your help to save one of my friends. She's enroute to Ganymede right now, on board a passenger liner named *Étoile.*"

As her brother spoke, Jenna hurried through *Pravedni*'s gunmetal-grey corridors, out of the cellblock. The floor was cold against her bare feet, and her lack of sleep was starting to catch up with her, so she struggled to keep up. O'Brien held her left arm the whole way, though she could not tell if it was to protect her, or to contain her.

PALE GREY DOT

"ESS already knows she's on board," Sienar continued. His tone was deadly serious. "I'm currently working under the theory that ESS leaked the information that led to the fleet's destruction at Jupiter Station. I don't have proof yet, but Cherny and I hope to find it soon.

"You have to ensure that Jenna makes it out of there and finds Ezza. If you need to convince her to surrender, send this transmission to her ... I ..." Sienar hesitated. Jenna had never seen him at a loss for words before. It was impossible, but she could have sworn Sienar was looking directly into her eyes. "Jenna, I'm sorry for everything that happened. Sal and Taylor were my responsibility. None of this is your fault." Sienar looked away. "I'm attaching my digital credentials to this transmission. Please, Gabrielle. You have to help her."

Jenna reached out towards him, but he vanished before her eyes. Her family was still out there, looking for her. Sienar said none of this was her fault. *Why would he say that? I already knew that.*

Sienar also said that ESS was responsible for the disaster at Jupiter Station. The United Fleet Admiralty and Her were often at each other's throats, but an outright attack against the fleet was unheard of. Still, Jenna had no problem believing it. *Should have figured that out on my own,* she chided herself.

"I need access to a transmitter," she said out loud. "I need to send something back to him."

The admiral halted, turning to face Jenna. "Not a chance. The operative won't be gone long. Listen to me, Jenna—Sienar took one hell of a risk by reaching out to me to begin with."

Don Miasek

"It's vital he gets this," Jenna insisted. "Go through my belongings. You'll find a drive with technical specifications. Get its contents back to him." Wrenching her arm free of O'Brien's grip, she reached out towards the admiral. "I'm giving you my codes to access it. I'm trusting you." The words did not come easily.

Cheng-Visitor slowly took her hand, accepting the codes. "I'll see what I can do, but for now, you and a squadron of my marines are getting off my ship. You're going to Uruk Sulcus. You are going to find Captain Jayens and her team."

"All right," Jenna said, unable to keep the surprise out of her voice. "What then?"

Cheng-Visitor resumed leading them through *Pravedni*. "If Sienar is right about your old agency being responsible for the destruction of twenty-seven ships and bringing the solar system to the brink of chaos, then it's going to turn into a war. And frankly, it's not one I'm sure we can win. With the fleet destroyed and the Syndicate rampaging throughout the system, the government's support is firmly behind ESS to clean up this mess. Once I deal with Ncube, I intend to set a course for Earth. I'm going to make my case directly to Premier Fairchild."

"I like you a lot more than I thought I would," Jenna muttered. *Leave it to Sienar to find an authority figure with an actual brain,* she thought. "Thank you for saving me." She couldn't remember the last time she'd uttered those first two words.

Cheng-Visitor grunted. "You can return the favour by getting me some actual evidence to back up Sienar's theory."

PALE GREY DOT

There was already a team of four soldiers in the battlecruiser's launch bay, crowded around the entrance to one of the mid-range shuttles. Jenna spotted the Special Forces emblem on their shoulders. Each was armed and armoured.

"I'm Commander Gus O'Brien. We'll have to handle the rest of the introductions later," O'Brien said, joining his comrades. Jenna noted his grey armour was immaculate, with not a scuff mark it on. She hoped he was more than just flash.

"Understand this, Jenna," Cheng-Visitor said. "The commander is in charge. You're there to advise on ESS protocol and follow his orders. Got it?"

"Yes," Jenna lied. She wondered if she was going to get armour and a gun. It had been a long time since she got to work with quality equipment. She smiled as she stepped through the hatch. Everything was back on track.

●

The solar system is collapsing, and I'm stuck here. Don't even know where "here" is, Cherny thought as he sat alone on the cafeteria bench. Like everything in the abandoned train station that served as Alexander Reuben's headquarters, it was dirty and on the verge of falling apart. To one side, Cherny watched as people lined up for their dinner allotment of noodles and slop. His own tray, sitting next to a plastic cup of vitamin juice, was still full of both.

It reminded him of his old job at Tsiolkovsky Spaceport.

He wondered how Minsk, José, and the others working the tarmac were doing. Violence—organized or otherwise—had broken out across the system. Ships carrying refugees were flocking back to Earth. The news reports said that all transit points off-planet had fallen under tight martial law to cope with the influx. Cherny bet that his old boss wouldn't take so well to having a soldier screaming in his face for every wrong move.

It hadn't taken long for the details of Cherny's origins to spread across the base, and all the Syndicate personnel were soon giving him a wide berth. He could overhear them, occasionally, whispering about the ESS operative in their midst. Sometimes it was out of fear for what he would do if he escaped, but a few were brave—they would gladly kill him had Reuben not expressly forbidden it.

To his surprise, Sienar had been willing to reactivate a few of his more harmless cybernetic functions. Limited access to MarsNet let him catch glimpses of the outside world and the chaos enveloping it. Though he still had no idea where on Mars he was, one of the first things ESS had taught him as a child were ways to turn limited network access into something dangerous.

As he picked at his noodles, he listened in on whichever transmissions he could pick up from the network and its users. They were all encrypted, but Cherny could guess which were health checks, which were status updates, and which were various cybernetics' background requests for information. *Progress,* Cherny thought. *Slow but steady.* He'd have been more confident if Sienar didn't also know all the

PALE GREY DOT

same techniques. He wondered if Alexander Reuben knew his cybernetics had been reactivated.

He also wondered if they were right about Her. He'd looked over the rest of Sienar's files on the matter. They detailed every action taken by the Syndicate over the past four decades, along with theories on how they could have acquired the information needed to pull it off. Each chain led back to ESS. It wasn't flawless, though. *You'd be hardpressed to definitively prove Her involvement.* Moreover, attacking the United Fleet outright seemed like a line even She wouldn't cross. Still, Cherny had never known Sienar to jump to conclusions. His eyes darted around the worn-down cafeteria. Surely the people here were incapable of launching a rebellion that threatened Earth itself.

Upon hearing a soft, rhythmic whirring, Cherny looked up from his dinner to see Kyle lurching in his direction. His robotic legs made him unsteady, but he eventually took a seat opposite him.

"Kyle," Cherny said. "I haven't seen you since Reuben's office."

"You mean since you collapsed on the ground, crying like a baby?" Kyle clasped his hands together and rested them on the metal table.

"How goes your glorious uprising?" Cherny glanced up at the flickering lights. He could hear the distant sound of water dripping. "Is it everything you hoped for?"

"I actually didn't come here to trade insults. Sienar asked me to check up on you. Lord knows why, though."

285

"He can come visit me anytime."

"He's busy working with Reuben. They're trying to clean up the mess you made."

"That *I* made?" Cherny leaned forward, stabbing his noodles with his fork. "I was exiled for fifty years. Don't go blaming me for whatever you think ESS has done. Hell, I'm probably the most innocent person in this entire base. Your husband was with ESS the whole damn time."

That must have struck a nerve, because Kyle glared at him with contempt. "The instant he found out what ESS was doing ... When he realized your master was trying to play both sides, he turned against ESS. He threw away his life when he saved the Syndicate at Uruk Sulcus. Why? Because Sienar is a good, decent man. You, on the other hand? You refuse to see the truth, even though it's so damn obvious."

"It's not that simple for me," Cherny said. *Jenna found a way to avoid the Pull. Ezza seems to have found a way. Sienar found a way. Only I failed,* he thought. *Me, Taylor, and poor Sal.*

"Oh, sure," Kyle scoffed. "That brainwashing I keep hearing so much about. Because of you and ESS, if Sienar so much as steps outside, a switch will go off in his brain and I'll lose him forever." He jabbed an accusatory finger towards Cherny. "Sorry if I'm not sympathetic to your plight, but with the misery that ESS puts others through, as far as I'm concerned, you've earned all that and more."

The cafeteria tables were filling up now as more of the dinner shift came in, and Cherny knew their conversation

PALE GREY DOT

would soon be overheard. *Who wouldn't want to hear the scary operative getting told off?*

"Do you know how Sienar describes you and the rest of your team?" Kyle pressed.

"I think you're going to tell me no matter what I say."

"He speaks of you as if you were family. He always talks about how many times his life depended on you, and how he'd gladly give up his to help you. He's so willing to forgive you for being a puppet, but as far as I'm concerned, you deserve whatever suffering this Pull gives you."

"If I deserve it, then so does Sienar. He's just as guilty as me. Besides," Cherny said, "I feel just fine. Hell, this is almost a relief to me."

"Oh?" There was suspicion in Kyle's voice.

"There's only one directive that comes with the Athena Protocols: do whatever ESS would want you to do." *Do what She would want you to do*, Cherny mentally clarified.

"Seems vague."

"It is, I suppose, but usually it isn't too hard to interpret. What would ESS want me to do right now?" Cherny shrugged. "There's nothing I *can* do. Sienar has seen to that. Oh sure, I could try to escape." He waved his cup of vitamin juice at the people who filed over from the serving line. "Maybe even kill a few of you."

Kyle scratched his chin nervously.

"But what would that accomplish? I'd be dead, and Reuben would continue on his merry way," Cherny took a swig from his cup. There was zero drinkable alcohol in this place. "As

287

Don Miasek

far as I'm concerned, being helpless is a gift. I won't be punished for failing to do the impossible."

"Or maybe ESS would want you to go out in a blaze of glory," Kyle said. "Make sure the oh-so-evil Syndicate can't extract any useful information from you."

Cherny's mouth twitched.

The dinner crowd grew thicker, encroaching on the seats around them. *These were the folks that didn't have the brains to abandon Reuben when they had the chance,* he decided.

Though his enhanced audial functions were disabled, it was impossible for Cherny not to overhear the chatter. The man three seats over was still worried about his ex; her ship went missing shortly after the attack on Jupiter Station. Another man was arguing with his friend, furious that the Syndicate members who abandoned Reuben had yet to be dealt with. The woman one table away from Cherny was muttering to anyone who'd listen about the stupidity of keeping "the operative" in their midst; someone, she said, should do something about it.

It was this last comment that had Cherny concerned. As he listened to Kyle, he watched the woman out of the corner of his eye. Two inches taller and as well built as Cherny ever was in his prime, she was clad in a skintight blue-and-gold suit. The thin metal strips that ran along her hands told of cybernetics that were once expensive. She might have been pretty, were it not for the hatred in her eyes—eyes that were the same shade of brown that Sal's had been.

Either put a stop to this now or wait until you find a shiv in

PALE GREY DOT

your side, Cherny decided. He glanced towards the woman, cutting her off. "If you have something to say, then say it to my face."

Her chair screeched against the floor as she pushed it back and rose to her feet, towering over him. "Are you really sure, Operative, that you want to push me right now?" she asked in a low tone.

Show no weakness, Cherny reminded himself. He remained seated, trying to put on an air of indifference as he looked up at her. "Let me guess, you're hoping to score some easy cred by threatening the big, bad ESS agent."

"Stace," Kyle said. Pressing his hands against the table, he awkwardly pushed himself to his feet. "This isn't a good idea. Reuben says—"

"Lay off, Kyle," Stace snapped. "ESS hasn't made you suffer the way I have."

"Reuben—"

"If Reuben has a problem, then he can come up here himself. This is between me and the operative." All eyes were on them now as she turned back to Cherny. "And as for you, you're owed a lot more than threats for what you did."

"And just what did I do?" Cherny asked. It was a hard line to walk between fearlessness and provocation. She was bigger, and she looked stronger. Her cybernetics looked modded—overclocked to mild combat grade, most likely. With his own disabled, that'd give her a big advantage. He hoped someone was running to get Sienar and Reuben.

"I was eight when I was woken up in the middle of the

Don Miasek

night by a commando raid smashing through the walls of our apartment. Apparently, my dad had been a bit too vocal on the Net, and some damn algorithm marked him as a Suspicious Person. I haven't seen him since. One calculation and you destroyed my family!"

"Pretty sure I'd remember doing that," Cherny retorted. He felt a pit in his stomach but did his best to ignore it. *There's no way to avoid a fight now. The only hope of getting out of here alive is to push her into doing something stupid.* "Though admittedly, after a while, all the raids start to blur together."

Cherny heard shouting from the crowd, urging Stace on. There was enough anger here to fuel a riot, and that was even without them knowing about his connection to the Martian Insurrection. It was only a matter of time before someone made a run at him. Better now than later.

"Stand up," she whispered. "I want you on your feet and ready for this. I'm giving you the chance you never gave my father."

Cherny gave Kyle a resigned shrug and swung his legs over then bench, climbing to his feet with an exaggerated wince as his bandaged side shifted. He prayed the woman would underestimate him. Even without combat cybernetics, his awareness training registered every twitch she and the crowd made.

Stace's right arm flexed, and Cherny moved. The woman's fist came straight for him as he brought up his metal arm. He felt a tearing in his side as he deflected the blow away from

Pale Grey Dot

his face. She was far stronger than he'd hoped. Staggering against the cafeteria table, Cherny lashed out with his foot, trying to catch her kneecap. She was fast, too, and jumped back to avoid it. The crowd was screaming at them.

Cherny kept after her, but she quickly proved that was a mistake. Her left slipped under his guard, striking him square in the gut. Cherny felt the wind go out of him.

A weapon. I need a weapon! Reaching out, he snagged his metal tray off the table and whipped it around as she charged towards him again. Noodles and slop flew, and a loud crack echoed through the cafeteria as Cherny made solid contact.

Stace screamed and fell to her knees, clutching her face. Blood trickled between her fingers from the gash running from her nose to her lip.

Ignoring the pain, Cherny struck again and again, slamming her to the ground with the tray. He gasped desperately for air as he brandished his bloodied weapon to the crowd. "Anyone else?" he spat.

Kyle lurched around the table as fast as his robotic legs would take him, trying to push through the people barring the way. He looked thoroughly panicked.

Cherny gritted his teeth. The strength started to drain from his arms. He could feel a wetness through his coat, and he knew the wound in his side had opened again. He stumbled backwards, ready to swing with whatever he had left at the next person to step towards him. He wondered how many others had grievances against him and ESS.

Don Miasek

"ENOUGH!"

The crowd stopped their advance, but the rumblings of discontent continued as Sienar emerged from the hallway. Cherny couldn't think of the last time he'd seen the man so furious, and it was a sight to behold. Threading through the crowd, he looked aghast as he laid eyes on the two combatants. "What the hell do you two think you're doing?" he snapped.

Stace took her hand away from her face. Blood was smeared down her chin and dripping onto her suit.

Cherny let the tray fall to the ground with a clatter and grabbed the table to support himself.

"We are on the same side here," Sienar said. He whirled around, now speaking to the crowd. "Do we not have enough enemies out there that we need to start making new ones amongst ourselves?" He reached out towards the injured woman. She grasped his hand with her bloodied one. Pulling her up, he kept his voice firm. "We can't afford vengeance, Stace."

With her free hand, she pulled a napkin off the table and held it to her nose. Her gaze was cast downwards.

"And you," Sienar now turned on Cherny with a look of restrained fury. "I thought you were smarter than this. I am trying my damnedest to keep you alive, and here you are picking fights with my people."

"It was going to happen no matter what I did," Cherny shot back. "If not her, then someone else." He remembered when the Athena Six were his brother's "people."

292

PALE GREY DOT

Sienar shook his head in frustration and disappointment. "Med bay, both of you. Let's go. Cherny, we've gotten word back from Cheng-Visitor."

Jenna. Cherny froze. She survived his betrayal. "What happened? Where is she? Is she all right?"

"Come," Sienar said as he put his brother's arm around his shoulders. The crowd parted for Sienar as he helped Cherny to the base's makeshift hospital.

There, Kyle carefully pulled the bandage off Cherny's left side as he sat on the medical slab. The wound was dark and sticky where the scabs had ripped open.

From the next bed over, Stace watched with grim satisfaction as Cherny winced. "Sienar, I'm sorry." She waved her hand in Cherny's direction. "I shouldn't have done that."

"Clearly," Sienar said, not taking his eyes off the monitor in front of him.

Stace shifted on her slab and looked to Cherny. "Maybe you weren't personally involved in my dad's disappearance, but tell me, Operative, tell me you weren't involved in countless others."

"I was," Cherny admitted. Back when he became old enough to realize he was in the ESS schooling system, the choice between heroically defending their grand society or living like a dredge had been so easy.

"So was I, if you'll recall, Stace," Sienar broke in. "And we managed to move past that."

"You risked your life to save the Syndicate on Ganymede. We'd all be dead or captive if it weren't for you." Stace jerked a

293

Don Miasek

thumb in Cherny's direction. "He's here because we dragged him here."

"He wasn't the one who started the fight," Sienar said tersely, stepping over to the medical printer. The new batch of tissue-regenerating nanites was nearly ready. "Cherny, you'll be happy to hear that Jenna escaped the trap that ESS laid for her."

Cherny looked down at his gash. Despite his best efforts, Jenna made it through. The Pull punished disobedience—not failure—and he'd never been so thrilled with failure before. "Does she ..." Cherny's mouth went dry. "Does she know what I did?"

"No," Sienar replied. "Or at least, if she does, she didn't hear it from me. She's on her way to Ganymede to meet up with Ezza."

Cherny closed his eyes in relief.

"Kyle, could you please give Cherny something for the pain?" Sienar asked. He gave his husband a firm look. "Something strong, if you could."

Cherny held out his arm, letting the physician insert a wire into one of the open ports.

"Jenna sent quite a lot of information, in fact," Sienar continued. "Journals of her travels since the insurrection. Theories on Her systems. Even grand plans to bring down ESS and all of Fairchild's administrations." Sienar smiled. "Our Jenna never lacked ambition. More importantly, though, she included the technical details on how she pulled off her greatest trick."

PALE GREY DOT

Without the adrenaline of the fight, the strength had drained from Cherny's limbs. "What trick? What do you mean?"

Sienar moved out from behind the printer, stepping towards him. "She designed the Athena Protocols. She implemented them."

"Wait …" Cherny felt lightheaded. He grasped for the wire in his arm, but no longer had the strength to pull it out.

"Leave it to Jenna to make a breakthrough in cybernetic technology, have it studied by the finest experts in the Earth Security Service, and still manage to figure out a back door in case it all went wrong," Sienar said.

Kyle held Cherny, gently lowering him onto the bed as he felt himself go limp.

When Cherny opened his eyes again, he was still in the medical bay. The walls were still covered in screens and terminals, the room was still lit by overhead floodlights, and the cables and computers still rested next to the decrepit pipes and grates. Kyle was looking down at him from above.

But Cherny felt different. He slowly reached up with his metal hand and found a new scar on the back of his head. He thought of Jenna, of Ezza, of Her, and of the Earth Security Service. For the first time since Tsiolkovsky Spaceport, his thinking was clear and his alone. The Pull was gone.

13

Haven't felt this good since before the insurrection, Jenna thought as she leaned back against the tunnel wall. It had taken a day for the Ganymede Travel Bureau to prep a train on the Uruk Sulcus line, but at least the man there had been surprisingly cooperative when they submitted the request. Though the Ganymede Nexus Habitat rooms were small and cramped, they didn't smell like those on *Étoile*. There was only one shower for each block of twelve rooms, but it was enough. She felt clean now. Even the recycled air of her armoured suit was almost refreshing, and setting her helmet's faceguard to opaque granted her a degree of privacy.

Jenna watched as O'Brien and his team worked to set up a barricade across the tunnel's width. Like hers, their armour had the United Fleet insignia above the right breast. *Hah,* Jenna thought, *never thought I'd see the day that I'd work with the establishment again.* It would be worth it, though, if it

PALE GREY DOT

meant getting Ezza back. Then they could go after Sienar—Admiral Cheng-Visitor must have some idea of where he was—and Cherny. Then it'd be onto Her. Jenna's comm system crackled to life.

"Jenna," O'Brien said. "Come on over here, if you wouldn't mind."

She found the marine unfailingly polite and got the sense he was deliberately being delicate with her. Jenna knew the others considered her unstable, but she'd long stopped caring about such things. She carefully skipped over in their direction, mindful of Ganymede's weak gravity.

One of the soldiers gestured to the devices planted on opposite sides of the tunnel walls. "The spikes are all set," she said. Behind the helmet was the face of a veteran. "The train'll lose power as soon as it crosses over them. You're sure this is the right spot?"

"Sergeant Nolan, is it? Getting really tired of you asking me that—of course I'm sure," Jenna replied. She and O'Brien had argued back and forth about exactly how to set up the ambush. Finally, he had deferred to her knowledge of ESS operations. "Any closer and they'd be in range of the Ganymede Nexus, and thus SecLink."

"Right …" Nolan said.

An alert flickered in Jenna's mind. O'Brien had opened another private channel to the rest of his team, but it hadn't taken her long to figure out a way to secretly listen in on their conversations.

"Don't let her get to you, Nolan," O'Brien said. "The

admiral says she's unbalanced. This is the woman who hijacked a civilian ship to save her own skin. But her info should be good."

"Understood, Commander," Nolan replied.

Jenna pretended she hadn't heard their exchange. Let them talk about her behind her back—it didn't matter. They only needed to do what they were told. Jenna turned and looked down the darkened tunnel. If their estimates were right, they had only a few short hours before Ezza would come back to her. Jenna ran a diagnostic check of her systems. The facilities at the Ganymede Nexus hadn't had all the equipment she'd needed, but she'd been able to get basic cybernetic functionality restored. *It'll be enough to see me through this.*

●

"The Athena Protocols were a risk we accepted," Ezza said. The locomotive rumbled around them as it sped through the tunnel. It had felt good to get back onto the train and shed her helmet.

To her left, in the engineer's chair, Bev Stroud sat cross-legged. The woman looked young, though Ezza knew that was an illusion. Her long hair had faint pink and blue highlights that would be suitable for a variety of youth-infiltration missions. Her expression, however, was one of stern experience as she steepled her hands beneath her chin. One of her four drones rested on the ground next to her. "It's a

PALE GREY DOT

shame it didn't work quite as well as She might have hoped," she was saying. "Still, they were a good first effort, and really, you should be commended for your amazing sacrifice."

"'First effort'?" Ezza had to fight to keep the surprise out of her voice. No matter how friendly Bev now seemed to be, Ezza knew it was always a competition between operatives. She was reminded of Brylan.

"Oh yes, of course they're trying again. I'm not familiar with all the technical details, but the next batch is expected to have some remarkable improvements."

"I see."

Bev smiled and reached over, gently patting Ezza's leg. "Don't let it bother you. You're going to be a celebrity now that you're back in the service. Well, we both are. Returning you to the fold is going to make Her very happy with me."

Happy enough to include you in the next iteration? Ezza wondered. She had signed on to the Athena Program without hesitation. The whole team had. It had been an easy choice to better serve the solar system. That, and to thank Her for everything She had done for them. Apparently, their failure wasn't enough to deter Bev from the same path.

"So, counting down the seconds?" Bev asked.

Ezza knew what she meant. "Yes," she admitted. In a few short minutes, they'd begin picking up transmissions from the Ganymede Nexus. From there, a few well-placed commands and she'd be back.

Bev gave a smile that was almost warm. "I bet you're looking forward to catching up with your old colleagues." Bev

299

lowered her hand, stroking the top of a drone as if it were a pet. "She recalled Cherny to active service a few weeks back."

"I know," Ezza replied. She remembered Adams sitting in that very seat, patting the control console in much the same way Bev was doing now with the drone. *This is the chance to prove your loyalty,* Ezza thought. *Or lull her into a false sense of security. Or ...* "The login module Sienar left behind included user IDs for myself, Jenna, and Cherny. Cherny's was already accessed, so you must have him, which means you'll soon have Jenna."

"What makes you say that?"

"Jenna reached out to me, and she no doubt reached out to Cherny as well. With him on your side, luring Jenna somewhere should be trivial. You haven't captured her yet, otherwise her credentials would have been used on Sienar's message, but it's probably only a matter of time."

A smile crept across Bev's face. "Spot on, Ezza. The last I heard, Jenna's whereabouts were located, and a United Fleet warship was working to bring her in."

"I doubt you'll be able to take her alive," Ezza said. Just saying it left a pit in her stomach.

"It's possible they won't succeed," she admitted. "But we'll see. You know, I truly am sorry about your men. Being out-numbered four to one meant I couldn't take any chances. You understand, of course?"

You don't sound very sorry, Ezza thought. Besides, she knew this was another test. The real question was whether she was still loyal to the United Fleet, or if the Athena

PALE GREY DOT

Protocols had kicked in enough to shift her allegiance to ESS. There was only one right answer Ezza could give. "Already forgotten," she lied. At least, she hoped it was a lie. Gole had served with her for the past two years. He had been a good, honest man. Adams had been far too young to die in some remote outpost on a desolate moon. And Nirali ...

"I'd like to be there when Ms. Kashem is debriefed."

Bev shrugged and glanced towards the backroom where the journalist was being held. "It won't really be up to me." They both knew there was no way Nirali would be allowed to go free. There were numerous possible fates for her, and all of them were final.

Ezza returned her gaze out the front window, wondering if she could do anything to help the woman. She wondered, too, what ESS had found in Sienar's message to Cherny, and if they were also now close to finding him, but she didn't dare ask. The support posts whirled past them. Then a flicker in the distance caught her eye. She cried out a warning and threw her arms up protectively before the shredding of metal filled her ears and she was slammed against her harness's straps. She heard something shatter, followed by the hiss of air fleeing the train.

●

"The target is down!" a marine shouted through the comms, as if it wasn't already obvious.

Jenna had watched the train break free of its railings and

301

Don Miasek

careen against the tunnel wall before ricocheting back onto the tracks. Her helmet's sensors audibly relayed the information, simulating the screeching metal. There was the brief flicker of fire, but it was extinguished almost immediately in the vacuum. Even before the train came skidding to a halt, Jenna rushed forward, determined to get there first. The others might do something stupid and get Ezza killed.

As she advanced, gun drawn, she absorbed a wealth of tactical information. The front cabin's seals were breached—the occupants wouldn't have air for long. The train's power had been completely cut—any scanners it had would be unusable. O'Brien's team surrounded the locomotive in standard United Fleet formation—there'd be no chance of escape. The only option any defenders would have was surrender or ...

Jenna halted as she saw the tiniest flicker of heat spiking up from within the train. A military-grade weapon. No ... four separate military-grade weapons. "Wait!" she called out. "Back!"

It was too late. The marine at the cabin's side entrance was thrown against the tunnel wall as the hull plating exploded outward. Tubular legs, long and thin, stretched out through the breach, pulling the rest of the drone through the opening.

The network feed told Jenna the soldier's condition in a bright red flash, but she didn't dwell on it. The drone twisted towards the rest of the group, energy projector focusing on its next target, only to shatter from a well-placed shot from the marine next to her.

Three more, Jenna knew, and she sent the data to O'Brien

PALE GREY DOT

and his team. Jenna blocked out the shouts from the others, instead listening for any electronics. *Nothing ... Nothing ... Wait, there!* The drones' controller was inside the train, moving from the front of the cab towards the back. A standard ESS cybernetic package allowed for numerous remote connections. Not Ezza—drones weren't her style. *Another operative, then?* Jenna checked her rifle and circled around to the rear.

Nirali! That was Ezza's first thought once the train finally came to a halt and her harness shoved her back against the padded seat. Her second was of their air slipping out into the void. She stretched forward, pushing against the straps as she grabbed her helmet. With a snap, it sealed around her neck, allowing her to draw deep breaths.

Bev had already unstrapped herself. Bright red lights flickered on her drones' sides as their weaponry activated. "Six of them, Ezza!" she shouted through the comms.

Ezza struggled with the buckle keeping her harness together. The damn thing had jammed. Through the window, she saw an armoured figure quickly sweep around towards the side of the cab. Ezza twisted as far as she could in her seat, watching as Bev vaulted towards the back and three of her drones positioned themselves next to the hatch.

An energy blast tore outward, ripping a hole in the locomotive's plating. From this angle, Ezza thought she saw one

Don Miasek

of the soldiers fall back. They didn't look like Ganymede Nexus Police. Ezza diverted power to her metal arm and tore the buckle off.

●

The locomotive's rear had been the first to rip off the track and scrape against the side of the tunnel, and Jenna saw that the armour plating had been nearly torn in half. She reached the back airlock and yanked the locking mechanism until it swung open. The inner airlock door didn't even need to cycle—it was already depressurized. Keeping her rifle up, Jenna climbed in, checking all corners for threats. Immediately, she spied a pressure suit strapped to the far wall. The figure inside threw up its empty hands defensively as Jenna took aim. Her comm buzzed.

"Wait, no!" the figure cried. The voice was female, and she sounded scared out of her mind. "I'm not with them! Please, help me!"

The hell? The suit was high quality but had no telltale signs of an ESS make. It looked civilian. "Tell me who you are right now," Jenna demanded.

"M-my name is Nirali Kashem. I-I'm a reporter for IDEA." She sounded like she was about to cry. "Don't hurt me, please!"

A dozen questions ran through Jenna's mind about how some journalist could have gotten all the way out here. A little voice in her head said to shoot her just in case. After a

PALE GREY DOT

moment's hesitation, Jenna decided against it. The woman was clearly unarmed, and her straps looked like they were locked. *A prisoner, then?* "Tell me how many there are."

"I—there's two. Ezza and another, up front. Please, the other one's an ESS operative! She killed Gole and Adams!" Nirali kept her hands in the air, as if she was afraid Jenna might change her mind.

Jenna felt a surge of adrenaline at the mention of her sister's name. She really was here. It had been so long since they'd been together. She had no idea who Adams and Gole were, but it meant this other operative already had blood on her hands. "Stay here," she ordered, moving towards the door. Her HUD registered distant gunfire, overlaid with the position of O'Brien's team. They looked like they were pinned down.

Nirali helplessly tugged at the straps. "She has drones ..."

I know, Jenna thought. She reached for the door handle, but then paused. The drone controller's signal was approaching rapidly. Jenna made a snap decision and backed up, crouching behind a crate of supplies that had toppled over in the crash. She cut all electronics, except the bare minimum needed to keep her suit's life support and comms online. Her readouts on O'Brien and his team vanished. *Sal was better at this sneaking thing.*

The door to the front cab swung open—Jenna could feel the subtle vibrations in the deck. *A drone? Its master? Or Ezza?* Without sound or sensors, there was no way to tell from her hiding spot. Jenna didn't rate her chances at

305

beating a drone's reaction time. The controller, though, was another matter.

"One of the soldiers was just here!" Nirali suddenly transmitted.

You cowardly bitch, Jenna thought. She tightened her grip on her rifle. *Wait ... no. The comm was on an open channel. Why ...?*

"Bev, w-where are you?" Nirali transmitted. "The soldier said she was going to circle around to the other side of the cab. Please don't hurt me ..."

Ah, this Bev is the controller and not there in person. One of the drones, then. The operative's name didn't ring any bells. Jenna stayed where she was.

There was silence on Nirali's part, as if she was receiving a reply. Then she said, "Oh, there you are. Bev, please, no. I-I've told you the truth. I didn't help the soldier at all!"

Jenna rose from her cover and took the shot.

•

Not again! Ezza thought frantically. She tried to rise to her feet, but even in Ganymede's gravity, her body felt like it weighed a tonne. *Help your fellow soldiers. They're United Fleet.* Of that she had no doubt. *No, focus on the mission. Focus on what She would want you to do! Maybe ... maybe you and Bev can subdue the marines without hurting them and make sense out of all this.* But in her heart, Ezza knew how ridiculous the idea was. The Pull couldn't be cheated.

PALE GREY DOT

Though her harness straps were off, she found she couldn't move. Ezza cursed her paralysis. *Don't make the same mistake that you did at Uruk Sulcus!* Through the cracked front window, she saw the soldiers take up positions against the drones. Her eyes saw the heat signatures flare up with each shot, just as her HUD displayed the status of Bev and her drones in bright red.

They're out there, fighting and dying for you, and you're sitting here helplessly, she told herself. *No, the decision was made for you when Adams and Gole were killed!* Her head ached as her thoughts went back and forth.

Wham, wham, wham.

Ezza vaguely registered Nirali opening a line to speak with Bev. Then she heard a sudden burst of static from the operative's comms. Outside, the surviving drones ceased their attack. Ezza's helmet went quiet. She twisted around in her chair as best she could. A new figure stood in the doorway.

The woman wore United Fleet armour over her pressure suit, with a standard-issue rifle magnetically clasped to her back; the heat signature suggested it had been recently discharged. Her helmet's faceguard was blank, but she looked back at Ezza for a long five seconds, head tilted as if pondering what to make of her. Then she approached, placed her hand on the armrest of Ezza's chair, and slowly swivelled it around so they were face to face. The woman reached forward and wrapped her arms around Ezza as her comms activated. "It's good to see you again," Jenna said.

307

14

"Five days?" Cherny exclaimed. "You had me under for five days?"

Kyle struggled to keep up. His left leg made a snapping sound each time he bent his knee. "The process your friend sent wasn't exactly simple. There are systems in you I've never even seen before. The chip alone … You should be lucky—"

"Fine, fair enough," Cherny said. He shoved open the stairwell door leading to the Syndicate base's deepest levels. After a moment's thought, he held the door long enough for the physician to catch up. As he waited, Cherny explored his newfound freedom. Gone was the omnipresent nagging sensation reminding him to do what She would want. He no longer had to carefully avoid thinking certain thoughts. It was liberating. *You've been given a chance,* he thought, *to make amends for betraying Jenna.* "Kyle, it's … Listen, I owe

PALE GREY DOT

you. You and Jenna have done what I thought was impossible. Thank you."

Kyle gave him a wary look as he hobbled down the stairs.

Once on the lower level, Cherny reached out and gave the man an awkward pat on the shoulder before storming down the hall. His side felt almost as good as new, though the bandages still remained. Stopping in front of the final door, he motioned for Kyle to hurry up.

While he waited, he reached out with his mind, connecting to the base's network. He was relieved to find the inroads he'd made into hacking the base's network were still intact. Odd that Sienar hadn't found them by now. *How long will it take before I can reach something vital?* Pull or no Pull, staying trapped by the Syndicate seemed like an eventual death sentence.

He stepped aside, letting the physician reach out and press his hand against the lock. The instant he heard it unlatch, Cherny burst in.

Sienar was already there with Reuben, bathed in the light of the single red bulb. The latter, towering over all others present, telescoped his optic in Cherny's direction. The gaze of his organic eye drifted about the room.

A smile grew on Sienar's face as he turned. "You're finally awake. We were getting worried."

Cherny doubted the "we" part.

"You'll have to forgive the little deception before your surgery. I couldn't be sure how you'd react if I told you we were trying to remove the Athena Protocols," he added.

Cherny waved his hand dismissively. "It worked, Sienar. It's gone." In addition to the trousers he'd been wearing, he'd only snagged a thin white shirt before barging out of the med bay, and he had to fight the urge to shiver in the chill of Reuben's office.

If Sienar shared any of Kyle's suspicions, he knew better than to show it. "Fantastic. You see, Alex? Getting Cherny on board was worth the risk. First Jenna, and now him. Everything is starting to fall into place."

The giant said nothing.

"Where is she now?" Cherny asked. *I have to make it up to her.*

"Gabrielle—Admiral Cheng-Visitor—freed her and sent her after Ezza, along with a team of her soldiers," Sienar said. "I expect they're on Ganymede by now."

"A dangerous risk," Reuben said. "There will be repercussions for a United Fleet admiral taking direct action against an Earth Security Service operation."

"We no longer have time to play it safe, Alex," Sienar said, looking over his shoulder at the cyborg. "Playing it safe is what let Her hack away at your control of the Syndicate over the past fifty years. What happened to the bold revolutionary that challenged the might of Earth with only a handful of pirates?"

"Time and pain," Reuben replied, "are powerful teachers." The red and black liquid sloshing through the tubes between his torso and life-support systems sped up. "Operative, if your programming is truly inactive, then I assume the

PALE GREY DOT

details of your master's plans can be freely divulged. If you have proof of Her complicit nature, we can disrupt it."

Cherny shook his head. "No, She didn't tell me anything about secretly taking over the Syndicate." Keeping information on a need-to-know basis was standard operating procedure. *But wasn't Sienar's motivation for sabotaging the Ganymede Blitz need-to-know? Either She didn't trust you as much as you'd hoped, or Sienar's theory is wrong.* He recalled Amanda's standoffish attitude towards him and wondered how much of that was Her.

"Inconvenient for us," Reuben declared. "Convenient for your master."

Cherny opened his mouth to retort that She wasn't his master but stopped himself. Reuben would never believe him.

"As much as I'd like to celebrate your liberation with you, Cherny, you've missed a lot," Sienar said. "The other Syndicate cells have struck over four dozen United Fleet targets over the past week. Ships, bases, and civilians. Even members of the Admiralty have gone missing."

"And once the United Fleet's crippled, ESS will have some breakthrough, eliminate the source of the uprising, and save the day," Cherny concluded. Though he found it easier to analyze the theory without the Pull tugging at his thoughts, he struggled with the idea that She would commit such a crime.

Kyle hobbled up next to Sienar, legs clicking with each step.

311

Don Miasek

"A clever plan," Reuben said. "But dangerous. Your master has taken great risks by attacking a rival governmental agency."

Cherny looked up at the Syndicate leader. "Don't tell me you're all that upset, Reuben. A part of you has to be pretty damn thrilled to watch ESS bloody the United Fleet's nose."

"All insurrectionist activities committed thus far are aligned with my goals," Reuben agreed. "The expanding powers of the Earth Security Service are not. Conjecture, however, is insufficient to convince those in power of a conspiracy. Proof is required."

A plan had already formed in Cherny's mind. "Where's Amanda?"

"One of my trackers spotted her leaving the Excalibur Hotel in Olympus Mons yesterday," Sienar replied. "I imagine she's still searching for you."

Cherny grinned. "You asked me before what Her weaknesses were, and Amanda is one of them. Their direct link is flawed. The time lag between Earth and Mars weakens the connection." Before, even thinking of Her as weak would have resulted in physical agony. "Amanda has been off Earth for over two weeks now, and I could already see her real personality beginning to slip through. Send me after her."

Kyle and Reuben's objections ran over each other.

"We can't just let him go!" Kyle shouted.

"Unacceptable," boomed Reuben. The man took two steps forward, gears creaking and servos straining. His neck ratcheted as he cast his optic gaze down upon Cherny. "The

PALE GREY DOT

operative Amanda agreed to be linked to your master. There is no reason to believe she regrets that decision."

Cherny wished he'd stop calling Her that. "So? Either I convince Amanda she's better off without Her in her mind, or we take her by force. Either way, we can pry the information from her."

"No. It is much more likely you would succumb to your brainwashing once more," Reuben continued. "There are imperfections in the cure your comrade has given you."

Doubt crept into Cherny's mind. "What imperfections?"

Sienar put his hand on Cherny's shoulder. "The Pull is fed to you through either the chip or SecLink. Yes, the chip is gone. Down here, hidden from SecLink? You're safe. But the instant you reconnect to ESS's network, you're going to feel it again, and I don't know if you're going to be able to resist it."

Just a month ago, the idea of returning to ESS seemed like a miracle. Cherny thought back to the reconstruction of Jenna's ambush against Marcus, and of his own theory that she had hacked into SecLink. "Jenna resisted it."

"Your friend has accomplished much that you could not," Reuben said.

Cherny glared up at Reuben, but the cyborg's eyes never wavered. *This monstrosity is standing between you and saving Jenna.* He felt his temper rise.

"Your proposal is rejected. The risks outweigh the reward."

"You robotic son of a bitch," Cherny spat. "You just want to let ESS and the United Fleet tear each other apart until you're damn well good and ready to take advantage of the situation. Go ahead and deny it. You're fine with everyone burning so long as your precious revolu—"

Cherny never would have guessed Reuben, with all his mechanical bulk and the tethers keeping him attached to his life support, could move so fast. In a flash, the man's arm was up, and a huge metal hand wrapped around Cherny's throat. Cherny could barely hear Sienar shouting, but Reuben's words came through crystal clear.

"I deny nothing, little operative," he intoned. "It is your friend who chose to ally himself with me, knowing full well that my goals are not his goals. I care nothing for the United Fleet. I care only for dismantling the twisted control that Premier Fairchild and all of Earth have inflicted upon us."

Cherny desperately clawed at Reuben's fingers, but his grip didn't relent. As the Syndicate leader pulled him close, Cherny could see that his organic eye was pale and blind. The thin hydraulics running along Reuben's arm didn't even twitch against Cherny's struggles.

"Mars once tried to escape Earth's grasp. The genesis for change was growing until you and your six butchered any chance it had." The blind eye rolled, looking in the wrong direction, while the robotic right remained focused. "Understand this: Though my Syndicate may be weakened, the ideals that it stands for remain strong. It can be rebuilt."

Sienar and Kyle were still shouting, but he could no longer hear them at all.

"You have misinterpreted who is in control, and it is not

PALE GREY DOT

your friend. You exist at *my* discretion. Do you understand now, Operative?" Reuben asked, looking down at him from above.

Struggling to suck in as much air as he could, Cherny could only frantically nod.

"Then the nature of our relationship has been made clear." The heavy machinery in Reuben's arm moved, and Cherny felt the pressure around his throat evaporate. Reuben ratcheted back to his desk and lowered himself into a seated position.

"Cherny ..." Sienar took a step towards him, but Cherny waved him off.

"No, go finish your strategy session," Cherny croaked as soon as his breath came back to him. He pushed his way past Kyle as he headed to the exit. Once out of Reuben's darkened room and into the hall, Cherny headed to the upper levels, ignoring the stares and suspicious looks he received from those he passed. As he crossed through the cafeteria, he spied Stace out of the corner of his eye. She looked none the worse for wear after their brawl. Cherny wondered if she had been punished for attacking him. He didn't stop, though; instead, he climbed the access ladder down to the track-level barricades. No one tried to stop him.

Up close, Cherny could see that the defensive wall had been rebuilt out of an old, broken-down vacuum train. Its brown hull was patched together with newly printed sheets of heat-resistant plastics, and a grated catwalk ran along its upper side. Reflective-grade holograms provided meagre

Don Miasek

protection against energy projectors. As Cherny sat on the rampart, dangling his legs over the edge, a guard clad in a Martian longcoat and a sensor mask watched Cherny with a wary eye, but did nothing to deter him.

Down the tunnel that led away from the Syndicate base, even with cybernetic vision, he could see only darkness. The encounter with Reuben had renewed his drive to leave. Cherny listened to the guard's footsteps. *He must be confident he can shoot me dead if I make a run for it.* Cherny bet more guards were watching from the other side of the comm centre's large glass windowpane overhead. He glanced dubiously at the gun drones perched on the wall beneath it. Some were ballistic and some were energy, but none appeared up to military standards. *None of this would stand a chance against a serious invasion.*

"What's your name?" Cherny asked the guard. The first step to escape was finding out where the hell he was.

Though his mask hid the man's expression, his tone was one of obvious contempt. "Hans Shultz. What's it to you, Operative? Making a list of traitors for when you get back home? *If* you get back home."

"Just making conversation," Cherny replied. "If you don't mind me asking, where are you from? I can't place your accent."

"Why do you care?" Shultz demanded.

"Because I have a very bad feeling that I'm going to be here for a very long time," he lied, "and I might as well make it as pleasant as I can by getting to know people."

Shultz shrugged as if it didn't matter. "Hellas York."

PALE GREY DOT

Cherny took a moment to look it up in his local files, but Shultz offered, "Little refuelling encampment on the eastern side of the crater."

"Phew. Can't get much farther from there than here," Cherny lamented.

"So?"

Lucky guess. Cherny mentally ticked off a few potential sites for his prison. The Hellas crater and Olympus Mons were practically on opposite sides of the planet. Chances were good he was still within the Tharsis province. "Hellas was hit pretty hard by the human-to-automation policy changes. You one of the old unificationists?"

Shultz crouched, getting down to Cherny's level. "You better believe it, Operative. Earth failed, and Fairchild would have dragged Mars down with it, so the entire planet came together in one drive for independence."

That, Cherny decided, *sounds straight out of their pamphlets.*

"But Earth can't bear the idea of someone actually standing up to them." Shultz shook his head. "Fairchild wanted a brutal example made of us, and Jesus Christ, did your kind ever succeed."

"Would you believe the original intent was to defuse the situation peacefully?"

Shultz laughed. "If the premier wanted the situation peacefully defused, she'd have actually listened to our requests. Independence! No more putting up with that Earth-first mentality. We'd get to decide who came to Mars,

317

Don Miasek

set the drone-to-human ratio, and become more than a teat for Earth to suck. She sure as hell wouldn't have sent in her ESS wolves if she wanted the situation 'defused peacefully.'"

Cherny looked out into the tunnels again.

"No answer for that, eh, Operative? You know, I bet you're just loving seeing us like this. The great revolutionaries reduced to living underground like rats."

"What, they don't let you head up to the city every now and then?" Cherny feigned surprise.

Shultz snorted. "It's an hour just to get to civilization."

"Mmm," Cherny replied. Inwardly, his mind filtered through hundreds of vacuum train stations, knocking off each possibility. Far from the Hellas crater, an hour—by train, Cherny assumed—to a major city. Shultz hadn't corrected Cherny's use of "the city," singular. The station would have to be far off the main lines to stay undetected for so long. Judging from the base's condition, he figured twenty to thirty years of deterioration. He cross-referenced this with the Martian Travel Bureau's advisories on station statuses. *Northwest of Olympus Mons, then? Towards Lycus Sulci? Thank you, Mr. Shultz, you've been very useful,* Cherny thought.

As Shultz returned to his patrol, Cherny resumed his attempts to break through the base's network to get full access. Every transmission was well encrypted, but he hoped at least one inhabitant hadn't been diligent about keeping their credentials secure. It seemed unlikely that Sienar could ever be so careless, but Cherny had already made more progress than he'd expected.

PALE GREY DOT

He spent a good fifteen minutes listening in on Shultz's idle transmissions. He still couldn't break the encryption, but with each message, he learned more about the network's security. *Getting there,* Cherny thought. *There's still a chance to get out of here and make amends.*

Cherny perked up at the sound of footsteps on the barricade behind him. He guessed who it was even before he turned to look.

Sienar slowly eased himself down next to him, letting his legs dangle over the edge. Minutes passed as the pair stared out into the darkness. The only sound was the shuffling of boots as Shultz patrolled back and forth.

Finally, Sienar spoke. "I need to head out into the tunnels. Make sure a couple of the forward sensors are configured for the next month. How about you come with me?"

There were a dozen ways to do that without physically being there, Cherny knew. "Sure," he said. The men climbed to their feet, and Cherny scratched at the bandages under his shirt on his injured side. It didn't hurt anymore, but it itched.

"We'll be back in fifteen, Hans," Sienar said.

The pair set off, lights flickering on as they passed each support strut. It wasn't long until they were alone. The sensors were well hidden within the small maintenance hatches that normally fed into the train system's network, camouflaged both visually and electronically.

Sienar pulled off the access panel from the first one, reaching inside to make the configuration checks.

"You really screwed this up," Cherny said.

319

Don Miasek

Sienar pulled his arms from the hatch, turning to face his friend. "Oh, I did, did I?"

"You allied with a murderous psychopath who's got you pressed so hard under his thumb you can barely breathe."

"It wasn't that simple, and you know it," Sienar said. "If you and Ezza hadn't gotten yourselves exiled, then maybe I'd have had more options."

Probably not, Cherny thought. It seemed more likely he'd have done anything to prove his loyalty and keep his old life.

"But no," Sienar continued, "you and Jenna were too unstable, and Ezza was already jumping ship to join the United Fleet. Frankly, it's a miracle I convinced Her to let you live out your lives and not wind up like Taylor." At Cherny's sudden silence, Sienar grimaced. "What, you thought She let you go out of the kindness of whatever passes for Her heart? Cherny, after all you've been through, you can't still believe that 'She loves all Her agents' crap." He scowled. "She loved us like pets, maybe."

"How …?" Cherny started.

"How did I persuade Her? It wasn't easy. Played to Her ego and convinced Her you two were no threat. She might try to set Herself up as some all-knowing goddess, but She's only human, Cherny. Technology and people—both are fallible. As for the Ganymede Blitz, if you think I had a lot of time after figuring out Her plans, then you're sadly mistaken. Stopping the takeover of the Syndicate was my only realistic option. It bought me time, and it bought me the gratitude of Reuben's forces."

PALE GREY DOT

"Time you spend sitting in Mars's basement while Reuben waits for all his enemies to kill each other," Cherny said. "And Reuben's trust doesn't seem to get you very much. What part of this doesn't scream 'screw up'?"

Cherny was almost disappointed that Sienar didn't lash out at him. Unleashing some pent-up anger would have felt good right about now, but the man was too damn reasonable. Sienar shook his head and reached back into the hatch. "It's not a great situation," he admitted. "It's such a classic ploy She's pulling, really. Declare some foreign threat to be the enemy and then tell the people you're the only one who can protect them. The only thing She's doing differently is actually feeding the enemy. We expose that, Fairchild will put an end to Her."

As he listened, Cherny ran through the list of user IDs he'd acquired through his network traces. *Come on. Someone here must have been careless with their access.* "And then Reuben's anarchists will have the run of the place. Not much of an improvement," Cherny said.

Access Denied.

Access Denied.

Access Denied.

"No," Sienar agreed.

"So when is Kyle going to operate on you? If I can't go after Amanda, then maybe you can once you're cured."

"He isn't," Sienar replied.

321

Cherny's surprise was genuine.

"Even if we could afford another five days for me to be unconscious, it wouldn't change the fact that you're absolutely right: Reuben gains everything by sitting here and doing nothing." Sienar stopped in front of another access panel. With a loud clang, he pulled it off and set it down on the ground before reaching into the hatch. "Unless ..."

In a flash, Cherny felt the sensor open up to him. Every byte flying between the abandoned vacuum train station, the sensor, and MarsNet passed through his mind. Cherny mentally prepared the necessary command to send a message to Amanda but found himself hesitating. "What are you ...?"

Sienar pulled his arms out again and slapped the hatch back on. He gave Cherny a grim smile. "You used to be so confident back in the old days. Trusted by everyone. Especially Her. I need you to regain that. After all, you're going to be the operative that eradicates the last of Alexander Reuben's cells."

"But ..."

"My greatest asset has never been intellect, strength, or charm. It's always been the team. You, Jenna, and Ezza— there's still fight left in you." When Cherny didn't answer, Sienar put a hand on his shoulder. "And don't worry. There's still fight left in me as well."

Cherny locked eyes with his brother, understanding the offer. Return to ESS. Resist the Pull. Save Jenna. Or stay here. A prisoner. Lose Jenna forever.

Cherny executed the command.

15

The door slid closed behind Jenna as she stepped out of *Starknight*'s surgical bay. She tugged at her gloves, tossing them in the bin as she passed. She was immediately greeted by three pairs of eyes staring in her direction. It was taking some practise not to be unnerved by all the attention.

"Well?" Nirali asked. The woman was sitting on the nearby medical bed. She had gained a deep purple bruise on her forehead, along with a black eye, though Jenna didn't know if she earned them during or before the train crash.

O'Brien stood near her. Though he said nothing, there was curiosity in his eyes that matched Nirali's question.

The third set of eyes were fully cybernetic. Rachelle Eday was apparently the second-in-command of this ship, though Jenna had only briefly met her. Overseeing a ship's computer systems while being simultaneously in charge of everyone couldn't be easy. Jenna remembered how hard it had been

323

to multitask on *Étoile*, and *Étoile* was far simpler than a warship. Rachelle sat perfectly still, no doubt distracted by her work.

"Went just fine," Jenna said. She couldn't keep the happiness out of her voice.

Nirali gave a sigh of relief.

"'Just fine' … meaning what, exactly?" O'Brien asked.

Meaning I'm beating Her. "It means it went better than I had hoped." She'd managed to walk a washed-up doctor from the Midwestern Wastes through the procedure decades ago when she'd had her own loyalty chip removed, but it felt good to finally get a chance to do it herself. "She should be up in a few hours."

"Will she remember everything she did?" Nirali asked. "When she was under their influence, I mean?"

It never quite worked like that, Jenna thought, but she didn't bother correcting her. "Yes. She'll remember everything."

Nirali nodded and gazed down at the floor.

Jenna took a step towards the medical table, getting a closer look at the reporter's bruises. She couldn't begin to guess why Ezza decided to bring a journalist on a secret mission to one of the most remote places in the solar system and let her be privy to so much sensitive information. Still, Nirali's quick thinking during Jenna's brief shootout with Bev Stroud had been convenient.

"We must now decide our next course of action," Rachelle said, finally breaking her silence. "I am still awaiting a reply from UFS *Pravedni*. Commander O'Brien, did the admiral

PALE GREY DOT

give further orders once you had secured the captain?" The cables running down the back of her head swayed as she spoke. Jenna found the full-convert cyborg unnerving—she reminded her too much of ESS's overwatches.

"No," O'Brien replied. "Once she dealt with Ncube, she was planning to head to Earth and meet with the premier to make the case against ESS."

Rachelle nodded. "Then in the absence of further orders, we should prepare to return to Jupiter Station so we can assist with the relief effort. Ganymede's orbit around Jupiter will create an optimal trajectory within two days. By that time, Captain Jayens will be awake, and we can consult with her."

"What?" Jenna protested. "We need to go to Earth! If Cheng-Visitor thinks she can get Fairchild to shut ESS down, we should be there. That's the only thing that matters right now."

"I don't see what benefit we would be providing the admiral. You failed to find Cheng-Visitor's proof at Uruk Sulcus-132."

Jenna opened her mouth to argue, but then thought better of it. "Fine. It's your ship. I'll be resting." As she started for the exit, she paused long enough to place her hand on Nirali's shoulder. "Watch over Ezza for me."

When she had come aboard, Jenna had managed to convince Rachelle to grant her use of Ezza's quarters until she was back on her feet. Space was at a premium on board *Starknight*, and Jenna had no interest in returning to hot bunking. Privacy was what she needed now. Jenna slid the door closed until she heard the click, then locked it. It wouldn't stop anyone with authorization, but at least it'd make it clear that she didn't want to be bothered.

Ezza's quarters were two by four metres, with a bunk and bed bag that could be configured for acceleration, rotational, or zero-g manoeuvres. Jenna lowered the bunk from the wall and sat down. *Sparse,* Jenna thought. Digging her hand into her pocket, she drew out a small data drive, taken from Bev Stroud in the aftermath of their fight.

You pulled this off once before with Marcus, she reminded herself. *That worked out all right.* Rolling up the sleeve of the United Fleet jumper they had given her, Jenna nervously ran her finger along the cracked and broken machinery on her arm. She wondered if she'd be able to get them fixed up once her mission was complete, or whether she'd go back to sleeping on the streets.

They need proof. That's what Cheng-Visitor and Rachelle said. Whatever memories were passing through Stroud's mind near the end of her life may have it. Jenna activated full debug logging for her cybernetics and carefully slid the drive into one of the ports as she lay back.

She was elsewhere now. The bed was different than the one in Ezza's quarters. It was far more elaborate, outfitted with overhead robotic arms and nanite scopes. A dark-haired man with a mechanical left eye looked down at her. Jenna's head rolled to the side to look at her metal arm. No, she looked at Bev Stroud's arm. It was silver and gleamed

PALE GREY DOT

in the bright lights of the surgical bay. Bev flexed her new metal hand. There was some scarring where the machinery met the flesh of her shoulder, but it didn't hurt.

"How do you feel?" the surgeon asked.

Bev broke into a wide smile as she curled and uncurled each finger. Power ran through her subdermal implants, feeding into the new cybernetics. It felt just like her old arm. "It's perfect," she breathed.

Jenna knew what this was. It was Bev's initiation into the operative rank. The enhanced strength, agility, and mental prowess that came with the machinery felt amazing. Jenna felt Bev's relief from passing the final hurdle. She was an operative now. The word alone demanded fear and respect from the common dredges.

The surgeon helped Bev to a sitting position. "You're to stay within the Tower for the next forty-eight hours for observation. Adverse reactions to the implants are rare, but they do happen."

"And after that?" Bev asked, holding onto his arm.

"After that," the surgeon smiled, "we can connect you with SecLink. You won't have to say a thing. You'll be able to feel Her."

Bev smiled with a mix of pride and nervousness. Everything she'd accomplished, from childhood to her service in ESS, was thanks to Her love and support. The idea of disappointing Her was terrifying, and not just because of the power She had over her life.

Back in Ezza's bed, Jenna gagged at the thought. It was

327

all too familiar. The surgeon's smiling face shifted, fading into the background as Jenna felt the medical slab vanish beneath her. *Where now?* Jenna wondered. A great window was between her and the endless field of stars.

Bev was clipped to one of the wall sofas in the Ganymede orbital station, gazing out into space. The window was artificial, of course—a projected simulation, both Bev and Jenna knew that—but the view was still beautiful. She wore a Ganymede Port Authority uniform—grey with blue highlights. A small bag of chocolate-infused café floated next to her, straw sticking out of the valve on top. There were others here. Bev's awareness training marked them all, though she gave no outward sign of it.

So, serving as an infiltrator at a way station, Jenna thought. *Not a bad job for an operative. Useful. Easy. Comfortable. Not so exciting, though, if that's your goal.*

Bev felt her subdermal implants buzz, and Jenna found herself holding her breath. *SecLink.* Jenna reminded herself that SecLink couldn't hurt her here. There was no risk of the Pull overcoming her. It was Bev connecting, not her. Still, Jenna's instincts were on edge.

//Hello, Bev. I need your help.//

Bev closed her eyes. It wasn't Her—She was back on Earth—but rather a fellow operative. //What do you need, Brylan?//

Jenna had recognized the "voice" even before Bev had thought it. There was a delay in the conversation. Twelve seconds passed between each message. In the back of her

PALE GREY DOT

mind, Jenna began calculating Brylan's possible locations. *When was this?* she wondered.

//Our wayward Ezza Jayens is heading your way. You are to collect her.//

//I'm already on assignment. My Syndicate contacts rely on me.//

//Not so important anymore. The fleet at Jupiter Station has been destroyed, and we have operatives across the system working to arrest the United Fleet leadership. Transmit your files on the Syndicate to the Tower. The overwatches can handle the coordination while you focus on retrieving Ezza.//

There! Jenna thought triumphantly. *Culpability!* Jenna felt Bev transmitting the data on her contacts, and Jenna's debug logging greedily slurped it up.

//I thought getting Ezza back into the fold was your job. You are right there with her, no?// A part of Bev wanted to push Brylan—really mock him for his failure. Jenna understood the feeling well.

//Ah, Bev. You know I'd have Ezza soon enough, but another wayward agent is coming my way. I regret I must leave the smaller fish for you.//

It took both Bev and Jenna a moment to realize what he meant. //You've found Jenna?//

Back on *Starknight*, Jenna shivered. A sense of dread began growing within her. She didn't know if she wanted to keep watching.

//She reached out to Cherny. Yes, I was surprised too.

329

Sentimentality, I suppose. She is on her way here, and I need to be ready.//

Jenna felt herself starting to hyperventilate. *Cherny couldn't have …*

//You need to get to Uruk Sulcus-132,// Brylan continued. //You'll need to travel by orbital drop. There can be no sign of your presence. Let Ezza access Sienar's final message and record its contents, then return her to the fold.//

//Did the team that reviewed his message to Cherny not secure the intel we need? What did it say?//

//It was heavy on misty-eyed notions of reassembling their team, along with a rant about his traitorous motives. Here's hoping for more substance from a message to his oh-so-powerful United Fleet sister.//

While Bev wondered whether she stood a chance against the legendary Ezza Jayens, Jenna's frantic thoughts were on Cherny. Maybe him telling ESS her location was part of some grander scheme. Maybe he knew Cheng-Visitor would secretly get a message to her. Jenna remembered how close she was to ending it all to avoid capture. Maybe Cherny had no choice. Maybe … But nothing else fit. *Betrayal. Memories don't lie.* Her breathing turned ragged.

Brylan must have picked up on Bev's long silence. //Her Athena Protocols have been activated, Bev. Oh, she tries to hide it, but I can see straight through her. Exploit that. And if you have to kill her, that is just fine. At the end of the day, she is not so important.//

Pale Grey Dot

Bev didn't seem convinced. She held the bag of café tightly, letting its heat warm her hands.

Jenna tried to focus, but the scene from Bev's memory was slipping away.

This is your chance, Bev thought. *Capture Ezza. Stop one of the six who hurt Her so much.* Jenna blocked the thoughts from her mind as best she could. On *Starknight*, she grasped at the data drive with sweaty fingers.

Bev and Jenna were elsewhere. They were at a club. Lights flashed down on them from above, and aromatic smoke filled their nostrils. No, she was on her back somewhere warm and soft. Her eyes were closed, but she could feel a man kissing her neck. The place shifted, and Bev was planning a route to Uruk Sulcus-132 that avoided detection. She was in the Tower, raising a glass with friends and colleagues. She was analyzing dossiers. She was fighting a man. She was stepping onto the surface of Ganymede … The places blurred.

Jenna finally managed to get a firm grip on the drive, and she yanked it from its socket. She sat upright, grabbing her head. Her hair felt greasy between her fingers. *Sentimental!* That's what Brylan had sent, and he had been right. *This is what you get for trusting anyone else. Even Cherny.* Jenna sniffed loudly. *You've let yourself grow soft these past weeks.*

There's no one else you can rely on anymore, she decided. *Only you.*

Don Miasek

Cherny was able to predict when it would happen. Two days after he triggered the command on the remote sensor, Sienar sent Kyle above ground to collect supplies and meet with contacts. It was a routine assignment, but the task usually fell to others, so Cherny recognized its significance.

He'd been spending his time drinking the watered-down, distilled crap they considered alcohol. Cherny found lowering his standards had been easier than trying to raise its quality. Sienar met with him only a few times. "Best they not think we're too close these days," he'd explained. They discussed the layout of the base's defences, which personnel were essential and which were disposable, and potential escape routes.

But just as often as not, their talks drifted to their childhood at the Kazan Institute for Education, and to Jenna. She had been the last to join their team at just ten years of age.

The educators had shoved her into their classroom and closed the door. She didn't stray from that spot all day, and stared them all down whenever they looked in her direction. While the others played with the VR system, completed their logic tests, or ran through their mathematics exercises, Jenna had watched from a distance. It was a day before she spoke a word to them, and longer before she truly joined them. But once she did, the six were inseparable.

PALE GREY DOT

"She needs your help, Cherny," Sienar had told him. "And you're going to need to resist the Pull from SecLink long enough to give it to her."

Most of the technical data Jenna had sent Sienar on the Athena Protocols was way beyond his comprehension, but Sienar had made it clear: even with the loyalty chip excised, SecLink would happily feed the conditioning to him should he ever be able to reconnect. There were theories on how to beat it, but in typical Jenna fashion, they were complicated. *She resisted it for decades. You can damn well do it until the mission is complete. You can't fail her again.* Despite the guilt, Cherny was relieved that she didn't know what he'd done to her. *You got away with your betrayal,* he thought.

It began with an alarm, through both the intercom and every subdermal implant in the base. Cherny was halfway through a piss when he heard it. He was alone in the bathroom, but he could already hear the shouts and commotion outside. He muted the virtual alert, but the real one was still blaring, echoing loudly in the enclosed space.

Cherny stopped in front of the sink, running his hands under the sanitation unit for a few seconds. He flicked them dry and approached the exit, pressing himself against the door. Through it, he could make out the sound of panicked footfalls. Five pairs. He took a deep breath and made his move.

Cherny burst into the hall without warning, hoping to catch them unawares. Three had managed to arm themselves, so Cherny focused on them after driving his metal fist into the face of the man closest to him. He crumpled into a heap as his friends reacted.

A woman—touting a newer SineWave targeting module and a LasTech Phoenix energy projector—was the top priority. Cherny barrelled through a pair of shocked defenders even as she took aim with her projector. There was a flash as the weapon went off just as Cherny reached for her. The lighting fixture in the ceiling exploded, raining sparks down upon them. For a brief moment, the alarm was drowned out by the noise. Cherny grabbed her arm and drove her face-first into the wall.

Cherny didn't bother reaching for the fallen weapon—it'd be locked to her implants—and instead whirled on the remaining three. By now, the element of surprise was gone, but there was only one person left with an actual gun. She desperately scrambled backwards, trying to use her compatriots as cover.

"Operative! Wait, no, we can—" she cried out.

A hulking freckle-faced man in Cherny's way took a swing at him with a lit evaporator torch. Reaching forward, Cherny caught the arm holding the weapon as it was brought down. The tip of the torch glowed bright white, and Cherny could feel the scorching heat just inches from his face. From here, it was a battle of strength, and Cherny's mechanical arm had that in abundance. He grabbed his adversary by the elbow and twisted him into the line of fire as the gunwoman pulled the trigger. The roar of the weapon echoed loudly down the hall. The freckle-faced man screamed in pain. The bulkhead behind them shattered.

PALE GREY DOT

Lucky, Cherny thought as he snagged the torch and let the man fall. *Four centimetres to the right and that would have been me as well.* Lunging forward, Cherny swung his weapon, catching the gunwoman square in the torso.

That left just one, and Cherny turned back towards her. He had already marked her as young. Sixty at most. She wore a faded red Martian longcoat, and from the way her suit bulged around the seams, she wasn't in decent shape. She had nothing resembling a weapon, and from the fear in her eyes, it was clear she knew she didn't stand a chance.

Cherny gripped his new evaporator torch with both hands and was unsurprised when the woman fled down the hall. He let her go. Killing random Syndicate members wasn't his goal here. Cherny flicked the switch on his torch and glanced at its display panel. The battery was nearly dry, but it would do for his purposes. He sprinted down the nearby stairwell and raced through the corridor at the bottom, stopping in front of the familiar door with its electronic lock. As expected, his stolen codes worked perfectly. Sienar would have made certain of that. The lock flashed green, and Cherny entered.

The room was as dark as ever, with only its single red bulb illuminating Alexander Reuben's life-support machinery. He was in the corner, interfacing with a console on the far wall.

"You have a way out of here, don't you?" Cherny called out.

Reuben turned, legs ratcheting as he faced the operative.

Don Miasek

His metal feet scraped against the floor, almost drowning out the distant sirens and advancing gunfire.

"Secret passages? An elevator to the surface? Something more exotic?" Cherny asked, stepping closer. With his systems fully restored by Sienar, he didn't need to wait for his eyes to adjust to make out the details of Reuben's form. As Cherny spoke, he registered every bolt running along Reuben's limbs, the servos that stood in place of flesh joints, and the armour plating protecting his vulnerabilities. Cherny calculated the reach of the man's robotic arms and the rotational limits of his shoulders. He remembered all too well the strength Reuben possessed.

The cyborg drew himself up to his full height, towering over Cherny. His optic telescoped and locked on to the intruder. Cherny wondered if he was being sized up as well. "You have brought them to us," Reuben said.

"Yep." Cherny brandished the evaporator torch with his metal hand. *Show no fear,* he reminded himself.

"Sienar has set you free."

Cherny didn't answer.

"And you believe you can capture me. To ensure the destruction of the Syndicate and the gratitude of your master."

"Close." Cherny's thumb flicked the switch on the torch, and it snapped alight as he held it out in front of him.

Reuben's optic focused on the tool. "You seek my destruction. Illogical. I am far more valuable to the Earth Security Service alive. You will not kill me."

PALE GREY DOT

"Only four people know that I've been cured of the Pull. Sienar, Kyle, me, and ..."

For the first time since he'd met him, Cherny believed he was able to read Reuben's expression. It was fear and comprehension. Reuben's hydraulics flexed as he took a lumbering step towards him. Cherny's enhanced vision showed a bright red power surge as Reuben brought his combat systems online.

Cherny had always hated this part of the job. He watched the cyborg carefully, wondering what was going through Reuben's head. "You should be thrilled. You're going to help me bring down ESS."

Reuben's arm, thicker than Cherny's leg, came swinging around far faster than someone with that much bulk ought to have been able to manage. This time, however, Cherny was ready. Ducking underneath the swipe, he lunged forward. It took all his strength to push the torch through the hard armouring on Reuben's chest. There was a crack, and the leader of the Syndicate slumped forward. The joints in his legs and arms seized up, preventing him from toppling over. The stench of burnt flesh and metal wafted from the body.

Leaving the torch lodged where it was, Cherny headed for the exit. He wasn't going to wait around for Syndicate personnel catch him here with Reuben's corpse. Cherny felt a buzz as his subdermal implants found a valid connection suddenly within reach. He opened his mind, and a full map of the Syndicate base flowed in. He could see the attacking force—the Martian Planetary Guard—throughout the base

Don Miasek

as they pushed through the halls. Icons denoting their status and armaments hovered over their positions. Known locations of the Syndicate defenders—both human and machine—were present as well, updated the moment any of the Planetary Guard spotted them.

War zones had never been Cherny's forte, but it only took him a moment to absorb the tactical data. Each defence point was quickly overrun by the power-armoured troopers. But there was one small team of Syndicate personnel sneaking their way through the upper halls. They evaded the lines of attack, only pausing to pick off the occasional straggler. *Sienar.* A feeling of dread came over Cherny as he broke into a sprint out of Reuben's office.

At the back of the invading force was a single blue icon marked by three simple letters: *ESS.* The icon, flanked by two soldiers, moved towards the only Syndicate team putting up a fight. They were marked in bright red.

Cherny vaulted up the stairwell at the end of the hallway, taking the steps three at a time. He sent a quick message along the Martian Planetary Guard network as he plotted a path to avoid as much of the fighting as he could. //This is Operative Cherny. Alexander Reuben has been eliminated. I'll be passing by your Hermes team within half a minute. The route looks clear.//

The flash of acknowledgement was almost immediate, and Cherny prayed their people were cautious enough not to simply shoot at anything that moved. Tactical overlay or no, trigger-happy idiots were always dangerous. As he raced

PALE GREY DOT

through the cafeteria, he saw soldiers decked out in matte-brown plating with arm-mounted energy projectors. They were processing the surviving Syndicate defenders, though the network was already preparing to send them deeper into the base for further combat.

The captives were having their hands shackled behind their backs and any cybernetic systems disabled. Those that hadn't surrendered had either been melted by energy projectors or torn apart by ballistics. Their fallen forms were strewn about the floor amongst tiny bits of metal that were once the cafeteria tables. Apparently, the defenders overturned the tables in a futile attempt to take cover.

One of the Planetary Guard soldiers, with hardly a mark on his armour, stood from where he was securing a woman's hands. "Hold, Operative! Are you hurt? We have a medic here who can—"

Cherny ignored the question and snagged one of the battered Syndicate rifles used in their ineffective defence. By some small mercy, it was unlocked. Cherny darted past the soldiers and into the adjoining hall that led to the base's comm centre. He knew exactly what Sienar was planning: fight down to the barricade and flee into the tunnels.

Cherny's implants buzzed again, but this time, the message was a much higher priority. SecLink. *"The chip may be gone, but SecLink will happily send you the protocols whenever you reconnect,"* Sienar had said. He summoned his courage and reconnected.

//Cherny, I need your help.// It was Amanda. //Sienar has

Don Miasek

disabled two of my teams and is making his way through the train tunnels. You are in position to outflank him if you hurry.//

Cherny stumbled, nearly dropping the rifle as he fought the Pull. It wasn't much farther to the comm station that overlooked the barricade guarding the tunnels. From there, he could drop down and … save Sienar. No, fight Sienar.

//Cherny, are you there?//

Sweat poured down Cherny's forehead as he forced himself onward. Gone was the light sensation of Martian gravity. Now his feet felt like they were glued to the floor. He leaned against the ruddy brown wall for support. *Just need a moment.* Cherny mentally transmitted, //I read you. I'm close. I'll get there.//

//Good. Stay connected. I'll feed you the necessary tactical data.//

Cherny grimaced and resumed his march. Disconnecting now would look suspicious. Sienar was fighting for his life over his decision to free him, but it would all be for nothing if Cherny let his cure slip.

The comm centre was dark, and Cherny had to squint to make out that the great glass pane overlooking the tunnel had been shattered. The last flicker of an energy discharge was reflected in the jagged shards that still clung to the window frame.

It was no brighter in the tunnel, but with his SecLink connection to Amanda, Cherny already knew what he'd find upon stumbling up to the broken window and looking

340

PALE GREY DOT

down. He could barely make out the rough shape of Amanda crouched behind the barricade, next to the wreckage of two makeshift drones the inhabitants had used for defence. She wore a Martian longcoat over black thin-weave armour and held an energy projector in her hands.

Beside her stood a full-convert combat cyborg with arms outstretched in front of him. External metal beams reinforced his limbs and torso, and his face was encased in a concealing helmet. Affixed to each forearm was a gun larger than most men. He was built and armed like a tank. The subtle glow of his optics provided what little light existed in the tunnel.

Scarcely thirty metres away was the fallen form of a second combat cyborg. This one was dead. His chassis had been split apart by explosives, leaving a greasy puddle on the tracks. Cherny could see the lone survivor of the Syndicate squad hiding behind it. From the way Sienar cradled his flesh arm with his metal one, it was clear he was injured. The energy projector in his cybernetic arm, however, was still primed.

"There's no reason to continue this, Sienar!" Amanda called out. "You know She will have mercy on you." She kept her eyes trained on Sienar's hiding spot. "You were one of Her favourites."

Sienar gave a loud, wheezing laugh that was interrupted by a coughing fit. "So was Taylor, and that didn't help him, did it?"

//Cherny, do you have line of sight?//

Cherny transmitted his affirmative.

Don Miasek

//Then shoot to disable. We'll charge in and take him alive.//

The rifle felt twice as heavy as Cherny slowly lifted it up and through the glassless window, careful not to make any noise.

"Taylor gave Her no choice. You were there, Sienar. You saw what he did."

"Yes, and we both saw what She did at Jupiter Station. You can't keep it a secret forever, Amanda," Sienar shouted.

The cyborg beside Amanda shifted his weight uncomfortably, but still kept his weapons trained on his target. Cherny's connection to Amanda told him that he was ready to fire the instant Sienar moved.

"Anything She did was the result of your failure on Mars," Amanda called out.

Sienar laughed again, though his voice was growing weaker. "I want you to tell Her that at least one of Her wretched children fought against Her every step of the way."

Cherny levelled the rifle, peering down the sights as he took aim. *Shoot him! He turned against Her! No, shoot Amanda! She wants to turn you against your friends!* Cherny started to pull back on the trigger.

"Or hell," Sienar suddenly snarled, "maybe I'll get the chance to tell Her myself."

A cacophony of shredding metal filled the tunnel as the left side of the barricade detonated, sending shrapnel flying into the combat cyborg's heavy armour plating. Cherny saw Amanda jump in the split second it took for the smoke and

PALE GREY DOT

dust to rush up to him. Cherny gagged, trying to hold his aim as he struggled to breathe. Metal crashed against metal as the entire rampart collapsed in on itself. The sound of repeated energy discharges snapped Cherny back into action.

Though he couldn't see more than three feet in front of him, Cherny leapt through the window. With the help of Mars's gravity, he hit the ground between the destroyed barricade and where Sienar had hidden. The air was even worse down here. Four steps in, he saw it.

Sienar's body was burnt nearly beyond recognition. The right side of his torso was gone, and the half-melted remnants of his cybernetic arm rested at an unnatural angle. Sienar's bloodied eyes stared straight ahead, lifeless. His body was coated in the white dust kicked up from the explosion.

Amanda stood over the corpse. Gently, she nudged Sienar's chin with her boot, as if to make sure he was really dead. Amanda looked at Cherny. "I'm sorry, but he didn't leave us much choice."

Cherny felt his eyes growing wet, and he swiped at them with his hand. *Tell her Kyle cured you!* Cherny stiffened and disconnected from SecLink as quickly as he could. There was no need for the tactical data anymore, and the thought of turning against Sienar made him feel sick.

"He was a traitor," Cherny lied. His voice was cracking, but he plowed ahead. "It had to be done." Cherny was certain Amanda would jump on his weakness, but to his surprise, she put her hand on his shoulder.

343

Don Miasek

"He was a fine operative, once," she said. "He just lost his way."

Cherny looked at her and saw the semblance of understanding in her expression. *She's becoming more human the longer she's away from Her,* he realized through the haze of his grief. Pushing the thought aside for now, Cherny knelt before his fallen brother.

"I think I understand what She saw in you." Amanda gave his shoulder a squeeze before letting go. "You've done an amazing thing here, Cherny. Jenna, Sienar, and now Alexander Reuben. Combined, the entire service has been looking for them for over two hundred years. You did it in a month."

But Cherny didn't reply, unable to take his eyes off Sienar's battered form. *For everything he did for us—everything he sacrificed here for me, so that I could escape this place—he deserved so much better.*

"Well," Amanda said, glancing back and forth between Cherny and Sienar, "I need to see to the processing of the surviving Syndicate members. I'll give you some time. Just … please, let me know when you're ready to go back to the Tower."

There was a hint of anxiety in her voice. *You want to go back to Her, but all your progress will be lost.* Cherny wished there was a way he could keep Amanda away from Earth, but it didn't seem possible. *Sienar probably could have thought of a way.*

Cherny took one last look. Sal, Taylor, and now Sienar.

PALE GREY DOT

There were only three of them left. He put on a brave face that he did not feel. "I'm ready now."

"It's no excuse," Ezza said as she sat on the edge of the surgical bed. The pale blue medical gown hung loosely on her body. Adams and Gole were dead, killed on a backwater moon as far away from civilization as possible, and it was her fault.

"Are you kidding?" Nirali said with a wide smile. "It's basically the greatest excuse in the history of humankind! Come on, Ezza. Mind control!"

"No, it isn't ... It wasn't quite like that," Ezza replied. "It was more of a rough directive. It ..." she trailed off. "Nirali, I attacked you."

"Wow, you really need to work on how you spin things. Just say 'mind control' and be done with it. I'm forgiving you."

Ezza couldn't help but smile, though it might have been easier if the reporter had told her off. "You're a much kinder person than I am."

"So ... you feel better now?"

"Yeah, I really do." Ezza reached up and felt the scar on the back of her head. Jenna had shaved a small patch on her scalp, but the rest of her hair sufficiently covered it up. Her mind felt free for the first time since Jupiter Station. She gave it a try. *ESS was behind the attack on the fleet,* she thought. Nothing. No

Don Miasek

pain. No overriding feelings coercing her into how to think. *Furthermore,* Ezza decided, *She is a hateful, spiteful bitch who deserves to rot in hell for Adams, Gole, Jupiter Station, and everyone else who's suffered at Her hands.* Again, nothing. Ezza's smile grew. It was far more amusing than it should have been.

"You're not just saying that?"

"Nirali …"

"All I know is that I'm going to get so many downloads when I file this story."

Ezza blinked.

Nirali raised her hands innocently. "I'm kidding!"

"Actually, it might come to that," Ezza mused. According to Nirali, Cheng-Visitor's *Pravedni* had yet to respond to their inquiries. Ezza had perused the most recent United Fleet channel transmissions. There were requests for orders, reports that nobody seemed to read, and a general sense of confusion. Compared to the anarchy that had settled over both the United Fleet and the solar system, the recent events at Uruk Sulcus-132 seemed petty.

Shouts could be heard in hallway. *Starknight's* surgical bay was insulated, but the pair of voices carried nonetheless. The first was a man Ezza didn't recognize. The second was all too familiar, and her heart skipped a beat when she realized who it was.

The hatch to the medical bay swung open. Nirali looked up, startled, as two figures stormed in.

"He betrayed us, O'Brien!" the first shouted. Damp hair hung around her flushed face. "For fifty goddamn years I

PALE GREY DOT

fought and suffered to set things right and that son of a bitch betrays us!"

"Jenna." It took a moment for the smile to fade from Ezza's face as she registered her sister's fury.

O'Brien was one step behind and just as furious. "You can't just barge in wherever you want," he was saying. "This is a military vessel. Security means we have a process for—"

Jenna cut him off. "Piss off. This is between me and Ezza. I knew her long before she joined your bureaucratic nightmare of an army. If it weren't for me, you and your team would be sucking vacuum on Ganymede."

The marine stood at his full height. He was easily a foot taller and likely four times as strong. "You don't give orders on this ship," he growled.

"Hey!" Ezza stood up from the bed. "Commander, thank you for bringing Jenna here. She's my responsibility, and I'll keep her out of trouble."

"Yes, ma'am," O'Brien replied.

"Well, I can see you haven't changed," Jenna muttered.

Ignoring Jenna's crack, Ezza kept going. "First, Jenna, thank you. I'd normally say that I can't believe you travelled across the solar system just to save me, but honestly, that's exactly the sort of thing you'd do." Ezza smiled in an attempt to reassure her.

"Second, I have no idea what the hell you're talking about. Who betrayed us?" Ezza suddenly remembered how thin her medical gown was. She glanced at Nirali and gestured to her uniform on the clothes rack.

"I went through Bev's memories," Jenna hissed. "That

347

Don Miasek

asshole Brylan said Cherny had turned, but oh, I knew better, I thought. 'Cherny would never betray us. Cherny knows the value of the team. Cherny has some goddamn integrity!' Well, it turns out he's scum, just like the rest of them!" Her eyes glistened between fury and despair.

Ezza took her naval jacket from Nirali and pushed her arms through the sleeves, regaining at least some semblance of dignity. Then she looked back at Jenna and waited quietly for the full story.

Jenna explained how she fought the operative Marcus on Earth and stole his memory drive, how she hitched a ride on *Étoile* for passage to Jupiter, and the joy she felt at finally being able to reach out to her surviving siblings. She described her failed attempt to flee Admiral Cheng-Visitor's *Pravedni*, how Brylan Ncube interrogated her, and how Cheng-Visitor and O'Brien freed her. Ezza repeatedly asked how in the world she'd managed to delve into an operative's memory drive, and everyone had stared in shock when she described hacking into SecLink. The technical jargon was leagues beyond everyone else's comprehension. Finally, she described her discovery within Bev Stroud's memory drive—the proof of ESS involvement in the attack at Jupiter Station, and of Cherny's betrayal.

When Jenna was finished, Ezza tried to keep a look of sympathy off her face. It wasn't something Jenna would appreciate, she knew. "Jenna, Cherny was reactivated. That

PALE GREY DOT

means the Athena Protocols were affecting him. You think he betrayed us? He didn't have a choice."

"Oh, spare me," Jenna snapped. "I resisted the damn thing for years before figuring out a way to slice it out of me. Didn't see *you* turning me in."

"No, I … Jenna, no." Ezza gave a nervous laugh. "You don't understand. I went through what he must have. I did my best. I really did, but I couldn't …" Ezza paused, composing herself. "There were so many times when I wanted to give up. The Cerebrol helped, but it wasn't enough. By the end, I would have done anything to sate the Pull." A part of her wondered if she should be telling Jenna this, but Ezza found she couldn't lie. "I wouldn't have lasted another minute. You're going to have to forgive him."

Jenna went silent. Ezza tried to decipher her implacable stare, but as usual, she was impossible to read.

Nirali and O'Brien exchanged nervous glances.

Ezza rubbed her temple with her cybernetic hand. Before she could say more, her subdermal implants buzzed. She switched the call to full audio.

"Captain, this is Rachelle." The cyborg came through clearly, but Ezza could hear the worry in her voice. "We've received word on *Pravedni*."

No sense putting off more bad news, Ezza decided. "Let's hear it, then."

*** FLEET-WIDE TRANSMISSION ***
*** SOURCE: THE TOWER ***
*** DESTINATION: ALL UNITED FLEET HOLDINGS ***

In the wake of the latest wave of attacks, the Earth Security Service, under direction of Premier Fairchild, has been charged with identifying and neutralizing the perpetrators behind the Jupiter Station attack. Preliminary investigation has already revealed widespread and systematic leaks in the United Fleet Admiralty by the Syndicate. Implicated flag officers have been brought into custody.

This investigation has also found evidence of Admiral Gabrielle Cheng-Visitor colluding with enemy forces, including facilitating the escape of a known terrorist. The admiral, formerly in command of extraplanetary fleet movements, has been arrested. Defence Minister Sebastian Havoic has also been temporarily removed from his post, pending further investigation.

All further orders to individual United Fleet assets will be sent from the Ministry of Public Safety, Earth Security Service branch, until this matter is resolved. The authority signatures of Premier Fairchild and Public Safety Minister Richter have been attached to this message.

Full cooperation with ESS personnel is expected. Normal operations will resume once the transfer of power has been completed.

United Fleet Command, Earth Security Service

16

//Welcome home, Operative.//

Cherny stopped mid-breath as he heard Her thoughts for the first time since he'd left Earth. SecLink meant the Pull, and the Pull meant being on the brink of failure. //Yes. I mean, thank you,// he sent. //It's good to be back.// Despite what he now knew, Her voice was still as smooth and comforting and terrifying as ever.

//You're still nervous.// It wasn't always clear when She was asking a question or making a statement. //Surely your past shortfalls have been redeemed by your recent successes.//

Cherny had returned to the Tower last night, and he had spent most of his time secluded in the small office set aside for his use. A chair, a desk, a data port, and a small holo-projector were all he really needed. //I still have work to do,// he finally sent. The best lies were nearly the truth.

351

Don Miasek

//You feel you still have something to prove.//

Another remark with more to it, and Cherny recognized the questions that lay beneath it instantly: Are you jealous of my connection with Amanda? That you've been replaced with the newer model? Are you concerned about no longer being my favourite? Cherny rubbed his forehead. A month ago, and the honest answer would have been yes to all. //Well, I ... // Cherny struggled to think of what to say. //We're always trying to prove we deserve to be the best.//

//Then I shall let you get back to it. Farewell, Operative.//

The line was severed, and Cherny breathed a sigh of relief. Jenna's write-up on the Athena Protocols had been invaluable. Yet another gift from Sienar. A half empty bottle of Cerebrol rested on the desk in front of him. It seemed to help.

Pushing himself up from his seat, he skirted around to the exit. As he stepped out into the hall, he spotted a familiar face. "Hey, Adrian," Cherny said. "What's brought you out of your lair? The place isn't burning down, is it?" he joked.

The overwatch stopped his awkward shuffling. His servos whined in protest as he turned towards Cherny, slowly and methodically, and the cables on his back jangled against the floor. In some ways, he reminded Cherny of Alexander Reuben, but with a mechanical body meant for data integration instead of physical strength. "Hey, Cherny," he cracked a smile. "On a café run. Esther gets cranky if she runs out."

Cherny grinned. "That'd be one disaster too many. We'd be hard-pressed to explain to the premier that the government fell because of a caffeine deficiency."

PALE GREY DOT

"Heh. You know it. Want to come with?"

"Yeah, sure." Cherny fell in line beside him. "How are the overwatches holding up?"

"Hanging in there. Lots more work. Civvy ships, renegade cells, Syndicate war bands, lost operatives. Billions of bugged assets throughout the system, only a hundred or so overwatches. Entire system is on enhanced monitoring. Thousands of new Suspicious Persons added to the database. Now we have to save the whole United Fleet?" Adrian remotely called for an elevator down to the nearest cafeteria level. "Glad we're in here and not out there. Poor fleet jockeys got their asses kicked."

After he had studied Sienar's theories on ESS's influence over the Syndicate, Cherny had deleted them from his local files. They were the last thing he wanted to show upon some security scan. It wasn't exactly ironclad proof, but he found it didn't matter. *If we're wrong, I'll be wrong with Jenna and Ezza.*

If it was true, it hadn't taken Cherny long to realize that the plan was not widely known. Apart from himself, he didn't know who else within ESS suspected it. Even the individual operatives, infiltrating their specific Syndicate cells, didn't seem to know the full extent of the overarching plan. Instead, control was exerted by the careful release of information to guide the Syndicate into certain actions. Subtlety was something She always excelled at. Adrian was just doing his best to help a compromised United Fleet.

A woman in a suit joined them in the elevator one level

Don Miasek

down. Her eyes visibly widened when she saw Cherny. "You're …"

Cherny smiled at her. "Hi there. I'm Cherny." He shook her hand. The atmosphere in the Tower had changed since he'd returned. Where assets and fellow operatives once avoided him in the halls or whispered behind his back, people he had never met before would now approach him just to express their admiration. The death of Alexander Reuben had been celebrated across SecLink, and everyone knew which member of the legendary Athena Six was responsible.

"Hi," she said, still awestruck.

Quickly rifling through his personnel files, Cherny identified her. Lem Woo. Data analyst. Training for operative status for the past fifteen years. "It's nice to meet you, Lem. I read about your work on the black VenusNet. Very clever manipulation."

Lem broke into a smile. "Oh, well," she giggled. "I had no idea that had reached the upper echelons."

Adrian rolled his optics.

If you ever want to make operative, you'll need to work on emotional control, Cherny thought. The elevator doors slid open. "This is our stop. Be well, Lem." He and Adrian stepped out.

Adrian pulled the wires trailing behind him so they wouldn't get caught in the closing elevator doors. "Fangirl?" He gave a robotic laugh.

I could get used to being a celebrity, Cherny decided. It reminded him of the good old days, back when the Athena

PALE GREY DOT

Six were the best ESS had to offer. The Martian Insurrection could be a minor blip on the radar soon enough. But it took only the thought of Jenna to remind him of his priorities. He imagined how scared she must have been when *Étoile* was boarded. *Don't fail Jenna like you failed Sal. Focus on your mission,* he thought.

//Cherny.// It was Amanda.

Adrian slowly looked up at him as Cherny nearly stumbled.

//Yes, Amanda?//

//I need you and the overwatch.//

//Right away,// Cherny replied. He quickly closed the connection, hoping his face hadn't gone pale. *A little warning would have been nice.* Glancing across at Adrian, he looked to see if there was any suspicion in the man's eyes. If there was, Cherny couldn't find it. Overwatches were not known for their social awareness. "Sorry, Adrian, we're being recalled."

"ESS can't survive if I'm away from my post for five minutes," Adrian said. "Can't argue."

Cherny chuckled despite himself. He almost would have preferred if Adrian wasn't there to remind him that ESS was largely comprised of decent human beings. Fighting monsters like Alexander Reuben was far easier. "You know what? Go grab a café and meet us back at your lair. I'll keep Amanda busy until then."

Adrian grinned and gave a mock salute before continuing to the cafeteria.

355

Don Miasek

Cherny watched him go. *Poor guy.* Like most overwatches, he'd grown comfortable with his lot. *It's not a bad life,* he supposed, *if you're more at home on the Net than in real life.* Cherny wasn't confident they could fight ESS without harming the innocent as well as the complicit. For now, he'd resolved to watch and listen. Ezza and Jenna were still out there, and a spy within ESS could become their best asset.

In the overwatch hideout, the holographic projector displayed a map of the solar system. Cherny recognized it as United Fleet holdings, from ships and stations to automated monitoring posts. Amanda stood behind Esther's left shoulder, hands clasped behind her back.

Esther stared straight ahead, but her eyes had a faraway look, as if not perceiving the map the same way that Cherny and Amanda were.

"Bev Stroud has missed her third check-in," Amanda said.

Hello to you too, Cherny thought. On the journey home, Cherny had watched Amanda slip away. Their ship was a high-powered, ultralight 1g transport, so the trip hadn't taken long. The closer they got to Earth, the colder she became. It was on the third day, thirty-two million kilometres from Earth, that she gave him the same look he'd seen when they'd first met. *Maybe if Reuben had let me go after her back when I wanted to ...* Cherny pushed the thought aside. Regret wasn't something he had time for anymore. Instead, he thought of it as another reason to stop this madness. "Then that's the second operative Ezza's beaten," he said.

Amanda did not argue. With a glance to Esther, the map

PALE GREY DOT

expanded, focusing in on the Jupiter locale. "Furthermore, we've received word that *Starknight* has filed a departure request with the Ganymede orbital station."

Cherny furrowed his brow. According to Sienar, Cheng-Visitor had been planning to plead her case with Premier Fairchild. Brylan Ncube had put a stop to that. With the number of ESS agents on board Cheng-Visitor's *Pravedni*, he staged a takeover. *What exactly are you trying to do, Ezza?* It took him a moment to realize that Amanda was looking in his direction, expecting him to answer that exact question. "She's getting desperate. You guys lost Jenna as well, so we can assume they've met up. Knowing Jenna, she'd want to find Sienar now that they're done at Uruk Sulcus-132. Remind me again why we were ever all right with them making it there in the first place?"

Amanda frowned in his direction. Cherny wondered if challenging her was a bad idea. Amanda may tolerate it, but She certainly would not. "Your former brother left a message for Ezza. We needed her to decode it."

"And since Bev hasn't reported in, we have no idea if he left her anything useful."

"No," Amanda agreed.

"Esther," Cherny said, "could you take us back out?"

The overwatch shifted in her seat. "You got it." A twitch of her hand, and the full solar system reappeared.

Cherny watched as the remaining fleet reappeared, scattered across the system. *That's it,* he thought. *That's what you're going to do, Ezza. You always were a leader.*

357

Don Miasek

"What is it?" Amanda had caught the look.

"Jenna and Ezza are trying to find Sienar," he lied.

"Unless whatever they found at Uruk Sulcus-132 gives them a clue, they wouldn't know where he is. Or rather, was. I fail to see how they are going to resume their search."

"Easily solved." Cherny faked a smile. "I'll just tell them."

Amanda tilted her head.

"They trust me. As far as they know, I'm still on their side." *You put Jenna in harm's way,* Cherny reminded himself. *It's your fault she suffered.* "Esther, start compiling all data on insurrectionist activity on Luna." The image closed in on Earth's moon. A hundred icons appeared, each denoting a cell, citizens tagged with the Suspicious Persons label, and other recent signs of organized disobedience. "Ah, this'll be easy. 'Dear Ezza and Jenna. I've successfully infiltrated ESS and found where Sienar is hiding out. He's on Luna, stirring up all the civil unrest shown here. Hope you're doing well. Hugs and kisses. Love, Cherny.'"

Esther laughed. Amanda did not.

"Well, you get the idea," Cherny told her. He desperately hoped she'd believe his bluff.

"The plan has merit," Amanda said after a moment's thought. "A course to Luna will bring them in our direction. Esther, prepare a transmission to UFS *Pravedni.*" The map focused in on the battlecruiser, now located halfway between Earth and Jupiter. Even as a hologram, it was an imposing image. Rows of missile ports ran along its frame,

PALE GREY DOT

broken up only by point-defence laser emitters. It boasted more weaponry than a half-dozen other warships.

"Tell Brylan to prepare his new ship for battle."

```
*** PUBLIC BROADCAST ***
*** SOURCE: UFS STARKNIGHT ***
*** DATETIME STAMP: 2510-03-11 23:03:21 ***
*** VIDEO FORMAT ***
```

[A woman stands before the camera, hands clasped behind her back. Her hair is slicked into a tight bun, and captain's bars rest on the shoulders of her crisp, pressed uniform. More than a few medals are pinned to her chest. A star field is visible through the small window behind her.]

"My name is Captain Ezza Jayens, commanding officer of UFS *Starknight*. Over fifty years ago, I served as an Earth Security Service operative. I mention this detail so you will understand that I have some experience in what I'm about to say. In the past month, we've seen our fleet assaulted from all sides. Twenty-seven of our ships were lost at Jupiter Station in a surprise attack, and that was just the beginning. Other ships have been ambushed, our cohesion has been disrupted, and our flag officers have been detained.

"You are no doubt confused and concerned by the Admiralty's silence in the face of the current crisis. There's been no word on the number of lives lost, no assessment of the extent of the destruction, and at this stage, most critically, no assurance of imminent defensive countermeasures.

"I know many of you are wondering how we could have fallen so far so fast."

[The captain's expression turns grim.]

"During a mission to Uruk Sulcus-132, I found out. This

is a coup by the Earth Security Service. ESS leaked intel that allowed the Syndicate to strike out at Jupiter Station, has permitted funds to reach their coffers, and has arrested anyone with the authority to stop the transfer of power."

[She holds up a small, silver data jack no bigger than her thumb.]

"Attached to this transmission are the technical readouts of a memory drive taken from an ESS operative. Examine it. See the proof of collusion for yourselves."

[The woman tucks the drive into a chest pocket and puts her hands behind her back.]

"In the absence of any remaining flag officer, I am taking command of the fleet. I mean to head for Earth, and ESS's *Pravedni* is in my way. Any other vessels still loyal to the United Fleet and Premier Fairchild ... well, I think you know what we need to do. We'll meet you at Earth, and we'll put an end to this."

"Captain Ezza Jayens, out."

17

Jenna placed the tip of the wire at the base of her wrist. Though *Starknight*'s chief cyberneticist had offered to replace the bent and cracked ports running up her arm, Jenna had said no. She preferred to take care of her own systems. With a sharp thrust, she jammed the wire into the socket. Around her, the quarters she shared with seven other members of *Starknight*'s crew vanished from her sight, replaced with darkness.

Then came a light. Virtual reality always took a moment to get used to. The avatars of those attending the virtual meeting were already there. There were six in total, floating in the void. Marked as a spectator, Jenna herself did not appear. Ezza and her cyborg second-in-command, Rachelle, were already there. Her sister's image looked as she had when she'd addressed the fleet—professional and perfect. Rachelle was a mere wireframe image of her usual self.

PALE GREY DOT

Ezza's message had added fuel to the solar system's fire. The United Fleet was nearly destroyed, and now one of their captains had publicly accused ESS of a coup. Jenna wondered how She was handling it all. *Maybe She's starting to feel Her precious control slipping from Her fingers. Maybe Fairchild has taken note.* It would be too much to hope that the premier would take action without real evidence, though. *Soon,* Jenna thought.

To Jenna's disappointment, only two other United Fleet vessels had responded to the plea for help. Jenna and Ezza had spoken only once since her outburst in the infirmary, but Ezza had argued that most ships were either damaged, out of range, or their captains had been unwilling to take a risk, given the chaos all around them. ESS had claimed control over the United Fleet with the premier's backing. Of course they would be reluctant to rebel, Ezza had said. Jenna knew better, though. They were cowards, all too willing to roll over and let their new masters rule. In the end, what did the pets care if their treats came from someone else?

They'd also received a secret transmission from Cherny just last night. "I'm still on your side," he'd said. "Come to Earth. I can help." He had even out laid a plan, and mentioned a decoy version he'd fed ESS. There were two problems that Jenna saw with it.

First, it didn't include Her death. *Unacceptable,* Jenna decided.

Second, the plan was a lie. It was just a trap to lure them

363

Don Miasek

in for Her. Jenna knew this with absolute certainty. He'd betrayed her once already.

She and Ezza had argued on both points. Arguing was something they still excelled at, and that little bit of contact had made Jenna feel nostalgic. But eventually, as they always did, they came to an agreement on how to respond to Cherny's offer of help.

One by one, the avatars of the other four participants lit up, nameplates highlighted underneath each. Captain Connie Danaboyina and Commander Lib Wong represented UFS *Mazur*, escort. Captain Reyansh Satō and Commander Reshma Guzman were in attendance for UFS *Talent*, missile destroyer. Both *Talent* and *Mazur* were five light minutes away from Starknight but were only light seconds from each other. The variable delay would make for awkward conversation. They would have a chance to discuss amongst themselves before sending the transmission to *Starknight*.

"We'll probably be accused of treason for responding to you, Jayens," Satō began. *Talent's* captain had a bulging gut, and his uniform struggled to contain it. With thin, dark hair and eyes that were too small for his wide and unshaven face, the virtual avatar did nothing to sugarcoat his appearance. Jenna wondered how he managed in the cramped confines of a warship. "This had better be worth it."

Over his shoulder, Commander Guzman folded her arms, looking down at *Starknight's* command. Seemingly unconscious gestures weren't the same in virtual reality. Everything was deliberate.

364

PALE GREY DOT

Ezza smiled. "You've read the contents of Bev Stroud's memory drive. Clearly you recognize its significance. This is a coup by the Earth Security Service. ESS is annihilating its only rival agency. That's why you responded to my call."

That or they had reached out on Her orders, Jenna thought. It would be such an easy thing for Her to have eyes on them at this very moment. ESS controlled the United Fleet now. Though Jenna had grudgingly accepted that Ezza's security measures on *Starknight* were solid, they couldn't say the same for *Mazur* and *Talent.* Any of their combined two hundred and thirteen crew members could be ESS assets. Their networks could be bugged. Their transmissions could be intercepted by any of the so-called refugee ships streaming back to Earth from Jupiter Station.

"Ah, yes," Captain Danaboyina said after the ten-light-minute round trip. She was a tall, lithe woman, and she kept her fingers steepled together as if in perpetual contemplation. "This memory drive of yours. My own technicians have assured me that they are impossible to decode. Why would we engage ESS in open warfare based on what may be manufactured evidence? Now, if we were able to examine the drive itself ..."

"But Captain Jayens isn't going to allow that, is she?" Wong, her second, said.

Fortunately, they didn't have to wait for the ten-minute round trip, as Captain Satō answered for her. "No, but she has good reason not to." The void between the six attendees lit up with a map encompassing everything from Jupiter to Earth. Between *Starknight*'s icon and Earth was the battlecruiser *Pravedni*. Six light minutes to the side sat *Talent* and *Mazur*. Convoys of refugee ships, coloured in grey, were making the trek back to Earth. "*Pravedni* has changed course. She's in position to maximize her firing time on *Starknight* should Jayens make for Earth."

"You don't know they mean to attack," Danaboyina said.

It must be frustrating for them to be able to talk amongst themselves before sending the transmission to Starknight, Jenna thought. But if Ezza was annoyed, she didn't show it. *She must be used to this sort of thing by now.*

"Oh, sure, maybe it's a peaceful firing solution," Satō muttered.

"Captain Jayens has transmitted her intentions to actively rebel against a lawful order from the premier. It would be within their rights to take *Starknight* by force."

Ezza finally had the chance to send her own reply. "I would have thought ESS would be happy to let us reach Earth to present our evidence. Let a few Ministry of Science techs take it apart. If it's fake, then they'd get a chance to prove it. Instead, they look ready to destroy *Starknight* and the memory drive with it. Now, why would they want to do such a thing if the truth were on their side?"

Ezza pointed a finger up at the four. "We lost an entire fleet at Jupiter Station, and ESS was certainly ready to capitalize on that. In just a month, hundreds of our officers have been arrested, Alexander Reuben has been killed after successfully hiding for centuries, our ships have been ambushed

PALE GREY DOT

by Syndicate forces that were somehow ready to attack the instant we showed weakness, the inner planets are under martial law, and the premier is shifting the entire United Fleet over to ESS command. What part of that doesn't seem suspicious as hell? And now they have the audacity to say the Admiralty is in collusion with the Syndicate?"

Jenna had to admit it was almost fun watching Ezza work. This was her element. As they waited the ten minutes for a reply, Jenna studied the other four participants. None of them looked trustworthy. Captain Danaboyina seemed ready to excuse anything *Pravedni* did. She and her second-in-command continuously looked at one another, no doubt sharing private conversations. Satō, on the other hand, didn't so much as glance at his own executive officer.

When the reply came, Satō scratched his belly. "Admiral Cheng-Visitor and I go way back. We were at the Tranquility Blockade together and more Syndicate rundowns than I can count. These allegations against her are BS." He shook his head. "Seems obvious something ain't right. Connie, you in?"

Captain Danaboyina frowned. "Why, what are you planning?"

Satō jerked his thumb towards Ezza. "I'm with her. I vote we demand that Brylan Ncube surrender *Pravedni* and let us meet with the admiral."

"And if he refuses?"

When he refuses, Jenna mentally corrected.

"A cruiser, a missile destroyer, and an escort against a

367

battlecruiser?" Satō gave a tight grin as he looked over his shoulder towards his second. "What do you think, Reshma?"

"I think we'd be screwed," she replied.

Jenna focused on the holographic battlecruiser. Though it looked small on the map, she knew *Pravedni* had enough power to reduce another ship to dust. She remembered how easily *Étoile* had been overtaken. Brylan Ncube was on that ship. Jenna hoped they'd get to kill him.

"You'd fire on another United Fleet vessel?" Danaboyina raised her hand to her mouth as she looked back at Satō. Jenna wasn't sure if she was nervous about their chances against *Pravedni*, frightened by the prospect of being labelled a traitor, or if the whole conversation simply hadn't gone the way she had hoped it would.

"Solar systems are made during moments like this, Connie," Satō said. "I'll not see the next two centuries under ESS's heel."

Danaboyina was silent for a moment. Their avatars flickered as she and her second conversed in private. After a minute, she looked back towards the gathering. "All right. We stand ready to assist."

Finally, it was their turn to reply. Ezza gestured to her executive officer. "Commander Eday will contact your ship overseers immediately to begin calculating our launch patterns."

Rachelle's wireframe model waved her hand over the map. Equations rose from the ships, detailing the projected paths of missiles, the planned acceleration of *Starknight* and how

PALE GREY DOT

it would impact mine deployment, and electronic jamming algorithms. Jenna didn't stick around to watch the hours of mathematics. Back in her bunk, she slid the wire from her wrist and opened her eyes.

Across the barrack, a marine sat on another bunk, chin propped up by her hands. The soldier wore a white tank top with *UFS Starknight* written across it in pale grey. When Jenna met her stare, the woman quickly turned away.

You're still a stranger here, Jenna knew. None of this was how it was supposed to go. She'd always imagined that the Athena Six survivors would hit the ground running. It'd be like it was in the old days. Cherny's treachery hurt her more than anything she'd faced over the past fifty-one years. Every morning, she'd wake up and have to remind herself that it really happened. Brylan's words echoed in her mind. *"Certainly didn't take him long to turn you in."*

Even Ezza was different. Distant. Professional, rather than warm. Ezza was United Fleet now. *She moved on with her life,* a little voice told her. Jenna wondered if Sienar had too, wherever he was. *Maybe they don't need you like you need them. Maybe the last fifty-one years of sleeping in gutters, trading fists with alley thieves, and running from anyone in authority had been for nothing. A wasted half-century of your life. Idiot. Why did you ever think things could be the way they were?*

Rising from the bunk, Jenna grabbed the straps of her beige travel bag. A second set of clean clothes swiped from the ship's commissary and a small pile of cybernetic drives were all that remained of her belongings. The clothes she wore now were civilian grey and ill-fitting, having been bought at the Ganymede Nexus. They would do. Slinging the bag over her shoulder, she left the barracks.

She met the reporter in the primary hull. Nirali was dressed in a bright blue-and-white suit—appropriate for a Jupiter Station refugee. "Oh, Jenna!" She broke into a wide smile. "How did things go with Satō and Danaboyina?"

"As expected," Jenna replied. While *Starknight* appeared secure from ESS's prying eyes, it was clear from the way ESS had neutered the United Fleet that the other ships were easy prey. Jenna wondered how much time and effort She had spent weaving Her fingers into the United Fleet's infrastructure. She certainly wouldn't have been capable of all this back when Jenna was in the service.

"You really think your friend Cherny will come through for us with this plan of his?"

Jenna ignored her use of the word "friend."

"No."

"Oh." Nirali's face fell. "Well, what now?"

"We have two weeks to figure it out, but for now, we play along," Jenna assured her. "Come on, Nirali. We have work to do."

Ezza double-checked the straps keeping her clipped to her command station. After three days of hard acceleration,

PALE GREY DOT

Starknight was back in zero-g. She had spent the past sixteen hours overseeing the deployment of a thick cloud of defensive mines. Momentum would keep them in front of the ship, and micro-thrusters would propel them to meet any incoming projectiles. With Rachelle's help, *Starknight* could control thousands of them at a time.

On the map in front of her, *Pravedni* was in their way. Like *Starknight*, the battlecruiser was on a course to Earth, but travelling slower. "Status?" Ezza asked, glancing to her right. She had to fight to keep the fatigue from her voice.

Tariq Lassiter, Adams's former second, looked up from his console. Though a century older than Adams, he was far less experienced. Tall and gangly, he had the look of someone trying not to seem out of his depth. She hoped he was up to the task of serving as primary. "*Pravedni* has changed course again to match us. Telemetry Control has us within *Pravedni*'s effective range for … uh"—he squinted at the console—"nineteen hours, forty-seven minutes. Their relative angle is plus two-point-seven degrees lateral, one-point-four degrees vertical."

"Let's give it another point-ten-second burst, then," Ezza said.

To her left, Rachelle acknowledged the command with a flick of her wrist. All along *Starknight*'s hulls, thrusters fired. Inside, the movement was almost imperceptible. Stretched across millions of kilometres, however, the difference was immense. Though a missile's straight-line range was infinite, each manoeuvre expended its limited fuel. Even better, the

Don Miasek

farther a missile travelled from the launching ship, the longer it took for updated calculations to reach it, making it easy prey for the target's defences.

"Manoeuvre complete," Rachelle said. "All mines have reported successful adjustment relative to our position."

"Telemetry Control has us within *Pravedni*'s effective range for sixteen hours, nine minutes," Lassiter said.

Soon Brylan would change course to compensate, Ezza knew, and that number would jump back up. So it had gone for the past four days. *Starknight* nudged itself, and *Pravedni* struggled to match it. Anything to eke out an extra hour of safety from *Pravedni*'s firepower. Manoeuvrability was their sole advantage.

Ezza reached into the holographic map with her cybernetic hand and spread her fingers, focusing on the two ships off to *Pravedni*'s side. *Mazur* and *Talent*'s approach on *Pravedni* would be simpler, as Brylan had done nothing to evade them. He was focused solely on her, apparently content to let his own mine clouds ward them off.

"Transmission received," Rachelle called out. "It's from the Admiralty."

"Anything new this time?"

Rachelle shook her head, and her wired hair glinted in the command centre's lighting.

"Then file it away." Since leaving the Ganymede Nexus, they'd received fifteen messages from the Admiralty—or whichever ESS-appointed official had replaced them. The first few were orders to halt all movement, but when it

PALE GREY DOT

became apparent that Ezza wasn't stopping, they became aggressive and threatening. The last several were demands that they surrender and declarations that other warships "still loyal to the United Fleet" were being sent to put an end to their "traitorous actions." That much, Ezza knew, was true. There were other ships on an intercept course, but they'd be too late. No, it was just *Starknight*, *Pravedni*, *Talent*, and *Mazur*.

Ezza hoped Satō and Danaboyina had truly been swayed. She hadn't met either of them in person before. Three ships against the solar system, and she didn't know if she could trust two of them. But there was no turning back.

"Status?" she asked.

"They've changed course again," Lassiter said. "Telemetry Control has us within *Pravedni*'s effective range for four days, nineteen hours, thirty-nine minutes. Plus two-point-six lateral, plus one-point-five vertical."

Ezza grimly began calculating the next round of manoeuvres.

So it went. When, after twelve hours, the primary shift grew tired, the secondary took over. When they, too, grew tired, the primary returned. Spaceship combat was as much endurance as it was intellect. On the fourth day, *Pravedni* fired its first barrage. Ezza was in the command centre when it happened. At thirty per round, it took very little time for the sky to fill between them. With the twenty-three-hour missile flight time separating the two ships, Ezza, Rachelle, and their technicians pored over each countermeasure.

373

Don Miasek

Shift *Starknight*, force the missiles to reestablish contact with *Pravedni*, use the momentary window of connectivity to try and breach their network security, jam the transmissions, overload the sensors, and force the missiles to rely on their own inferior onboard computers.

Ezza had launched their own missiles as well, though theirs would be running on closed communication throughout. *Starknight* hadn't the computational resources to devote to a futile attempt to physically break through *Pravedni*'s own defences. Satō and Danaboyina had the job of dealing damage, and their missiles were already en route.

Ezza was in the mess hall with Carmen after a fourteen-hour shift, sucking vitamin-infused meat paste through a straw, when she received a new transmission. Ezza knew the importance of being seen by the exhausted crew under her command, and so no matter how fatigued she felt, she refused to let it show. Appear confident. Appear tireless. Appear invulnerable. Excusing herself with a smile that she hoped didn't look fake, Ezza pushed off from the table and floated through the halls back to her office.

Clipping herself to a safety tether, she saw the dead guard's breather looking back at her from where it was vel-tacked to the wall. Even without the Pull, Ezza still wanted the reminder. Folding down the desk, Ezza accessed the transmission.

"Mademoiselle," Brylan said. His smiling face appeared in the small holographic display before her. "I have been asked to reach out to you to negotiate the terms of your surrender.

PALE GREY DOT

This comes from Premier Fairchild herself. I am told she has finished transferring control of the United Fleet over to ESS and has directed us to bring an end to this distasteful act of insurrection."

The image pulled back, and Ezza saw that Brylan was wearing a United Fleet uniform. There were admiral's bars on his shoulder. "It has been no small task, but so far, ESS has succeeded in securing Earth, Mars, the Luna bases, the Venusian Twins, and the major asteroids. So many thousands of people are seeking to vent their anger against the premier. Much of that is thanks to you and your theatrical broadcast." Brylan shook his head. "Disappointing that you would deliberately cause so much chaos, but that is why ESS is needed to maintain peace, order, and good government, no?

"There is only one last pocket of resistance, spreading lies and propaganda, and that is you. The premier's technical advisors have reviewed your claims, and it is clear that your evidence is faked. ESS memory drives cannot be accessed by anyone other than their owner.

"The premier would prefer to end this peacefully. As would She, of course." Brylan stressed the pronoun. "Consider your life, the lives of your crew, and the stability of the solar system. Operative Brylan Ncube, out." He gave a final smile before the transmission ended, leaving Ezza alone with her thoughts.

Much of what Brylan said was true. The physical memory drive had been a last-ditch effort at staving off the takeover.

375

Don Miasek

Ezza gave the breather mask one last look before making her way back to her quarters to sleep.

Ezza made sure she was in the command centre when the first salvo was due. Electronics had shut down three of the thirty. Ezza met Lassiter's and Rachelle's gazes before returning her attention to the map. Twenty-seven bright red, holographic dots met the green cloud of mines. Each of *Pravedni*'s missiles worked in conjunction with one another—one would manoeuvre to draw as many mines away as possible, to create an opening for its brothers, while *Starknight*'s mines fought to outsmart the attackers. Days of analysis, second-guessing, and mathematics played out in sixty seconds. There was a flash on the map for each missile they brought down. *Flash, flash, flash.* Eventually, only one remained, but Ezza knew that was all it would take.

"Activating lasers," Rachelle announced.

Though the beam itself was invisible, the result was not. After two seconds of concentrated fire, the final dot flashed its demise.

Lassiter raised his hand to his forehead as a relieved smile passed over his face.

Ezza felt like a weight had been lifted from her shoulders. The defensive screen could hold, at least for now. Accessing *Starknight*'s intercom, she announced, "This is Captain Jayens. *Pravedni*'s first salvo is down." *We'll all survive another twenty-eight minutes.* "Begin preparations for the next wave. Captain Jayens, out." Closing the line, she looked in Lassiter's direction. "Status?"

376

PALE GREY DOT

"We're in their effective range for another three days, eighteen hours, fifty minutes. Negative one-point-two lateral, plus two-point-five vertical," he reported. "We're going to do it," he said as his smile grew. "We have a chance."

They began working on the next set of manoeuvres.

Four hours and eight barrages later, *Talent* and *Mazur*'s initial salvo hit *Pravedni*'s own screen. They barely made a dent, and none of the missiles made it close enough to be shot down by defensive lasers. But it was additional computational time and manoeuvring considerations that Brylan had to waste. Moreover, even the battlecruiser didn't have infinite mines to deploy. If it only bought *Starknight* an extra minute of safety, it'd be worth it.

That night, halfway through a five-hour rest, Ezza's subdermals buzzed her awake. The good news had come through. The technicians had run the numbers. Assuming nothing else changed, they had a seventy-eight percent chance of surviving the missile salvos before *Talent* and *Mazur* broke through *Pravedni*'s defences. Ezza had thanked them, readjusted her bed bag, and gone back to sleep.

An hour later, something changed.

Ezza awoke again to an alert from her implants. Instinctively, she connected to the network and realized what was wrong. Unzipping herself from her bed bag, she slid open the door to her quarters and floated towards the command centre. Rachelle was already plugged in, and Lassiter's second, Adaeze, was still on duty.

Don Miasek

"Let's see it," Ezza said as she pulled out her station's harness and clipped it to her belt.

The holographic map showed *Talent* and *Mazur*, with bright red icons flashing on the latter.

"*Mazur*'s latest missile salvo changed course shortly after launch," Adaeze said. Ezza could tell the woman was trying to stay calm. "At that range, they overloaded *Talent*'s mine cloud and scored a direct hit on the primary hull."

"Damn," Ezza whispered. She wondered if Danaboyina had always been siding with the ESS-led United Fleet from the start. Or maybe Brylan had convinced her to switch sides. Maybe he'd offered her power in the new regime. Maybe he'd threatened to annihilate her and everyone she loved. Or maybe she simply realized that three spaceships against the entire government was only ever going to end one way. In the end, Ezza knew, it didn't matter. "Survivors?"

"The primary hull has been obliterated," Adaeze said. "The secondary hull has breaches along its central side. I …" She shook her head. "There's no way there's anyone left."

Ezza could only spare a moment's thought for Satō and his crew. "And *Mazur*'s current in-flight missiles?"

"They're heading our way now. ETA for the first salvo is twenty hours."

"Should we power up the transmitter to contact Captain Danaboyina?" Rachelle asked, but Ezza shook her head.

"She made her decision, and she isn't going to change her mind again. Adaeze, let's see the current status of our minefield's fuel reserves."

PALE GREY DOT

"Our current supply of mines will be unable to sustain a barrage from both *Pravedni* and *Talent*," Adaeze said. "Updated calculations show an eight percent chance of survival until we escape *Pravedni*'s effective range."

"Deploy everything we have left, then," Ezza said.

The colour drained from Adaeze's face. Ezza knew it was a death sentence. Eventually, the mines would either run out of fuel or become depleted by successful interceptions. Then *Starknight* would be defenceless.

"Well, then," Ezza smiled with false confidence. "Rachelle, Adaeze, we have twenty hours to calculate the dispersal of our remaining mines. Shall we get started?"

As they worked, their focus changed from escaping *Pravedni* to staving it off for as long as possible. A renewed round of transmissions from the Admiralty and Brylan were received shortly thereafter. There were offers of clemency and demands for surrender. There was calculated proof of *Starknight*'s inevitable destruction. Ezza dismissed them all. Of course they'd rather she surrender. Then they could scour the ship and secure Bev Stroud's memory drive, rather than assume its destruction. *They'll never get that chance*, Ezza told herself.

Ezza decided to forgo changing shifts. Adrenaline and café would keep her going. She, Rachelle, and Lassiter plotted each subtle course change to force the incoming missiles to expend fuel, to reorient *Starknight*'s mine cloud, or to keep their ship away from *Pravedni* and *Mazur* for at least a little while longer. With each move, they sacrificed the long term for the short.

379

Don Miasek

Ezza's stomach growled as they worked through the final details. The on-the-go meat paste had gotten very old very fast. There were dark circles under Lassiter's eyes, and even Rachelle looked exhausted. Interfacing with the ship for this long was gruelling work. Ezza remembered when she suspected the cyborg of being Brylan's source of information, back when the Pull was affecting her mind. *Just a little longer, Rachelle,* Ezza thought.

"Five minutes," Lassiter announced.

Fifty bright red dots cruised towards *Starknight*, and the mine cloud moved to destroy them. Impact flashes appeared on the map, and Ezza thanked whatever powers that be for each one. A quarter of the missiles swooped to the side, drawing off a segment of mines to create a gap for the remaining projectiles. *Flash, flash, flash.* Then it was over.

"Six are through," Lassiter said.

"Lasers," Rachelle announced. *Flash, flash, flash.*

Ezza held her breath as the lasers focused on the remaining three. Every crew member on board, she knew, was doing the same. *Flash, flash.* A single missile was all it would take to obliterate the ship. The laser emitters refocused on the last as it corkscrewed wildly, trying to evade the lock. The collision alert sounded across *Starknight's* intercom and every crew member's implants. Ezza closed her eyes and gripped the railing tightly. The ship shuddered from the impact, and Ezza felt her harness retract, keeping her pinned against the wall of her station. The ship was spinning now, and a flood of damage reports flew into her mind.

PALE GREY DOT

"The missile broke apart at the last second," Rachelle called out, "but we have a partial debris strike along the central deck."

"Breaches?"

The cyborg was silent as she pored through the wealth of information from every corner of *Starknight*. "Pressure has been lost through C deck. Airlock doors from connector struts one and two are jammed. Three and four are still secure. Atmospheric pressurization may be possible. Wait ... processing. Processing. Secondary hull has also reported seventeen microbreaches. The nuclear pulse engines have stalled, and we're in a one-point-two rpm roll. Casualty report pending."

"Oh God," Lassiter said.

Entire sections of the holographic *Starknight* flashed red. Manoeuvring thrusters, three missile launchers, the laser emitters along the primary hull's forward section ... The list kept growing. Ezza expanded the holographic map to include her minefield. More than half were sending fuel alerts, and a fifth had been shut down by *Pravedni*'s electronics. Ezza saw dozens of gaping holes in the cloud. Twenty-three minutes before the next barrage would arrive.

We're dead in space. Brylan will disable the ship. He'll board us and tear through the place for the memory drive. Or he may simply let his next salvo kill us all. Ezza cleared her throat, remotely activated the ship's intercom, and said, "This is Captain Jayens to all hands. We're abandoning *Starknight*."

381

DC FORTRESS

WASHINGTON, EARTH

March 23, 2510

Re: Urgent analysis

Dear Premier Fairchild,

Per your request, my cyberneticists have looked into it and agree that Captain Ezza Jayens's claims were indeed plausible, though analysis of the physical device would have been required to confirm.

Sincerely,

Liu Wahid, Minister of Science

18

Ezza is probably dead.

The thought had been haunting Cherny for the past week, ever since they received the report from Brylan Ncube that *Starknight* had been obliterated. There were escape pods, but not enough to support the full crew. It would take time to track them all down. Cherny had run some calculations, taking into account which pods had been ejected, the impact point of the first missile to breach *Starknight*'s defences, the distance from the command centre to the nearest pod, and a dozen other variables.

When the numbers came back with a thirty-eight percent chance of survival, Cherny tweaked the values. Ezza was fast, he'd reasoned. She was born in space. Navigating a broken spaceship in a firefight would be second nature to her. Her crew's distribution throughout the ship's twin hulls may have been altered for the battle, giving her a better chance of

383

having made it into one of the launched pods. The number had only inched up to forty-five percent.

Cherny had kept a stiff upper lip around his ESS colleagues even while his innards crawled. "Sad, of course," he'd said, "but she gave us no choice." Ezza's broadcast had initially plunged the Tower into disarray. The public accusation of ESS involvement in the Jupiter Station attack meant damage control efforts had taken priority.

Ezza is probably dead.

As he dwelt on the thought, Cherny pressed his hand against the window of the helicraft, rubbing away the fog on the glass. Through it, he watched the confused and disorganized masses far below him. The Bronx Spaceport was not unlike the Tsiolkovsky Spaceport back in Hawaii. The sprawling array of landing pads had been added piecemeal over the decades, creating a haphazard layout. Each was equipped with their own machinery for refuelling and repairs, though the thick smog forced Cherny to lean on his cybernetic vision to make those out in the distance.

Thousands waited for their turn to pass through Earth customs and immigration. Armoured soldiers and hovering drones herded them through the process. Cherny watched a woman with two children in tow pass underneath one of the large metal arches stretching across the walkway. The arch flashed green, signalling their presumed innocence. Others were not so lucky. Using SecLink, Cherny could have easily picked out those in the crowd who were listed as Suspicious Persons. He'd know who would get through to the next stage

PALE GREY DOT

of their life—reassignment to wherever the Ministry of Industry deemed necessary. He'd know who would be taken aside and never released. Luckily, Cherny wouldn't need SecLink again if their plan worked.

But even without the Pull, Cherny still found himself sympathizing with Her. She didn't develop the Athena Protocols. She didn't make Taylor think that wiping out hundreds in Olympus Mons was worth it to get Griffenham. *We caused Her so much pain and grief, and yet She was willing to let us go.* Amanda had told him that She protected them in the aftermath of the insurrection. *Likely true,* Cherny admitted. *You can't blame your sympathies on the Pull anymore.*

And Jenna? *She had been out there, trying to reunite the survivors against all odds for half a century, and you gave her up within seconds. Sienar died to give you this chance to redeem yourself. Ezza fought a lost cause somewhere between Earth and Jupiter for you.*

An alert flashed in his mind, snapping Cherny out of his thoughts. The shuttle was due to arrive in twenty-one minutes. He sent the command, and his helicraft lowered itself onto one of the Bronx's few empty landing pads, lurching as it hit the tarmac.

Cherny slipped a breather over his head and sealed it. It was a bad one out there. The door slid open and Cherny stepped down. Air coolers in his black suit hummed softly to counter the intense heat as he cleared the landing pad and crossed the catwalk leading to the traffic control tower.

Inside were three dredges in orange coveralls, one a

Don Miasek

full-convert cyborg. Augmented windows let them oversee their sector of responsibility despite the fog. In the middle of the room, a holographic map showed the landing pads, each assigned to a shuttle or hopper.

"Who the hell are you?" The supervisor was marked by a blue card on her chest. Though not nearly as big as Minsk had been, her smarmy, egotistical tone was no different.

Cherny transmitted his credentials, and the woman immediately stiffened.

"I ..." She looked at her compatriots, but they pretended not to notice. Focus on your work and don't get involved— Cherny knew the strategy well.

Cherny stretched his cybernetic hand out towards her. He kept his breather mask on—being faceless had its advantages.

The supervisor looked at the outstretched hand but didn't take it. "Yes, no, I ... I get it, you're ..." she trailed off.

"Protocol requires that all ESS credentials be verified, Ms. Li," Cherny said. "The security of the solar system is everyone's responsibility."

Li gave a defeated sigh and grasped Cherny's hand, making the connection. Within moments, the authentication was complete, and Li drew back her hand. "Yes, yes, you're an operative."

"You have no reason to worry, Ms. Li. I am not here for you or any of your workers," Cherny said. It was such an easy act, pretending to be the feared.

Li did not look reassured.

Cherny stepped up behind the full-convert cyborg. A

PALE GREY DOT

quick command overrode his terminal, and the holographic map zoomed in on one of the landing pads. The pad's type, available facilities, and schedule scrolled past it. All this information could have been pulled from SecLink, but they needn't know that.

Li wiped her forehead with her sleeve. "I ... Is something wrong? I promise you that each shuttle has been fully marked and registered with the Ministry of Public Safety. We've filed everything we had to. If there's anything else we can do, then we—"

"In fifteen minutes, orbital hopper flight NY1467 is due to set down from Gagarin Station." Cherny kept his voice aloof, as any good operative should.

"Yes, that's correct. We've filed everything we had to," Li repeated. "The Ministry of Transportation is in full compliance with the new protocols. If we did anything wrong, please tell me and I swear we'll—"

"I told you," Cherny said, "I am not here for you or your workers. I'd rather not have to tell you a third time."

Li swallowed and again looked at her companions, but they kept their focus on their terminals once more.

"Redirect the hopper to pad 17C and have two teams meet me there. I will oversee the screening personally."

"Yes, of course. You can oversee it. Not a problem. Thank you, sir." Li started to bow, then salute, before finally failing to do either.

Without another word, Cherny stepped back out onto the catwalk and returned to the landing pad. Looking up, he

Don Miasek

could see the hopper overhead. It was an older model, and its mismatched paint scheme, patchwork armour, and rough handling spoke of well over a century of service. Cherny waited impatiently at the edge of the platform. Jenna was on board that ship, and as he watched the spacecraft descend, he thought back to the last time they'd spoken.

They had just been recalled to Earth. Sal was dead, along with hundreds of Martians. Taylor had been locked away. Cherny remembered the dread he'd felt back in the Tower. They'd failed their mission in the most brutal way possible. Execution for all of them seemed likely. Cherny had never seen Her so furious. At the time, Cherny thought it was over the Martian deaths, but decades of reminiscing made him wonder. Ezza and Sienar had been sullen and silent, but Jenna had been hit hardest of all. Cherny remembered her frantically poring over her technical specifications of the Athena Protocols as they awaited their fates, trying to find out where it went wrong. Cherny had taken her aside and told her it wasn't her fault. He remembered how grateful she'd looked when he said that. Not long after, she slipped out of the Tower and was never seen again.

Thank goodness she doesn't know what I did to her, Cherny thought.

●

Jenna gripped the handhold tightly as she felt the hopper dip. There were thirty of them in just this passenger space alone.

PALE GREY DOT

Jenna could have reached out and touched a half-dozen others. The smell of so many unwashed bodies reminded her of the alleys of Toronto. Twelve minutes until touchdown, she knew. To her left, pressed up against one of the few windows, Nirali stared out in awe. There wasn't much of a view, and what could be seen rapidly vanished with each dip. The most polluted air hung low to the ground. Still, the reporter kept her nose to the glass, ducking and weaving to get a better angle.

This was, as she had told Jenna countless times already, her first visit to Earth—virtual reality didn't count. On that point, Jenna had agreed. Some things couldn't be replicated, like the oppressive, grimy air that made you feel sticky after just a minute outside, the fear that the next security arch would destroy your life, or the threat of violence from your fellow displaced. It wasn't the same when you could just unplug to make it all go away.

Over the course of the sixteen-day journey, the reporter had asked how the Pull worked, what the rest of the Athena Six were like, who "this mysterious Her" was, and what Jenna's old job at ESS had been like. She'd even asked about her personal life—marriage, friends, biological family. Jenna had deflected each question and was grateful when Nirali eventually gave up. Ezza had asked her to bring Nirali safely to Earth, and Jenna had agreed. For all their arguing, she hadn't wanted to part ways on a bad note. Besides, the reporter was now important. While Jenna and Nirali snuck aboard a refugee ship heading back to Earth, Ezza

Don Miasek

was running distraction. *She might already be dead*, Jenna thought sadly.

"Hey, I think I see our pad!" Nirali exclaimed. "Weird …"

"What is it?"

"All the other pads have like twenty soldiers around them. Drones too. Ours has probably twice that."

Jenna forced her breathing to remain steady. The landing shocks cushioned the blow as the hopper touched down. A ship-wide announcement went out across the intercom and each passenger's subdermal implants. Standard disembarking orders. Business as usual. Jenna knew better. "When we get off, stay with the herd. Follow orders. Submit to every security demand. Don't do anything to stand out from the crowd."

"Yeah, I know."

"This isn't Jupiter Station. This is Earth. Assume everything you do is being watched. Even when you think you're alone, you're not."

"I got it," Nirali replied.

Jenna studied her face. *You better not screw this up.*

●

Cherny stood with his hands clasped behind his back as the hopper touched down. He remained perfectly still, flanked by two security teams wearing masks and armour. Each had a pistol in their holster. With an operative looking over their shoulders, he was sure they'd perform their duties thoroughly.

390

PALE GREY DOT

The hatch opened and, one by one, the passengers disembarked. More than a few without breathers wrinkled their noses at the smell, and some covered their mouths with their shirts to avoid inhaling the airborne particles. Most wore old Jupiter-style clothing—colourful in their reds and blues, but ill-equipped to deal with the rigours of the Earthen environment.

The squadron captain's voice was amplified to be heard over the roar of the engines from the other pads. "Each passenger will be examined for identity, health, contraband substances, and any illegal cybernetic packages. Initial scan is done manually—if you have anything to declare, make sure you do it before then. Secondary scan will be handled automatically. Ensure all wireless requests from me and my officers are promptly accepted. Once through, you will be transferred to a Ministry of Industry compound for reassignment."

"Is it normal to go through two scans?" one woman called out. Sweat poured down her forehead from the heat. "Does this have anything to do with Captain Jayens's transmission?"

The captain hesitated before looking over at Cherny with a nervous eye. When Cherny said nothing, he pretended not to hear the woman's question. "Oh, and welcome to Earth," he said, addressing them again. "You'll find it a lot nicer than people say."

The closest guard grabbed the arm of the first passenger and hauled him forward, while another ran a scanner over his body. After a moment, they waved him through the

Don Miasek

security arch. He stumbled through, and the arch flashed its acceptance. One new expat back on Earth.

"Get a move on," the captain shouted to the next. "Weather bureau's ordered rain within the hour. I don't want to be caught out in it, and Lord knows you unprotected stains don't either."

Cherny kept his gaze on the hatch as passengers continued to step out onto the tarmac. A short woman emerged. Her brown hair was down to her shoulders, and she wore a suit and breather that looked new. Ezza's reply to his plan had been short, but from it, Cherny knew that this was Nirali Kashem. Though he didn't give her a second look, his heart began to race. If the reporter was here, then nearby must be ...

Jenna stepped out next. Despite the heavy breather covering her face and slumped shoulders, Cherny recognized her instantly. Her hair was scragglier than it had been when he'd last seen her, and it looked like she'd lost weight. Malnourished, even. Through the semitransparent visor, he saw her eyes nervously darting left and right. Unlike Nirali, she wore a dull grey jumpsuit and had a travel bag slung over her shoulder. The words *Ganymede Nexus: The Pride of Jupiter* were emblazoned across it.

"Go on, ma'am," the guard ordered Nirali.

The reporter looked at the arch apprehensively before stepping through.

Though Cherny had complete confidence in Jenna's forgeries, he had to fight to avoid holding his breath. Fortunately,

PALE GREY DOT

the arch flashed green, and Nirali joined the rest of the passengers huddled on the other side.

Jenna slowly held her arms out as the guard ran the scanner over her. After a moment, she was shoved through the arch. Jenna stumbled and turned.

"You have something to say?" the guard asked. His breather gave his voice a mechanical inflection.

"No," Jenna said, casting her eyes downwards. "I'm sorry."

The guard moved to the next passenger.

"Hold." The instant Cherny spoke, everyone on the landing pad froze. He knew the image he was cutting—a man in black overseeing the work that would determine each passenger's fate. Some of them might have even guessed he was ESS. Cherny strode up to Jenna, looking down as if examining her.

Jenna cast her eyes elsewhere, as any good refugee would.

"Captain," Cherny said to the lead officer, "seize this woman."

Immediately, two guards grabbed Jenna's arms. She didn't resist.

"Secure her cybernetics. Bring her and any belongings to my craft."

"Yes, sir," the captain said.

Cherny did not have to explain his reasons. "Oversee the rest of the scans. I have what I came for."

"Of course," the captain said. He looked relieved to have survived intact. "Jain, Bedi, do as the operative says."

The instant the words were said, a worried murmur ran

Don Miasek

through the remaining passengers. Cherny could guess their thoughts. *Who is this woman? How close are we to being hauled off to some godforsaken hole? Maybe she's secretly United Fleet. Maybe the rumours of a coup are true.* Nirali stood at the edge of the crowd, watching in silence as Jenna's hands were bound behind her.

Cherny strode towards the catwalk leading to his helicraft. The guards shoved Jenna along, as if being rough with the prisoner proved their loyalty. *Just a little bit farther, Jenna. Then we can drop the act.* Cherny remotely unlocked the ship, and the guards forced Jenna through the side hatch. His helicraft was small, with two pilot chairs up front and a rear bench seat. They hadn't changed much since his original run with ESS.

"The Earth Security Service appreciates your cooperation," Cherny said to the guards before climbing in. The door slid closed, locking into place. The helicraft's rotors began to whirl, and within moments, it was airborne. Cherny slid the breather up over his face and tossed it aside with a grin. "We did it!" he exclaimed.

Jenna said nothing.

"Hold on." Cherny waved his hand, and the shackles keeping her arms bound behind her slid off.

Jenna undid her breather mask and set it down on the bench beside her. Carefully, she rolled up her sleeve and began working on the mechanical ports along her arm, making sure each peripheral was securely attached. Her face was unreadable.

PALE GREY DOT

"I almost didn't think it would work!" Cherny said. He spun one of the pilot's chairs around and sat down so he could face her. "Jenna, there's so much I want to say. When you left … When you left the Tower all those years ago, none of us had any idea what happened to you. We were all scattered. Ezza went off to the United Fleet, you were gone, Sienar was still in ESS, and I was stuck in Hawaii …" Cherny realized he was rambling but didn't stop. "I assumed you were dead."

"Where's Ezza?" Jenna asked. Her voice was barely above a whisper.

Cherny's smile vanished. "I don't know. Her ship was destroyed, but … but there's still hope. Brylan is searching the escape pods. There's a good chance she—"

"And Sienar?"

"Oh … Jenna." A knot was growing in Cherny's stomach. "I was captured by the Syndicate and brought to an underground Martian base. Sienar was there, trying to bring down ESS. He was working alongside—or … or against—Alexander Reuben. ESS found the base, but Sienar helped me escape. Listen, Sienar's plan—"

"Is he dead too?" Jenna tugged her sleeve back down to her wrist.

Cherny licked his lips nervously. "I'm so, so sorry." He knelt down and reached out to hug her, but stopped when she pulled back.

Instead, Jenna looked out the window towards the dirty clouds. Toronto was far below them now, so all they could make out were the shadows of the stratoscrapers.

"Sienar died so that we would have a chance at beating Her," Cherny said. "And we can do it, Jenna. I've made all the arrangements with a contact in Premier Fairchild's personal scientific advisory. We have Bev Stroud's memory drive. You can show them the proof that ESS was behind Jupiter Station. Then we can negotiate with Her. We'll be safe. She'll be safe. Nobody else has to die." He was getting excited again. "You do have it, right?" He reached for the travel bag, but she pulled it closer to her body.

"Jenna," he said, confused. "You fought for us for over fifty years, and now we're so close. You have to be feeling so—" His subdermal implants buzzed, and Cherny mentally reached out to the helicraft's systems. "Something's wrong." The deck vibrated, and he felt his weight shift as he stood up.

Jenna was still looking out the window, watching the buildings as the helicraft changed course.

Cherny stopped midstride to the control seat. His face went white as he stared at Jenna in horror. There was a high-priority request from SecLink.

//Operative.// Her words were as soothing as ever. //After all I have done for you ... from taking you under My wing when you were a mere child, to forgiving you for your crimes in Olympus Mons.//

Jenna finally looked away from the window, though Cherny had no idea if she was aware of his sudden connection to SecLink.

"No ..." he said out loud. Cherny held on to his fear, using it to focus away from the Pull.

PALE GREY DOT

//Despite all the love I have given you, you still betray Me in My hour of need.//

"Jenna, I need your help. She knows where we are!" Cherny looked frantically over his shoulder. The Tower loomed before them through the helicraft's front windshield. The pitch-black exterior panel closest to them, several storeys high, split open to reveal a docking bay. "Jenna!" he shouted.

Finally, she looked at him. "Exactly how long did it take you?"

"What?" Cherny croaked.

"How long did it take you to betray me to Her when I asked you for help?" There was venom in her tone.

//There were others, My dear, sweet Cherny, who felt I was too kind with the Athena Six, but I always felt I could rely on you,// She whispered.

She knows what you did. "I …" he trailed off. It was getting hard to think again. Cherny tried to sever his connection to SecLink but fumbled with the mental commands. "I'm sorry. I'm sorry! I tried to fight it, Jenna, I swear I did. But the Pull! It was—"

Jenna sprang from her seat, knocking him to the deck. His head hit the pilot's chair as she landed atop him. "I spent half a century trying to put our team back together!" Her hands were around his throat now. Cherny grabbed her fingers, trying to muster the strength to break free, but she held tight. "I trusted you!"

//Did you think I would not be watching you? My love for My children has never made Me blind.//

A shadow passed over the helicraft as it lurched into the Tower's docking bay. Already, the wall was closing behind them.

//Perhaps you thought I could be distracted by your show in deep space?//

"Jenna ..." he struggled to choke out the words, though he could barely breathe now. "The drive ... We need to get the drive ..." She wasn't a large woman, but it felt like a tonne of bricks was resting on his chest.

"Forget about the damn memory drive!" Jenna spat. "I'm here for only one reason. I'm going to kill Her."

Cherny's eyes went wide as he begged with his failing breath.

•

Jenna slowly unwrapped her fingers around Cherny's throat as the helicraft settled on the landing pad. It'd been a long time since she felt such indecision. Strangling him hadn't been as satisfying as she'd hoped. *Kill him, or no?* He was almost pitiable, lying on the floor with his head resting against the pilot's seat as he struggled to suck down air. *Damn him.* It'd been so easy when she was a mere fugitive. It was her against the solar system. It wasn't so easy now that she had family to betray her. Maybe Ezza had been right, and Cherny was as much of a victim as Sal and Taylor had been.

Pressing herself against the helicraft's bulkhead, Jenna peeked through the side window. Heavy-maintenance

PALE GREY DOT

machinery hung down from the ceiling, and refuelling tanks lined the walls. Two dozen guns were pointed at the ship's doorway. Each member of the security force wore light armour. A woman in black, not unlike Cherny's uniform, stood at their lead. Her long blonde hair was tied back, and a handheld energy projector rested on her hip. Jenna recognized her from Marcus's memories.

She gave Cherny one last look before making her decision. Reaching out, Jenna undid the latch and pulled the helicraft's side door open. All guns were raised in her direction as she stepped out onto the pad.

"Jenna Doe," the blonde woman called out. "Welcome home. We'd rather—"

"Shut up, Amanda," Jenna snapped. "I want to speak with Her."

If Amanda was surprised that she knew her name, she showed no outward sign. "Odd that you think you can make demands right now."

"Yeah? Then go ahead and shoot, you bitch."

All guns remained trained on her. Amanda didn't so much as twitch.

"No? What's wrong?" Jenna yanked the travel bag off her shoulder and held it up front of her as if it were a shield. "Oh, you want this, don't you? You think I don't know how She thinks? She wants Bev Stroud's memory drive. She'll want to fake some proof that Ezza was lying. She'll want to know how I beat Her. How I beat Her damn encryption. I die and this thing burns."

399

To Jenna's disappointment, Amanda didn't look concerned. "It's true, then?" the operative asked. "You managed to gain access to an operative's memory drive?"

Jenna didn't reply. Instead, she scanned the troops. The typical security guard was mere fodder compared to an operative. Though their faces were covered, she could see the nervousness in their body language. Brylan had said ESS considered her a legend, and Jenna suspected he had been truthful about that. Still, they were many, and she was one. They had weapons, and she had only the small energy projector within her cybernetic hand. Jenna answered Amanda's question by giving the bag a shake. "Don't have much interest in talking with a lackey. I want to talk with Her."

"Behaviour like this," Amanda replied calmly, "is why you were always Her favourite." She must have transmitted orders, because one by one, the soldiers lowered their weapons and filed out of the docking bay.

Though it was just the two of them now, Jenna knew better than to think she could fight Amanda alone. They would have left nothing to chance. "I want to talk to Her," Jenna repeated.

There were footsteps from the helicraft behind her. Jenna whirled instinctively as Cherny stepped down onto the deck. His neck was still red where her fingers had pressed into it. The look of desperation in his eyes was gone, though Jenna couldn't tell if he was simply resigned to his fate.

"Operatives." Her voice filled the docking bay.

Jenna shivered and cursed herself for doing so. It was not

PALE GREY DOT

often that She spoke, but the thought of feeling it in her mind made Jenna want to throw up. No, better it be aloud. "I'm not one of Your damn operatives anymore," she shouted.

"And you, Cherny? I wonder if you still possess the capacity for loyalty. You sacrificed Sienar. You sacrificed Ezza. All for failed misdirection." She was like a mother reprimanding a child. "I can have your Athena Protocols fixed, Cherny. I can ensure you will never stray again. Come with Me."

Jenna glared at him. The coward was being given an out.

But to her shock, Cherny didn't so much as hesitate. Reaching for his left wrist, he pulled out his transmitter and let it fall to the ground. "I'm with Jenna," he said.

"My sweet, innocent Cherny," She intoned. "You misunderstand. I was not giving you the choice."

Amanda moved for her energy projector and Jenna wasn't fast enough to react. A bright flash struck her mechanical arm, and Jenna felt the strength go out of it. Her bag slipped from her grasp and landed on the deck with a thud as her implants shut down. Amanda was already moving towards them, energy projector in hand. From the corner of her eye, Jenna saw another shot strike Cherny. He hit the side of the helicraft and slumped to the ground.

She was nearly on them now. Her calm, confident expression hadn't changed. The operative knelt to snag the straps of the travel bag.

As Jenna tried to bring power back to her dead arm, she lunged forward and drove her right fist towards Amanda's face, but the other woman caught it in time.

Don Miasek

"Maybe if your systems weren't so rotted," Amanda said. "Maybe if you were still in your prime." The operative rose to her feet. Jenna struggled against her, but it was no use. Her shoulder nearly dislocated as her arm was twisted behind her.

Jenna fought to free herself, but a knee in the back sent her face-first into the side of the helicraft. Blood dripped down her cheek, and she whirled around just as Amanda grasped her neck with her mechanical hand. The energy projector was back in her other, pointed at Cherny's face.

Cherny stared back at the operative as he slowly pushed himself to his feet.

Jenna gagged, struggling in vain to loosen the fingers around her throat as Her voice filled the room once more. "Now, let us see where I went wrong with you."

●

"What were you like, Amanda?" Cherny called out, trying to keep the desperation from his voice. His wrists, ankles, and neck were strapped to the interrogation table as they wheeled him and Jenna through the Tower's halls. His gaze was forced up towards the ceiling, and every time he tried to move, the bindings would bite into his skin. Having been on the other side of enough interrogations, he knew breaking free was impossible. "What were you like before you tied your mind to Her?"

Amanda was at the head of the procession, examining

PALE GREY DOT

the small, silver memory drive squeezed between her thumb and forefinger. The operative slowed enough to look over her shoulder at him. Cherny had hoped she'd at least show some reaction to having her secret exposed to the rabble, but she looked unconcerned.

"Well, Sienar told me," Cherny pressed. "He said you were warm and friendly. Then you suddenly turned into a goddamn machine. Whoever you were before was gone. Face it—She killed you. You're just Her wearing another woman's face." He knew the Tower's layout by heart, and despite his restricted view, he had no doubt where they were being taken.

Amanda motioned to the guard behind Cherny.

Stinging pain shot through his body as the stunner was jabbed into his side for a good ten seconds. "Do you even remember Mars?" Cherny could hear his voice cracking. "You were actually able to feel again. I should ... I should have figured out some way to keep you away from Earth."

Out of the corner of his eye, he could see Jenna strapped to her own table. He tried to catch her eye for support, but she just kept staring up at the ceiling. *She has to know where we're going,* Cherny thought. The Tower's surgical facilities had uniquely specialized equipment. *Come on, Jenna. They're going to tear our minds apart. Why the hell are you so calm?* It wouldn't take them long to figure out a way to reinstall the Pull. *Or maybe they'll just dissect our brains and be done with it.* "I hoped you wouldn't return to Earth, Amanda. But no, you let Her kill you again," he wheezed.

403

Amanda went back to ignoring him, though Cherny knew if he kept pushing her, he'd get another shock for his trouble. He wondered if the pain was worth the extra five seconds of life it might buy him.

"Why?" Jenna suddenly spoke.

Now Amanda stopped and turned, placing the memory drive in an inner pocket. The procession halted as the operative stepped over to Jenna's table so she could look down and meet her eye to eye. She apparently did not need Jenna to elaborate. "What better way to thank Her for everything She's done for us?" she asked. "You of all people should understand. Surely that was your reason for developing the Athena Protocols to begin with."

"Agreeing to that was the worst mistake I could have ever made. They're an abomination, and whatever this new procedure is will be too."

"Flaws can be corrected, Jenna. You shouldn't be fighting this. You're going to be part of the family again. Isn't at least a part of you excited?"

"What I'm going to be," Jenna snarled, "is very happy when I break out of here and kill the lot of you."

It was not often that Cherny saw emotion from Amanda—on Earth, at least—but here he saw the briefest hint of sadness in her eyes. "You know, She really does think highly of you. I'd like to think we'll get to know each other better soon enough."

They resumed their march. Their path must have been cordoned off, Cherny realized, as the Tower's halls were devoid of the usual foot traffic. Soon he heard the surgical

PALE GREY DOT

bay doors opening, and he was wheeled in. Cherny squinted against the bright overhead lights. "No, no, no," he whispered as he felt his resolve starting to disintegrate.

"Ah, there they are," he heard a man say. "Come, bring them over. We are almost ready." There were footsteps as the man approached, stopping at Jenna's table.

"Please, don't. Please, I'll do anything …" Cherny begged as they pushed his table to the centre of the room. Great mechanical arms hung down from the ceiling, dangling over his head. Some were tipped with scanners, others with syringes, and others with scalpels.

Cherny heard footsteps by his table. A moment later, a man wearing a white surgical mask filled his view, looking down at him. His eyes were mechanical, well suited for precision work. A bright red light shone from his left as he scanned his patient. "Do not worry. You will feel nothing. Once we have found out how your colleague evaded her Athena Protocols, we can work to fix it in both of you. Then we can see about adding you to the direct network. Our dear Amanda needs colleagues on her own level, no? Soon you will be better than new."

Cherny flinched as he patted him on the shoulder. "Jenna, can you hear me?" he called out. He tried to crane his head towards her, but the bindings held him tight. "I'm so sorry for all of this. It's my fault."

"Shhh," the surgeon said. "Rest. You can … hrm." He moved out of his line of sight, leaving Cherny to stare up at the scalpels and syringes above him.

Don Miasek

The seconds ticked away, and Cherny wondered when the instruments would descend upon them. Two … three … four minutes went by. Still, there was nothing but silence. Both Amanda and the surgeon had gone quiet.

Then Cherny heard two sets of footsteps moving away, followed by the surgical bay doors cycling.

Are we alone now?

"Jenna?" he called out again. "Please tell me you're there. I need to hear your voice."

Jenna didn't answer, though Cherny could hear her fidgeting on the table.

"Listen to me. I regretted turning you in the moment it happened. I got your message and the Pull … I …" Cherny found it hard to compose himself while the instruments of his imminent dissection hung above him. "Jenna, after we were exiled from ESS, I was lost. Our team failed, and over a thousand died on Mars because of it.

"I spent the last fifty years stuck in a dead-end job, praying that our exile would end. When She contacted me again, of course I jumped at it. I should have realized it was a mistake, but I didn't." Cherny stopped to give her a chance to reply, but he only heard the sound of metal slowly scraping against itself. *What is she doing over there?* "Jenna? Can you hear me?"

When she didn't answer, Cherny went on, describing his job at the Tsiolkovsky Spaceport, how he eventually lost faith that he'd ever get pulled back into ESS, and how he thought he'd never see Jenna, Sienar, or Ezza again. He confessed how happy he'd been when he was recalled back to service, how he feared being sent away again, and that he'd wondered how the other Athena Six survivors were doing. He even told her of Sienar's final moments in the Martian tunnels, and how he had fought to the very end against Her.

Eventually, Cherny ran out of things to say, and he finally went silent. *How much time has passed since Amanda and the surgeon left us? An hour? Two?* His neck was getting sore from being stuck in one position for so long, and he was starting to lose feeling in his feet.

A moment later, the floor shook, as if the Tower was hit by an earthquake. Cherny felt himself pressed against his straps. The cabinets lining the walls and the apparatuses above him rattled. The floor rumbled again, stronger this time. Cherny felt the table nearly tilt to one side. "Jenna?" he called out. Whatever it was, it was getting closer.

The door cycled, admitting a series of panicked footsteps. Cherny struggled and failed to turn his head to see who had entered. The footsteps stopped near Jenna's bed. "What did you do?" the surgeon shouted.

Cherny heard metal snapping, followed by the man screaming. Gunfire filled his ears, interrupted only by loud thuds as heavy objects hit the floor. He winced, praying that a bullet wouldn't find him. Ten seconds later, all Cherny could hear was his own breathing.

Then Jenna's face appeared above him. There was a maniacal glint in her eyes. When she reached out and tore off the bindings keeping him strapped to the interrogation table,

Don Miasek

Cherny saw that her arms were covered in red streaks. She grasped his hand and pulled him up. The broken bodies of the surgeon and a pair of guards were crumpled on the ground, blood pooling around their heads. "I thought about it," she said, "and I'm going to give you a chance to fight for my forgiveness."

19

Jenna reached into the metal tray beside her interrogation table that held her peripherals. Carefully, she inserted each transmitter and attachment back into the proper slots in her arm. As power started to flow back into her systems, she began charging the small energy projector in her hand. The guards' weapons would be locked to their own cybernetics, and there wasn't time to rip through the security. *Our wits and onboard systems will have to do,* she decided.

Another rumble ran through the Tower, and this time, the walls and ceiling shook. Jenna grabbed the interrogation table for stability. *It'd almost be hilarious if this whole place came crashing down with us in it. At least it'd kill Her along with everyone else.*

Cherny was just now getting up from the surgical slab. "What did you do, Jenna?" There was surprise and fear on his face.

409

He always was one step behind me. "If you had your transmitter, you could figure it out yourself." A jumbled mess of information was overflowing on EarthNet, and she barely knew what to focus on first. Selecting the state news outlet, Jenna smiled in satisfaction. Helicrafts belonging to the Earth Planetary Guard were swarming the Tower. All transports were being routed away to make room for the advance of heavy tanks. Hundreds of government alerts blared, warning all civilians to evacuate the block. "It's beautiful, Cherny."

"Bev Stroud's memory drive," Cherny said as a look of realization washed over him. "You never had it."

Jenna grinned wildly and looked to the ceiling. "Hear that, You psychotic bitch? 'Failed misdirection' my ass! Gave the real one to the idiot civilian, and now Fairchild's coming for You!" After a moment's pause, she added, "Nothing to say to that, eh? Well, don't worry. We're going to have a nice, short chat about it in person soon enough."

The speakers crackled as She spoke. "Operatives. You should think about what you are doing."

Even this deep within the Tower, Jenna could hear the sound of distant gunfire. On the newsfeed, she saw helicraft boarding rams smashing through the dark walls of the Tower. With each impact, their surroundings rattled. "Oh, I've thought about it. I've thought about it every goddamn day for the past fifty-one years." She jerked her head towards the door. "Come on, Cherny."

Cherny looked down at the surgeon and guards she had killed. It'd been a messy job. Jenna wondered if he was

PALE GREY DOT

regretting siding with her, but eventually he looked up and nodded his assent.

Jenna stormed out into the hall, checking each corner as she went. Cybernetic hearing allowed her to make out footsteps in all directions. She heard a security team on the deck above them rushing to where the outer wall had been breached. The soldiers had six entry points already, and more were coming. Firefights had broken out across the Tower. The attackers had the element of surprise, and Jenna knew it wouldn't be long before the security forces and whatever few operatives were stationed in the Tower were overwhelmed.

Her cybernetics consolidated the mess of physical and virtual data together, and Jenna plotted a path of least resistance. She motioned for Cherny to follow. One level down, she saw that one of the second-wave helicrafts was carving into the side of the Tower. Security teams would already be on the way to intercept, she knew. The corridor leading to the elevator shaft looked clear, though. *Ought to be able to slip through before the fighting moves up.*

Cherny moved with her, covering the corners she couldn't. Despite herself, it felt good working with one of her brothers again. They had no need to signal one another as they swept through the Tower, always knowing what the other would do before they did it.

Jenna burst through the doorway that led to the elevators. The sound of weapons firing beneath them was deafening, but they pressed onward. Any hopes she'd had that

411

Don Miasek

ESS would be pushed back quickly were dashed. *No matter. If we're lucky, we can—*

The entire deck beneath her feet suddenly gave way. All Jenna could do was cover her head as she plummeted. She barely heard Cherny shouting her name amidst the roar of snapping metal beams. An instant later, and she hit the floor amongst broken tiles and dirt. Her systems flickered off from the impact. Struggling not to make a sound despite the pain, Jenna forced her eyes to remain open. Dust and smoke filled her vision, and there was a sharp, stabbing pain shooting through her left foot. It took her a moment to register what had happened—someone had detonated explosives, though she didn't know which side had done it.

Gunfire ripped over her head, and Jenna pressed herself against the ground in desperation. Even moving that much made her foot scream in agony. Her enhanced vision took a moment to readjust to its surroundings, and she saw the bright red icon of the last member of an attacking the Planetary Guard squadron. She turned her head the other way. It wasn't an ESS security team, but rather a pair of hulking drones, three times the size that Bev Stroud's had been. Their powerful spider legs were taut, clamped to the walls and floor to keep them steady. Their primary weapon emitters swivelled upwards as they manoeuvred for a clear shot.

Their guns flashed as they launched volleys of energy at the last guardsman, nearly blinding Jenna. The man was obliterated in seconds. Unmindful of their victory, the drone nearest to her skittered closer. Its chassis was marred

PALE GREY DOT

by bullet holes and dirt, but its systems seemed unaffected. Jenna rolled onto her back, trying to drag herself away from the machine while it brought its scanner to bear. Jenna felt the power starting to flow back into her hand-mounted energy projector. *Just a few more seconds!*

The drone's controller apparently made a decision, and its weapon projector tilted downwards towards her face. Jenna instinctively flinched, and a split second later, the drone's body spasmed as it was lit up from above. The legs wobbled before the entire machine toppled onto her. Air rushed out of Jenna's lungs from its weight, and her foot suffered another wave of torment. With her vision filled by the metal bulk of the drone resting on her chest, Jenna heard a second and third shot, followed by the sound of the remaining drone collapsing.

There was a thud as Cherny landed beside her, crouching down to cushion the impact. The drone's weight was lifted as he heaved its corpse off her.

Jenna reached up and took his extended hand. She winced as she tried putting weight on her left foot. "It's fine," she said preemptively. Her cybernetics flashed a brief medical diagnosis: two broken toes and a hairline fracture. *Not enough to stop me. Not after all this.*

But Cherny was looking over her shoulder. Jenna turned to see a lone overwatch standing in terror near the corridor doorway. This one was little more than a circuit board with four data-port riddled tentacles and a human face. He stared at them in shock, tentacles squirming nervously.

Jenna wondered if this was the man controlling the

413

drones that tried to kill her, but then decided it didn't matter. She raised her hand and took aim, but Cherny calmly pushed it back down.

"Go find the nearest Planetary Guard squad and surrender yourself to them," Cherny called out. "They'll keep you safe."

The overwatch nodded vigorously before shuffling away as fast as he could.

Kind-hearted idiocy, Jenna thought. She was reminded of her decision to let Marcus die and decided not to press the issue. The overwatches didn't matter. The security guards didn't matter. Hell, even other operatives didn't matter. The only thing that mattered was Her. Jenna hobbled onward, trying to wave the dust out of her face with her cybernetic hand.

Cherny gave one last look in the direction of the fleeing overwatch before taking Jenna's arm and putting it over his shoulders. It helped to support her weight while her systems worked to numb the pain.

They hadn't gotten far before speakers above them activated. "Jenna," She said. "You need to know that I saved you. After the Martian Insurrection, there were demands to punish those responsible. Of course there were, given the catastrophe."

"Liar!" Jenna snapped. They had reached the central elevators now. "You blamed everything on Taylor and killed him!"

Cherny let Jenna go and ripped off the control panel,

PALE GREY DOT

attaching the wires within to his arm. For a brief second, they heard the elevator descending to their position, only for the power to shut down. The doors remained stubbornly closed. "Dammit," Cherny muttered under his breath as he removed the wires. The Tower and all its functions belonged to Her.

"Would you have preferred that I blamed who was truly responsible? Tell Me, Operative, was I the one to design the Athena Protocols?" She intoned. "Was I the one to install them? Was I the one who helplessly stood by as Taylor and Sal's madness drove them to cause the deaths of so many Martians in a misguided attempt to please Me?"

Cherny gave her an apprehensive look, and Jenna glared back at him. "She killed him," she repeated through gritted teeth.

"And it pained Me greatly to harm one of My children," She said. "But it was one of you or all of you, Jenna. I stood up for you against the premier herself. You know I only ever do what is best for you."

Jenna motioned for Cherny to back up as she took aim at the elevator doors. A bright beam from her hand lashed out against the metal as she slowly carved her way through.

"Jenna, Fairchild's army is here," Cherny said. They could hear shouting and energy weapons firing one level up. The slow, methodical footsteps of heavy, military-grade power armour were unmistakable. "There's no reason for us to go after Her ourselves," Cherny pressed. "I've plotted a path to the nearest external wall. We can sneak our way there, sur-render to Fairchild's forces, and—"

Don Miasek

"I'm going to kill Her," Jenna interrupted. "You can either help or abandon me again." *Come on,* she urged impatiently as she finished slicing a circle in the door. Jenna awkwardly pressed her shoulder against it and pushed with all her strength, careful to keep as much weight off her bad foot as she could. The carved metal gave way and fell into the elevator shaft. It took some time before she heard the echoing sound of it hitting the bottom.

"There's no need for this, Jenna!" Cherny retorted. "Listen, She's done horrible things, but even She deserves fair justice."

Jenna didn't answer. Instead, she reached through and grabbed the closest cable with her metal hand. Dangling in the shaft, she looked back at him, waiting for his decision.

After a moment, Cherny muttered a curse and reached through the breach.

●

Cherny gripped the line tightly as he crossed the threshold. He relaxed his hand just slightly, and the pair began the long descent. The sound of metal fingers scraping against the cable was awful, but he put it out of his mind. It was pitch-black inside the elevator shaft, but his cybernetic vision allowed him to take in their surroundings.

"Wait! Stop!" Cherny suddenly called out.

Jenna squeezed tight, coming to a halt as she looked back up at him.

PALE GREY DOT

"Do you hear that? The air circulation's off."

Jenna's expression turned gleeful. "Fairchild's shut down the main power. Must be dawning on Her that there's no escape."

It hurt to watch Jenna like this. Cherny wondered if she even cared about the engineered war between the United Fleet and the Syndicate. *Or is it only hatred driving her?*

After what felt like an eternity, their feet hit the bottom of the shaft. There was no sound of gunfire. There was only their breathing, their footsteps, and the sizzle of metal as Jenna sliced through the elevator doors.

He stepped up beside her. "I don't suppose you've given any thought to taking Her alive," he said. He doubted there was any way to convince her, but he felt he at least owed Her enough to try.

Jenna responded by pushing the doors open and clamouring up into the hall.

There was no more light in here than there'd been in the shaft, but leaning on his cybernetic vision allowed Cherny to make out the rough, industrial-scale cables strapped to the ceiling. The power and data needed in this part of the Tower was immense, and the backup generators couldn't do them justice.

The air was dry and cool but had a stale smell to it. Aside from the technicians needed to maintain Her systems, people did not often venture this deep into the Tower. Cherny himself had only been here once before, back when he had first become an operative, but the way was burned into his memory.

So close now. Jenna had to remind herself to stay calm. With her next step, she tried putting more weight on her foot. *Good.* Any sensation in it was nearly gone, and Jenna found she was able to limp along at a decent clip.

"Ah, there you are," She said as one of the hallway's overhead speakers activated. "My clever Jenna, have you reconsidered Olympus Mons? The burden of Taylor's and Sal's deaths rests on your shoulders as much as Mine."

To her surprise, Cherny answered before she could. "Jenna didn't wipe out the United Fleet at Jupiter Station or take over the Syndicate so You could prove to Fairchild how indispensable You are. Sienar told me that the only thing You ever cared about was Your own safety."

All of this so She could keep Her goddamn job, Jenna thought. She nodded her thanks to Cherny.

"Then Sienar was wrong," She replied. "The only thing I ever cared about was the safety of all of ESS. That includes the both of you. Jenna, on the other hand, has murdered two of your fellow operatives already. My children, we can work this out."

"Do you still have access to the Tower's network?" Cherny asked. "Get ESS's security personnel to surrender. Premier Fairchild will—"

"Kill me," She interrupted. Her voice was softer, and Jenna could have sworn She almost sounded nervous. "Perhaps

PALE GREY DOT

not today, but eventually. You know this to be the case. Make no mistake—if you continue to move against Me, it is an execution. Please, Cherny."

Jenna raised her hand and, with a quick burst, blew out the speaker. *Idiot. Shouldn't be wasting power like this.* Still, Jenna had found the pleading in Her voice gratifying. There was white light up ahead where the hall opened into a small chamber. All power and data cables ran through there, buried deep enough to avoid being cut.

Jenna gave Cherny one final look before limping slowly down the hallway with him. They both kept their hands outstretched, ready to fire at whatever came their way. But instead of gunfire or threats, Jenna could only make out the sound of murmuring.

"It'll be okay," Amanda was saying. A short set of stairs led down to the chamber's recessed floor. The room was circular, with all walls focused on the human-sized capsule in the middle. It was metal on all sides, save for the glass window on top, and was securely fastened to both the floor and ceiling, with thick cables running between it and the Tower's infrastructure. The dim lights in the walls peeked through the wiring, causing a jumble of shadows to play across the room. Amanda caressed the glass gently as she spoke in a soft tone. "A team is working to clear a path to the underground. We can get Us to safety," she whispered.

Jenna and Cherny crept up to the precipice before dropping to the lower level. Though her cybernetics were nearly drained of power, Jenna diverted what she had left to her

419

energy projector and tried to steady her nerves. After so long, she could hardly believe it was nearly over.

"Oh," Amanda said to the capsule, replying to some unheard voice as she ran her metal fingers along the glass. "Yes, I suppose We have no choice now."

Just as she mentally pulled the trigger, Jenna's arm was yanked to the side. The energy burst flew wide, striking the cable junction on the opposite wall. Fire erupted from the electronics as Jenna's arm was pinned to the magnetic grappling clamp that had emerged from the maintenance panels beside her.

Amanda's pistol was already in her hand and aimed at Cherny. The pair fired simultaneously, and Jenna squeezed her eyes shut in the sudden flash of light. Opening them again, she saw the two operatives locked together. The smoking remains of Amanda's weapon lay on the floor before the capsule.

Jenna struggled against the clamp, but her arm didn't budge. Reaching up with her free hand, she tried to pry off the panel next to it in an attempt to shut it down. On the opposite side of the room, foam shot from the ceiling, smothering the flames from her errant blast.

"All of this is your fault!" Amanda shouted as she slammed her fist into Cherny's gut. "Your failure on Mars nearly killed Us!"

Cherny knocked her second strike aside before throwing a punch of his own.

Amanda jumped backwards to evade, landing on the

PALE GREY DOT

lower level before the capsule. "But Mars wasn't enough, was it? The Ganymede Blitz would have fixed everything, but again, one of you idiots ruined it!"

"You mean ruined ESS's chances to take over the Syndicate," Cherny retaliated.

"Yes! Think about it, Cherny. We could have played both sides forever. Think of the casualties We could have prevented!" As she rose to her full height, Jenna saw her surreptitiously draw a dagger from her boot. Cherny instinctively raised his metal arm to block the weapon as it flew through the air. The blade buried itself to the hilt in his circuitry.

"*Preventing* casualties? I'm sure everyone on Jupiter Station will be thrilled to hear it," Cherny hissed through a clenched jaw. Jenna saw that his arm had become dead weight, but he still managed to swing it around, catching Amanda in the side of the head. She went down, slamming against the capsule. With his free hand, Cherny wrenched the blade free and hurled it.

Jenna ducked as the weapon slashed through the wiring just above her head and embedded itself in the panel. The telltale sound of the magnetic clamp losing power filled the chamber, and in an instant, she was free. Amanda was also back on her feet. Jenna forced her injured foot to work as she stood on her toes, reaching up and yanking the dagger out of the wall.

Cherny grunted as he tripped over the stairs behind him. Amanda's fist slipped under his guard, and Jenna could hear ribs cracking. Gripping the dagger's hilt as tightly as she

421

could, Jenna limped past the capsule, and before Amanda could react, plunged it between her shoulder blades. It took all her strength to break through the thin-weave armour beneath Amanda's suit. Amanda barely made a sound as the air rushed out of her lungs and she slumped against Cherny.

Jenna pulled her off him and pushed her aside, not bothering to check vitals. The operative wasn't why she was here.

"Jenna," Cherny said through laboured breaths. He held his chest in pain.

As she looked down at him, she couldn't help but feel pity. His blood stained the steps, and his breathing was growing more ragged. In his eyes, she saw such a sad desperation. "Appreciate your help, Cherny," she said. "I'm glad I gave you another chance."

Jenna then looked away, licking her lips as she hobbled up to the capsule. *This must be what it's like to open a present on Christmas.* She had to fight the urge to hyperventilate as she peered through the glass.

Her naked body was emaciated, with greying skin shrivelled around Her bones. Though the movement was subtle, Jenna could just make out Her ribs gently rising and falling as She drew shallow, respirator-controlled breaths. Loose strands of hair were splayed across the padding for Her otherwise bald head. Her skeletal arms rested at Her sides, and gnarled fingers curled over Her palms. Her eyes were closed, and from the yellowish crust that covered them, Jenna doubted She was even capable of opening them anymore. Jenna didn't know how old She truly was, but she had been

PALE GREY DOT

born long before the development of effective anti-ageing techniques. Cherny was calling out to her, but Jenna didn't listen.

"Wait." Though Her overhead speaker crackled, Her body and mouth remained motionless. Her voice, Her strength, and all of Her power came from the vast network that permeated the Tower and stretched beyond to the farthest reaches of the solar system.

Jenna drew her metal arm back.

"Look at your brother," She said. Her voice, normally so in control, faltered.

You're just stalling for time, Jenna knew. *Trying to buy another second You don't deserve.*

"Ask him. Look him in the eye and ask him whose fault it is that Taylor, Sal, and a thousand human beings perished."

Jenna kept her fist poised but glanced over her shoulder. Cherny had crawled over to Amanda's fallen body. His hands were pressed around the dagger in her back, trying to stem the tide of blood. Jenna saw fear on his face as he looked up at her. "Go on," she hissed. "Tell Her that She pressed us into action too soon after the Athena Protocols. Tell Her that She pressured Taylor into doing whatever he could to make Her happy!"

Cherny opened his mouth, but no words came out.

"Tell Her, Cherny!" Jenna shouted.

He shook his head before dropping his gaze back to Amanda.

Fury welled up within her and she felt tears on her cheeks.

423

Don Miasek

Jenna looked back at the capsule and smashed her fist through the window. The shattered glass left cuts on Her face, but there was precious little blood. Her eyes twitched. Lips that had not moved for decades struggled to form real words.

In one fluid motion, Jenna thrust her fist forward again, this time into Her ribs. It felt like breaking through a stack of dusty paper. Jenna closed her eyes as she slowly withdrew her hand. Though it felt like a great weight had been lifted, it wasn't as satisfying as she'd imagined. With Her last words, She had managed to ruin even this.

Jenna spared one last look at Her broken body before turning away. Cherny was still with Amanda. She wondered if he would have tried to stop her, had he not been injured.

"We can still save Amanda," he said. He took long pauses as he struggled to steady his breathing. "Jenna, I need your help. There should be a medical kit somewhere. Please, can you …?" he trailed off.

She stepped past him, gripping the stair railings for support as she climbed. "Have to admit, Cherny, I hadn't really considered what to do afterwards," she said. "I'll have to give it some thought." It'd be maybe fifteen minutes before Fairchild's army broke through to the lowest level. *Should be enough time to climb back up, regain network access, and plot a way out of here.*

Jenna didn't look back as she fled.

424

DISPATCH FROM THE PREMIER OF EARTH
*** HIGH PRIORITY ***

Fifty-three days ago, our society was tested by the catastrophe at Jupiter Station. Since then, there has been much misinformation being spread throughout the solar system, including falsified transmissions and lies spread throughout the planetary networks.

The truth is this: The Syndicate uprising has been quelled. Their leadership, including Alexander Reuben, has been killed or captured. The strength of our military and intelligence apparatuses have, once more, proven both unified and resilient. The gratitude of the government has been extended to the Earth Security Service and the United Fleet.

All residents within the solar system, whether planet-bound or in our extraplanetary locales, should know that they are protected. In the wake of this victory, the government will be reallocating its military and intelligence personnel to better suit a world without threat from the Syndicate.

This includes a strengthening of the United Fleet's intelligence branch and the disbanding of the Earth Security Service. The Ministries of Defence and Industry will ensure all eligible ESS members remain gainfully employed.

Mary Fairchild, Premier of Earth

20

The halls of the DC Fortress were devoid of ornamentation. There were no windows to the outside world, works of art on the walls, or any other distinguishing features to identify one corner from the next. Any signage was virtual only, and Cherny's cybernetics had been disabled the instant he was taken into custody. The floor was dark grey plating, while the overhead lights were glaringly bright. They passed no others.

Two soldiers walked behind Cherny, each wearing face-concealing helms and wielding stunner rifles. At each crossing, they ordered him left, right, or straight. Cherny had tried asking them questions—where they were taking him being the first—but they had simply ignored him.

The past two weeks had been a string of interrogations.

"Why were you summoned back to the Earth Security Service?"

PALE GREY DOT

"What was your relationship with the head of ESS?"

"Why did you and the operative Amanda go to Olympus Mons?"

"How did you break free during your capture on Mars?"

"How was the former operative Sienar killed?"

"What happened to you during the siege of the ESS Tower?"

One interrogator would ask, followed by a second asking the same, followed by a third. Again and again, they hammered the same questions, all while his cybernetics were hooked up to machinery designed to read every hint of doubt or deception in his mind. His old training may have been enough to help him get away with a lie or two, but he didn't bother trying.

Throughout it all, Cherny's mind kept returning to Jenna and Ezza. The last he'd seen of Jenna, she was limping down the corridor away from Her chamber while he desperately worked to save Amanda's life. He wondered if she'd escaped.

Ezza's spaceship had been destroyed, but he didn't know if she'd survived. He'd asked about them both as often as he dared, but each time the interrogator would simply shake their head and move on with the questions.

As they marched him through the halls, he thought about where they could be taking him. There were at least three ministry offices they could have reached by now. The guards stayed focused on him, but they didn't seem nervous, so he figured he wasn't being taken to an execution.

Finally, they stopped in front of a door. The first guard

427

inserted a robotic finger into the lock. Three seconds later, it swung open. The guard stepped aside and motioned Cherny through.

The office stood in stark contrast to the sterile corridor behind him. Beneath his feet was plush carpeting. Tapestries hung on the walls, depicting the construction of the space elevators, the first underground bases on Mars, the colony fleet to Alpha Centauri—chronological images of Earth's progress since the solar system fell under one government almost three hundred years ago. An overhead holo-projector hung from the ceiling. Off to one side was a coffee table surrounded by sofas. The lighting was warm and friendly. Cherny felt like he was stepping onto another planet.

He glanced behind him, but the door was already closed. Turning back, Cherny looked at the wooden desk in the centre of the room. Piled on it were stacks of papers— actual, real paper, Cherny noted. His focus, though, was on the man behind the desk. Sebastian Havoic, Minister of Defence, second only to Premier Fairchild in military matters, motioned for him to step forward. The last Cherny had heard, he'd been removed from office along with the rest of the United Fleet's leadership. His fortunes had clearly changed.

Cherny had never seen him in person before. Physically, Havoic was not a large man, but the intense way he sized Cherny up gave him pause. A thin strip of silver cybernetics running along his forehead glinted in the light. Havoic

PALE GREY DOT

reached over to one of his piles of papers and drew out a folder, briefly reviewing it. Cherny caught sight of his own name at the top.

"Mr. Fender," Havoic said before setting it back down.

Cherny wasn't sure what he was supposed to say, so he started asking questions. "Where are Jenna and Ezza?"

"We will get to that," Havoic replied. "But first, I owe you my gratitude. If it weren't for you, ESS's coup would have been successful, and I'd be either imprisoned or dead. The United Fleet would have been destroyed, and the Syndicate would be a puppet force, utilized as a system-wide bogey-man whenever Karla felt She needed more power."

Cherny blinked in surprise, and Havoic tsked.

"Come now. Any fear Karla once inspired in others was extinguished when your colleague put a fist through Her chest. It serves nobody to continue with any theatrics on Her behalf. She was a relic from a bygone era, and if the premier had let me have my way, She would have died a long time ago. In the end, She was merely human, and I've no intention of letting Her ridiculous mystification survive Her." Havoic leaned forward. "You disapprove?"

"No," Cherny lied. It felt wrong, hearing Her name. It would have been unthinkable for an ESS operative to speak it aloud.

"Mmm." Just when Cherny thought Havoic would call him out on it, the minister changed the subject. "During your incarceration, the government has been working to settle the disorder that swept across the system. ESS has

429

Don Miasek

been disbanded, and so it falls to a broken United Fleet to pick up the pieces."

The overhead holo-projector flashed, and suddenly, the comfortable office surroundings were smothered by the solar system. Beside Cherny was the sun. Mercury and Venus circled in front, with the other inner planets cresting around Havoic's desk. Beyond, the constellations hung in the air.

Havoic reached up and plucked Earth out of its orbit. "Earth was easiest, of course. Martial law isn't far from the status quo." He tossed the planet back into orbit.

Status quo. Cherny thought of Sienar. *He'd have been devastated to know that after all this, we've only managed the status quo.*

Jupiter hurtled past the minister, and he caught it with both hands. "It will take Jupiter and its moons decades to recover after the loss of Jupiter Station. Tens of thousands will suffer because of Karla's desperation."

He let it go and reached for the next planet. "Poor Mars. Earth's trough. No wonder the Syndicate thrived there after you bungled the Martian Insurrection. I've seen projections suggesting they may sue for independence again. Certainly, the weakness exposed in the government by your Athena Six will embolden them. Tell me, any concerns about how it ended there with your friend Sienar?"

"No regrets," Cherny lied again. "I would have liked to have brought him in alive, but ultimately, he betrayed Earth when he joined the Syndicate. I'd like to know what

PALE GREY DOT

happened to Jenna and Ezza. And I'd like to know what you're planning to do with me. Sir."

Havoic let Mars roll out of his hands, where it rejoined its brethren in orbit. "I'm not going to have you killed, if that's what you're worried about."

Cherny could breathe easy again.

"I've been receiving counsel on how best to pick up ESS's pieces. I've been told by someone I trust that you can still be of use." Havoic must have transmitted a command, because the side door slid open.

Cherny's eyes lit up as she walked in.

She wore a pressed United Fleet uniform. Her hair was tied back, and she walked with confident purpose. She didn't pay the soaring planets and asteroids any mind as she stood next to the minister.

"Cherny," Ezza said. A wide smile graced her features.

Cherny had to stop himself from running over and throwing his arms around her.

Havoic glanced between them. "Admiral Jayens will oversee your briefing. You're dismissed."

"I—y-yes!" Cherny stammered. "Thank you, sir."

Once they were back in the stark halls, Cherny reached out to Ezza. It felt good to hug her again. Made it all seem so real. They embraced for nearly a minute.

When they finally pulled apart, Ezza placed her hand on his shoulder. "Here, let me return your senses."

Cherny felt strength flow through his body as his systems came back online. The previously blank walls suddenly

431

sprang to life with information. Virtual signs marked the paths to the farthest corners of the DC Fortress, data streamed by from the newsfeeds, and constant status updates illustrated the twisted web of bureaucracy that kept the solar system running. After weeks without it, Cherny felt like a blindfold had been removed from his eyes. Rather than focusing on that, though, he kept his attention on Ezza. "I thought you had been killed."

"Still here," she replied, beaming.

"Has there been any news?"

Ezza didn't need him to elaborate. "No word on Jenna," she said in a quieter voice. "But she survived over half a century on the run from ESS. I'm sure she's out there."

"She'd better be." Cherny looked Ezza's uniform up and down. "Admiral, eh? Does this mean I have to salute?"

"Don't be ridiculous, Cherny. Only when others are watching."

He laughed.

Ezza put her arm around him as she led him through the halls. "Come on. We have a lot of catching up to do."

●

The Public Servant sat a half-hour north of the perimeter wall that bordered the DC Fortress. The four-storey inn and cafeteria served as either the final respite for those travelling to the claustrophobic capital, or as the first taste of freedom for those leaving it. The paint on the walls had long been

PALE GREY DOT

scoured off, and the floorboards creaked. On an admiral's pay, Ezza could afford the classier, more upscale lodgings not far from here, but she had picked it for the privacy of its booths and the discretion of its servers. They kept the blinds shut, though there wasn't much to look at outside beyond a seemingly unending dust storm.

"Ten days of uncertainty," Ezza said. "I sent everyone off in different directions so they'd have to track us down one by one to search for Stroud's memory drive. Our escape pod just had me, Ensign Adaeze, and Crewman Guthrie packed in a cramped space with nothing to do."

To her right, Nirali stared with her hands over her mouth, as if she didn't already know the ending of the story. Ezza hadn't wasted her time trying to get the reporter into DC Fortress.

Cherny, sitting across the table, kept his hands wrapped around his beer as he listened intently. Ezza had scrounged up a grey longcoat for him.

She still wore her United Fleet uniform, and she considered herself lucky that, after everything that had happened, she was still able to do so.

"The pod didn't have quite enough range to pick up transmissions from the nearest relay station, so we had no idea what was going on. Ten days, Cherny, of wondering whether you, Nirali, and Jenna had managed to pull it off. All we'd get was the occasional cut-up signal from the long-range Net. And the only thing it told us was that the solar system was still on the brink of tearing itself apart." Ezza grinned and waved an accusing finger at both of them. "For all I knew, She had snagged all three of you and 'proved' Her innocence to the premier."

The door to their booth chimed before sliding open. The server slid their food across the table. Cherny looked at his eggs, bacon, and toast as if he hadn't had a good meal in ages. He had ordered the good stuff—processed and coloured to look like the real thing. His hair was thinner, Ezza thought, but the rest of him was thicker than when she'd last seen him. Filled out, perhaps.

Once the door was shut, Nirali reached over for one of the nutritional paste bars. "Hey, Cherny, did you ever hear about an operative named Brylan Ncube?"

"Only second-hand."

Nirali looked to Ezza, and so she picked up the story from there.

"Well, picture the smuggest asshole you can imagine," Ezza said. "Give him the solar system's most powerful warship and add in all of Her authority and self-righteousness. Now imagine the look on his face when he found out I didn't have Bev Stroud's memory drive and he was about to lose everything."

Nirali sighed. "I sort of wish I had been there to see that."

Silence settled over the table as they picked through their food. Ezza was last here eight years ago, and it tasted like The Public Servant's cloning tanks hadn't been cleaned since. There was that grainy, starchy flavour and overly chewy texture that came with low production values.

PALE GREY DOT

It was Cherny who eventually broke the silence. "Where do you think she is now?"

Ezza took a deep breath. She'd been wondering the same thing ever since she found out what transpired in the basement of the Tower. "Fled to Europe? Off-world? Hell, I don't know, Cherny."

"ESS apparently suspected she'd been hiding out in the Midwestern Wastes for most of the past fifty years. Might make sense that she'd head home again."

"Could be." Ezza suspected that if Jenna didn't want to be found, she wouldn't be. "You want to go after her, don't you?" Ezza found that even after all these years, she could still read him.

"The last thing she said to me was that she'd have to think about what to do now that She's dead," Cherny said between forkfuls of egg. "She could still be a threat."

"But that's not why you want to find her," Ezza prompted.

"No," he admitted. "I hurt her, Ezza. She reached out to me for help, and I barely lasted a second before turning her in. I have to make it up to her. See if there's any way to reconcile things between us."

"Cherny, the Pull—"

"Is a damn lousy excuse."

"Maybe," Ezza conceded. She thought back to Uruk Sulcus, and how willing she'd been to join Bev Stroud. Gole and Adams paid the price for her failure. She glanced at Nirali, wondering if she was thinking the same thing. Looking back at Cherny, she added, "But you did risk your life to plan Nirali and Jenna's safe passage to Earth. You confronted Her and Amanda."

"Against my better judgement. If I'd had my way, we'd have bolted out of there the instant we freed ourselves and let the army take care of it."

"Yes, I read your statement on that," Ezza replied with a chuckle. "You really need to give yourself more credit. You found and stopped Alexander Reuben. Regardless of his war with Her, his death can only be a good thing for the solar system."

"Also against my better judgement. Sienar practically forced me into the role."

Ezza cast her eyes down at the mention of his name. *I would have liked one last chance to say goodbye to him.* The reports had described Sienar's death in detail. It had been an agonizing read. Ezza decided not to say so to Cherny. "For as long as I've known you, Cherny, you've always worked best when someone throws you in the deep end of the pool."

He laughed.

"I'm going to be staying on Earth for a while," she continued. "Oversee the efforts to pick through the remains of the Tower and see if there isn't something that can be salvaged from this mess. The United Fleet's in shambles, thousands of ESS assets are missing, the Syndicate has fragmented further without Her influence, and people just saw their unflappable government shaken to its core. You heard Minister Havoic— there's going to be more violence to deal with."

Nirali shifted uncomfortably in her seat.

PALE GREY DOT

"Pretty tall order," Cherny said. "But I think they have the right person for the job."

"I appreciate that, but it's not something I can do alone. Tracking down lost ESS fugitives certainly falls under my new purview. What do you say, Cherny? Are you willing to be thrown into the deep end once more? The last of the Athena Six working together on one final mission? It could be like old times."

Cherny smiled. "Are you sure? I got fired from my last job."

"I'm willing to overlook it. Unless you'd prefer to try finding Jenna by yourself?"

"Thank you, Ezza. Of course I accept."

Nirali reached for another bar, and Cherny turned his attention to her. "How about you, Nirali? What are your plans now that you've seen the glorious homeworld?"

"Oh, I hate this place," she said cheerfully. "Even with a breather, the air smells awful, there are security arches every ten steps, drones buzz by your ear nonstop, and it's too hot all the time. But my brother is somewhere on this godforsaken planet. As soon as I find him, I'm going to get out of here."

"And you're going to stay out of trouble," Ezza reminded her.

"Sure. Of course."

Cherny set his fork down. His eggs and bacon were gone. "Don't underestimate how careful you need to be. You're damn lucky you had a high-ranking United Fleet officer pulling strings for you, but that only gets you so far."

437

Nirali turned several shades towards red. "What makes you think she—"

"Because I know Earth, and I know how security works," Cherny interrupted. "You're a reporter, Nirali. Of course you're being watched. Just because ESS is gone doesn't mean everything is sunshine and rainbows now. Ezza would have had to fight on your behalf to keep you out here with us."

Nirali gave Ezza a suspicious look.

In truth, Ezza hadn't needed to argue too hard. After her battle with Brylan Ncube's battlecruiser, she was finding she had a lot more clout than she'd ever had before. The admiral bars on her shoulder were proving useful. "The government was very appreciative of your efforts to expose ESS's threat to the stability of the solar system, Nirali. But Cherny is absolutely right. You need to be cautious."

Nirali frowned and went back to nibbling on her nutrition bar.

Ezza knew what she was thinking. "I know you're frustrated, but solving all of society's problems isn't a two-month job. Just know that the solar system is better off than it was before."

Cherny shoved the last few bits of toast into his mouth and leaned over to the blinds, using his free hand to gently separate two of the slats. "Dust storm's letting up."

Ezza transmitted her payment authorization and tossed her napkin on the table. "No sense sticking around, then."

The booth unlocked and the three of them slid out. Ezza grabbed her breather and slipped it over her head, making sure the seals clipped together under her chin. Nirali had finally gotten the hang of putting hers on.

They stepped into the lobby and through the doors that led outside. A wave of hot, muggy air instantly hit them, along with the few lingering particles of sand still blowing in the wind. Ezza put the discomfort out of her mind as they made their way to their helicraft, which had earned a few more nicks and scratches in the storm. Its doors slid open for them, and Ezza took the front seat.

With an admiral's air-traffic privileges, it'd be about forty-five minutes to Toronto. From there, the real work of tying up ESS's loose ends, rebuilding the fleet, and restoring civility to the system would begin.

As the helicraft's thrusters lifted them up into the air, Ezza glanced into the back. Nirali was slouched to one side, head on the armrest, already half asleep. Cherny had connected to the United Fleet network and was no doubt poring over the stack of new files in his mind.

Ezza looked to the path ahead of them. *We still have a long way to go.*

ACKNOWLEDGEMENTS

Despite what one might think, writing a book is not a solitary activity. No, it involves many hands and many eyes. Thus, I am eternally grateful to my beta readers: Kirby, Pat, Jennifer, and my number one fan, Suzanne. They convinced me to not make the plot a labyrinthian maze from which even a minotaur could not escape. My second round of readers—Randal, Anahita, and Michelle—smoothed off the rough edges for me.

Of course, thank you to Turnstone Press for their support. They have a quality-comes-first attitude, and the book is better because of it. Thank you Sharon and Jamis for your efforts in bringing *Pale Grey Dot* to life. Additional credit goes to my editors: Adria, for trimming away words that needed to be trimmed, and Melissa, for her extraordinary patience and laser-like attention to detail.

Last but not least, I must thank the Toronto Sci-Fi and Fantasy Writers group. They provided feedback, support, advice, and companionship. Justin, David, Michelle (again), Peter, Adrienne: thank you. And to anyone else in the group who fixed a word, nudged a sentence, or offered a better idea: you have my gratitude.

—Don

Don Miasek writes from smack dab in the middle of Toronto, Canada. An Aurora nominated editor for *TDotSpec*, he's had a hand in bringing Amazon bestseller *Imps & Minions* and *Strange Wars* to market, as well as *Speculative North* magazine. He is a proud member of the Toronto Science Fiction & Fantasy Writers Group. *Pale Grey Dot* is his debut novel.